"Is This What You Wanted?"
He Asked Softly,

pulling her to him and bending so that his lips met hers. His mouth moved on her own and her heart stopped. "Is this what you were after...Alethea?"

And then his lips closed on hers, warm and hard and soft all at the same time. She felt as if she were submerged in sensation, melting. The anger in her turned into passion, the shame into desire. Surprised at the strength of her own feelings, she tried to fight them; but they were too strong. She felt herself relax in his arms. He felt so strong, so warm, so good.

"Yes," she whispered when he drew back a little. Their eyes locked. "This is what I wanted." His lips closed on hers again, blotting out all thought.

Dear Reader:

We trust you will enjoy this Richard Gallen romance. We plan to bring you more of the best in both contemporary and historical romantic fiction with four exciting new titles each month.

We'd like your help.

We value your suggestions and opinions. They will help us to publish the kind of romances you want to read. Please send us your comments, or just let us know which Richard Gallen romances you have especially enjoyed. Write to the address below. We're looking forward to hearing from you!

Happy reading!

The Editors of
Richard Gallen Books
8-10 West 36th St.
New York, N.Y. 10018

Gentle Betrayer

LYNN ERICKSON

PUBLISHED BY RICHARD GALLEN BOOKS
Distributed by POCKET BOOKS

Books by Lynn Erickson

This Raging Flower
Sweet Nemesis
The Silver Kiss
Gentle Betrayer

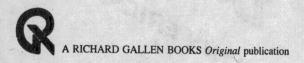 A RICHARD GALLEN BOOKS *Original* publication

Distributed by
POCKET BOOKS, a Simon & Schuster division of
GULF & WESTERN CORPORATION
1230 Avenue of the Americas, New York, N.Y. 10020

ISBN: 0-671-45146-4

First Pocket Books printing July, 1982

10 9 8 7 6 5 4 3 2 1

RICHARD GALLEN and colophon are trademarks
of Simon & Schuster and Richard Gallen & Co., Inc.

Printed in the U.S.A.

To
Jerry Friedenberg,
in gratitude for his invaluable assistance

Chapter 1

Thursday, December 1

Several dark heads turned as the maître d' led the slim, brown-haired woman to a small corner table in the crowded Aphrodite Room. She supposed it was unusual to see a woman dining alone here in Athens, much more so than in her native city of New York, but the raised brows bothered her no more here than they would have at home. She was in this plush, red-draped dining room for an excellent reason.

The maître d' seated her with a flourish, rattling away in Greek and English, smiling broadly. Automatically, her hazel eyes swept over the table setting: Belgian linen tablecloth, fine bone china, Waterford crystal wineglasses. Then she raised her glance, looking around to absorb the decor: the Corinthian columns of gleaming white marble, the gilded frieze depicting ancient Grecian warriors, the marble fountain with a stylized sculptured fish spewing a stream of water. The atmosphere juxtaposed European Baroque with the simplicity of ancient Greece.

Nice. Very swank, she decided as she printed each detail on

her mind like a photograph to be recalled later. This was her job. And it was glamorous, exciting work for which she had a natural flair. She thoroughly enjoyed writing her column for *The World's Fare*, seeing her name in print: Alethea Holmes. The travel was marvelous, the people she met were gracious, warm, and sometimes even opened their homes to her. She was only twenty-five and could pursue her career for years and still raise a family later.

She studied the menu carefully, trying to pick those items that would give her the best idea of the restaurant's quality—those difficult dishes that separated the good from the great.

It was too bad she wasn't one of those people, those lucky few, who could eat all they wanted without gaining weight. Her job was terrible for someone like her who had to watch the calories but adored good food. She had to work at keeping her figure, but it remained slim and neat—not exactly voluptuous, certainly not mannequin-thin, but nicely curved where females were supposed to be curved.

Her clear eyes rose from the menu to see the maître d' approaching again, grinning brilliantly. The Greek people were certainly a friendly, cheerful lot.

"Mademoiselle, do you mind to share your table with a gentleman?" he was saying. "This night is so crowded, you see." He gestured eloquently with his hands at the full, candlelit dining room.

Alethea was about to object, but a small stab of curiosity led her to say "Yes" before she even had time to examine her motives. Why not? It was her last night in Athens. It might be pleasant, different, to have some company, even if she had to struggle along with her five words of Greek.

The maître d' was coming back, leading her unknown dinner companion. She watched as he made his way toward her past the splashing marble fountain. But she couldn't see the man, as the white columns and tall potted plants in antique urns maddeningly kept hiding him from view.

The maître d' pulled out the chair opposite her, stepped aside, tellingly raising his eyebrows, then withdrew with a sweeping bow.

The man remained standing for a second, and she couldn't help staring up at him. The first thing she noticed was his lopsided grin, slightly mocking, as if he were laughing at himself, the situation, the whole roomful of people. Then he sat down with the quick, fluid motion of someone who was completely at ease with his body, an athlete, perhaps.

"I assume you're not Greek," he said in pure American. "Maybe French . . . or English. Am I hot or cold?" The grin widened. She noticed how the laugh lines crinkled around his eyes—deepset blue eyes, amiable-looking now, but with a distant, guarded depth to them.

"Only cool," she replied, falling instantly into the same light, bantering tone. "I'm half American, half French. Not bad at all for starters."

"Well, at least I don't have to struggle along in Greek. My French is a bit better."

Suddenly, she wanted to ask him a thousand questions. What was he doing here? Why was he, too, alone? Where was he from? He was obviously from the States, but with no telltale regional accent. East Coast, she guessed. And then she couldn't help but notice his impeccably cut dark suit, American in style, and worn well. His dark hair curled slightly over the collar of his blue shirt. She noticed him watching her closely. Was he trying to guess her thoughts?

"Now it's my turn," she said, very aware of the pleasure of having a man, a very attractive man, sitting across from her at the table. It made the meal ahead an adventure rather than just an assignment. "East Coast, U.S.A. Somewhere between New York and Washington, D.C. Close?"

"Yes. Philadelphia, but I work in D.C.," he answered. "I'm impressed."

"Oh, it's nothing." She laughed.

The man leaned toward her conspiratorially, and she became intensely conscious of the male scent of him, the way the candlelight glinted off his rich brown hair and created brilliant pinpoints of light in his unusually blue eyes.

"Now that we're through with the preliminaries, can we get down to basics? What's your name and what in hell is a nice girl like you doing in a place like this—alone?"

Alethea grinned. "Typical male question. I'm working."

"Quite a job you've got, dining out in style."

"I'm a writer for a gourmet magazine. I do a monthly column on European restaurants."

"Ah. And the other basic?"

"Oh, my name. Alethea Holmes. And yours?"

3

"Nick DeWolff."

They looked at each other then for a long while, almost solemnly, as if this casual encounter were something more. She couldn't help the curious feeling that this meeting was due to fate. And that was a totally alien feeling to her. Normally, she wasn't the least superstitious.

The waiter broke into the moment as if a pebble had been tossed into a still pond, shattering the perfection of the surface. Alethea ordered, then had a sudden thought. "I wonder if you'd mind ordering something different from what I'm having? That way, I can taste yours, too. It would be better for my article. That is, if you don't mind."

"Great idea. As long as I get some of yours. And how about an *ouzo* to start with?"

"I thought a white wine would be better—"

"No way. We'll go native. *Ouzo* it is."

"Sure, why not," she conceded, smiling at him, feeling carefree. It was surprising how easily he'd done that to her.

After the waiter left, Nick leaned forward, folding his arms on the tabletop. "What magazine do you write for?"

"World's Fare, based in New York."

"I'm afraid I've never seen it. TV dinners are more my style," he teased lightly.

"Isn't this a little out of your league then?"

"Absolutely. I'm treating myself." He paused at her disbelieving smile. "But seriously, do you always travel alone? Don't you need a photographer or something?"

"My column is strictly reviews. An occasional recipe if I can squeeze it out of the chef. Once in a while, I'll include photos if a restaurant has its own."

"I see. Does this restaurant realize what you're doing here?"

"No. Otherwise, I might get special treatment. Some people do it differently . . . maybe they like the fanfare."

Funny, Alethea realized, she didn't mind answering the questions she'd been asked so often before. He really did seem interested.

But what about him? Somehow it seemed important to know what his job was and what he was doing in Athens.

He hesitated for a split second when she asked him. It struck her that he withdrew a little, that his smile became the tiniest bit fixed.

4

"I work for the government. And as for why I'm in Athens, I'm on vacation. Always wanted to see the Parthenon."

"Oh, is your job exciting?"

Nick laughed. "Don't I wish. No, I'm only a dull paper-pusher, part of the huge bureaucracy, that's all."

Alethea cocked her head to one side, studying him unabashedly. "You don't look like a bureaucrat," she mused.

"Appearances can be deceiving," he replied lightly. *"You* don't look like a magazine writer."

"Why not? What do I look like?" She bristled with irritation. Another macho type who thought he knew where all women belonged.

"Oh, I don't know. Maybe an artist, a painter or sculptor . . ."

"That's funny. My mother was."

"Was what?"

"A painter."

"Is she the French one?"

"Yes. *Was,*" she corrected.

"Oh, I'm sorry," he said, instantly contrite.

"It was years ago. I've adjusted to it now."

"Were you raised in the States or in France? I only ask because you have a vague sort of foreign look about you."

"Mostly in the States, but I still spend time in Paris. My mother inherited a small apartment on the Left Bank that's mine now. I stay there whenever I have to work in Paris."

"And your father?"

"Oh, it's so complicated, you really wouldn't be interested."

"Yes, I would," Nick said simply. His statement held a depth of feeling that belied the triteness of the words themselves.

Alethea flushed at the intensity of his gaze. Then his question reminded her, brought back the nagging worry. She frowned.

His blue eyes imprisoned her glance. "What is it?" he asked softly. "Something's wrong."

"Oh, really, you wouldn't—"

"I said I would," he interrupted.

"Well," she paused, then went on, "if you really want to hear it. My father works for the Abjala Petroleum Company. Do you know—?"

"Yes. Small Arab emirate on the Persian Gulf. Very rich."

"Well, anyway, my dad is an engineer, really a very smart man, a genius. Several years after Mamma died, he took this job.

They've given him unlimited funds to do research with. He's been there about two years now." Why on earth was she telling all this to a man who was virtually a stranger to her? How unlike her normal reticence. But his sympathic gaze urged her on. He *was* a good listener. "My father loves it there, says he can do so much work. I really don't know what his research involves though, it's so technical, but it's something to do with refining oil." She paused, thinking back. "And then the other day he telephoned me at my hotel here in Athens. And . . . it was very strange."

"Why?" came Nick's soft voice.

"Well, he asked me to come to Abjala to see him, insisted. He knows how tight my schedule is. It seems we never see each other anymore." No point dwelling on *that*, she realized. "Anyway, I have to be back in New York on Monday, so it was really hard, but I finally said I'd get there over the weekend. I mean, it's not as if Abjala is around the corner. But he sounded so odd . . ." Her voice trailed away with the memory. "He wouldn't tell me why, just kept repeating he had to see me. A telephone wouldn't do this time. He's never done that before. So, naturally, I'm worried. I think he might be sick."

"I see. Do you have any other family?"

"No. Just Dad and me, and we've been apart so much lately. Well, I'm nervous. He's never done anything like this before."

"I can understand that. But you said you're going to Abjala, so you'll find out soon enough, won't you?"

"Yes, of course, but meanwhile I feel like I should be doing something."

"Did he ask you to do anything?"

"No, just to come as soon as possible."

Nick reached across the table and gave her arm a quick pat. "Then quit worrying. It never did anyone—"

"Any good," she finished. "I know, but that's easier said than done."

"I understand how you feel."

Alethea sensed he really did understand. It was a decidedly remarkable sensation. Why, she hardly knew the man. She couldn't believe she'd told him the story at all. But it had helped. She felt relieved.

Then Alethea couldn't help but wonder why this very attractive man seemed to care about her problems. It wasn't as if she were beautiful. She had a nice face, but it wasn't sensational. Its only really good points were a fine white complexion—that *never* tanned—and deep-set, almost slanting, darkly fringed hazel eyes. Although she knew her honey-brown hair was one of her best features—softly waving and shiny—tonight it was too business-like, pulled back tightly into a severe bun. Damn! Why tonight, of all nights, hadn't she taken more time with her appearance?

Suddenly, Alethea realized that she was being rude, brooding over her too-plain face, talking about her own worries. What about him? She met his gaze levelly. "That's enough about me." She gave a nervous little laugh. "How about your family?" Abruptly, she wished she hadn't phrased it quite that way. He'd think she was asking the obvious, about a wife, kids. Still, she admitted to herself, she *was* curious . . .

Her heart sank as Nick hesitated, pinioning her with a quick, hard gaze. Finally, he smiled ruefully. "Not much to tell, really. Never did get around to marriage." A corner of his mouth lifted into a knowing smile. "My folks ramble around in a huge, echoing mansion outside Philadelphia. I rarely see them."

"Why not? You're so close, living in Washington."

He gave a short, harsh laugh. "Frankly, I'm not very welcome."

"Aren't you past teenage rebellion yet?" Alethea asked jokingly, but saw right away that she had touched on a sore nerve.

"It's a fifteen-year-old argument. It's simple. I refuse to go into my father's law firm."

"It can't be that simple . . . But maybe it's none of my business."

"It's the same old story," he continued pensively. "Disillusioned Vietnam vet throws years of Harvard Law School away. Can't seem to make his peace with the Establishment."

"But your job now must be just as dull as law practice."

Whatever Nick was going to say remained unspoken, for just then the waiter came and placed two tiny glasses of clear *ouzo* in front of them. She was almost glad for the interruption, as the conversation was becoming uncomfortable. Nick raised his glass as if for a toast, but Alethea eyed hers warily.

"Come on," he said warmly. "To unexpected encounters."

She lifted her glass, clicked it against his, took a sip and gasped. The stuff was like fire—pure, slick, licorice-flavored fire!

Nick laughed deeply. "You'll get used to it."

"Never!" she breathed, wrinkling her small, straight nose. "I'm leaving tomorrow and that's the last *ouzo* I'll probably ever have!"

"Not if I can help it," he said, quirking one dark brow.

"What's that supposed to mean?"

"How about we go out on the town tonight and have a few more? It's my last night here, too." He hesitated, looked questioningly at her. "That is, unless there's someone . . ."

"No, there isn't," she said levelly. "But really, this is so sudden—"

"And I hardly know you," he finished, giving her that boyish, crooked grin. "So what? I hardly know you, either. You might even attack me."

"You never know," she agreed, laughing, enjoying herself. "Okay then, we'll do it."

"Good!" said Nick, and then two waiters appeared next to their table with trays of exotic, delectable dishes. "Well, Miss Holmes, here you are. Now you can go to work . . . so to speak." And he grinned at her, his blue eyes dancing with merriment.

Chapter 2

Thursday, December 1

After the meal, which was excellent, they left the Aphrodite Room together. A lovely feeling, thought Alethea, walking out of a crowded restaurant with a tall, good-looking man. She felt a tingle of excitement just knowing she was going somewhere with Nick. And she was dressed for any occasion, anywhere he might take her. She'd worn her good black suit with a shell-pink silk blouse, and her tan, camel's hair coat.

He led her to a green Porsche, which rather surprised her. Tourists usually took taxis in Athens—the traffic was murder. He slid in behind the wheel and looked over at her in the darkness of the chilly December evening. It was very intimate, the two of them alone in the car while the heavy, noisy traffic of Athens swirled and eddied around them.

Alethea shivered, pulling her collar up around her neck.

"Cold?" he asked.

"Yes, a little. I thought Athens was warm and exotic."

"Only in the summer. Now it's cold and exotic." He started

the car and pulled out expertly into the traffic. He seemed to know precisely where to go. His driving was impeccable, efficient. He appeared to know Athens perfectly.

"Where are we going?" she finally asked.

"The Plaka. It's the old quarter of Athens, all jumbled up against the base of the Acropolis. Very picturesque, very ethnic. Personally, I think they built it all a few years ago for dumb tourists like us."

"You don't strike me as a 'dumb' tourist, Nick," she said quietly, fascinated, watching the way his strong hands held the wheel and shifted the gears so smoothly.

"Oh, I am, as dumb as they come," he replied lightly, giving her a sidelong glance as they drove.

They pulled up in a street that climbed toward the base of the Acropolis, the high mount that was crowned by the lordly Parthenon. She'd heard about the Plaka but had never been there. The minute she stepped out of the car, Alethea could hear a lilting Greek melody coming from a nearby *taverna*. The street narrowed, winding among small, square ancient buildings, piled one on top of the other like children's building blocks. Attached to many buildings were patios, roofed by latticework, obviously for use in the warmer months.

"It must be heavenly in the summer," she observed.

"Yes, it must."

Music was everywhere, emanating from several *tavernas* as Alethea and Nick walked up the street. The air was filled with the aromas of olive oil and garlic, fish frying and wine. A trio of Greek men stumbled out of a doorway, laughing, then disappeared into the night shadows.

"Come on, I have a favorite hangout," said Nick, taking her hand.

His touch was warm and strong. His fingers held hers confidently. A surge of pleasure coursed through Alethea, and she felt her spirits soar. She would always remember this city, this night, this man. The whole evening was one of those momentous turns of fate, the crucial congruence of two individuals' paths of which the result was far more than the sum of one and one. It was truly a kind of magic.

Nick led her up a side street, even narrower, impossible to drive on. The haunting music of a *bouzouki* poured from the door of a small *taverna*. There was a sign over the entrance. She couldn't read the Greek letters, but the picture was unmistakable: the Greek satyr, Pan, evilly eying the world, goat's legs instead of human, his pipes held to his lips.

As Nick opened the door for her, a blast of hot air, mixed with smoke and noise and the sharp aroma of Greek wine, hit her in the face like a soft blow.

She stood there stupidly, overcome for a second. She sensed Nick at her shoulder. When she turned, he smiled down into her eyes reassuringly and squeezed her hand.

"Nicko!" shouted a gravelly voice. "Nicko, my friend!" A short, heavyset Greek trotted up to them, throwing his arms around Nick. *"Willkommen!"*

"Philo, *kalispéra,*" Nick said. "May I introduce my friend, Alethea?"

Philo took her hand, kissed it, then looked deeply into her eyes. He was perspiring. He smelled of strong tobacco and *retsina*, the tangy, resin-flavored Greek wine. *"Kalispéra, good evening, belle mademoiselle."* And then to Nick, "Come, sit here, the dancing comes *vite*, quickly."

He led them to a table, waved a hand, and golden wine was poured into glasses that appeared miraculously. "Drink, *mes amis*. I must go now, to start the dancing, the *hazapiko.*"

Alethea noted Nick's expression was contained, but frank amusement escaped from his eyes. Finally, he burst out laughing and raised his glass to her. "To Philo. Wait till you see the dancing here, Alethea. It's wonderful."

"Why are you laughing?" she asked, her brow furrowed in confusion.

"Your face. You looked so . . . amazed."

"Well, I haven't seen this part of Athens before—"

"That's why we're here. I wanted to share it with you."

She smiled into his blue eyes. He said such nice things. Was he just fishing for a response, a one-night stand with another American? But she sensed that he was sincere—why, she didn't know. In fact, she thought, he was somewhat of a mystery. Perhaps it was the smooth way he handled himself, the self-assurance he emanated. But there was more. There were little things, like his knowledge of Athens and his close relationship with Philo. Nick certainly didn't seem like a typical tourist . . .

He took her hand that lay on the table. "It's more fun with someone, don't you think?"

"Oh, yes."

Then Philo began to play his *bouzouki* and the center of the floor cleared instantly. The twanging notes of the stringed instrument were powerful. The traditional tune made fingers tap unbidden, feet itch to dance, hearts thump in rhythm. It stirred the blood. Then, as the music soared, one man stood up and began moving, gracefully, unselfconsciously, to the music, repeating over and over the intricate, ancient steps to the folk dance. His eyes were closed as if in a trance. Soon more men stood to dance, forming a swaying line, stepping delicately to the music, their bodies moving in unison. There was strength and exuberance in these Greek men that Alethea had never seen in European or American men.

She watched, fascinated, and sipped her wine. When the dance was over, Philo sat with them, beaming, sweat beading his cheerful face. They had to drink to the dance, to the men, each and every one, to the song, to his beautiful *bouzouki*. Her head began to swim. The evening took on a blurred quality. The music was the sweetest she'd ever heard, the dancers more spirited, the smoke and din more exotic, Nick DeWolff more virile, his white smile more meaningful. Alethea knew she was laughing a lot—at Philo's polyglot use of language, at Nick's jokes, at anything. It was so hot in the *taverna* that she took off her suit jacket and rolled up the sleeves of her pale pink blouse.

Philo pulled them both to the center of the floor where they danced to the *bouzouki* music. She lost herself in sensation, moving to the tune with Nick, who seemed to know the complicated steps so well. He had taken off his jacket, and she saw that he moved beautifully, his tall, broad-shouldered frame lithe and supple, like an ancient trained Olympian. The Greeks stood in a circle, flashing their white teeth under bushy, black mustaches, urging them on, clapping. It was a bacchanal, a Dionysian orgy. Alethea kicked off her shoes to dance better, loosened her hair until it fell to her shoulders, moved to the music as if she were wedded to it, possessed by it. The *retsina* lost its strange, bitter tang and tasted like ambrosia. It went down so easily . . .

Then, later, much later, Nick was saying goodbye to Philo and pulling her out into the cold Athenian night. It sobered her like a slap in the face.

"Was I too awful?" she asked Nick suddenly.

"God, no, you were wonderful. They loved you!" He pulled

her close, kept his arm around her as they walked down the lamplit street.

"I never do things like that," she said wonderingly.

"There's always a first time. Anyway, I'm glad it was with me." He stopped suddenly, put her at arm's length, his hands on her shoulders. He studied her face for an endless moment. "Are you glad you came?" His deep voice was gentle.

The light from a nearby window struck one side of his face, illuminating the strong line of his cheek and jaw. His eyes were dark pools. She noticed for the first time that his nose was slightly askew, as if it had been broken at some time. He had an aura of mystery about him that she could not put her finger on—something hidden, dangerous perhaps, but not dangerous to her, no, never to her.

"Yes, I wouldn't have missed it for the world," Alethea answered, feeling a surge of warmth for Nick fill her.

"Good, I wouldn't have either," he said simply. "Will I see you again?"

"I'm leaving tomorrow."

"So am I. Can I drive you to the airport?"

"You really don't need to go to the trouble . . ."

"It's no trouble, Alethea," he said firmly. "I want to." He paused, then went on. "When will you be back in New York?"

"Monday. Nick?"

"Yes?"

"Is this something we want to pursue?"

"Yes. Why not?"

"I . . . I wonder . . ."

"Alethea, I'm not a child. I don't play games anymore. I know when I like someone."

He smiled then, a slight uptilting of his strong mouth. His dark head bent toward her, and she knew instinctively that he was going to kiss her. She felt a tingling in the pit of her stomach as his lips brushed hers in a kiss so light she wasn't at first sure that their lips were even touching. The feeling was heavenly. When she had been kissed before, there had always been a bit of nervousness, especially the first time. But Nick's approach to the art was entirely different, thoroughly refreshing.

For endless moments, he did nothing more than move his mouth against hers in the same feather-light touch. But then, finally, he placed a large hand at the back of her neck and slowly pressed her lips to his more firmly. And then his other hand came around to the small of her back, and she was drawn up against his lean frame while his lips parted hers and his tongue began to savor her, search her mouth with mounting urgency.

Alethea's heartbeat quickened and unexpectedly her knees weakened. She leaned against his warm body, placed her arms around his neck, feeling the dark curling hairs where they touched his collar. She grew mindless of the cold night, of the dimly lit street on which they stood locked in their embrace. Nick moved a confident hand beneath her coat and touched the side of her breast covered only by the thin silk blouse. His calculated touch sent waves of pure pleasure coursing through her veins. And then his hand cupped her breast tenderly and she moaned weakly.

He took his mouth away for an instant. "You're beautiful," he whispered softly, and his mouth found hers again in a hard, demanding kiss.

Her senses were flooded. Nick was taking possession of her mind and her body as no man had ever been able to before.

She stiffened abruptly. What was this stranger doing to her? She drew her lips away from his. Her breathing was shallow, and she couldn't meet his eyes. It was all too quick, too foreign to her nature, letting this man control her body and her emotions like this. Why, she had known him for only a few short hours. It was all too fast.

Nick must have noticed her tension, because he pulled back and looked at her, merely looked at her, quietly, his eyes unreadable in the dark. She sensed his gaze on her. His large, warm hands still held her arms above each elbow.

She shivered inadvertently but not from the cold.

Alien fear filled her. She was afraid she'd wake up tomorrow and find it all a dream, and he would no longer be attractive to her. It would all be spoiled. "I better get back to my hotel," she said stiffly.

He drove her back through the nearly deserted streets to her hotel. They were silent, as if they both thought along the same lines. At last they pulled up in front of her hotel.

Nick shut the motor off and turned to face her. "Want a nightcap at the hotel bar?"

A nightcap, and then what? she wondered. "No," Alethea replied finally. "I think I'll try to get some sleep."

"Alone?" Nick smiled charmingly.

"Yes . . . alone." He must think her a terrible prude, she thought abruptly.

Nick studied her for a moment, then opened his car door and stepped out. He helped her onto the curb and took her elbow as if he were going to walk her to the entrance.

He stopped, hesitated. "I wish you'd change your mind about a drink."

They stood near the car, away from the lighted entryway. There were a few passersby but no one seemed to notice them.

Alethea met his eyes. "Tomorrow's going to be a long day," she said, feeling suddenly quite stripped of defenses standing there alone with Nick, wanting to say yes to him but somehow afraid, sensing it wouldn't be quite right—not yet.

He smiled patiently down at her. "I guess I'll have to take no for an answer."

She nodded.

"This is a terrible blow to my pride," he teased. His hand touched her chin, tilting her head up to his. Slowly, he brought his mouth down to hers and kissed her again, thoroughly.

Alethea responded instantly, and when he began to draw away, she let her lips linger on his for a brief moment, telling him more than she had wanted.

Nick grinned knowingly, then took her arm again and walked her to the door. He gave her a chaste kiss on the cheek in front of the doorman. Somehow it disappointed Alethea a little. She longed to feel his strong arms around her again, his face close to hers.

As she rode up the elevator to her floor, she suddenly remembered her father again and felt guilty, as if forgetting him for a few hours had somehow done him harm. And then she felt angry that he should make her go all the way to Abjala. It was all so inconvenient, so unsettling. He was old enough to know better than to play these games!

By the time Althea reached her room, exhaustion had set in. She was dizzy and the taste of *retsina* filled her mouth still. She threw her coat and purse onto the bed, kicked off her shoes and sank into a chair. Her hotel room was oppressively, coldly empty.

A watery sun blinked down on Athens the next morning. Alethea was grateful. A bright sky would have made her head ache even more. And she was so nervous. First over her father, a nagging worry that never quite released her from its upsetting hold, and then over the fact that Nick DeWolff was going to pick her up soon to drive her to the airport.

He'd phoned earlier, waking her from a restless sleep, sounding brisk, cheerful, efficient. She was afraid her own voice had been a weak croak. And to be honest, she hadn't expected him to call.

"Alethea, I'll be there at ten. My flight is an hour later than yours, so it will work out fine."

"Are you sure you want to bother? I can still take a cab."

"We've been over that ground before. I'll be there at ten sharp."

"Okay, sure. Thanks."

"You all right?"

"Sure. A little tired, that's all."

She heard his deep laughter over the wire. "You're not in practice."

"I'm not at all sure I want to be."

"See you later." He chuckled.

"Okay."

She took a shower, hoping it would wake her up, wash away the cobwebs. She brushed her teeth vigorously, fluffed her soft brown hair dry. For a change, she decided, she'd wear it down instead of in a bun. It fell in soft waves to her shoulders. She chose a beautifully tailored tan suit and a silky, green, short-sleeved blouse from her small wardrobe, knowing it would do for both a cool day in Athens and a hot day in Abjala. And she knew it was flattering to her slim figure, too. Not that her father would notice. No, the fuss was all for Nick, Alethea admitted to herself. She did care what he thought of her, how he remembered her.

She never wore much makeup, but today she put on some mascara, though she hardly needed any, and a little blush on her clear white skin. Shalimar, too. It had been ages since she cared so much what a man thought of her looks. It was kind of fun . . .

Her phone rang precisely at ten, making her heart jump into her throat. She felt like a sixteen-year-old on her first date as she hurriedly stuffed clothes and toilet articles into her suitcase, checked her plane tickets, passport, schedule. It was a familiar routine—packing the few select items of clothing that she almost always took along. One set for winter, one for summer. She had it down to an exact science by now. She had even found the perfect suitcase, lightweight, sturdy, yet ample for her things. She had learned quickly never to travel with more than she could handle herself.

Alethea snapped the bag shut, took her customary last look around, not really seeing anything. She was distracted. She hadn't felt this way in years.

He was waiting in the lobby. Her heart gave a great, joyful lurch as Nick turned, saw her, walked toward her. He was just as she remembered: not perfect-pretty or too handsome but so very masculine with his lopsided, boyish grin, his lovely blue eyes, slightly bumpy nose and dark waving hair that looked the tiniest bit rumpled. He wore a well-cut tweed sport coat with leather patches on the elbows, gray flannel pants, a white turtleneck sweater. From a distance, he gave the impression of youth, but she knew he must be thirty-five, maybe more.

"All ready?" he asked, taking her suitcase effortlessly.

On the drive to the airport, Alethea found herself watching his every move, as if to impress his memory on her mind: his strong hands, the firm line of his neck, the way his jacket fit his broad shoulders. He turned the Porsche rental in at the airport and checked their luggage. He was obviously used to traveling. He was certainly an odd sort of tourist, much too well versed in the routine, much too . . . smooth.

And still, her mind turned to her father in Abjala, perhaps ill or hurt. Nervousness began to consume her as the departure of her flight grew near. She knew she was preoccupied, too quiet.

"Worried?" Nick finally asked.

"Yes, frankly, I am."

"I know."

"Nick, I'm sorry if I'm not very good company . . ."

"Hey, forget it."

He asked for her address in New York, wrote it down on a piece of paper Alethea was sure he would lose. "I'll call you when you get back," he said. "Then you can tell me all about your father and how you were upset over nothing."

"Sure." She tried to smile, but her face felt wooden. "Nick, thanks for everything. You've been wonderful. I had such a great time last night." She paused. "I hope you do call . . . soon."

"I will."

Her flight was announced. She felt suddenly stiff and heavy, as if she wouldn't be able to get up and walk to the gate where she would take a shuttle to the plane.

Nick stood, his blue eyes filled with an emotion she could not name. "That's your flight," he said inanely. He pulled her toward him, held her for an impossibly long, agonizing moment. "Goodbye, have a good trip."

"You too," Alethea replied, trying again to smile, but instead, ridiculous tears welled up behind her eyelids. She whirled around and walked blindly to the gate, afraid to turn again.

Well, she told herself firmly, Nick was behind her now. She had to turn her mind to her father, her normally open, guileless father, who was waiting for her in Abjala, consumed by some odd problem of his own that he had not been able to confide to her over the phone.

Unexpectedly, it seemed sinister to Alethea Holmes.

Chapter 3

Friday, December 2

Alethea's father had not been at the Abjala airport to greet her. It had been an anxious hour since she had finally landed. She had waited patiently at first, thinking that her father had gotten tied up for a short time, but then the patience had turned into irritation and the irritation into worry. It was not like him to forget anything this important. Since he had called her to come, it was certainly disturbing.

As she sat in the airport now, images of her father lying in a hospital filtering through her mind, she felt the grip of panic tighten around her heart. And here she was, alone, unable to help him, while the dark Arab men stared at her unblinkingly. Then she tried to think logically. Maybe he was perfectly fine, maybe he forgot, maybe he thought it was tomorrow, maybe . . . oh, maybe anything! Dammitall!

This was ridiculous! There was some simple explanation. She had to find out where her father was, and if he couldn't meet her, she'd take a taxi and go to him. Very logical.

Alethea pulled her wallet out of her shoulder bag and searched through the many small, folded papers until she found the right one: Abjala Petroleum Company and a phone number. Certainly they would be able to locate him. Why hadn't she thought of it right off?

She walked to a pay phone, then found she would have to exchange some bills and get change. How irritating! And then it seemed to take the young teller forever to change her money.

Finally, she dialed the number, wondering what she would do if the person who answered spoke only Arabic. Her heart hammered loudly, squeezed with apprehension, as the phone rang. Then, as she feared, a female voice came on the line speaking in the native tongue. Alethea did, however, recognize the word "Abjala."

"Do you speak English . . . or French?" she asked anxiously.

"Oh, yes, of course," the woman said in English.

"Oh, thank goodness." Alethea heaved a great sigh of relief. "My name is Alethea Holmes," she began slowly. "My father is Dr. Craig Holmes. Do you know him?"

There was a long pause. Either the woman knew him or she didn't. What was the delay? Finally, she said, "Yes, I know him. Please . . . where do you telephone from?"

"I'm at the airport—stranded, I'm afraid. My father was supposed to pick me up over an hour ago. I was hoping someone there would know where he is."

There was another long hesitation. "Oh, I see. May I put you on hold for a minute, Miss Holmes?"

The phone buzzed quiet static into Alethea's ear while she waited, biting her lower lip. The minute seemed to stretch out infinitely while the phone echoed and clicked.

Finally, the woman came on again. "Miss Holmes?"

"Yes."

"I'm going to connect you with the oil minister, Suliman Akmet. Will you hold, please?"

"Yes," she managed to reply, wondering how on earth she had rated speaking to the oil minister himself! Maybe her father was tied up with this Suliman Akmet. That would explain the delay, wouldn't it?

The phone clicked dead again. She waited, shifting her weight from one foot to the other, watching a giant jet take off with a shimmering roar. It had been a long day—first Athens, then switching planes in Riyadh, and now this. She had almost forgotten what she was waiting for when Suliman Akmet's voice broke into her thoughts.

"Miss Holmes? Dr. Craig Holmes's daughter?" he asked in a well-educated, British-accented voice.

"Yes. I'm so sorry to disturb you, Mr. Akmet, but my father was supposed to meet me at the airport. I've been waiting for some time. Is he with you?"

There was no immediate answer. Alethea felt her nerves grow raw, her palm grow clammy against the warm black receiver.

After a while, the oil minister said, "Your father is not here, Miss Holmes. If you'll but be patient for a few minutes longer, I shall come myself."

"Oh . . . but that's not really necessary for you to—"

"I insist. I'll be there shortly."

"Well . . . all right." They clicked off. The oil minister was coming to pick her up himself? Amazing.

And now she was waiting again, waiting for Suliman Akmet. A man who was a complete stranger. It all seemed very strange. And she was more positive every second that something dreadful had happened. Maybe it was a good thing she had come. Her father might need some care and medical attention. Maybe she'd have to fly him back to the States. God! Why didn't this Akmet get here?

After endless minutes, a long, sleek, black Cadillac limousine with small diplomatic flags fluttering from each side pulled smoothly up to the main door of the airport. The driver got out and approached the entrance. Inside the vehicle, Alethea caught a glimpse of a man seated in the corner of the backseat, wearing a white headcloth, dark glasses.

The driver was walking toward her, asking politely, "Miss Holmes?" He took her suitcase, then ushered her out to the car, while she got an impression of people's heads turning, staring at them in awe. And, she admitted, she was a bit awed herself.

When the door was opened, she stepped inside, and the door clunked shut, enclosing her in a hushed, semidark, air-conditioned interior that smelled of oiled leather and an aromatic tobacco, and . . . power.

"Miss Holmes." The voice was deep, elegantly smooth.

"Mr. Akmet?" Suddenly, Alethea became aware of her wrinkled suit, hastily done-up bun, the sticky feel of nervous sweat under her arms and on her hands.

"I am so glad to meet you." He held out a perfectly manicured hand. "Your father said nothing of your visit."

She could not help but notice that Suliman Akmet was a striking figure, impeccably dressed in the latest Gucci suit. His white headcloth contrasted sharply with his dark features, making his face seem all the more compelling. His nose was prominent, high-bridged, yet straight and even. His lips were thin and turned slightly down at the corners. He wore a thin mustache and well-trimmed beard. But she could not see his eyes, as he wore sunglasses which reflected back to her only distorted, fragmented images of herself.

"It was a last-minute plan," she said finally, clenching her fists unconsciously. "My father—is he all right? Where is he?" The note of worry revealed itself clearly now. She could no longer make a pretense of hiding it.

Suliman Akmet took one of her hands in his. She noted unthinkingly that his hand was quite cold. He removed his sunglasses carefully and looked directly at her, his face smoothly handsome, a slight frown on his brow, his large, dark eyes unreadable.

"I'm so sorry, Miss Holmes. Your father has had quite a serious accident . . ."

A low moan of dismay escaped her lips. "How bad is it? Is he in the hospital? Can I go to him?"

"Miss Holmes, your father—"

"No!" she cried, knowing instantly what Akmet was going to say. "No!" She could feel a dread fear swell up behind her eyes, choke her throat.

"I'm so sorry. It was an accident. In his lab. A fire . . . everything destroyed." The smooth voice sounded so concerned.

"No," she whispered, drawing back into a corner of the huge car. "I don't believe it. I want to see him." A darkness fluttered in front of her eyes.

"I have taken the liberty of seeing to the details," he went on slowly, carefully. "There will be formal services held here Saturday. The American chargé d'affaires will handle this end. What a dreadful time for you to arrive. It only happened yesterday."

The voice went on, each sentence like a blunt nail driven into her brain, wounding, stunning, dazing her into a cold, suffering immobility, taking her far away into a place where everything was

22

unreal, nightmarish, frozen, unendingly bleak and cold, so cold.

She heard the Arab's voice continue, but now she could not make out his words; they were so distant. She sensed his hand on her arm. She saw his brown eyes fill with sympathy for her. She heard a long, quavering breath and realized it was her own.

Reality began to filter back in small ways—the slanting afternoon sunlight outside, the smooth jolting of the car, the tall, new buildings beginning to bunch together along the modern street they traveled, Akmet's voice, low and soothing.

"I know this is a terrible shock. Please accept all my sympathy. Your father was a wonderful man, a brilliant scientist. We will miss him."

Was Akmet really talking about her father? Was? He was gone, then? Never to be seen again, spoken to, joked with, hugged, laughed at. And dead, not from quiet old age, or disease, but in a roaring, explosive fire.

Alethea shuddered, goose bumps rising on her arms. Her eyes closed and hot tears squeezed out from under the lids, burning liquid paths down her cheeks. She could not fit her thoughts around the stark knowledge of finality.

"I can't believe it," she choked out. "Please, please, let me see him. You must be mistaken—"

"I wish I were, believe me. I would give anything if I did not have to tell you this frightful news." His voice was fervent. She had to believe him. She knew it was true. She was only lying to herself, trying to escape the inevitable truth.

"Miss Holmes, we're going to the Hilton, where I have taken the liberty of making a reservation for you. If you wish, I can send someone up to stay with you?"

A stranger? To share her grief, her sudden loneliness and pain?

"No," she said, trying to regain control of herself. "Nobody, please. I don't want anyone."

"Will you be all right? Perhaps one of the American wives—"

"No," Alethea repeated firmly. Her nose was running. She sniffed, tried to wipe the tears away. Akmet pulled a spotless silk handkerchief out of his pocket and handed it to her. It smelled obscurely of aftershave and Gauloises. "I'll be fine. It has to all sink in. I'm not going to slash my wrists or anything. It's just such a shock."

"Of course. I understand."

23

The limousine pulled up smoothly in front of the imposing Hilton. Akmet handed her out to the driver, who whisked her into the hotel, up a hushed elevator, into a suite of rooms done in cool blues and greens.

She sat, dazed and spent, on one of the double beds, her hands playing idly with the strap of her purse. What was she to do now? Go home, back to work, as if nothing had happened? Or spend days, weeks, sobbing and tearing her hair? She felt so empty, so totally without direction. There was no one to call on, not a soul she could think of beyond acquaintances.

"I got these from the hotel doctor."

Her head snapped up. Suliman stood before her, holding out a small plastic bottle. He read the label. "Take one before bed." She took the bottle and sat looking at the Arabic words until they blurred and danced in front of her eyes, unable to make sense of the strange, curling characters.

The warm whisper of his breath touched her hair. "They're sleeping pills. Just in case you need them. They might help."

"Thank you, but really . . ."

"Just don't take too many." His face split in a thin smile as he bent over her. "I will have your dinner sent up. Ring the front desk for anything you want, please. The staff is aware of your . . . ah . . . situation. I have given them orders that you are to be well cared for. And feel free to phone me at any time, for any reason whatsoever." He handed her a card with his name and a phone number, then seemed to hesitate. "Would you prefer that I stayed with you for a while?"

"Oh, no. I'm just going to take a bath and try to relax. I don't think I'll need these things. I'll be all right." She suddenly wanted to be alone. She wanted to cry for a long time without having anyone look at her with pity, or make her think about anything. Afterward, she'd be herself again and know exactly what to do.

"Don't forget to call if you need anything. *Anything*. I will be here tomorrow morning at nine to collect you. There are some things to go over, some calls to be made abroad, I'm sure. And then I shall take you to the services at the consulate."

"Tomorrow at nine. All right," she said absentmindedly, her thoughts focused inward to the welling anguish.

Her mind kept circling one painful thought like a vulture, ready to pounce but wary. Then she could no longer keep from touching on it. She hadn't seen her father in almost a year—since last

Easter in Paris. She had put her own career, her own wants, desires, needs above her father's well-being. Perhaps if she'd seen him more often when he was still living in Boston, made more of an attempt, but that was absurd. It would not have changed what happened. It *would* have made her feel better, less burdened with remorse, yes, and even a kind of guilt. She could not indulge in pure mourning. It was too mixed with self-blame. And it was too late now.

She sat on the edge of the bed and cried for her father, wrapping her arms around her body and rocking back and forth in misery. She felt so alone. There wasn't another living soul in the world she belonged to, or who belonged to her.

The room was growing dark as evening approached. Still, Alethea did not move. Her sobs died down and she began to feel calmer. She told herself that death was a common occurrence. It happened every second of every day and left someone bereaved. But everyone recovered from grief as life went on. She knew she would bear it: the service here, and then a flight home, a funeral there. She'd bear it, just as everyone else did. It would take time, but she would survive.

It was then that Nick DeWolff's face appeared unbidden in her mind's eye. She felt a sudden surge of longing for him. He would be able to comfort her, say the right words. Just his presence would be so good. Alethea knew it, even while telling herself she hardly knew him, that he was a virtual stranger. Still, she wished with every fiber of her being he was with her.

The evening light slipped in through the blinds, falling in golden stripes across the room as Alethea eventually found the energy to get up and take off her clothes. She lay down on the bed, pulled the sheet up to her chin. It didn't hurt quite as much anymore. It wasn't quite as shocking.

Life would go on.

Chapter 4

Saturday, December 3

Nick DeWolff heard the familiar dull thump of the newspaper as it hit the front door, then bounced back down the apartment steps. He unfolded his lean frame from the couch, placed his morning cup of coffee on the table and opened the door.

Sure enough, there was the *Washington Post* lying in the middle of the sidewalk. Barefooted, naked except for his robe, he went down the three concrete steps and picked up the thick bundle.

God, it was cold out, he thought a moment later while slamming the door behind him and tossing the paper casually aside.

He strode into the small kitchen of his Dupont Circle apartment and poured himself more steaming black coffee. He should be writing a report for Skip Porter, not lounging around. That business in Athens had been sticky, and his boss would want a full report on his desk Monday morning. The National Security Council was like every other government agency—they didn't give a damn if you'd just spent two weeks nearly getting your head blown off. They wanted a report, in triplicate, no later than yesterday.

Hell, thought Nick, picking up the newspaper as he dropped himself easily onto the couch. The report could wait.

He began scanning the front page. Same old stories: Uprising of Guerrilla Troops in Central America, Hostages Taken, President Meeting with his Advisers on Explosive Mideast Issues. On and on it went, and who the blazes was out there to stop it?

Skipping the editorials, his eyes came to rest on a small column on page three headed, "Scientist Killed in Abjala."

Abjala. Suddenly, it brought to memory the attractive woman in Athens, the one who had managed to bring him out of his tired, lonely mood. The evening had been surprisingly perfect—Alethea, a pure pleasure. She could be very special. Funny, he recalled, didn't she say her father worked in Abjala?

And then the name, Dr. Craig Holmes, flew up from the dark print to meet his eyes.

"Lord," he whispered. What a damn pity. Alethea must be terribly upset. He remembered her concern, then wondered if she had gotten there before or after her father's death.

Nick scanned the first paragraph of the article that listed Dr. Holmes's credentials, then slowed his reading.

. . . a tragic laboratory accident . . . explosives ignited Thursday . . . funeral to be held on Sunday in Boston, Holmes's hometown . . . arrangements being made by the oil minister, Suliman Akmet, who expressed to the press his deep sorrow over the loss of the renowned scientist . . .

Thursday, Nick thought. So Alethea's worry had been well founded. And they had been out dining and dancing while he selfishly made light of Dr. Holmes's phone call!

An accident was a little too coincidental for Nick's taste. It just didn't fit. Alethea had said it was uncharacteristic of her father to ask her to come to Abjala. Whatever he had wanted, he'd been unable . . . or afraid . . . to communicate it to her over the telephone. And then this so-called accident. Pretty damned unlikely.

Nick closed the paper and rose, pacing the room like a pent-up tiger, unable to relax. He recalled Alethea's image: high forehead, straight nose, small, pointed chin, a smooth white, almost translucent, complexion. Not a spectacular beauty, but the kind

27

of girl who grew on you with time and familiarity. The kind of face that was not all on the surface, but was subtle, demanding emotional attachment to unlock its beauty. How was she taking all this? She had told him that her father was her only living relative.

Nick strode purposefully into his bedroom and began looking through his trouser pockets. Where in hell was that scrap of paper? If only he could keep an address book on him, but who ever heard of a top-security agent having one of those?

Finally, he found it. Alethea's New York telephone number hastily scribbled, the numbers jumbled in a familiar pattern, on the back of a matchbook cover.

He sat down on the bed and dialed. Of course, if the funeral was in Boston on Sunday, it was doubtful he would reach her. Yet he felt he should at least try.

The number rang and rang. An accident, his mind kept repeating. Very strange . . .

He placed the receiver back onto its cradle with a deep frown creasing his brow. He could try to call her overseas, in Abjala—she might still be there—get hold of her through that oil minister mentioned in the *Post*. But that wouldn't be wise.

Some time later, Nick showered and dressed snugly in a pair of jeans and an Irish knit pullover. Leaving his apartment, he walked through the damp, cold air down to the neighborhood grocery. After buying enough food to last him the weekend, he returned home and whipped up three eggs, bacon and a pitcher of orange juice. But his mind was not on the mechanical functions of living. He was growing more edgy, more tense with each passing minute.

He shoved his food aside and went into the bedroom again. Maybe he could get Skip Porter at home, Nick thought as he dialed.

"Hello?" came a small child's voice, probably Mandy, he decided.

"Is your father there?"

No reply, just a clump that echoed in his ear. But the line was still open and Nick could hear muffled voices in the background.

Finally, his boss came on. "Yes?"

"Nick here."

"So you're back. Good. How did everything go?"

"You were right. Our friend was a bad boy." Nick referred to a fellow agent, gone sour and selling classified documents to the East Germans. The man had committed suicide after a chase that ended in Athens.

"Did you . . . correct him?"

"In a manner of speaking. He corrected himself. Permanently."

There was a pause at the other end of the line. Eventually, Porter said, "It was for the best. No need to air our dirty linen and all that."

"No, sir. No need at all."

"Have a full report on my desk Monday morning."

"I will. Listen, Skip, something's come up and I'd like to see you for a few minutes."

"Is it important?" Porter hesitated. "Look, Alice and I have a wedding to go to at four. Can you stop by at, say, three?"

"I'll be there. And thanks."

Nick knew that Skip hated to be disturbed over the weekend, but this business about Alethea's father wouldn't hold until Monday. At least, thought Nick, he wouldn't be able to rest until he had voiced his suspicions to Porter, who might have input on the subject.

He arrived at Porter's Silver Spring home a few minutes before three. Mandy answered the door, opening it a shy foot.

"Can I come in, Mandy?"

"Hi," came the piping voice of the five-year-old who finally allowed him entrance.

Porter was dressing, or so Nick gathered from the child who led him into the kitchen and asked him to reach the cookies for her.

"Am I going to get in trouble?" Nick asked, smiling warmly at the dark-haired girl.

"Oh, no. Mommy said I could."

"You better go ask your mother again," Porter said from the doorway.

Mandy scurried out. "Sorry to disturb you," said Nick, his blue eyes meeting those of the distinguished, gray-haired man. "It's just something I'd rather not sleep on."

"Let's go into my study."

Nick followed Porter into his hushed, ruby-carpeted study. He sat down in a wing chair facing Skip's desk. "I met a woman in

Athens," began Nick, half-smiling at Porter's raised brow. "Anyway, she was on her way to Abjala, to see her father, Craig Holmes. Apparently, he was some sort of a—"

"Genius," finished Porter easily. "Used to have top-security clearance when he worked on one of our government projects. I read about him in this morning's paper. Terrible waste."

"Yes," Nick said, then went on to tell Porter about Alethea's fears and the strange telephone call she had received from her father.

Porter was silent for a while after Nick finished. "It does seem a trifle coincidental . . . but you may be making a federal case out of nothing. You do," he paused, leveling his eyes at Nick, "have a flare for the dramatic."

Nick smiled tightly. "I'm seldom wrong, though. You've said it yourself. I've got a nose for trouble and I feel it, Skip, in my bones this time. Holmes's death was not an accident."

"Say you're right. Now why do you suppose he was . . . murdered?" Porter clasped his hands in front of him, staring intently now at Nick.

"That's a good question. Wish I knew the answer."

"Forget it, Nick." Porter rose hastily, checking his watch. "Take a few days off this week. Get some rest. You're naturally tired out."

The interview was obviously over. "Maybe," Nick said thoughtfully, walking to the door.

Porter's voice stopped him. "Is this Alethea Holmes attractive?"

Nick laughed, showing even white teeth. "Very."

Porter shook his head. "I thought so."

After giving Mandy, who sat in front of the television, a conspiratorial wink, Nick left the NSC adviser's house and drove back toward Washington. He should have known Porter would be skeptical. He always was. At least they understood one another. They were men playing the same game, holding the same dangerous cards. This time, though, Nick knew he was right.

As he steered the green BMW through the heavy weekend traffic, he thought about Porter and about how easily Porter had dismissed him. Nick remembered a time he had returned to Washington badly banged up. Skip had visited him in the Army Hospital and said something that had stuck firmly in Nick's mind. "You're lucky you're alive," he had said. And then, "You take too many chances . . . You're a thrill junkie."

A thrill junkie. What a wonderful way to describe your life! But it had a ring of truth to it. Maybe, Nick thought now, it was true. But wasn't that what they paid him handsomely for—for his expertise, his education, the years spent in Nam with Naval Intelligence, and afterward, in Africa, South America. Besides, somebody had to do the dirty work. Men like Porter wouldn't. They preferred to sit behind their desks and push buttons.

By the time Nick got back to Dupont Circle, he was feeling like a caged animal, depressed and jumpy.

If only Alethea were home, he could find out a little more about her father and his work for the closemouthed oil sheiks.

Nick pulled the green car smoothly into a spot in front of his apartment, the empty place he occasionally rested his head and sarcastically called "home." When did Alethea say she was returning to New York? Monday, he was sure. Something about an article due for her magazine. But Monday was forty-eight hours away. A long time.

And what the hell did he care about some girl he met passing in the night? Oh, sure, he'd like to see her again, but conjuring up a murder case in his mind as a pretext to phone her *was* going a bit far.

He turned the key in his lock. A thought drifted over him darkly. This job of his was getting too much like the endless waiting between missions in Vietnam, the oppressive, sick feeling that the calm wouldn't last . . .

And the feeling didn't go away. It hung over him as he tried to catch up on routine paper work. At last he gave up and pushed his chair away from his rolltop desk. No good. His body yearned for action, his mind for a challenge.

He paced the floor, taking bites out of an apple he'd absent-mindedly picked up, glanced at his watch: 4:43. The afternoon and evening stretched out ahead of him bleakly.

He could call the folks and invite himself up for the day. But he quickly dismissed that idea. He always felt a little guilty leaving them—his mother with so many unanswered questions and his father with caustic retorts that were still unspoken. They hadn't come to terms with him since he'd returned from Nam, a disillusioned vet who'd seen too much carnage in the field and incompetence in high places.

When they started in on his present job, that always clinched it. His mother would cry and say it was too dangerous and his father would ask again, bitterly, why they'd wasted so much money sending him to Harvard Law School.

They couldn't understand that the war had left him with a need for excitement, that he couldn't stay away from it, and they also refused to believe that most of his job was routine, boring paper work.

Needing to distract himself, Nick ticked off possibilities in his mind and vetoed them one by one until he thought of Catherine. Of course, Catherine would be perfect. That is, if she weren't busy on a Saturday night. And knowing Catherine, he couldn't imagine her without a date. He dialed her number.

"Hello?" came her low, husky voice. Even over the phone it promised unspoken pleasures.

"Catherine. It's Nick."

"Nick, love! So good to hear your voice!"

He plunged right in. "You busy tonight?"

There was the slightest pause. "It just so happens I'm not. I was going to stay home and do my nails."

"Dull. Go somewhere with me instead."

She laughed throatily. "How can I resist when you ask me so gallantly?"

"Great. I'll pick you up at eight. Dinner, then dancing or something."

"I'll be waiting with bated breath, darling."

He was in luck. Catherine was always deluged with men. And no wonder. She was a top fashion model—tall, lissome, pale silvery blonde hair, high-cheekboned Nordic face that had been on more magazine covers than he could count. They had once been lovers, but passion had changed to something that satisfied both of them even more: friendship. He didn't have to pose with Cat. She knew him too well.

A few hours later, Nick found himself telling her about Alethea over coffee in a Georgetown restaurant. "So the poor kid must be devastated. She's all alone. I tried to call even though I knew she wasn't supposed to be back till Monday anyway."

Catherine's huge blue eyes widened. "How awful. And to be so far from home—where did you say?"

"Abjala."

"Yes. Well, just keep trying to get her. She'll need your sympathy."

"I will."

"Nick, are you serious about this girl? You sound—"

"Cat," he interrupted, "have I *ever* been serious about a girl?"

"No, darling, but thi time you sound, well, anxious."

"I only met her two days ago."

"Don't you believe in love at first sight? I fell in love with my first husband in a split second."

Nick snorted. "No, I damn well don't!"

Catherine leaned across the table and flicked a long finger under his chin. "You poor thing. No romance in your life at all!"

"I had enough of that stuff in Nam to last me," he said darkly.

"I know, Nick, love. You told me about Mei Ling, but that was years ago. You can't go running from relationships forever because of her."

"Okay, Dr. Freud," he said sarcastically. "What's your professional advice?"

"Oh, if you're going to be like that . . ."

"Come on, where do you want to go now, Cat? Let's have some fun."

It was nearly two in the morning when Nick stopped his car in front of Catherine's high-rise. He walked her through the elegant, hushed lobby and up to her apartment door.

"Want to come in for a while?" Catherine asked, her blonde, curved eyebrows arched questioningly.

He'd been waiting for her to ask. He had decided he was going to say yes, when something stopped him. He bent, not very far, to kiss Catherine's cheek. She smelled delicious. "No, not tonight, Cat. I've got a headache." He grinned wickedly at her, knowing she understood him perfectly. Besides, why ruin a good friendship?

She threw back her head and laughed that low, husky laugh of hers. He joined her. It was good to have a friend with whom you could laugh, even if it was at yourself.

Chapter 5

Saturday, December 3

As it turned out, Suliman Akmet was very thoughtful. He took care of Alethea as if she were a member of his own family. He picked her up at precisely nine in the morning and drove her to his plush office in the Abjala Petroleum Building. There he quietly, efficiently placed calls to Boston: the funeral home, the airport, the newspaper, even an old friend of her father's who would be there tomorrow to meet Alethea's overnight flight. That was always the worst part, all the arrangements, the paper work. It was terrible and morbid when you couldn't think. Suliman, she came to realize, was a heaven-sent blessing.

Afterward, they left his ultramodern office building, which towered above the low, squat buildings of lesser government officials, and drove to the American Consulate, where the chargé d'affaires held a short service before members of Dr. Holmes's staff in Abjala and a few other Americans whom Alethea didn't know. Everything went smoothly, quietly, dully.

And still it was ghastly. The chargé d'affaires was a sunburned, cherubic-faced young man, terribly ill at ease with her, obviously wishing himself far from this uncomfortable situation. The service was held on the well-tended lawn. The weather turned chilly, with a desert wind kicking up plumes of the ubiquitous brown dust from the surrounding streets.

Alethea did not cry. She stood still, ignoring the wind that snatched at her skirt and whipped her hair into long, ragged streamers. She heard the words of the service, but they were faint and unreal. She shook hands, smiled politely at the people who spoke to her.

It all seemed so ridiculously useless, like a long-outdated custom that had lost all meaning. It all seemed like a farce.

Suliman stood close by her side. He did not intrude on her thoughts or feelings, but she felt his presence. It was very kind of him to spend so much valuable time with the daughter of a man he knew so slightly, Alethea thought.

And then they went inside to a meal she barely touched. They left and he drove her several miles across the expanse of bright, barren desert to the American complex where her father had lived. Alethea was terribly afraid she'd break down again when she saw his things, but mercifully the three-room apartment was so austere, so devoid of any personal touches, that she felt it could have been a stranger's. There was only one bad moment—when she saw his old paisley bathrobe, rather tattered now, hanging on a hook in the bathroom. The familiarity of it hurt like a knife twisting inside her.

"Is there anything here you wish sent on the plane to Boston with you?" Akmet asked gently.

"No, not really. Give his clothes away. I have no use for them."

"I'll have his books and papers boxed and sent to your home. It's in New York, didn't you say?"

"Yes. New York. I'll leave you my address . . ." It was then that she saw the picture on a dresser. It was a silly one, taken at least ten years before. She and her mother and her father, on a pebbled beach in Italy with a quaint village rising behind them. They had all been laughing at the antics of the young boy taking the picture. She had been a skinny, immature teenager, maybe fifteen. A sudden gust of sorrow swept her. Never again. Her mother first, but at least she'd had someone to lean on then. Now her father, and she was totally alone.

"I . . . I think I'll take the picture," Alethea said, feeling her eyes turn hot and scratchy. She clasped it to her chest, as if to press the pain into herself, to hug the ache to her.

Suliman took her arm silently, led her out into the glaring sunlight, into the cool, dark cavern of the limousine, and spoke rapidly to the driver in Arabic.

They drove along the shoreline that had looked so ragged from the airplane, through dry salt flats. Brown hills rose into sandpaper-rough mountains to the west. The turquoise water rolled lazily into shore. Ancient, triangular-sailed dhows plunged on their way to ports further east. Suliman described everything. It became more and more evident to Alethea that this man, his land and his culture were vast worlds away from hers. He pointed out modern structures of steel and concrete that rose off the desert floor and pierced the pellucid sky. His voice rang softly with a passion born of an ancient pride, of an emotion that was as elusive to her as a breath of wind.

"Would you care to see more of Abjala?" he asked, leaning close to her, his breath fanning her cheek.

"Yes," she said honestly, "I would."

He instructed the driver to take them through the older sections, the still-untouched, winding streets of the ancient city.

"As you can see, Alethea," his hand gestured out the window, "we have a long way to go to truly enter the modern world . . . a very long way."

Her eyes took in the scenes of poverty, of unlivable structures, of children in rags wandering above open sewers in the streets, of a marketplace unfit to enter. "It's depressing," she whispered.

"Yes. More so for a man in my position," he replied. "But someday all of our people shall share in the wealth. It is a promise I have made myself."

"Very noble." She meant it. The world needed men who cared, who could open their eyes to the obvious problems their people experienced.

"You must be tired," he said, then instructed the driver to return to the hotel.

The car inched its way back through the old district and out onto a wide, modern boulevard lined with palms and superstructures whose many windows glinted in the late desert sun.

This was Suliman Akmet's world, not the awful districts he had just shown her. Alethea became intensely aware of him, of his dark, compelling good looks, his all-encompassing aura of power. Yes, she thought, a man like Suliman could truly bring his people out of bygone ages.

He asked her if she would care to dine with him that evening.

"At eight, then," he said, taking her hand as the sleek black limousine stopped in front of the Hilton. "I do not wish to press you, but it is better for you to get out, be busy, see people. It will take your mind off your grief."

He still had on those dark glasses, making it almost impossible for Alethea to judge his expression. He had a kind of contained intensity that frightened yet attracted her. What was really behind those opaque lenses?

That afternoon she fought taking one of the little sleeping capsules. In spite of her raw nerves, she slept quickly, but awoke shortly later with a start and a throbbing, groggy head.

She tried reading, but the words blurred and ran, and she found herself looking at the same paragraph twenty times over without comprehending a single word.

Finally, she took a long, relaxing bath, then dressed mechanically for dinner.

Suliman picked her up shortly after the *muezzins* ended their haunting call to evening prayer. It was dark but only faintly cool outside the hotel as she stepped into the long black limousine, handed in by the chauffeur.

"Good evening, Alethea." Akmet's deep, resonant tones emerged from the darkness of the car. The usual cloud of strong smoke surrounded him, the perpetual Gauloise dangled gracefully from his lean brown fingers. "I hope you enjoy our evening before your flight. I have chosen a very special place for you. It is one of my favorites." His lips split into a white smile. "Tonight is all for you. Abjala must leave you with some good memories."

He had finally removed his dark glasses. His eyes were large, dark, limpid. He looked younger.

The restaurant was posh. They ate in a private dining room curtained off from the outside world. Almost like a harem, Alethea thought fleetingly—the elegant gold hangings, the thick Persian carpet, the soft lighting, even a small, blue-tiled fountain that dripped into a tiny stone pool. It occurred to her to write about the place for *The World's Fare*, a conditioned reflex, but she pushed the thought aside. Not tonight.

Three boys in white robes and headcloths waited on them, not uttering a word the whole time. It was eerie. They brought course after course of fantastically prepared tidbits: tahini salad, dips and cucumber slices, skewered pigeons, stuffed vegetables, minute shishkebabs. No wine was served, according to Muslim custom, although Suliman had asked her if she wanted any. Then the main dishes arrived. Lamb in a delicious sauce that defied description, flat bread still hot from the oven, piles of steaming white rice, yogurt, a vegetable mélange with dill and lemon. It went on and on, slowly, serenely, suffused with a thousand years of tradition.

"I know you are a connoisseur yourself," said Suliman between courses. "Of course, your father told me about your most fascinating job. I hope all this is to your liking."

"It's absolutely marvelous. I'd love to write it up sometime for my magazine."

"It can be arranged with the management. I have only to say the word."

"Oh, no, I'd need more time, but thank you anyway."

"Tell me, Alethea," he said, leaning toward her, his almond-shaped eyes resting on hers. "What will you do now?"

"Oh, after the funeral I'll go back to New York, take a little time off, I guess. Then to work again."

"Is it not an empty existence? Do not women need a home and children? Or are you too modern for all that?" He smiled at her, making him appear not rude, but simply interested.

"It isn't at all empty. I have an interesting job, friends, my own life. I'll probably want to get married someday and have children. I'm just not ready yet. There's so much to see and do, so many experiences I haven't had yet."

"Ah, yes, I know that feeling. It was the way I felt when I first left my country to go to school in England. Open to everything, desiring every experience, every sensation. That is youth speaking."

"You lived in England?" she asked, interested in this strange man who was half Western and half Eastern.

"Yes, for several years, and in the United States also. Oxford, then Cal Tech. I learned very much from both. I learned 'wog' in England and a few rather more rude words in the States. I also learned how to make my country a world power in oil. That was perhaps the easiest thing I did learn in your world."

"I suppose it was hard for you. People can be so cruel." She was embarrassed for the narrow-minded bigots he must have run into.

"It was not all like that. When you have money, and my family supplied me with that liberally, you can always find people who will be your friends."

"Real friends?"

"Some of them, yes. I still keep in touch with men all over the world in high places who were at school with me. We make quite a little international clique."

"Fascinating."

"Yes, and lonely, too, at times."

"Do you prefer living here?"

"Infinitely. This is my home. I love every grain of sand with a passion, and will protect it with my life, if need be."

Suddenly, it occurred to Alethea that she had no idea whether Suliman was married or not. There had certainly been no evidence of a wife, but perhaps customs were different here.

"Do you have a family?" she asked.

"No." He smiled, his thin black mustache lining his upper lip pleasingly. "I am, alas, wedded to my job, as you are."

She could find no rejoinder for his comment. She hoped he hadn't seen through her question, or thought her too forward. Perhaps she'd better change the subject.

"Your job must be very challenging. I wonder how you've found the time to spend with me. I'm very grateful."

He spread his hands in a characteristically Mideastern gesture. "When something tragic happens, one must be prepared to take the time. And, also, I have enjoyed your company so much. It is not often that I have the opportunity to dine with a beautiful woman, especially here in Abjala." His dark liquid eyes glowed warmly at her in the dim light.

"Thank you, but—"

"No, thank *you*, Alethea."

There was a short silence broken only by the splashing of the tiny fountain, a sound that seemed momentarily to fill the curtained room. Then Suliman spoke again.

"I want you to know that your father was a genius. We had such great hopes for his research." He hesitated. "Did you know anything about his work?"

"Not really."

"He was working on a very complicated new process. It would

have brought us great benefits—also the rest of the world." He looked concerned now. "It is a terrible tragedy for everyone that he is . . . gone."

It was good to hear that her father had been held in high esteem. Somehow it helped, if only a little. At least he'd been appreciated.

"Can you salvage anything from his lab? Papers or anything like that?" she asked.

"We have tried. We can find nothing that was not destroyed. Perhaps, if you find anything at home, you would be so kind as to let me know?" Suliman gave her a sharp look, disconcerting her a little.

"Of course. But I don't remember ever having seen any of his stuff in New York."

"Probably not, but one never knows, and it is of such vital importance." Akmet smiled again. "Now let us change the subject. Tell me about your work."

So the evening continued. Alethea found him an interesting man, a strange mixture of East and West. A man full of the knowledge of his own power and wealth, one who knew his way intimately in the corridors of many world capitals. Yet he accepted her as an equal. It was very flattering. She could grow to like this man very much, given the opportunity to meet him under different circumstances. He was extremely attractive with his dark eyes, his perfectly trimmed goatee and mustache, his high-bridged aristocratic nose, his beautiful British accent.

When he took her back to the Hilton to pack her suitcase, it was late. The black limousine pulled up to the hotel's doors and double-parked, disregarding the angry horns of other drivers. Suliman took her hand, leaned toward her. She was terribly afraid he was going to kiss her, but he didn't.

"You will get over your father. He will be a happy memory soon, and more beloved for being so. He was a genius and will be missed, but you must go on without him now. I know you will be successful at anything you choose to do, and it is because of his influence that you will be. Always remember that."

Alethea went to her room and collected her things while Suliman's words drifted in and out of her thoughts: you'll be successful . . . because of your father's influence. A nice, comforting thought. It fortified her.

When she returned to the limousine, she took Suliman's polite gesture of handing her into the car for granted. She was already growing accustomed to it.

They drove the short miles to the airport, and when he brushed her hand lightly with his lips and had the copilot seat her in the first-class compartment long before anyone else was permitted to board, she took that for granted, too. He even waited in the plane until the other passengers boarded. He made small talk, smiling often. Only once did he mention any business.

"I hate to bring this up again, Alethea—the project your father was working on. Should you get back to America and think of anything, or perhaps come across any of his papers, you could mail them to me and we could complete his work. You'd like to see that, wouldn't you?"

"Yes, certainly," she answered without hesitation. "I'll do anything I can to help you."

"Goodbye then. I hope we meet again. I have a feeling that our paths will cross sometime, don't you?"

Alethea laughed. "I'm not much for believing in fate. I think we control our own destinies. Perhaps we can *make* our paths cross. I would hate to think I'd never see you again."

"Good. Then we'll keep in touch. Have a pleasant journey."

His tall dark form disappeared from the plane, leaving Alethea in a vague turmoil. What had she started now? And then there was Nick . . . Would he really call her in New York?

There were so many things to think about, so many new facts to sift through and put in their mental places. She settled back in her seat, not even caring that the dusky men surrounding her turned in their seats to stare at the Western woman who traveled alone and who had been escorted onto the plane by Suliman Akmet, one of the most powerful people in their tiny country.

Nor did she notice the two men in dark glasses who sat on the other side of the aisle behind her, and who never took their eyes from her for the entire trip.

Chapter 6

Monday, December 5

"Chin up" came to mind as Alethea's cab jerked to a neck-snapping halt in front of *The World's Fare* Building on West Fifty-fourth Street.

Alethea had a racking headache and felt like her body had been through a tornado. She was done in: empty, lonely and miserable inside. She hadn't written another word on her article, not since the flight to Abjala, and was only stopping by the office to see her editor and tell him she needed some time off. Surely someone else in Alan Dunbar's stable of writers could finish the piece from her notes. This was the first time she'd ever missed a deadline.

Stepping out of the cab, Alethea put on sunglasses to cover her red, sore eyes.

She had to wait to see Alan, and sitting in his outer office, leafing through magazines, didn't help. Any situation that left her idle for a few minutes increased her anxiety. In desperation, Alethea tried to organize a pile of receipts for her expense account. Even so, her mind turned back to her father's funeral the day before in Boston. It had all been very proper, very quick, just as he would have liked it. His old friends from the years he'd worked in the aerospace industry were all there, somber and polite. It had been painful, and she hadn't slept much the night before on the long flight from Abjala. But it was all over now. When she got home, she could sob all she wanted, in private, away from people unsure of what to say.

Once Alethea was able to see Alan, he kept her for twenty minutes with a lecture on pulling herself together, time being the best healer, etcetera.

She rose to go. "Thank you, Alan. You've been very kind. I think I'll pick up my mail and just go home and sleep for a week. I'm really beat."

"Of course you are. Take all the time you want." He stood and put an arm around her shoulder while they walked to his door. "You just let me know when you're ready to come back."

"I will. And thank you again. Really."

"No problem."

Her next stop was the third floor, where the pool secretary, Miss Worth, kept Alethea's mail for her while she was abroad. There was a stack of it, as usual. It must weigh twenty pounds, Alethea thought, noticing several food and wine magazines that Alan insisted his writers review.

It took the cab thirty minutes to weave in and out of the rush-hour traffic and make its way down to 34 West Ninth Street in the Village where Alethea kept an apartment. She'd had it since college. It was rent-controlled, and she wouldn't give up the place for the world. Oh, yes, there was the Paris apartment, too, but New York was her favorite city even though she spent so much time in Europe on assignment.

Wearily, she climbed the four narrow flights to her apartment on the top floor. It was a tiny place, really only two rooms if you didn't count the kitchen and bathroom—and she never considered them, for who would call an area a room when you couldn't turn around in it?

Entering the apartment, Alethea tossed the mail on the coffee table, deposited her small bag on the bed, kicked off her shoes and decided to have a large glass of wine to dull the edge of her exhaustion.

When she half-fell onto the couch and picked up the mail, she sighed deeply and a measure of tension ebbed from her body.

Tossing the junk mail aside, she glanced through the bills, decided they could wait, and looked over the single personal item in the stack. It was a card from Leysin, Switzerland, with a picture of the ski slopes on the face. She'd know that scrawled handwriting anywhere. Nobody could possibly desecrate handwriting worse than Clair, her oldest and dearest friend. Clair was a jet-setter. They'd first met in finishing school in Switzerland, and had seen each other frequently during the ensuing years. Trying to decipher the words, Alethea finally got the gist of the hastily written card. Clair had rented a chalet for December in Leysin and wanted Alethea to visit.

It would be nice to ski again, but to get on a plane again? To try and keep up a happy face in front of Clair? Maybe later in the month, when she felt a little better.

Picking up the full wineglass, she took a long drink, then let her head fall back on the couch and closed her eyes. She craved sleep. Maybe it would relieve this awful void within her.

She rubbed her eyes, they felt so swollen and scratchy. It didn't help. Starting to rise from the couch, Alethea picked up the mail again and noticed one envelope thicker than the others. Curious, she slipped the strange envelope out of the stack of magazines. How odd. It was addressed to her in her father's handwriting in care of *The World's Fare* and postmarked from Abjala. Alethea stared blankly at it for a long moment, forcing herself to remember that her father was dead now. It felt strange holding the packet in her hand. Lightly, she traced her finger over the handwriting, a tear burning a path down her cheek, a tightness forming in her chest.

Finally, she slipped a fingernail through the seal. It would be hard to read something from him now, very hard.

"Oh, Dad . . ." Alethea whispered aloud.

Taking a deep, ragged breath, she began to read the letter attached to the bunch of papers underneath.

"Dear Thea," it began. Tears spilled over and dropped onto the first page, blurring the words. With great effort, she read on.

> I realize you'll be here in a couple of days—can't wait to see you, hug you. It's been too long! By the time you get back to New York, you'll already know pretty much about everything, but I thought it would be safest to send my papers on ahead. Hang onto them

until I figure out the best way to make my discovery available. I've been busy with my job here, nearly done, though. And then, of course, I've been working on the final specifications for my "biggie"—a system which will make gasoline use almost a thing of the past. Can you imagine it, Thea? I know my notes will bore you to tears. Chemistry, as I recall, was not your "thing"! But to put it in layman's terms, I've developed a cheap, practical way to convert the gas engine into a hydrogen-burning engine.

As you know, hydrogen is the most abundant element in the universe, and it burns beautifully, cheaply, efficiently, without pollutants. In the past, storage was either expensive or very dangerous. That problem has been solved. I've invented a system so *anyone* can get all the fuel he needs by simply equipping his car with a water tank, a special carburetor, a supply of chemical additive, and *my* extremely secret semiconductor used to "dope" a magnesium bed. Lost you, didn't I?

That was for sure, she thought, but read on doggedly, fascinated.

Men have been experimenting with hydrogen-burning engines for years. My contribution is practical and affordable usage. Maybe it's not that special, but I just love bragging to you!

How like him, Alethea thought, to add that touch of humility. He had spent a lifetime at his work; mostly, though, as a rocket engineer in New England. Everything about his work was always so hush-hush. It had made her dad seem like some sort of a spy. It had been glamorous, exciting to think of him that way. And now it had apparently paid off for him.

It boggled her imagination.

Ever since your mother died and you started your career, I've been fooling around with this system. I just wish I could have completed my work out in the open, but as you can well imagine, the oil-producing nations would frown on my development, thus the secrecy. I'm not even so sure the U.S. of A. will be happy about my invention, but at least I have nothing to fear from them. I'm not so sure about Abjala. Just remember, Thea, should anything happen to me, find a way to keep these notes out of any single country's hands. I poured my life's blood into this project for mankind, and so far no one knows anything about it except you and me. It would kill me to see it gobbled up by one greedy country that could then virtually control the world.

Alethea scanned the beginning of the long letter again. Her father had been terribly upset when he wrote this. Oh, he tried to cover it up, but she could read between the lines. What did he mean by being careful . . . if anything happened to him?

She was grief-stricken reading his words, but now she was confused, too. Hydrogen engines had nothing to do with oil refining in Abjala.

Her brain reeled with thoughts, but nothing seemed to quite jell.

In case I'm not afforded the opportunity to explain the development of my discovery, I'm going to write it all down for you, Thea. I'd like you to read it, to better understand the direction of my life. When you're finished, remember it's imperative to hide these notes safely away until I get back to New York.

Alethea's spine began to tingle. The void, the emptiness, was slowly being replaced by uneasiness. She read on quickly, skimming the technical jargon, her mind straining to understand the full picture.

You were still a little girl when I left the company. I had been offered a high technical management position in the moon program. I didn't realize it then, but deep in my subconscious an idea—*the* idea—had taken root and was slowly gestating. It took years to break through the heavy workload of the Apollo program, then more years before the oil crisis fertilized the idea to the point of fruition. And it was only the time and financial support of the Abjala Petroleum Company that allowed it to ripen into maturity, right here in the laboratory where I am writing this.

Alethea remembered something—a silly memory—out of her distant past. One night in Boston, her father had invited a few of his colleagues over for dinner. Afterward, they had sat around the fireplace, laughing, drinking brandy. And she slipped in, ready for bed, carrying a blanket. Her father scooped her up onto his knee. She had asked him what they were talking about and he told her a story about a man driving into a gas station, pulling up to the water hose and saying, "Fill 'er up," to the attendant.

The story had been a joke, to her, but now she knew her father had been serious.

She trained her eyes back onto his letter.

. . . so keep these enclosed notes safe, dear. I haven't any copies for obvious reasons, and redoing them would be a helluva lot of work.

It's time for your dad to turn in, and you'll be here in a couple of days anyway. We'll have a long chat then. Can't wait.

> With all my love,
> Dad

The full impact of his work finally struck her like a brick tumbling from the sky. He had developed something so completely earthshaking that it took a while to comprehend the scope of it all.

But it *was* real. His notes, his scribbled papers, his letter were here in black and white, dangling from her hand. She looked at the thick wad of papers, shuffling through them. One was labeled: 4.1.1.3.1. Formation of Hydrogen Energy Constants. She didn't understand a word of the chemistry, the jargon, the diagrams, but it didn't matter. These papers contained all that was left of her father. It was the culmination and meaning of his life. That it was also a miracle that could help millions, no, *billions* of people did not escape her either.

Was this why he had wanted her to come to Abjala? To tell

her about this? Then why, *why,* had he sent his one set of notes to her?

And then it dawned on her, quickly, terrifyingly. No wonder he had sounded so strange over the phone!

Her mind racing now, Alethea knew, deep down in the pit of her stomach, that his apparent worry had been well founded and that . . . he must have feared for his own life.

Sudden terror hammered at her heart and crawled up her spine. It was not an accident. Could it be true? Or was she completely crazy even to think such a dreadful, horrifying thing?

Alethea stuffed the papers back into the envelope and began pacing the small living room in the dim evening light, her thoughts racing and jumping, but always coming to the same conclusion. He must have been murdered. There had been no accident in his lab. The damning proof of his concern, his worry, was lying on the coffee table, screaming the simple, undeniable facts.

But who in God's name would do such a monstrous thing? Who had a motive strong enough actually to kill her father?

She walked into the bedroom, back out into the living room, finally forcing herself to sit down and remain calm. Otherwise, she might go crazy.

Alethea found her thoughts dwelling on her father instead of trying to figure the mess out. She couldn't stop envisioning his face, his smile, the way he always laughed teasingly when he called her "Thea." And then she couldn't think anymore. The tears came, racking her body in a torrent of sobs that left her spent.

Evening turned into night. Alone in the darkness of her tiny apartment, she was aware neither of time nor her surroundings. It was as if acknowledging the possibility of murder had plummeted her into a state of shock that took the place of reality. At last, mercifully, she dozed. Exhaustion overtaking her, she let the numbness carry her into oblivion, a faceless, dark world where thought and pain could not touch her.

Sometime during the small, tender hours of morning, she awoke with a start and was flooded once again with confusion and grief. Still, even after the rest, she found thinking too difficult, too painful. Automatically, in the dark, she rose and went to the bathroom where she unconsciously filled the tub with hot water, pulled off her clothes and sank deep into the warmth where she wished she could stay forever.

Gradually, her mind began to function. There was something about his papers, not just that she had them, but something else . . .

She rose and wrapped a towel around her, then went into the living room, reaching down and touching the envelope, running her fingers over it as if it would tell her something.

That was it! Good Lord! Suliman Akmet had asked her about them! He had said something about an unfinished project. Did he know what was really contained in these papers? Was that why her father sent them out of Abjala? Was that why he had been so tense? Was Suliman Akmet somehow involved in the lab fire?

"Calm down, girl," she whispered, feeling her heart pound furiously in her chest. She was leaping to conclusions that might not be true at all. She'd have to back up a step or two and review the facts as she knew them.

Alethea did exactly that. She forced herself to go over everything as objectively as possible from the moment her father had asked her to come to Abjala.

Dawn crept over New York City in a blanket of gray, pushing the shadows in her living room back into the corners. She sat pensively on the couch. As the minutes ticked unendingly by, Alethea concluded that there was truly something very wrong in the death of her father. Her spine tingled coldly. It was true. His discovery was priceless, and Suliman Akmet wanted the papers . . .

Alethea rushed to her closet and pulled on a loose, Irish knit turtleneck, socks and jeans, then raced into the living room and snatched up the phone.

She had to call the police!

But after a long moment, she replaced the receiver. She really was going nuts! How in God's name could New York City's finest help her? Why, they'd laugh in her face!

Yet she had to get help—tell someone. But who?

She felt shaky, cold all over her body, and tried rubbing her arms briskly against the chill sweeping her.

Pacing the room like a nervous cat, Alethea racked her brain with a list of people she might call. But each name, each organization that flew into her mind was quickly dismissed. She walked tensely to the window and pulled back the interior shutters, looking out unseeingly over the quaint street. *Who* would believe and help her?

On the sidewalks below, people were walking hurriedly on their way to work, their faces bored, as if this were just another day filled with sameness.

Her eyes roamed the street at random. She had to think of whom to phone. She had to take some action against her father's murderer.

Inadvertently, not really seeing him, Alethea fixed her stare on the only unmoving person in the tide of bodies. If the man hadn't turned his dark face upward and looked directly at her window, she never would have truly seen him.

"Oh, my God! No!" It wasn't possible . . . but there he was, obviously an Arab, nervous and watchful, looking directly, unmistakably at her!

Her mind racing, Alethea slammed the shutters back together and clamped her hand over her mouth in horror. She thought her heart was going to burst. This was too ridiculous to be believed. And yet the fact remained, she was being watched. And Suliman Akmet had sent the man.

Think, Alethea, think! How could she get out of her building, escape somewhere with the papers? But if there was somebody in the front, surely there were others. And if they caught her with the papers . . . They'd take them and her father's life would have been lost in vain. She couldn't let that happen. She wouldn't!

Maybe she was imagining things. Perhaps the man had only been waiting for someone and she was being paranoid. Alethea again pulled aside the shutters a fraction of an inch. There he was, standing near the front door of her building, trying to appear nonchalant. Nobody noticed him. It was New York, after all, no one would. No one but Alethea herself.

Then she began to think in earnest. Should she try to disguise herself? A possibility, but fraught with the danger of being caught. Should she just try to wait it out? But she couldn't sit in her small apartment forever.

She'd have to get help—that was the only way. But the police would ask for explanations, treat her like a suspect herself. They probably wouldn't believe her anyway. This sort of thing was not their responsibility, and no doubt the Arabs would have diplomatic immunity.

Alethea fixed herself a cup of instant coffee just for something to do, then sat down at the kitchen table and took a sip. Damn!

She'd forgotten sugar. On the way to get some, she was drawn to the window again. Yes, he was still there, reading a paper now.

Having forgotten both the sugar and her coffee, Alethea sat down on the sofa and tried to go through the rest of her mail, but it was hopeless. What lay outside occupied all her thoughts. Dropping her head on the back of the couch, she massaged her eyes and tried to relax.

Suddenly, the ringing phone rent the air like a knife. She froze for a split second, paralyzed. Slowly, her hand reached out toward the shrieking black instrument. It shrilled again, twice, three times. She snatched it up.

"Hello?" Her voice sounded weak and shaky, even to her own ears.

"Alethea? Is that you?"

"Yes, who is this?" The male voice was vaguely familiar.

"Nick, Nick DeWolff. Remember? Athens last Thursday?"

Her breath released in a short exhalation. She had not even known she was holding it. "Nick? Oh, my God, Nick?" Her voice was shrill, saturated with relief.

"Yes. I've been trying to get you since Saturday. What's wrong? You sound strange."

"Oh, Nick, I'm so glad you called."

"I read about your father in the paper, and just wanted to say how sorry I am—"

"You know?" Alethea asked, thunderstruck.

"That your father was in a lab accident? It was in the *Washington Post*."

"Oh."

"Listen, Alethea, what's wrong? Is it your father?"

"No. Yes. Nick, there have been such strange things going on . . ." Unexpectedly, it struck her. Nick DeWolff worked for the federal government. "Whom do you work for?" she asked, knowing how strange the abrupt question must sound but not caring.

"What? Alethea—"

"Tell me, whom do you work for?"

"A government agency. Is there a problem?" His voice sounded wary.

"It's so crazy. Will you believe me if I tell you the story? I'm quite sane. I have to find someone who will help me."

"Whoa! You're going too fast. Slow down. Take it one step at a time."

"Will you believe what I tell you?" she demanded.

"Yes, you know I will."

So Alethea told him about her suspicions, about Suliman, about her father's papers, about the Arab watching her apartment. She tried very hard to recount the events in logical order, to make sense.

There was silence on the line when she finished.

"Nick?" she asked fearfully.

"Yes. I'm here. Look, your story may have something to it. I'm going to call a man who can help you—maybe. Sit tight, keep your door locked. Don't let anyone in, not *anyone*, understand? I'll get back to you as soon as I can. You okay?" His voice was brisk, efficient. He sounded like he knew what he was doing. It was infinitely reassuring.

"Yes. I am now. Oh, thank you, Nick. Call back soon, please."

"I will. I promise."

Hanging up the phone was one of the hardest things Alethea had ever done. It cut off her one link with Nick, with help. Please don't take long, Nick, she thought. She couldn't bear the waiting. Minutes stretched on, endlessly, each second a bead on the thread of time, passing rounded and full, seemingly in front of her eyes. Automatically, she retrieved her cold coffee. It was still sugarless and bitter.

She was about to give up hope when the phone rang. Even though she was expecting it, hoping for it, the ring startled her into spilling a few drops of coffee onto the table. She grabbed the receiver.

"Nick?" she cried.

"It's me. I promised, didn't I?"

"Oh, thank God."

"Now listen carefully. I'm coming to New York to get you out of there. Okay?"

"Yes, Nick, but that Arab—"

"Don't worry. Just wait for me. I'm driving, so it'll be a few hours. Just keep your door locked. Have you got one of those police locks?"

"Yes, but—"

"Good. When I get there, I'll knock, but don't let me in until I say, let's see . . . how about 'The Pipes of Pan'?"

"Philo's *taverna?*"

"Yes. That's something no one else would know. Then, and only then, do you let me in. Understand?"

"Yes. Oh, please hurry."

"I will. And Alethea . . ."

"Yes?"

"Stay away from the windows."

Chapter 7

Tuesday, December 6

It began to sleet somewhere between Baltimore and the Delaware Memorial Bridge on Interstate 95. Nick automatically slowed his speed, cursing under his breath. He wondered if the roads would be bad all the way up the New Jersey Turnpike and on into New York. Still, he was glad he had driven, as Kennedy International would be a mess in a snowstorm. This way, at least he would get there, even if he were late.

The traffic was terrible, inching along as the sleet built and froze on the dark road surface. He switched on his wipers to high and fell in behind an endless line of four-wheelers.

Dusk fell like a gray gauze curtain, and the miles ticked by tediously. All the while, he knew Alethea would be watching the clock, waiting, a bundle of nerves. At least one good thing would come out of the delay. He'd have time now to mull over in his mind exactly what he would say to Alethea about his job. It would be obvious, of course, that he'd lied to her in Athens, telling her he was a "paper-pusher." She would already know that, if she'd given any thought to why he, himself, was coming for her. How much of the truth should he sprinkle in to convince her? There was always the old standby line—he was a messenger type, hand-delivering documents, things like that, around the country. It sounded innocent enough, but would Alethea buy it? If she had an ounce of sense, she wouldn't.

Nick pulled the forest-green BMW out of the line of traffic and passed several trucks. The stream of slush from their tires made it impossible to see. He pulled back into the right lane and checked the time. Two or three more hours at this rate.

Maybe he should just tell her the truth—that he was an agent. Surely Alethea would understand why he had lied to her in Athens. Or would she? More than likely she'd back away from him as if he were a man to be feared. Somehow he didn't want this particular woman to think that of him, even if it were true.

Well, anyway, Nick told himself, he'd just have to judge the situation when he arrived at her apartment. He would try to handle her with kid gloves, win her trust back if indeed he had lost it by the lie.

Porter would get a big kick out of Nick's current dilemma—the fact that he was concerned about the women's reaction to him. And it was out of character for Nick, comical, really.

What had Porter said on the phone earlier? Nick thought back over their brief conversation.

"So you're still on that Holmes girl thing . . ." Porter had begun.

And then Nick had carefully explained all he dared over the telephone. "I spoke with her only minutes ago. She's in possession of documents vital to us if I understand her correctly."

"Sure she's not a kook?"

"Not in the least," Nick had replied. "As proof, she told me about a suspicious type outside her window—from the country mentioned at your home on Saturday."

Porter had hesitated, then become more interested. "Is she quite sure?"

"Absolutely. And she's scared. Wants help."

"Now listen," he had said cautiously, "do you think these documents are worth my time?"

"Positive. A nice feather in your cap if they're valid."

"All right. Drive on up there and bring her in. I just hope this isn't a wild goose chase."

"It would be faster to fly," Nick had said.

"No, no. Bad weather forecast. Drive. You'll have more leeway."

As it turned out, Porter was right. The weather had gotten worse, almost certainly causing indefinite delays at the airports.

Suddenly, Nick laughed. He could picture the Arabs standing in front of Alethea's building during their first snowstorm. There was nothing worse than a stakeout, even on a pleasant day.

Then his smile faded. Maybe they weren't waiting anymore. Maybe they had forced their way into Alethea's apartment and were at this very minute trying to get the papers from her.

Abruptly, his knuckles white on the wheel, Nick pulled out into the icy, sleet-covered passing lane and depressed the accelerator to the floor.

Alethea went into her bedroom and looked out the window carefully, remembering Nick's last words. It was beginning to spit snow instead of sleet as the afternoon turned grayer. God! Would Nick ever get here? It had been several hours since he'd called. Maybe he'd had an accident on the icy road, hit a traffic jam in the Lincoln Tunnel. Anything. And then what would she do?

She walked aimlessly around the apartment, sat down, tried to read, but she couldn't comprehend the words. Her eyes kept drifting back to the clock on the kitchen wall. The hands had crawled slowly all afternoon, so slowly that she thought sometimes she'd scream from the tension. And the dark man, shivering in the cold, still kept watch under her window. At least he was staying down on the street. If he'd made a move toward her building, she was afraid she'd panic and run screaming out of her door.

Then Alethea thought back on what Nick had said, going over every word again. She would go to Washington with him. He would save her from this awful predicament. Her practical mind took over, and she began to grab a few things from her drawers to take with her. Most of her stuff, of course, was still packed in her suitcase, but at least it gave her something to do.

She got out her big, zippered bag and filled it with the contents of her purse: wallet, credit cards, passport, makeup, comb and brush. Then she added the things she'd pulled from her dresser. It all fit and could be easily carried like a shoulder bag. Considering what to wear for the trip would give her something else to do.

She took off her clothes and threw them into the hamper. She took a long, hot shower, washed her hair leisurely, let the relaxing streams of water slide over her body. Carefully, Alethea kept her mind off the man outside and dried her hair, put on clean underwear, then chose a pair of navy-blue wool slacks and a pale green turtleneck sweater. They would be warm and comfortable.

She finally allowed herself to look at the clock again. It was after six. He should be arriving soon, very soon. A surge of excitement gripped her heart. She never dreamed she'd be seeing Nick again! The last few days had completely erased him from her mind. But he had thought of her, obviously, had even called her. A sudden image of him came to her: Nick dancing in the *taverna*, his white teeth flashing in a grin, his fingers snapping to the music. How had she traveled so fast from that distant, joyful world? Had it ever really happened at all?

The soft tapping at her door abruptly drew her attention. Her heart leaped.

"Nick?" she cried, running to the door.

There was no answer. Her heart jumped again, this time in terror. It was the Arab!

Faintly, through the drumbeats of her heart, she heard Nick's voice. "Alethea?"

Suddenly, as her hand reached for the door handle, she remembered his instructions. *Don't open the door for anyone.* Her hand drew back as if a snake lay coiled around the doorknob.

"Alethea, can you hear me?" came his muffled voice.

"Yes," she whispered, then louder, "yes."

"The Pipes of Pan," he said through the door.

It took her forever to undo the police lock, slide back the chain latch, turn the doorknob, open the door. Her hands fumbled, not wanting to work. Time stubbornly stood still.

Finally, the door swung open and Nick stood there, filling the doorway with his reassuring presence. Wordlessly, he stepped in, closed the door behind him, and redid all the locks carefully. Then he turned to her, smiling. "Sorry it took me so long to get here. The roads were awful."

"I know. I was so worried when I saw it snowing." She was relieved, but suddenly a little shy, a little awkward. She didn't know how to talk to him. Would he kiss her, or shake her hand?

"Come here," he said easily as the corner of his mouth quirked into a reassuring grin.

Tears sprang into her eyes—a flood of relief—as Alethea took comfort in the security of his strong embrace. She buried her head in his shoulder, her breath ragged with emotion. And then she felt his hand under her chin, tilting her head up to meet his gaze.

It was odd—and it should have been the last thing on her mind—but she wondered, suddenly, how she could have forgotten how very blue his eyes were, blue like the deep Atlantic waters on a sunlit day.

Nick kissed her. For a few wonderful moments, Alethea was able to forget her fear and respond to the firm, sensual pressure of his lips moving expertly against hers. It was as if she were melting, instantly, her whole being consumed by flames. She reached a hand up and caressed the smooth skin at the back of his neck, savoring the feel of him, reveling in the strength of his corded muscles as his arms encircled her waist, almost lifting her off her feet. In their nearness, pressed to each other, Alethea could feel the firm male bulge beneath his trousers. Her breath caught in her throat at his sensuality, his complete virility. If only, Alethea thought wildly, she could stay locked in these arms for an eternity, never to return to the reality of the past few days!

But almost as soon as the thought filled her mind, Nick moved his mouth from hers and traced a burning path up her cheek until he kissed her more lightly on the nose.

He drew back, holding her now at arm's length. "Better?" he asked softly.

It was a long moment before her heartbeat slowed. Finally, she managed to whisper, "Yes . . . I do feel better."

He dropped his hands altogether from her arms. As if a lifeline had been severed, her spirits sank. Alethea's hazel eyes searched his face. Strange, but his expression had changed somehow. He was so . . . so remote, so businesslike now.

Silence seemed to hang in the room oppressively. Alethea felt suddenly nervous again, awkward in his compelling presence. She tried to calm herself, to meet his eyes levelly. She smiled weakly, regaining a small measure of control, but still knew that her heart was pounding too furiously after only a simple kiss.

Nick was saying something. She tried to focus on his words. "What?"

"Has anything happened . . . with your friend down there?" He gestured toward her front window.

Alethea realized he wasn't going to touch her again. "No, but he's still there."

"I know. I saw him when I came in. There's another farther down the block."

"How do you know?"

"I looked," he answered shortly, with no humor. "Now, we have to get you and your father's papers out of here safely. I'm afraid we'll have to drive back tonight. This can't wait."

"But how are you going to avoid those men?" Alethea asked, a little stunned by his brusque, distant manner. This wasn't like the Nick she remembered from Athens. He had changed somehow.

"Don't worry. I'll take care of that. Look, can you fix me some coffee? That'll help keep me awake tonight."

"Sure," she said, glad to have something to occupy her hands. Out of the corner of her eye, she could see him go to the window, move a shutter, check the front of the building, then stare across the street at the opposite apartment building. Was there someone there, too?

Alethea watched him closely from the kitchen as his back was turned. He was wearing gray flannel slacks, a pale blue crewneck sweater over a shirt, and a thick English tweed sport coat. She couldn't help noticing that his broad shoulders tapered to narrow hips, and that he had a tight, cute rear end when he leaned forward to look out the window better.

"Coffee's ready," she said. "Sorry all I have is instant."

"That's fine." Nick closed the shutter and came over to the kitchen table, pulled out a chair, sank down into it, rubbing his eyes with a thumb and forefinger.

"No milk, either."

"Never mind. Damn, that drive was nasty," he said, running a hand through his dark hair.

"And now we'll have to go all the way back. Can't we stop somewhere along the way? You'll be dead by the time we get there."

"No, I won't. I'm used to this kind of thing. I'll manage."

She sat across from him, sipping her own coffee, studying him. His face was drawn, the lines that went from his nose to the outer corners of his mouth deeply etched, his blue eyes a little dull from tiredness. But he puzzled her. What did he mean he was used to this kind of thing? What exactly was Nick DeWolff's job in Washington? A mere bureaucrat did not go gallivanting around in blizzards to pick up women who were being watched by Arabs.

He looked at her then, meeting her eyes squarely. "I'm sorry about your father."

"I appreciate that."

"I tried to call you all weekend to tell you . . ."

"I just got in yesterday. The funeral was in Boston, where we used to live."

"I see."

They were just making small talk. It was totally unlike their rapport in Europe. Alethea felt she had to break down his reserve somehow. "Do you make it a habit of rescuing damsels in distress?" she asked, trying to sound lighthearted.

His expression hardened, turned wary. He forced a smile to his lips. "Not really. I was just handy today."

"Whom did you call—the man you said could help me?"

His gaze did not waver, but a kind of remoteness turned his face into a stranger's. Then, suddenly, his eyes filled with a strange expression that she thought might be pain. Nick turned his head away for a moment, then met her eyes once more, and he was the man she knew again. Alethea was vastly relieved.

"I guess I better tell you everything. You'll find out soon enough anyway."

"Find out what?"

"Look, I'm an agent for the National Security Council. My job is a little more involved than what I told you." He paused. "I'm sorry I lied to you. But it's part of our job to tell little lies like that. If everybody knew who we were, we wouldn't be much use to anybody. I hope you understand."

"I see." Alethea looked at her hands that clasped the coffee cup, unable to meet his gaze. It explained so much: his intimacy with Athens, his efficiency, even his well-tuned body. She tried to grasp exactly what this new knowledge meant but it eluded her. She couldn't even remember exactly what the National Security Council did, only that it had something to do with security, spy stuff. "Now I understand."

"I'm glad I called. I would have done something even if I were an insurance salesman. You were so upset. Please believe me, Alethea." His hand touched hers, warm and comforting and gentle.

"How do I know you're not lying again?" Her hazel eyes met his, searched them, found no evasiveness.

"You can see my ID if you want . . ."

"No, that's all right," she said, quickly snatching her gaze from his. "I believe you."

"I have some calls to make first and then we can get started. Are you all ready to leave?"

"Yes."

He went to her phone, dialed a number, deliberately turning his back to her. She tried to hear what he was saying, but mostly it made no sense, as if it were in some kind of code. She got the impression that he was reporting to somebody. After looking at her phone book, he made another call. This time it was quite understandable. Her mouth opened in astonishment.

"There is a fire at Twenty-nine West Ninth Street," he was saying. "I can see it from my window. You better get here fast!"

He wasn't even looking out the window. How could he know there was a fire?

Nick hung up, a grin on his lips. "That should hold them up some."

"But what—?"

"Watch."

Within five minutes, they heard the wailing of the fire engine sirens, and then the first truck careened around the corner in the growing darkness. Soon the street below was lit up diabolically by red lights, crisscrossed by fire hoses, and totally blocked by three huge fire trucks.

"Come on, time to leave," Nick said. "Don't forget the papers. And leave the lights on."

Alethea put on her coat, grabbed her zippered bag, checked for her father's manila envelope in it, then followed Nick out the door. She felt a sudden fear, as if she were threatened by just leaving her apartment. They slipped out the entrance into the large crowd that had already gathered. There were no Arabs visible. They walked around the corner to Tenth Street where Nick's car was parked.

"But they'll follow us," Alethea said as they got into the BMW. "They were watching all the time."

"No they won't, not with those fire trucks blocking them in."

Of course not, Alethea told herself, admiring the simplicity of his ruse. He really knows what he's doing. It had all been so easy. And she never would have thought of it in a million years.

"I hope you didn't expect a shoot-out," Nick said, pulling out into the empty street, heading toward the Lincoln Tunnel. "We try not to get into those. They're messy." His voice was full of humor as he turned to catch her expression.

Nick drove as skillfully and effortlessly in New York as he had in Athens. Soon they were crossing into New Jersey, heading south. They hadn't said much to each other. Nick's attention was obviously on the wet highway and slanting snow. Alethea's was on other things.

She watched the hypnotizing sweep of the windshield wipers and the glare of oncoming lights while her mind worked furiously, digesting all the new information that had been thrown at her.

At first she had been so glad to be rescued that she had not questioned anything. Now, feeling calm and secure in Nick's car, far from the Arabs, Alethea began to think logically again. Suliman had wanted her father's papers enough to kill for them. Someone else might want them just as much, someone like the National Security Council, which in this case meant Nick DeWolff. Suddenly, she remembered, with a strange lucidity, that her father had expressly written that his discovery was not for any single country, not even the United States. Oh, God! In her terror, she'd forgotten that completely. If any one country got the papers, her father's life would have been lost in vain. The NSC could not have the notes.

In an instant, her decision was made. She was not going to Washington.

Alethea glanced sideways at Nick's profile as he drove. His hair was a dark mass, his eyes shadowed, but she could see the little bump on his nose that she'd longed to touch in Athens, the strong, clear line of his jaw, the capable way his hands handled the steering wheel. She should have known there would be a flaw in the first man that she had ever felt so comfortable with and genuinely *liked*. Damn! Well, she'd certainly never see him again after tonight. It was too bad, but some things were more important than a possible romance, no matter how wonderful the man, and Alethea knew what her priorities had to be.

She'd have to be extremely careful. Nick was no amateur. She'd already seen him in action. He was cool, smart, probably ruthless. For the present, she'd act innocent and naive, scared, dependent. Didn't men always fall for that? They did in the movies, anyway.

"Are you exhausted?" she asked, opting to be friendly—the first step.

"I'm all right." Nick turned his head, glanced at her, focused back on the road ahead. "How are you?"

"I'm not driving." She paused. "I'm awfully sorry, but that coffee . . . Could we stop somewhere?"

Nick was silent. Did he suspect her? Or was he wondering if they'd been followed or estimating the time they'd been making? Finally, he said, "Sure. I could use another cup of coffee anyway."

About twenty minutes later, they came to a brightly lit rest area. Alethea breathed a silent prayer as they pulled into the parking lot and stopped. Nick stiffly got out of the car, stretched and waited for her. She noticed that he kept an eye on her bag. It was an automatic action for him. It was his job.

The snow was still falling. It was piled up in corners, glistening and icy. The wind was sharp but it felt good, waking Alethea up after the long drive. Nick put a casual hand on the small of her back as they walked toward the cafeteria. She hoped that he couldn't feel her muscles tense up under his touch. And she didn't even know whether she loved his touch or feared it.

As they entered the building, she noted the location of the restrooms—down a hallway to the left. There must be a door or window at the end of the hall or in the bathroom itself. There were plenty of cars and trucks around. She'd approach someone, say her car had broken down and she needed a ride. It didn't even matter where they were headed. Nick would never be able to find her on this dark winter night. She'd be gone. She had all she needed in her bag—passport, money, credit cards, checkbook. She could go anywhere.

The fluorescent lighting made them both blink when they sat down in a booth. Almost instantly, the waitress was ready with coffee.

"Nick," Alethea began, "I haven't even thanked you for what you did. I was so scared that I couldn't think."

"It was a good excuse to see you again, wasn't it?" He grinned at her, looking younger and more relaxed than he'd been in New York.

"You didn't have to drive hours through a storm to see me, Nick. There are easier ways."

He shrugged. "The situation sounded serious. It's better not to take any chances."

"Do you really think those men were watching me? Right now it seems ridiculous. Maybe they were after someone else . . ."

"I'd say it was likely, but it's not my job to decide those things. I just do what my boss tells me." He leaned back against his seat, stretching his long legs in front of him under the table.

Now was the time. "Excuse me. I'll be back in a minute." She slung her zippered bag over her shoulder, slid out of the booth, turned and walked toward the hallway. She imagined his eyes on her every step of the way, burning a hole in her back. Any second, she expected to feel his hand on her arm, his low, teasing voice asking her where she thought she was going. Her heart beat furiously in her chest.

But nothing happened. As soon as she was safely around the corner, Alethea began searching desperately for a way that led outside. There were two doors. One said "private" and was locked tightly. The other said "men's room," and she just didn't have the guts to open it and see.

Quickly, she went into the ladies' room. Damn! A tiny window, but sealed with a grill.

Could she get out the front door without him seeing her? Then she remembered that Nick was *facing* the entrance, while she stupidly had sat down with her back to it. Tears of frustration filled Alethea's eyes. It was impossible to slip away.

For a few seconds, she leaned on a sink, willing her tears to subside. Then she splashed cold water on her face, practiced her smile in the mirror, and started back to the booth.

She'd simply have to keep trying.

Washington was only about a half hour away when Alethea noticed another truck spot coming up.

"Nick," she said, "I'm really embarrassed, but I have to stop again. Coffee always does that to me. Do you mind?"

"Okay. I probably need to stop anyway," he answered. "Getting stiff again."

It could have been the same harshly lit cafeteria, and Alethea quickly took the seat facing the hallway. She was learning.

She excused herself again, walked toward the restroom sign, but this time his eyes weren't on her. That small detail alone made her feel better, more clever.

The hall could have been the same, so could the door marked

"private" and locked. Damn! Didn't anyone leave their doors open anymore? She went into the ladies' room and instantly her heart began a slow, measured thud. There was a window, an old-fashioned, two-section window that began to open in jerks when she pushed up on it.

There was a woman in one of the stalls, so Alethea combed her hair and waited until the woman left. Then she quickly raised the window completely, sat on the sill and swung her legs over and out into the cold, wet night. She let herself down gingerly until her feet touched ground. Alethea pulled the window back down and looked around to see if anyone had noticed her. No one was around. It was the back of the building, away from all the lights and trucks and people.

She tried to picture Nick back inside, waiting and waiting. It wouldn't take him long to figure out what she'd done. She'd better hurry. She imagined how angry he'd be. Thank God she'd never have to face him again. Yet, Alethea felt a sense of loss. She'd never see him again, never see his blue eyes rest on her, his lopsided, boyish grin, his laugh lines crinkle at something she said. Her heart squeezed with self-pity. It could have been good between them.

Walking to the corner of the building, she stopped and peeked around it to see if anyone would notice her rather unusual appearance from the rear of the restaurant. Good, no one was looking in her direction. They were all busy buying gas. Now she had to find someone to give her a ride. Ugh, she could see herself ending up alone with some weirdo on the road at night. Well, it would just have to be done.

Trying to seem casual, she walked through the slushy ruts to a group of truckers standing around talking while their tanks were being filled. She went right up to them before her nerve failed her.

"Hey, you guys, I need a lift. My car broke down and I've got to get back to the city. Anyone going that way?" She put a bright smile on her face and kept it there.

"What city, lady?" asked a heavyset man, grinning.

"Oh," she waved her hand airily, "any city."

"I'm going to New York," put in a tall, thin, side-burned trucker. "Leaving right away." He gave her an assessing look.

"Would you mind if I came along?" Alethea asked.

"Hell, no, might keep me awake."

"Oh, thank you!"

"Come on then." He stopped and eyed her warily. "It's just you, no boyfriend or family or anything?"

"Oh, it's just me," she said brightly.

He led her over to a huge rig that was pulling a refrigerated trailer with the words "Chesapeake Seafood Company" emblazoned on its sides. He helped Alethea climb up the steps to the cab, which sat high above the ground. It was another world inside: gold-framed pictures of a wife and kids, fringe, pale blue upholstery.

"My name's Bernie, what's yours?" he asked as he swung himself into the driver's seat.

"Oh, Jane. My name's Jane," she said, her heart beating quickly at the lie. She'd had to use this ruse a couple of times in Europe. She usually traveled alone, and once or twice she'd had a breakdown with a rental car or a lonely train ride through a long dark night. It paid to have a story handy . . . just in case.

"Hello, Jane." His gaze traveled slowly over her, leering a little.

Here goes, she thought.

Bernie began all the complicated steps to get the big semi moving, pulled out into the feeder lane and gradually picked up speed. The rig rode surprisingly smoothly and easily through the inky night.

"How come a little girl like you is stuck out here on a night like this?" he asked after a while.

"My car, I told you."

"Come on!"

"No, really, I have to get back."

"Lady, you didn't even care what city you got back to!"

"Okay, I guess I can tell you the truth," she said, praying her story would convince him. "I just had a terrible fight with my boyfriend at that truck stop and I skipped out on him. Let him rot in there!" She tried to make her voice emerge angry and upset.

"I get it. So what's the fight about?"

Alethea hesitated, then began dramatically, "I'm pregnant and he won't marry me." Then she put her face in her hands and managed a few racking sobs. She was so frantically tense that she could have turned on tears with no trouble at all . . . or hysterical laughter.

"Oh, you poor kid. Look, maybe I should take you back there

and you can make it up . . ." Bernie's voice was suddenly full of concern.

Alethea straightened up abruptly. "Oh, no! I couldn't stand to see him again, ever! I just want to go home! Please."

"Okay, it's your life, Jane."

The huge rig rumbled on through the dark wetness, and Bernie didn't try to lay a finger on her. As the miles rolled away behind her, Alethea began to feel a great sense of relief. Now she knew exactly what to do. She'd take the first plane to Paris and stay in her little apartment there for a while. Perhaps she'd fly by way of, say, Rome or Berlin as a precaution. But before she left New York, she'd mail the envelope to a perfectly safe place—a place no one but she herself would know about, a place where it would be absolutely secure until she could feel free to get it.

And suddenly Alethea knew exactly where.

Chapter 8

Tuesday, December 6

Nick turned around in the booth and glanced again at the doorway leading to the restrooms—still no Alethea.

He checked his watch. She must have been gone ten minutes by now. Either the ladies' room was crowded or Alethea was taking a helluva long time with her makeup. Of course, he thought, growing more suspicious by the second, she didn't wear much makeup. There was also the fact that she had been terribly quiet, withdrawn, since they had begun the drive. He had attributed it to her nerves and the fact that she was mourning her father, but now he wondered . . .

A frown tugged at Nick's mouth as he came swiftly to his feet, threw a bill on the table and walked purposefully toward the ladies' room. He knew he couldn't just barge in and make a scene so he waited, impatiently, hands on hips, until a woman appeared.

"Excuse me," he began, "but I wonder if you would mind seeing if my wife is still in there?" He shot her a false grin. "She wasn't feeling well and I . . ."

The woman smiled. "Sure. What does she look like?"

He indicated her height with his hand. "About five-five, shoulder-length brown hair. She's wearing navy-blue slacks and a sheepskin jacket."

"All right." The woman disappeared through the swinging door.

However, Nick was sure by now that five would get him ten Alethea wasn't there—probably never was.

What an idiot he was! A blind, stupid idiot!

The lady reappeared, sticking her nose out the door, shrugging, nodding negatively.

"Well, thanks anyway," he said. "She's probably in the car." He forced a smile.

Furious, Nick strode out into the cold night. The huge parking lot was wet, reflecting the overhead lighting and distorting his vision. Still, he couldn't see her anywhere. Was she out on the highway, hitchhiking? Was she *that* stupid? But no. Not Alethea. Most likely she was long gone, maybe in a private car. But judging by the vast number of semis parked in the lot, she probably had asked a truck driver for a ride. But which way? The restaurant sat on an island splitting the highway; she could have gone north or south.

"Damn," he murmured, thrusting his freezing hands into his pockets. Why in hell had she pulled such an insane stunt? He'd done absolutely nothing to intimidate her!

Angrily, Nick strode toward the car. No, he reasoned, it wasn't anything he had done. It must have been the idea of going to Washington which had scared her off. Of course, he might be giving her the benefit of the doubt. Maybe she had realized the possible monetary value of her papers and decided to do a little bartering. After all, she appeared to be a smart woman. Alethea hadn't seemed the greedy type, but on the other hand, who knew *what* went on behind those innocent hazel eyes? At any rate, she had changed her mind somewhere between her apparently sincere plea for help on the telephone and the stop at this restaurant. What did it matter anyway? The little twit was gone and he'd been made to look like an ass!

Nick turned the motor on. Which way?

He decided on north, back to New York. She would flee to an area she knew, certainly not to his terrain.

As he pulled the car onto the highway, he wondered if he

weren't misjudging her. Maybe she was cleverer than to run home. Somehow he doubted it, though. Alethea wasn't a professional like he was. Still, the idea that she might outsmart him made his blood boil. And here he had thought what a nice, sweet little female she was!

By the time Nick reached New York again, he was thoroughly tired, fed-up and still fuming with anger. Alethea had used him to rid herself of the two Arabs and probably figured he'd be far easier to dupe. The idea brought a sour taste to his mouth.

It was late—actually early in the morning—when Nick pulled into a parking spot around the corner from her apartment house. Naturally, if he were to find her there, it would border on the miraculous. Nevertheless, it was a starting point.

He walked around the corner. It was snowing more heavily now. He reached 34 West Ninth and stood looking casually around the empty street. The Arabs were gone.

Funny, Nick realized, but he hadn't actually noticed her neighborhood before. It was a nice part of the Village, cozy, with a treelined street. Her building, too, looked inviting, tidy, with its little wrought-iron gate. It was a four-story red brick building— a walk-up—a beautiful house which showed its owners' pride. The windows on the second story had iron grill boxes, holding miniature evergreens covered with snow. On the top floor, where Alethea lived, were neatly painted white interior shutters. Somehow the building suited Alethea.

Four flights of steps later, Nick stood before her door. He didn't bother knocking but was surprised to find it unlocked, easily swinging open on its hinges.

An intuitive, familiar prickling sensation crept up the back of his neck. Something was very wrong . . .

He backed away from the dark entrance, his brain telling him to take it cautiously—trust his instincts.

Nick reached inside his jacket and pulled out a gun, bent his arm close to his chest and carefully, slowly, rounded the corner of the doorway in a half-crouch.

It took him a long second to find the light switch. When he flipped it on, he took in the whole room with a quick sweep of his eyes. No one. He knew the other tiny rooms would be empty, too.

However, the apartment was in shambles. And there was an overpowering scent of perfume in the air, as if a bottle had been overturned. Surely she hadn't done this. That left the Arabs. It fit.

As an extra precaution, Nick checked the rest of the apartment and returned to the wrecked living room. Picking up an overturned photograph, he fixed a cushion on the couch and sat down with the picture in hand. A middle-aged man and Alethea sitting around a pool together—Alethea and a lover? Or Alethea and her father? Probably the father, Nick surmised by the way they sat comfortably together and sported the same short, straight nose and oval-shaped hazel eyes. She looked quite pretty, in an old-fashioned sort of way, with her hair a natural shade of medium brown hanging in soft curls around her shoulders. His gaze took in her figure, too, the long, well-shaped legs and flat stomach, the nicely curved bust in the bikini top. Not bad at all, he thought. It was a shame she had turned out to be so deceitful.

Nick rose and rechecked the bedroom. Alethea's clothes were strewn all over the Oriental rug and hanging loosely out of the open closet. The bedding was torn apart and the mattress was pulled half off the frame. A horrible thought struck him: Had she returned and found the Arabs here? Or had they come in when she was already gone?

Think, Nick told himself, back up and think. If you made your way into the girl's apartment and were looking for vital material, you wouldn't bother tearing the place up if she were here. No. You'd twist her arm or whatever it took to get it out of her—and Alethea certainly wasn't the type to withstand torture—few people were. A mental picture of faceless dark men holding the girl down and beating the information out of her disturbed Nick more than he cared for. Quickly, he erased the ugly scene from his thoughts.

Turning, he searched the bathroom. Although the medicine cabinet was torn up and hanging open, nothing seemed to be gone, nothing he could notice, at least. A large bottle of Shalimar perfume was broken in the sink.

All Nick's instincts told him that she had never returned.

Going back into the living room, Nick picked up the overturned phone and dialed Porter's home number in Silver Spring. The phone rang several times—Skip would love being awakened at this hour!

"Porter here," came his groggy voice.

"Nick. Listen, she's disappeared . . . gave me the slip."

"Great!"

"You don't have to tell me!" Nick yelled, angry at her, himself, even Porter.

"All right then." Porter hesitated. "Where do you think she's gone to? Any ideas?"

"One very good one."

"Where are you now?"

"Her place. Looks like the Arabs may have been here."

"Could *they* have her?"

"I don't believe so," replied Nick.

"This is a stupid question," Skip paused, "but do you think they might have the papers?"

Nick laughed. "You're right . . . it's a stupid question."

"Okay then, find her. I don't care how. How in God's name could she have given you the slip!" It wasn't a question. "Well," he said irritably, "what's done is done."

"Look," Nick replied smoothly, "I'll find her."

"The minute you do—"

"I'll report."

"Listen, Nick . . . when, and *if*, you find her, let's give your lady friend a little time . . . Watch her. See if she's up to something."

"Like what?"

"Maybe she's selling to the competition . . . Who knows? But I'd like that information before I see her."

"All right," Nick agreed, thinking that he would rather just bring her in—be done with it.

"Keep in touch. Close touch."

"Will do." Nick replaced the receiver on its cradle.

He'd find her. It always sounded so simple but often took days of pounding the sidewalks and going without sleep to accomplish. Thank God he wasn't chasing a pro . . . or was he?

Sitting down on the couch, he reached over and sorted through her scattered mail: bills, magazines, junk mail, a postcard. He looked the card over. On the face was a ski area scene and when he flipped it over, he found the contents to be hastily scrawled out and hard to read.

Marvelous skiing for so early . . . you must come up when you're in Paris . . . too dreary there . . . love and kisses, Clair.

* * *

72

The tiny writing on the card said Leysin. Nick hadn't been there but he knew the approximate location of the small Swiss resort. There was a chance Alethea might have gone there. But something told Nick she hadn't. At least not yet. He had a very good idea of her destination.

He glanced at his watch; it would be light soon. Nick wondered when *The World's Fare* offices opened in the morning. He wasn't about to head to Kennedy until he checked one more thing out and hopefully got an address. It might be a waste of valuable time but it would be worse if he flew across the Atlantic and found she didn't have a phone. It might take days then to find an address.

What he needed was a cup of coffee. Nick started to rise when his eye caught sight of a little blue book lying under the coffee table. He reached down and picked it up, turning to the first page. It was her diary, he registered instantly. He hesitated but then thought it might provide important information and began to read from page one, scanning the dull parts and concentrating on those items which revealed more about her.

About halfway through, he'd come to the conclusion that Alethea was an extremely sensitive woman, almost a romantic in her view of life. It was hard for Nick to believe that the girl who had outwitted him saw the world through such rosy glasses, but she obviously did and was plainly naive considering the amount of traveling she'd done. And she was honest with herself, writing, "I often feel like a child inside but do a good job covering my tracks with a smart tongue . . . at least Dad always says I do!"

The only dark side that emerged was the mention of her dead mother. The apartment in Paris, it seemed, had been first her grandmother's and then her mother's. Her mother was, Nick recalled, French. Alethea wrote of a great sadness in that apartment and of missing her mother dreadfully.

Nick looked up for a moment; he felt ashamed of himself for digging into her private life. He'd expected to read about the girl's conquests, travels. Not to delve into her soul. He felt cheap, dirty.

He glanced over at the photograph of Alethea and her father, at the finely chiseled features that seemed to fit the girl in the diary who felt so often like a child. It was strange to discover this side of her; outwardly, she appeared so confident.

Looking down at his watch, Nick wished the magazine's offices would hurry up and open so he could get out to the airport. If he'd figured out her trail so easily, then surely others were on the scent, too.

He glanced back down at her diary. He'd gone this far . . . Nick read on to where she finally mentioned a man, and for an instant he felt an odd emotion sweep him. It was almost as if he were jealous. How ridiculous! Shrugging off the thought, Nick read on about her affair with Bill, apparently a New York literary agent, whom she had seen on and off for a year.

She wrote of him as not very attractive . . . safe . . . single . . . made her laugh. But the part that interested Nick was after she'd broken up with this Bill and thought about seeing a shrink, writing:

> *I'm certain now that it's me. Maybe I am frigid, but I can't pretend to feel something that's not there. At least I'm honest. In this day and age you would think I could enjoy the* act, *but still, nothing. I'm making myself blush crimson but I'm positively going to ask a shrink as soon as I'm back from Greece."*

So, thought Nick, she does have some dark sides to that rosy world of hers, and then, like every healthy male, he fleetingly thought that it just took the right man . . .

The memory of Alethea's kiss, her slightly reluctant response to him, rose unbidden to his mind. The way her supple body had molded to his instantly when he had arrived at her apartment, the sweet taste of her lips as they had parted beneath his, the feel of her hardened nipples against his chest. How was it possible that this sensual woman could conceive of herself as "frigid"? Not a chance, Nick thought, recalling her uneven breathing, the feel of her abdomen pressed tightly against the telltale swell beneath his trousers . . .

"Brother," he muttered, thinking what an idiot he was. The woman had just played him for a total fool!

He rested his head back on the couch in exhaustion. He closed his eyes—just for a moment.

Suddenly, it was ten o'clock. Nick cursed and reached for the phone. After several minutes, he was through to the offices of *The World's Fare* magazine.

"Ah, yes . . . I'm trying to locate an old friend of mine," he said, very businesslike, rubbing his tired, scratchy eyes. "Her name is Alethea Holmes."

"Just a moment please," the receptionist said. "I'll switch you over to editorial."

Nick remained on hold for several minutes, listening in irritation to background music.

"This is Miss Worth, may I help you?"

"Yes. The name's Nicholas DeWolff. I'm an old college friend of Alethea Holmes and I've been calling her apartment for several days now. She doesn't seem to be in. Perhaps you might tell me her whereabouts?"

"Well . . ." She paused. "You're the second to call already today."

That figured. While he dozed, the Arabs had been busy. He was dying to ask the woman if she'd told them anything, but instead he said, "It's quite all right, I assure you, Miss Worth. I ran into Alethea in Paris last month," he took a shot in the dark, "and she made me promise to look her up when I got to New York."

"Oh, my goodness. You've probably missed her completely. She's most likely back in Paris by now. Turned in her article Monday, said she needed some time off. Her father died recently. She almost always vacations in Paris."

"Seems destiny is against us." Nick forced a rueful laugh. "Say," he went on, "I've got business there next week. I wonder if you might have her address?"

"Mr. DeWolff, I'm sorry, but I can't give you that information. You understand."

"Of course," he said politely, swearing under his breath.

"But you could telephone her. I'm sure it's in the Paris directory."

"Wonderful," he said quickly. "I will."

Well, that took care of that problem, and as it turned out he could have flown to Paris hours ago. Still, it paid to be careful. Now all he had to do was check the airlines to see if she'd been listed on a late-night flight. It would be easy. No way would she have a false passport—she had to have used her own name.

Nick left the apartment. It was sleeting out now and he felt the icy fingers of winter creep into his bones as he turned on the car, letting it warm into a purr.

While he drove impatiently through the noisy city traffic, he felt certain that it would only take a few minutes at Kennedy to find out that she had indeed flown to Paris. He was glad now that he'd taken the time to bring along his passport and some extra clothes—he always did—no telling for how long or how far this girl was going to run. And Paris was *damn* cold in December.

Eventually, his anger over the heavy traffic subsided; there wasn't much he could do about it anyway. He sat at a stoplight watching the sleet blow diagonally across the side window, distorting the view of cars and lights and tall buildings. His mind drifted back over the hours and he imagined Alethea fleeing New York in terror. Those delicate hands must have shaken, and the fear had surely played in her hazel eyes. Funny, but it was hard to stay mad at her. Suddenly, Nick felt tension seep into his limbs and up the back of his neck. He couldn't get to Paris fast enough now. Her tails would probably already be there, maybe at her place right this moment, forcing her to hand over her father's notes . . .

Abruptly, Nick was seized with a strange hope. He wished that he was wrong about her location and that the Arabs would be, too. He hoped that Alethea was smarter than to go to the most obvious of all places, her own. Still, he doubted it, and cursed the three-thousand-mile ocean that he had yet to cross.

Chapter 9

Thursday, December 8

Stretching her limbs languidly, Alethea tried to rid her body of the stiffness of sleep. She rolled over, facing the back of the couch, and snuggled up again into a warm ball.

Suddenly, her eyes flew open and she was instantly fully awake, her heartbeat increasing by the second as the memory of the past two days flooded her consciousness.

It was daylight already! She must have overslept. Glancing quickly at her watch, Alethea saw it was nine o'clock. She'd slept twelve hours and here she had planned to be far from Paris by morning! Now it would be better to wait until dark.

Kicking the blanket off, she rose from the couch, ran a hand through her tangled hair and looked down at her rumpled slacks. Thank heavens she kept some extra clothing in Paris. She'd use the communal bathroom down the hall and take a nice, hot bath. But first, coffee.

While Alethea waited for the water to boil, she instinctively went to the window overlooking rue Monsieur-le-Prince. No dark men; at least none that she could see. But just because there were no obvious watchers didn't mean there weren't any there. Not at all.

She dropped the white lacy curtain back into place and fixed some *café au lait* in a bowl, in the French fashion. As Alethea sat at the small kitchen table, she looked around the high-ceilinged, two-room apartment. It was typically Parisian, with the kitchen and living room bunched together forming a large square. Though she had painted the walls white to cheer the place, she had left alone the old Persian carpet covering the wooden floor even though it was getting a touch threadbare in several places. With a Persian, that was all right. Anyway, it went with the antique furniture. Over the squat couch, she'd hung many paintings, most of which were original oils inherited from her mother, and then several etchings Alethea had fallen in love with and had had to purchase.

It was a homey room, Alethea decided. Even if the century-old plaster on the ceiling was peeling, she still adored it.

Alethea sipped on her coffee, then leaned back in the chair and pulled the curtain carefully aside one more time—still no suspicious-looking men hanging around. She let the lace fall back into place and couldn't help but notice how shaky and white her hand was. Of course, her skin was always so pale it looked as if she never got any sun. That was the *gamine* look her mother had said was so feminine.

As the minutes ticked endlessly by, Alethea couldn't stop thinking about her parents, and that wasn't good. If only she weren't so alone! But whose fault was that? It was *she* who had decided on a career, letting the few men in her life slip through her fingers like so many grains of sand . . .

Well, she was going to have to put aside her grief and worry and do some decision-making. There were very few paths open and she'd have to carefully think things out before making a move. Staying in Paris was impossible. Not only had she told both Suliman and Nick about the apartment, but yesterday, when she'd placed an overseas call to *The World's Fare,* the editorial secretary had some disturbing news. Two parties had already called that very morning inquiring after her. Of course, not knowing any better, Miss Worth had told both callers that Alethea most likely was in Paris.

Nick must have been one of the callers, and the Arabs, no

doubt, had been the other. Alethea was convinced she couldn't stay in Paris much longer.

She placed the empty bowl in the sink, found her robe, a change of clothes, and went down the hall. A nice, hot bath would make her feel so much better, and once her hair was washed she'd feel more human.

But as she lay back in the tub, the urgency of her situation took hold again and she was soon toweling herself off and pulling on a clean pair of jeans. Falling asleep on the couch had been a mistake. After the call to Miss Worth, she should have grabbed her bag and run. But she'd been too confused, too weary to even think.

Well, after a night's sleep, it would be easier now to form a plan of action.

Letting herself back into her tiny apartment, Alethea carefully locked the door behind her. She fixed herself some regular coffee and sat down near the kitchen window again, where she could keep a close eye on the street below.

She had taken all yesterday to go over and over in her mind the events that had turned her life into a nightmare and brought her to Paris. She was positive that she'd done the right thing by getting away from Nick. It had been stupid to tell him about the papers in the first place. The only thing telling Nick had accomplished was to make this whole mess more complicated. And of course she had ruined any hope of a relationship between them. Or perhaps, she realized, he had ruined it by simply being in the profession of his choice—a spy. His life would always be filled with lies and deceit. Alethea sighed in resignation. She should have suspected in Athens that he was too good to be true. No man handled himself the way Nick did, or was so damned attractive, and was only a bureaucrat, a "paper-pusher" as he'd described himself.

She wondered what he had done when she had given him the slip in that truck stop: Was he furious? Or had he been worried?

The image of Nick—his boyish grin, the sun-crinkle lines around his eyes, that silly bump on his nose as if it had been broken—filled her mind's eye. He always had a pleasant male scent surrounding him—not aftershave, but a pure, natural body scent made up of things like leather, wool, good health. A very *male* odor she loved.

"Stop it!" Alethea whispered aloud. What possible point was there in dwelling on a man like that? He was no better than those two Arabs in New York. Nick had chosen his world. It was not hers.

And then it occurred to her how easily he might be below, now, hidden in the *patisserie*, or perhaps the *boulangerie*, watching her apartment, those wonderful blue eyes of his straining up toward her window.

A chill ran through her limbs and she trembled just to think about the possibility that anyone, even Nick, could force her to reveal the location of the papers. They did those sorts of things, didn't they? It wasn't just in the movies . . .

Alethea's stomach suddenly gnawed with hunger. She glanced down the street at the pastry shop. She could almost smell the flaky buns and sweet, layered cakes from here, but she didn't dare to venture out. Damn! Well, she'd have to resort to canned goods. Ugh. Here she was half-starving, an authority on the better European restaurants, and she was forced to eat canned string beans!

She managed finally to consume a few bites and then automatically tidied up the apartment while she began to form a plan in her mind. The most pressing problem was where she could hide for a few days until she was certain no one was following her. Then she would retrieve the papers, and later she'd make certain those filthy murderers in Abjala were punished. She would need help for that—help from an independent source, someone powerful who didn't owe allegiance to any particular country. Small task, Alethea told herself bitterly. There was no such person or agency.

It was early afternoon when Alethea sank down despairingly on the couch, realizing that there was no one she could turn to. The one blood relative, the one person she really had trusted, was dead now—her father. Well, she wasn't going to resort to tears again; the past days had been filled with sudden crying spells and a lot of self-pity. No, that had gotten her nowhere. And by dark, she had to be away from here.

It was then that Alethea remembered the postcard from Clair. If she went to Leysin, all she had to do was ask anyone if they knew where the best, most flamboyant après ski party was and she'd find Clair. Clair, the proverbial "hostess with the mostest," the fast-lane heiress. Yes, it would be easy to find her chalet.

Alethea was turning over the idea of staying in Switzerland for a while when a light rap at her door made her heart come stabbing to a halt.

She jumped up from the couch, fear gripping her, and looked frantically around as if there were an exit from the apartment, an exit that she'd never seen before. The rapping sounded again.

"Miss Holmes?"

Alethea froze, staring in horror in the direction of the strange foreign voice, her eyes fixed on the door.

"Are you there, Miss Holmes? Alethea? Please answer . . ."

She threw her hand over her mouth to keep from screaming as the hammer-beat of her heart pounded in her ears. Where had she heard that voice before?

"Please, Miss Holmes . . . I know you're in there. This is Suliman Akmet."

Oh, my God, she thought furiously. Why was *he* here? If only the earth would open up, swallow her, carry her away from all this!

"Miss Holmes, I've been terribly concerned about you. I tried to get a hold of you in New York. Please don't be afraid . . . We must talk. I'm your friend, you *must* believe me!"

Liar! she screamed inwardly. Filthy, murdering liar!

Quickly, Alethea moved toward the phone. The police would arrest him. Oh, how could she have been so taken in by him?

"Alethea, we have no time for these games. There are important things I must speak to you about. I've come a long way. . . . It's about your father's death. . . ."

Her hand froze on the dial.

The cultured, British-accented voice continued in a low, hypnotic tone. "I know you are afraid right now. And you have a reason." He hesitated. "Please just say 'yes' if you hear me, please."

Gingerly, she replaced the receiver. Was there something about her father's death Suliman could tell her now? He had said it was an accident, but what if he were innocent and had learned differently? What if he wasn't involved, after all? Still, she prayed he'd leave her alone. She swore her heart was going to burst at any second.

"Alethea?"

She walked to the middle of the floor, wringing her hands fitfully in front of her. "I'm here," she half-sobbed. "Please . . . go away . . ." There, it was said—he knew she was there anyway.

Gathering a measure of courage, she spoke further, "If you don't leave, and take your men with you, I'm going to call the police."

"My men?"

"Yes," she cried. "Your men! I know they're watching me . . . I'm not an idiot!"

"Of course you aren't, Alethea. Please open the door and let me explain—"

"No! I'm going to call the police now." Again she went to the phone, but this time she knew she was bluffing. How would she explain this mess to the *gendarmes* without mentioning her father's discovery? And then they, too, would want the papers for themselves. The horrible feeling of loneliness swept her again. If only there was someone she could lean on, confide in . . .

"Perhaps," said Suliman through the door, "you should call them. You see, I think you may need protection . . . that's why I sent men to New York, to protect you. I tried to call you there to explain, but you were gone."

Feeling that her heart would burst, Alethea listened with growing hope while her mind whirled at Suliman's calm words. Was he telling the truth? He had been her father's friend . . . He seemed such a nice man . . .

She found herself saying, "How do I know you're not lying?"

There was a moment's silence. "You don't, Alethea. But you'll have to trust someone, sometime. All I can tell you is that I'm not the enemy. But there may be some in my country who are . . . That's what we must find out, isn't it?"

"I don't know . . ." Confused tears glistened in her eyes.

"Trust me. Open the door."

Trancelike, Alethea walked slowly to the door and with shaking hands undid the latch, praying feverishly that she wasn't making a mistake—knowing that desperation was driving her to seek a friend. "You can't come in," she said, opening the door a crack.

"I understand completely. Perhaps we could talk someplace else where you'd feel more comfortable."

"Yes," she replied. A public place would make sense. She relaxed a little.

"You'll need a coat." He spoke kindly, protectively.

Alethea closed the door and went to the closet, pulling down her heavy Irish knit sweater from the top shelf and grabbing a plaid tam to keep her head warm.

When at last she was out in the hall with Suliman, she felt

terribly foolish and insecure. She couldn't be certain whether he was a real friend or not.

Her eyes turned upward timidly. Alethea saw him entirely differently this time. He was tall, quite tall, and well proportioned, actually handsome in a Machiavellian sort of way, with a neatly trimmed beard and deep-set, intelligent eyes that did not seem to fit the smile on his thin lips.

"I am so glad you are putting your trust in me, Alethea. We're friends, after all."

"Well," she replied hesitantly. "To be honest, I don't know about trust."

"Of course, of course. How could you at this point?" His hand went carefully under her elbow and they began to walk down the steps. "Where would you like to go? A restaurant? A café?"

"Well . . . a café, I guess." The cold, damp air of December struck her in the face as they walked out onto rue Monsieur-le-Prince. The chill refreshed her in a way, but she felt shaky and weak, knowing she looked as pale as death.

Suliman stopped at the corner. "Where would you prefer to go?"

"How about the Café Toujours, it's just on the next block," said Alethea, feeling the presence of his hand still supporting her elbow. It was a strong, familiar hand that promised security and hope or, perhaps, she thought nervously, danger.

Chapter 10

Thursday, December 8

A faint movement of the lace-edged curtain in the second-story window caught Nick's eye just as he felt an enormous urge to yawn.

Yes, it must be Alethea. He got only a quick glimpse but the image of her small, scared face and her soft, waving brown hair stayed in his mind's eye. So she was here. He had been almost positive, especially yesterday when he had finally gotten into Paris, and then found the quaint, narrow little Left Bank street on which she lived. There had been a light on in that second-floor front apartment. It had seemed almost too easy. The girl was an amateur, no doubt about that. All he'd needed to do was look her name up in the Paris directory: Holmes, A. 20 rue Monsieur-le-Prince.

No one suspicious had entered or left the building since last night when he'd parked across the street from the entrance. Only the usual: a couple of middle-aged maids with their string bags, some schoolchildren leaving early in the morning, a few petite Vietnamese.

God, he was tired! The never-ending airport delays—that damn snowstorm. It had taken twice as long to get to Paris as it should have, and then the long night of waiting and watching. Oh, he should be used to it by now. He had been on stakeouts in steaming, infernal jungles and on long, boring, usually cold nights all over the world. Guess he was out of practice. Well, he'd soon fall into the pattern again—the unending patience, the ability to remain unnoticed on a busy street, the half-unconscious skill of spotting the one person, or the one move, for which you had been waiting days, even weeks. It all came flooding back.

Nick shifted his weight on the dark red upholstery and thought again that perhaps he should have rented a less noticeable car like the drab, ordinary, European sedans that lined one side of the narrow old street. The color of his car was fine—a burnished, dark steel-gray—but the Saab Turbo was a bit too classy for this middle-class neighborhood. Might cause a few too many heads to turn. Oh, well, it was done, and he had rented it expressly because of its smooth power and expert handling, especially in city traffic. He just might need its speed and quick turning ability.

His mind returned to the business at hand—Alethea Holmes.

Why had she run? And if she meant to evade him, why had she gone straight to Paris, where he could so easily find her? Had she just been panic-stricken? But why on earth had she run from *him?* She shouldn't have been afraid of him at all. Not after Athens. Was she here to meet someone, sell the so-called discovery to another interested party? Porter had thought she might. Maybe he was right.

There were too many unanswered questions. Either Alethea was totally, stupidly innocent and afraid, or was already pitting the U.S. against the Arabs for a sale. Either way she was dangerous—to her country, to whoever *might* have killed her father and especially to herself. He'd give her one more hour. If she didn't make a move or meet with anyone by then, he'd simply knock on her door and find out exactly what she was up to. He couldn't sit in the car on this street for too much longer.

Paris was raw and damp in December. He hunched down into his trench coat and started the quiet purring motor, putting the heat on high for a few minutes. Cold muscles don't react well—better stay warm and loose.

The hour was nearly up when Nick's practiced eye spotted a tall, elegantly dressed figure striding down the opposite side of the street. Didn't quite fit into the standard local population of students, shopkeepers, middle-aged women.

As the man approached the entrance to number 20, he paused and looked up as if to read the address, and Nick could see him quite well. The man was a dark Semitic type with a neat black goatee, a perfectly fitted suit, camel's hair topcoat, polished glove-leather loafers. It could be Suliman Akmet.

He turned into the doorway, pushed the buzzer, then disappeared into the shadows of the building. Nick felt his blood quicken.

He waited motionlessly, yet he felt every nerve in his body tingle, every muscle fiber prepare to contract, every sense widen to absorb whatever data he might need. It was as if an unseen entity within him had shifted into high gear but kept a foot on the clutch, gunning the motor to a straining point.

Nick didn't have long to wait. A few minutes later, the Arab reappeared, his head turned back as if he were listening or talking to someone as he politely held the door open. It was then that Alethea walked out onto the narrow sidewalk, blinking her large, dark-lashed eyes in the light gray Paris afternoon. She wore some kind of heavy white sweater and a pair of jeans. And on her head perched a ridiculous little plaid hat—ridiculous, but somehow charming on her, a bit old-fashioned. She looked pale, a little frightened. She hugged her arms around her waist to ward off the chill. The tall Arab took her elbow protectively and they entered the throng of people heading toward the corner of the Boulevard Saint-Michel.

What in hell could she be up to now? Most probably setting up a sale . . . yet she didn't exactly look like a person in command of the situation. In fact, she looked nervous as hell.

Poor Alethea, Nick thought to himself with an inadvertent flash of pity. She's in way over her head.

Then he caught himself. Poor Alethea, my ass! She's probably bargaining this very moment with the Arabs, then it'll be the Russians, the Chinese, then she'll play one against the other and milk them all dry, us included. Maybe she looks sweet, but you can't judge a book—

The two figures had nearly reached the corner when Nick nonchalantly got out of his car, stiffly unfolding his height, feeling his cramped muscles. Casually, he strolled along with the crowds, seemingly oblivious, but with every sense tuned toward the couple ahead of him. He easily kept Akmet's head in view as the pair turned onto the wide boulevard and began to walk north past cafés, *charcuteries,* lingerie shops and bookstores.

Nick hoped they wouldn't turn into some rabbit-warren of an old building; there was no way to follow them into the dark confusion of one of these narrow-fronted old monstrosities. But they didn't turn off until they reached the Café Toujours, where they selected a small, round table in the back corner.

Nick sauntered past the café once, noting where they sat, the arrangement of empty chairs near them; then he searched for a suspicious-looking person at another table—someone who did not *quite* fit into the scene. There was nobody he could put a finger on. For a moment, he studied the window of a *patisserie* next door, thinking of how to keep an eye on Alethea and Akmet. It was imperative to keep them in sight. They might leave to do business somewhere else. Or, the thought struck him, maybe Akmet had some other, nastier plans for the girl. Nick felt his heart contract in fear for her. He'd have to be very careful not to let his emotions cloud the hair-trigger sharpness of his senses. He couldn't let his protective feelings for Alethea get in the way of duty, of his job.

Glancing around, Nick noticed a newspaper kiosk nearby. He sauntered over and began looking at French magazines, always facing the café. He could see the two of them at a table in the glass-fronted room, talking earnestly. Damn. If Alethea didn't know him, Nick could sit next to them and eavesdrop. This way, he couldn't hear what they were saying.

Suddenly, Alethea began to gesticulate angrily. Nick hoped she wasn't dumb enough to tell Akmet she suspected he'd killed her father.

Suliman remained imperturbable. When she finished her tirade, he smiled thinly and leaned his dark head close to hers. Obviously, he was trying to persuade her of something. Akmet's fine, long-fingered, aristocratic hand, with a cigarette dangling, swept the air in a graceful gesture and the girl nodded her head. Nick's frustration mounted. Now they were talking like old friends. It was understandable if she was negotiating with him, selling the papers to the oil sheiks for cold cash. Nick didn't want to think she was capable of that, but still . . .

Akmet put his hand on her arm and leaned even closer, talking sincerely, convincingly. A hot flash of jealousy assaulted Nick, uncontrollable and unexpected. The strength of his reaction confounded him. My God, he thought, what's wrong with me? This is a job, just a job.

But it hurt somehow to watch them together, sipping their coffee as if nothing were wrong, as if she'd completely forgotten that she suspected Suliman Akmet of murdering her father. Nick felt that he was the one who should have been sitting at the table reassuring her, touching her.

Get a hold of yourself, Nicholas James DeWolff the Third, he told himself. This is no time to go all soft and mushy.

They rose shortly thereafter, leaving the café together, and Nick had another chance to observe her up close. Alethea appeared slightly relieved, a faint smile gathering at the corners of her mouth as she listened to Akmet. They turned back the way they had come. Suliman was taking her home, Nick assumed. Never assume anything in this business, he told himself, Akmet may be going to knife her, kidnap her or, for that matter, make passionate love to her.

Nick trailed well behind them and walked slowly back to rue Monsieur-le-Prince, easily spotting Suliman's dark head at the entrance to number 20. Alethea went in, the door closed behind her and the Arab walked away. As he passed a large dark sedan parked on the street, he nodded almost imperceptibly to the occupants, then continued on, turning the corner and disappearing into the crowd.

Nick walked past the car Suliman had so briefly acknowledged. There were two dark heads inside, one drinking a Coke, the other watching Alethea's building from behind an Arab-language newspaper.

Thoroughly unprofessional, obvious. So Suliman wasn't convinced the girl had nothing . . . He was going to wait and see, follow her. But why not simply nab her? Have those dolts in the car force her to talk? Should be simple . . . But then Nick realized that he was thinking about an oil minister, not some cheap thug or fanatical terrorist. Apparently, Akmet was going to play it cool for a while, do things the quiet way—make as few ripples as possible.

Deciding to phone Porter and fill him in while hopefully Alethea stayed put for a few minutes, Nick left rue Monsieur-le-Prince.

He found the nearest *poste* and let himself into a booth. It seemed to take the overseas operator forever while he waited impatiently for the call to go through. It should be about nine in the morning in Washington. Porter would be in his office at least. Finally, the buzzing, electronic-sounding ring was answered. He recognized the voice of Porter's secretary.

"Joan, get me Porter right away. This is Nick—"

Instantly, he heard a click, then Porter's voice.

"Go ahead, Nick."

"I'll make this fast. Our little bird has made her nest in Paris."

"Oh?"

"Yeah, and she's had a visitor—the very same Akmet character that she told me she suspected of killing her father."

"Akmet? How the hell did he find her so fast?"

"The same way I did, Skip, the girl's an amateur."

"I see . . . I see. Listen, Nick," Porter paused briefly, "I'm baffled. Why would she run from us and then let Akmet around her?"

"Two possibilities from what I can gather," replied Nick. "Either she's selling, or Akmet's won her trust. From what little I can gather, I'm opting for the second angle."

"I'm not so sure, maybe she's going to play us off against each other."

"Possibly . . . but I have a gut feeling that Akmet has managed to fool her. Somehow I don't picture this kid turning around and selling him something."

"Maybe," Porter said thoughtfully. "And I better tell you that I've done some more checking on this guy. Seems he's a ruthless s.o.b.—went right to the top in the oil racket, leaving more than a few heads behind. If he thinks she's got something of her father's that he wants, he'll stop at nothing . . ."

"Then we better cut this short."

"Exactly," Porter agreed, reading Nick's mind. "I'm also convinced there's validity to these papers she claims to have, checked out Holmes's credentials some more and—Why else would Akmet be in Paris?"

"No reason I can think of. Listen, Skip, I know it's risky, but let's give her a bit more time to play out this hand—a few days to see if she's selling to Akmet or if she's an innocent kook. If I drag the kid in for nothing, we could have those bleeding hearts on the Senate subcommittee down our throats again for harrassment."

"Good point. But keep in close touch. If what you originally told me is true, I want those papers. Got that? Don't let her slip away now, and watch that oil minister for chrissakes! He's evidently a dangerous customer!"

"Roger. I'll be in touch."

Nick hung up the phone and was back in front of 20 rue Monsieur-le-Prince in a matter of minutes. Briefly, pulling his collar up against the damp Paris chill, he wondered if the pretty girl knew, or even cared, that she was playing with fire.

Chapter 11

Friday, December 9

The insistent ringing of the phone forced Alethea to open her eyes. But this time she was prepared. "I will not panic," she said aloud. "I will cope. This is not another crisis, only a phone call, that's all."

She sat up in bed, deliberately slowing her motions to dispel the thought that there might be something to worry about, and walked over to the table where the telephone sat, still shrieking its impersonal message. She tried to force her heartbeat to even its jagged rhythm, but her hand seemed to have a mind of its own and shook slightly as it lifted the receiver.

"Hello?" Was that really her own voice, so timid-sounding?

"Alethea? I was afraid you . . . weren't home."

It was Suliman Akmet. She could not mistake his now-familiar voice. It brought back instantly the day before at the café when he had seemed so rational. "I'm terribly sorry about all this, Alethea. After you left Abjala, one of my men told me about the final police report . . . about the possibility that it wasn't an accident. I've got a team at this very moment working with the police investigating every facet of this terrible thing. If there is anything amiss, rest assured we will find it and I shall let you know immediately."

That had certainly taken her aback, made her even more uncertain what to believe. And when she had asked him to call his men off, the ones that had watched her in New York, he had hesitated, then smiled, his sculpted lips turning up warmly. "Of course, Alethea, my dear girl. They were only for your protection, but if you insist . . ." He had spread his hands in a mock-helpless gesture, then frowned and shook a brown finger at her. "But you must promise to call me if you are afraid or if you need any help whatsoever."

Alethea brought herself back to the present conversation with a wrenching effort.

"Oh, hello. I just slept late," she managed to say.

"Awfully sorry if I woke you, but I had the strongest urge to ring you. I guess I still feel a bit protective. You understand. I feel responsible until this matter is cleared up."

"There's no need to feel that way . . . Suliman. I'm quite able to take care of myself. But I appreciate your concern." What did he really want? She thought she'd convinced him yesterday she had nothing. He couldn't possibly be interested . . .

"Yes, I suspect so. But still, I hate to think of you here in Paris, all alone. It worries me. I thought we might have dinner together this evening."

Did he mean what he said? Was he merely being friendly? Or did he have ulterior motives? Did he still think she had the papers? Oh, God, whom could she trust? If only there was someone, *someone* she felt sure of, someone she could talk to. She was alone, so alone.

He was speaking again. "I'll fetch you tonight at eight. I know what you're going through, really I do. Everything will be quite out in the open. So you don't have to worry. Believe me, I understand your doubts. They're only natural."

He sounded so concerned. Maybe she was crazy to doubt him. She was exhibiting typical paranoid behavior. That was it—paranoid! Imagining things, shadows, men around every corner. But it wouldn't hurt to have dinner with him. In fact, she really should, if only to find out when he was leaving Paris, to make sure he'd keep his promise about the tails. Maybe it was a good thing she hadn't left the previous night.

"All right. I'll be ready at eight."

"Wonderful. I'll see you then, Alethea."

As the phone went dead in her ear, she convinced herself that Akmet would never risk his status by doing something so crude, so stupid, as murdering a man. Oh, no, not Suliman Akmet. She could imagine him using his power, perhaps having to fire people, force them to do something against their will in the business world . . . but murder? No.

Over dinner maybe she could even feel him out some more, make a better judgment as to his real motives. Maybe he was just hot for her body, maybe it was as simple as that.

Alethea realized she was still holding the phone in her hand, as if it would tell her something more.

"Silly old thing," she said aloud, putting the receiver down.

It was hot and stuffy in the apartment, and automatically she began to open a window when suddenly she froze. What if those men were out there? But Suliman had promised. Yes, but what if there were others, maybe even Nick. If Suliman had found her so easily, then Nick could find her, too.

"Oh, hell," she said to the walls, "if you're out there, so what. What am I afraid of? That you'll shoot at my profile on the curtains? Come on!"

She pushed up the wide, old-fashioned window and leaned on the sill for a minute, feeling the cold, damp air wash over her. There was no one on the street who appeared to be the least bit suspicious.

"How 'bout a cup of tea?" Alethea said, smiling again as she realized she was talking to herself. They say that when you're alone too long . . .

Waiting for the water to boil, she thought some more about Nick. If he had followed her here, he would have just knocked on the door, just asked her to go back with him. He didn't have any reason to skulk around.

Alethea made her cup of tea and sat down at the small kitchen table, still in her nightgown. She was hungry and there wasn't a damn thing in the cupboards. She'd simply go out and buy something!

A long, crusty *baguette,* some fresh, pale yellow butter, maybe a *salade Niçoise* for lunch. Here she was in the middle of the gourmet capital of the world and afraid to go out and buy anything! Absurd.

She'd wait until midmorning, when the streets were full of ladies shopping. She'd wear her old trench coat and a scarf over her head, the collar pulled up—in case anyone was looking for an American girl in jeans—and she'd buy whatever she wanted, including a newspaper! This business of retreating from the world, of being afraid of every shadow, would have to stop.

But then there was the problem of when she could retrieve the notes, if they had even gotten there yet and weren't lost. The thought made her shudder. How long would it take until she was certain, without any doubts, that no one was following her? Was she clever enough to spot someone in a crowd? Dammit! She couldn't hang out in Paris forever, studying faces, looking over her shoulder every moment. Eventually, and soon, she had to get the papers, and then, of course, figure out whom, or what organization, to give them to.

Well, tonight she'd know what Suliman planned and she would firmly tell him again that she needed no protection. Then, tomorrow . . . what should she do?

Alethea thought about her friend Clair. And Leysin, Switzerland. She really should go there. It would be far easier to recognize someone totally out of place at the resort than it would be here in Paris. Alethea pictured the snow, the blue sky, the absolutely breathtaking scenery, some good physical therapy, too—skiing. Maybe she'd meet someone interesting there—a lovely, tall, handsome, charming, tanned skier, on holiday. Maybe they'd end up together some evening in a cozy Swiss chalet with a bottle of good strong Dôle, a fire. You never know. She could use a pair of nice warm arms around her right now. Yes, a brief interlude wouldn't hurt at all.

Leysin—the perfect place. She'd definitely go tomorrow. Her ski suit and boots were in the closet. Yes, she could borrow skis from Clair, no need to drag them along. A wonderful idea! Perfect!

She should have thought of it right away. The clean, snow-washed mountains of Switzerland, the pure peasant, down-to-earth practicality of the Swiss.

Alethea felt much better. She'd made a decision, formed a plan of action now, and she knew it was a good one. Clair wouldn't even think of prying. They could relive their school days and the other times they'd gone skiing together, looking for men. It would be fun. The dirty, winter-gray streets of Paris were far too depressing.

But there was still tonight. She'd have to be cautious, not drink much wine, watch him carefully, weigh his words, gauge his reactions. An interesting man, so European, yet so thoroughly Arab-looking. The type to gallop out of the desert on an Arabian stallion, a flashing scimitar in hand, but also the type to be the perfect host at a cocktail party. What had her father thought of him? What, really, did she think of him?

Chapter 12

Friday, December 9

Alethea watched from her window as Suliman climbed out of a taxi. She could almost imagine his voice, smooth, deep, instructing the driver, *"Attendez ici."*

When he crossed to her apartment house, she saw him turn the collar up on his heavy camel's hair coat. It was a raw, bitter evening; she didn't have to be outside to know that.

Finally, Alethea heard his light rap on her door. "Just a moment," she called, grabbing her dressy black coat with its fitted lines, diagonally buttoned front and small mandarin collar. She allowed another second to straighten her slip and panty hose underneath the smartly cut black dress she wore. Of course, Suliman would be properly attired, so she had chosen this particular dress for its elegant, flattering waist above the flared skirt. She smoothed the nylon around her knees and thought to herself that she did have nice legs, trim, well shaped.

And then, as she unlatched the door, it touched her mind that Suliman would find her terribly American.

"You look lovely," he said, taking her coat and helping her on with it.

"Thank you," was all she could find to reply.

They walked carefully down the dimly lit staircase and out into the bitter Parisian night.

"You must detest this sort of weather," Alethea said.

"Yes," he replied, taking her arm lightly, "I must admit I do. Europe can be miserably cold and depressing this time of year. It reminds me of the time I spent at the university in England. The land there is blanketed in a cold, damp gray mist for months. It's oppressive."

"Yes, I know," she said, thinking of how temperate and bright it must be in Abjala right now.

Once in the warm interior of the taxi, Suliman asked her where she'd like to dine.

Alethea selected the restaurant, Le Relais de la Butte, telling him that it was one of her favorites in Paris and that she'd written it up once in her column and wouldn't have to analyze the dinner this time—just enjoy it. She laughed then, some of her earlier tension was easing during the drive to Montmartre. That, she guessed, was good. If they were going to relax at all and really talk to one another, it was important to let Suliman know she felt at ease. Even if she wasn't, she couldn't let him know.

Minutes later, as they entered the Montmartre restaurant, she saw that he was faintly surprised at the simplicity of her choice. Le Relais was done in rustic, rather quaint decor, with gaily colored curtains and whitewashed walls—a country-style atmosphere that apparently took Suliman unawares.

"Do you like it?" Alethea asked.

"Quite nice," he replied as they were led to a private corner away from the kitchen's swinging door.

He took the wine list from the maître d' and asked her if she had a preference.

"I'm an absolute klutz when it comes to wine," she admitted. "I'm forever meaning to take a few classes on wine selection, but there never seems to be time."

"You're a busy woman, I can see. Fascinating," he said pensively.

"I guess we Westerners do seem that way to you," she answered with a hint of sarcasm.

He smiled in reply, nodding his head, and Alethea knew he must be thinking how very unfeminine a working woman was. Suliman must like them well rounded in body, at home, awaiting the summons of their man. How was it the Mexicans put it? "Barefoot and pregnant." Yes, that was how he would want a woman, she suddenly thought.

Alethea suggested the veal, and Suliman ordered a bottle of white wine, a vintage Hermitage Blanc, to accompany the dinner, telling her that his ulcer would no doubt revolt. After returning the menus to the waiter, he looked solemnly across at her. The soft candlelight flickered across her skin and lit her hazel eyes. She knew by his intent gaze that he was attracted to her. The knowledge was somehow exciting, making her feel light and breathless. And, Alethea wondered, did he know how thrilling his aura of power and dark good looks were to her?

They ate the meal, making small talk over the delicious food. Suliman questioned her about the seasonings and preparations, even admitting to her his frequent bouts with his cursed ulcer, and Alethea wondered why he felt comfortable enough to tell her such things. She was certainly calm this evening, quite removed from the frightened distrust she'd felt yesterday at the café. She almost hated to get down to business. Things were going so pleasantly right now.

It was Suliman who first brought up the subject. "Alethea, I spoke with the chief investigator of the lab accident this afternoon . . ."

An alert look came to her eyes, a faint furrow creased her brow.

He continued, "What was originally thought to be a plastic substance found after the accident turned out to be a part of your father's inventory and—"

"Are you saying," she interrupted, "that it *was* an accident? I don't believe it!"

He let his hand fleetingly brush hers on the tabletop. "But it's true, Alethea. You should be relieved, although I promise I shall do even more checking to satisfy you."

She met his words with suspicious silence.

"Alethea?" His deep-set eyes fixed on her. "I wish I could impress on you the importance of the project your father was working so hard on."

She snapped to full attention. What was he up to?

"If one were to read his papers, he or she might well misinterpret them. Your father was working on a new, more economical oil-refining project for us, but it seems so technical, confusing to the untrained eye."

"Excuse me, Suliman. But I haven't any idea what you're talking about," she lied tightly, feeling suddenly hot in the close restaurant. Would he believe her . . . or would he know that she was playing dumb?

"For the sake of argument, Alethea, let's say you had these papers we're looking for, say your father mailed you the original copy and kept one for himself . . ."

"Why would he do that?" Her breast was rising and falling more rapidly now under the black dress; she wished she could regain control.

"Quite simple, my dear. He worked hard on the development and wanted to impress you, although I'm certain you wouldn't comprehend a word of his technical mumbo jumbo." Suliman covered her hand gently, reassuringly, with his strong one. "Are you certain he sent you nothing? Please . . . try to think. It's important to my country, and of little value to yours."

Alethea slid her hand away from his grip. She needed time to sort this all out. But he was watching her so closely right now, she couldn't. If only he wouldn't press her so hard! She'd have to put Suliman at bay . . . and do it firmly.

Finally, she spoke. "I've made a decision. I'm going to Switzerland to visit a friend. When I get back, I'm going to work again. You've been very kind, but I'm afraid we can't help each other, and frankly," her voice took on an angry, defensive tone, "I don't appreciate all these questions about my father's work."

"I didn't mean to press you."

"I'm sure you didn't. But still, I've been terribly depressed and I'm thoroughly sick of thinking about all this, sick to death!" She lifted her wineglass and drained it, then spoke again, her voice becoming more heated. "I'm sick to death of everyone asking me about my father's research! I have had nothing, nothing! Please, let's just drop the whole thing."

"I've been a fool, Alethea."

She could sense his unease. Why had she said *everyone?* He would know now that someone else had asked her about the papers. She may have made a dreadful error in telling him about going to Switzerland.

"Alethea," he said, "you must allow me to fly you to Geneva in my Lear. It's the very least I can—"

"No. But thank you anyway," she stated flatly, praying that she was handling him properly.

The waiter interrupted them, mercifully, thought Alethea as she saw her grip on the conversation slipping further, beyond her reach.

"Dessert, *monsieur?*" asked the waiter.

"Alethea?" Suliman said.

She shook her head negatively, but suggested, "Why don't you try the *cerises flambées?* They're excellent."

"No . . . no. My ulcers, you understand. But I should love to indulge otherwise." He smiled politely up at the waiter. *"Merci, mais non, pas ce soir."*

"Très bien, monsieur. Le compte?"

"Merci."

Suliman turned his attention back to Alethea. She sipped on her wine, feeling that he was tense now.

"Do you ski, Alethea?"

She smiled matter-of-factly. "Yes, since I was a child in New England."

"How marvelous," he replied thoughtfully, in a distant tone.

On the ride back from Montmartre to the Left Bank, Suliman did much of the talking, surprising Alethea with his knowledge of Paris—its buildings, districts, history—affording her little time for thought. It did not escape her attention, however, that by going to dinner with him, alone and unprotected, she had placed herself in a trap. He could abduct her at any minute if he so chose. But he hadn't. And certainly if Suliman were responsible for her father's death, he would have made his move already.

Alethea glanced out the taxi window. They were on the Left Bank. It sure looked like he was taking her directly home. She felt relaxed, turning her attention back to his conversation.

". . . and so the edifice was erected in 1469 over the spilled blood of many," he was telling her.

"You're very knowledgeable about Parisian history," she commented, smiling, watching his long, aesthetic fingers as he lit another Gauloise.

The sweet-smelling smoke wafted up to his nostrils. "I know much about many cities. You understand, it is my business to be well versed in many subjects." He paused, pinning her with his gaze. "May I tell you something?"

"Yes," she replied, curious.

"You must tell no one. It will be our secret."

Alethea laughed at his uncharacteristic comment. "I won't tell a soul."

"The traveling, the people I meet, it most often bores me."

She lifted a smooth brow. "Bores you? I'm afraid I don't—"

"You must understand that I am forced to endure many long journeys and then longer conversations with my associates. I'm afraid," he smiled evenly, "that we are a very dull lot. All business and no play, as you might put it. My world is a deceitful world, far more deceitful than American politics. We must always be so cautious, keep our eyes turned in all directions."

Alethea assimilated his words in silence. Yes, she thought, buying and selling oil on world markets and then always having to protect the interests of his small emirate, making sure he wasn't gobbled up by OPEC or the ever-present Communist threat. It would certainly give her ulcers, too!

"I guess I'm fortunate," she said pensively. "My line of work is based on honesty."

Suliman emitted a curt laugh. "Honesty? You mean to tell me that a restaurant owner will not try to bribe you? I'm not so naive, my dear."

Not exactly sure why, Alethea took offense. "You're right, of course, it happens all the time. But how long would I be in business if my readers tried one of the restaurants in my article and found the food entirely different? My job and my credibility depend on my word."

"That's very noble. But surely *some* columnists are not above a little bribery."

"Lots of them take all sorts of bribes," she explained patiently. "They accept anything from money to expensive side trips. But I don't. And, frankly, that's why I'm at the top and they aren't," she finished without a hint of modesty.

"Excellent!" he exclaimed. "You are quite a woman, Miss Alethea Holmes."

She smiled weakly in reply, wondering how he'd done that to her—made her say such a vain, conceited thing.

He reached over, placing his hand on her knee; it was warm,

gentle. "I wish I could say my world was as simple as yours. You see, Alethea, I must always protect my people, at all costs. Take for example your father's project." Here he goes again, she thought dismally. "Had his work been completed, Abjala would have gained strength in the oil emirates—indeed, in the world. It is like a chess move: we advance, our opponent must go on the defensive."

"Things change quickly."

"Ah, yes. So they do! And there is the game!"

"The refining project you say my father was working on . . . was it so important that you would want it for your country only?"

"Of course," Akmet replied evenly.

"Then when you told me there were *some* people in your country who might have wanted my father's so-called discovery to themselves . . . could *you* also have wanted that?" Yes, Alethea realized, it was like chess, only this was a very dangerous game.

Suliman smiled thinly, stubbing his cigarette out in the ashtray. "Quite the contrary. It is simply that there are people who would stop at nothing to make certain that your father's discovery remained in Abjala. You understand?"

"Yes." Did she ever! Suddenly, she couldn't stop herself from asking the inevitable. "Wouldn't you, Suliman, want to keep his work to yourself? Surely it was more important to you, the oil minister, than to anyone else." Alethea held her breath as the taxi pulled up in front of her building.

He studied her closely for a long, agonizing moment. Finally, he said, "That is an astute assumption, my dear. Quite frankly, I am very glad you have brought out in the open this touchy subject which stands between us. I admit I want very much to possess his discovery, but as oil minister I must keep my hands clean. I must remain above suspicion. Were you to check with my peers and associates, they would tell you of my honor. I hold my honor dear and human life is precious to me."

Alethea let him take her hand as they stepped out into the now-misty night and walked to the door. How she would love to believe him!

He walked up the steep flight of stairs to her door, still holding her hand. Then he placed his other hand on her shoulder and carefully turned her around to face him. "You *do* believe me, don't you, Alethea?"

He was so terribly close now she could feel his warm breath

fan her cheek. "I . . . I'm still not sure what to believe, Suliman. I do want to believe you."

Then, just as she had known he would, he bent his head toward her. What would his lips feel like? she wondered. And then his mouth touched hers, a lingering brush of his lips. She remained motionless, unaffected by his caress yet strangely wanting to feel something, anything; the smallest response would have heartened her. Suliman moved his mouth deliberately over hers for an endless minute and still she remained passive to his touch. His hand stayed on her shoulder, though he didn't press her to respond. Did he sense her coolness, her inability to feel, to warm to a man's caress? And yet, as his mouth possessed hers, she recalled one man whose very nearness did send waves of pleasure coursing through her . . .

Akmet took his lips slowly away from hers. "I cannot tell you how sad it shall make me when you go away to Switzerland. Stay in Paris, Alethea."

"I . . . I can't," she breathed shallowly.

"Why not?"

"I need a rest, a *real* vacation. Surely you can understand."

"I don't, my dear. But it is your choice, of course." He stepped back.

"Please, I appreciate your concern," she said carefully, "but I couldn't stand the idea of being followed by your men, even if I need protection. Please give me your word."

"You have it, of course."

She unlocked her door and stepped partway through the entrance. She turned back to face him. "Goodnight, Suliman. And thank you for the evening." She began to close the door.

"Alethea?" he said quietly. "I should not like to think you are not being honest with me about your father's notes. I hope you have grown to trust me. You must make me a promise that you will think this over in Switzerland. His project was of little value to the United States but would mean so much to Abjala. You understand?"

She nodded hesitantly, wanting so desperately to believe this compelling man. Still, she found herself saying, "I really have nothing of his. Whatever you are looking for must have been destroyed in the fire."

She cast her eyes away as he met her words with a stony silence.

Finally, he said, "Call me when you return to Paris."

"You'll still be here? I may be gone a while."

"I have extensive business matters to attend to while in Paris. No doubt I'll still be here. Have a pleasant holiday, Alethea."

"Thank you." She smiled politely and closed the door, leaning her back against the hard wood as she listened to him retrace his steps down the hall. She let her breath out then. It was as if she had been holding it all evening, she realized suddenly.

Chapter 13

Saturday, December 10

The snug double windows of Clair's rented chalet looked out across the Rhône Valley to the Dents du Midi, a row of jagged white mountains that did have a slight resemblance to a set of molars. They were as awe-inspiringly beautiful as Alethea remembered, jutting like blue-white specters into the sky.

Lucky it was sunny today, she thought as she swung open the two sets of glass panes to breathe in the fresh, crisp mountain air. Yesterday had been overcast and spitting snow when she got off the quaint little cog railway at its highest stop—Leysin-Feydey. But today was one of those perfect days that are rare for the Alps in December.

She looked down the mountainside at the steep picture-postcard streets of Leysin that wound, tumbling picturesquely, below her. The Swiss *hausfrauen* already had their *duvets*, their precious down quilts, hanging out of the windows to air. They were like a set of fluffy white pillows pasted to the windowsills, Alethea thought, the comforting, tradition-laden peace of the small village already seeping into her.

The chalet was giving off faint morning sounds through its thick walls: water running through the pipes, the tinkle of silverware in the kitchen, the thump of a door closing. It sounded familiar, reminding her of the many times she'd been skiing with Clair before, mostly during their years together at finishing school in Lausanne.

Clair had been thrilled to see Alethea the night before when she had staggered in the door breathlessly, having lugged her suitcase up the steep road to the chalet.

It had been so good to see Clair again. It had been a few years since they'd talked except by phone. Alethea never knew where Clair would be. She was truly one of the jet set, spending the winter here, the summer there, turning up without fail in all the best places, the new spots that the beautiful people discovered a season later than Clair had been there. If Alethea did not know her so well, she would have been thoroughly jealous.

Clair was a tall, thin woman, with long blonde hair. Her features were not beautiful but striking, and her body was lean and kept in a state of taut fitness.

"Never thought you'd really show up, Thea. God, I'm glad to see you!" Her long, trim form had been vibrant with excitement, the glass of hot mulled wine in her hand spilling drops all over in her happiness. "But guess what?" She leaned close to Alethea and made a distasteful face. "Lisa's here, too."

"Oh, well, we can keep out of her way, can't we?" Alethea asked, remembering with great clarity Clair's older half-sister. Both of the girls had always hated Lisa's man-crazy, superior attitude. In a word, Lisa was a snob.

"Sure. She's bound to find some guy and then she'll be out of our hair."

"Hasn't she mellowed any? She's not a teenager anymore."

Clair sighed. "Not a bit. She's going to be the big three-o next year and I think she's frantic to get her hooks into some poor unsuspecting soul before then. But, hell, forget her. What's new with you?"

Somehow it had been embarrassing to explain about her father, that she had come to Leysin for some R and R. It seemed an awful thing to do, to burden fun-loving Clair with her grief. And she certainly couldn't explain the real reason she was here.

"Poor Thea," Clair had said. "How awful. But I'm so glad you came. There's nothing like these mountains to make you forget. Come on, I'll show you to your room."

They had lounged on the big double bed in Alethea's room, drinking the hot, spicy wine, growing lightheaded while Clair gabbed, asked questions, cried a little for Thea's father. They'd talked for hours and Alethea had enjoyed it, relaxing totally for the first time in a week. Just an old-fashioned schoolgirl gab—no words to watch, no insinuations to catch. And Lisa hadn't shown up at all. "Probably got herself a stud for the night," remarked Clair.

Leaving the window, Alethea pulled on her long johns, turtle-neck, black one-piece suit—might be a little too warm for it today but tough, that was all she had along—and stepped out onto the balcony overlooking the rustic, wood-paneled living room. The chalet was venerable, old, smoke-darkened, carved with Swiss motifs wherever possible. Leave it to Clair to rent such a marvelous place, and leave it to Lisa to tag along.

Alethea went down to the big country-style kitchen and found Clair at the table, sipping hot chocolate.

"Hurry up and grab a bite. We better get going before the gondola line gets too long. It's gorgeous out. Boy, you're lucky to hit good weather. It's been spitting snow all week."

"Hi, guys!" Lisa's breezy, booming voice filled the room before she actually entered. "Heard you were here, Alethea. Nice to see you again."

Clair made a face that Lisa fortunately couldn't see. Alethea hid a smile, not believing a word Lisa said, especially the "nice to see you" part.

"Hi, Lisa. It's been a long time." Lisa looked the same as Alethea remembered: tall, lean body like Clair's, but she had a head of wildly curly black hair and pale blue eyes in a large-featured, expressive face.

"Hey, you two going skiing? Can I come along? I hate to ride the lifts alone." She popped a stale piece of bread into her mouth.

Clair sighed to Alethea, then turned to her half-sister. "Sure, Lisa, I guess so."

"Thanks, guys. I'll be ready in a sec. Just have to put on my face. Wait for me."

"She's really kind of pathetic, isn't she?" Alethea said.

"Pathetic! You jest, my dear. It's all an act—for our benefit this morning, for someone else's later. Who knows? *She* doesn't even know anymore." Clair shrugged and Alethea loved it. It was fun to be girlish again, to gossip, to be carefree. Clair had done that to her.

The walk to the *téléférique*, which would take them to the top of the Berneuse, was short. The ruddy-cheeked Swiss, the tanned tourists, the stenciled patterns on the wooden chalets and shop-fronts charmed Alethea anew. Nothing was more enchanting than this Swiss village. There wasn't an ugly corner anywhere; every building was sparkling clean, cared for like the precious possession it was.

There were a few people in line already waiting for the four-man gondola and more straggled up to join them. Everyone looked happy, thrilled with the sun and the promise of a day of skiing. Certainly no one looked out of place, Alethea thought in relief, deciding she would enjoy this day thoroughly.

But Clair and Alethea noticed that Lisa kept turning around, watching, as if there were something, or someone, interesting behind them in line. Eventually, it became embarrassing because Lisa's height, her great mass of black curls and her skintight red suit made her quite obvious.

"Lisa, what in heaven's name are you gawking at back there? You're making a spectacle of yourself!" Clair hissed to her.

"Don't bug me now, sweet sister. There's a man back there, and is *he* attractive! Must be new. Haven't seen him around before. He isn't the pretty type, but he's got something, kid—the old sex appeal. He's pretending he doesn't see me, but you know he does. Must be the shy type. I love him already!"

"Oh, God, here we go again!" said Clair, shaking her head.

"Hey, here *I* go again. *You* aren't interested, remember?"

"Sure, Sis."

Lisa ignored her sister, her eyes trained behind them. "Come on, let's slow up. Maybe he'll catch up to us in line and we can go up the gondola together. Perfect! Wonder if he's French, German, English? Hard to tell. But without clothes, who cares!"

"Well, I'll be damned if I'm going to turn around and look! You'll have the poor man's pants off before you even know his name!"

"What's in a name, Clair?" Lisa nudged her sister in the side with her elbow, threw her head back and laughed loudly while Alethea did her best to ignore the whole conversation.

As slowly as Lisa dawdled, the man never did catch up with them. They got off the *téléférique* and Lisa decided her boots needed some major adjusting, so they waited by the lift exit while Lisa bent over, presumably fixing her boots, and sticking her tight, round, red rear in everybody's face as they left the lift building. But she didn't succeed in finding the man, and pouted for the next few minutes.

"Come on, Lisa, lay off. The world's not going to end. You'll see him later."

"Yeah. He's probably lousy in the sack anyway. The good-looking ones always are."

Not all of them—not Nick DeWolff, thought Alethea suddenly. He was awfully good-looking and, she was absolutely sure, would be wonderful in bed. For the right woman, though, she reminded herself dismally. She wondered briefly if he skied, but then asked herself why on earth she was even thinking about him. She'd never see him again anyway. Obviously, he wasn't the one who had called *The World's Fare* and he'd never picked up her trail after that awful night on the turnpike. She almost felt sorry for him, found herself hoping that he hadn't gotten in trouble with his boss because of her. He'd been a real man, not a super-macho chauvinist, but a real man nevertheless. Too bad he worked for the government. Regret suddenly seeped into Alethea's happy mood, coloring, but not spoiling it.

The three women skied the top of the mountain all morning, slicing through the few inches of new snow, carving around the checkerboard moguls, swooping down the wide bowls. Lisa kept looking around to see if the man was following them, and she saw him a few times, as she informed them, but quite far off. Whenever Lisa attempted to follow him, or steer their path nearer to his, he seemed to disappear into thin air.

"Elusive hunk, isn't he?" she commented thoughtfully one time. "But, hey, the skiing's great. Let's do the Piste Bleue and go all the way to the bottom this time, then lunch, and if he's in the restaurant, I'll have another go at him."

They skied hard, trying to upstage each other, picking all the expert trails, and on the lift back up, Clair and Alethea made mock-suffering faces at each other as they were forced to listen to Lisa's inane chatter about the "gorgeous male" she'd been trying to catch.

At lunch, Alethea realized she was exhausted, wind- and sunburned. Her legs ached from the unaccustomed exercise. It would take her a few days to get in shape.

"God, Clair," she said between sips of wine, "I'm really sorry but I'm beat. I think I'll ski down and take a long, hot bath this afternoon. I'm not in condition yet."

"Great. I'll come with you."

"Hey, you don't have to—"

Clair laughed. "My best friend comes to visit and I can't take an afternoon off! Besides, I've been out every day. Enough is enough."

"You sure?"

"Absolutely."

They sat around a table in the restaurant at the top of the Berneuse finishing the cheese fondue and a bottle of local *Fendant*. The pungent melted cheese was delicious, the wine cool and faintly sparkling, made from grapes grown in the valley just below Leysin. It was heaven.

Alethea let her mind wander, absorbing the amazing view from the restaurant. She had been right to come to Leysin. Already she felt cleansed, more normal. The sick terror and grief seemed very far away, quite ridiculous now. It was like turning over a rock so that the sun touched all the slimy, dark, crawly little things that lived under it. As soon as the light hit them, they disappeared and it was just a rock and some clean dirt.

Of course no one was following her! What a fool she'd been! She'd been watching all day and saw only the usual holiday skiers.

And it was so nice to have a real friend around. Good old Clair—always loyal and dependable regardless of her crazy life-style and huge trust fund. Alethea was tempted to tell her the whole story, but that would be useless and cruel. And up here, in the unpolluted atmosphere of the Swiss Alps, it seemed slightly ludicrous. No, she'd just enjoy her vacation and keep a very sharp eye out.

"Well, you ladies can go down but I'm staying," broke in Lisa. "I'm going to find that guy if I have to fake a broken leg right in front of him."

"You do that," Clair said distastefully.

"You wait and see. I'll invite him to the party tonight."

"Party?" Alethea asked.

"Oh, just some people coming over, pretty casual," explained Clair. "It'll be fun, good for you."

Later, luxuriating in the huge bathtub back in the chalet, Alethea went over the situation in her mind again. She'd go back to Paris in a few days and call Suliman, tell him that she was returning to New York to work. Why shouldn't he believe her? Then she'd calmly rent a car, or maybe take the train, and collect the papers. It would be simple. What wasn't so simple was where to take them. Someone or some organization that was utterly irreproachable and international: the Nobel Committee, or the United Nations. Something like that.

When that was taken care of, she could turn her attention to her father's murder. She was certain his death hadn't been merely an accident; even Suliman hadn't quite given up the investigation. And if no one helped her, she'd find out who had done it even if it took all her life.

Suliman's story about the explosives left in the lab didn't ring true. Oh, he probably meant well. But the police in Abjala obviously weren't too efficient. They'd overlooked something. Naturally, Suliman wouldn't admit that. He probably felt he had to take their report at face value. But *she* didn't.

First, though, she had to take care of the papers . . . for her father. One step at a time . . .

And maybe, Alethea thought, playing with the idea, she'd even have the opportunity to have dinner with Suliman Akmet again. He was a fascinating man, showing her a side of life of which she'd had no experience before: the life of the rich and powerful, the leaders of the world. It was very attractive.

As she got out of the tub, feeling pleasantly relaxed and a little sleepy, she decided to take a nap. Then she'd have to make a big decision—the biggest decision of the day: what to wear to the party tonight?

Chapter 14

Sunday, December 11

When Nick skied off the ramp that afternoon, amiably waving goodbye to his gondola partners, he was hardly surprised to find the girl's round, perfectly shaped fanny wiggling enticingly before him. Alethea's friend was bent over, supposedly adjusting her binding, all but blocking his path. Alethea and the third girl were nowhere to be seen.

"Damn," he muttered irritably under his breath, trying to get around her.

But Nick didn't know Lisa. "Oh, my!" she called in a female-in-distress tone. "Do you speak English?"

Nick slid to a stop in front of her. "Yes, I do," he replied roughly, his eyes scanning the area for a sight of Alethea.

"It's my binding," she cooed. "These bindings are always getting too loose!" Lisa straightened to her full, shapely height, ice-blue eyes meeting his boldly.

"Here," he muttered, reaching down to tighten the toe screw with a coin.

"Oh, I'm so glad to find someone who can help. They've been bugging me all day."

And then, without looking up, Nick thought to ask, "Skiing alone?"

"Why . . . yes, I am. My sister and her friend were skiing with me but decided to call it a day and went on back to our chalet. Guess I'm all by myself now." And then Lisa feigned a loss of balance, placing a gloved hand on Nick's shoulder to steady herself, leaning her full weight on him, her slim thigh against his side. "Sorry," she said innocently.

Finished adjusting her binding, which had seemed fine in the first place, Nick rose back up to his full height. Well, at least he knew where Alethea had gone. This girl was smiling provocatively at him. He had to admit she did have a lovely mouth. And what the hell, he realized abruptly, surely Alethea would stay in one spot for a couple of hours. He didn't have to keep an eye on her continuously . . . And maybe Alethea's friend knew her plans. He could try.

"Are you taking another run?" she asked, batting long dark lashes at him enticingly.

Nick checked his watch. There was no way Alethea could catch the last daily railway back down to Aigle and there were no rent-a-cars here, so she was stuck in Leysin, at least for the night. "Sure," he replied, smiling for the first time, seeing the girl's pale eyes light up with excitement.

"Mind if I tag along?" she asked. "I just hate skiing alone, don't you? By the way, my name's Lisa."

"Hello, I'm Nick."

She skied expertly, carving perfect turns down through the mogul field in front of him, her backside in the red pants almost glowing—a neon invitation against the white snow.

It struck Nick as he followed her lead easily that the hunter had somehow become the hunted, and by such a raven-haired, ruby-lipped, totally formidable female! He was not at all sure he liked it, although, he had to admit, it might be interesting.

They stopped at the summit of a steep, narrow ravine which few skiers could manage. "Look at those two!" giggled Lisa, pointing below at two heavily clad bodies wrapped around each other halfway down the steep pitch. Obviously, they had collided and were unable to stand, much less get their skis unscrambled.

Nick almost burst out laughing; it was the Arabs, the man and woman who had been recklessly tailing Alethea all day. Suliman really should have found better skiers! Although he doubted that there were too many accomplished skiers in the desert emirate.

"Do you think they need help?" Lisa asked.

"They got into the mess," Nick replied, "let them get out of it. Besides, it's the only way to learn, isn't it?"

"I suppose so."

Nick shot them an amused glance as he carved an expert turn beside them and headed down the slope. They wouldn't recognize him. In fact, none of the Arabs knew he was around—at least, not yet.

At the bottom of the trail, Lisa stopped again, breathless. "You ski wonderfully," she gasped. "How long will you be in Leysin?"

"That depends."

"On what?"

In reply, Nick grinned, showing even white teeth.

"I wonder if you'd like to come over to my chalet tonight," Lisa said. "We're having several people in après ski. You know, hot wine, soft music, a cozy fire . . ."

"Sounds lovely. But I can't say for sure."

Lisa quirked a dark curved brow.

"I meant," he began again, "that I sort of told some other people I'd dine with them. Maybe I can get out of it."

"Do try." Lisa batted her thick lashes again and Nick thought she was like the female black widow spider, a man-killer. And he was her chosen victim, caught in her web, waiting to be mated with, to suffer, to die a glorious death . . .

"I'll try hard," Nick replied, feeling himself already hopelessly entangled. Oh, well, he thought, it was time to meet Miss Alethea Holmes face to face again. He was certain Porter would agree, too. The girl had had enough time, more than enough, to display her loyalties. It was time for her to fork over the information and make the trip to Washington.

At the base of the slope, Lisa gave Nick directions to the chalet—of course, he already knew exactly where it was; he'd spent a miserable night watching the place from his hotel window.

"I'll try hard to be there. All right?" He slung his skis easily over his shoulder.

Lisa lifted her dark goggles up onto her ski cap. "I'll be waiting." And then she rose up in her boots and placed a warm kiss on his cheek. "At six?"

"If I can," Nick said, giving her a heart-melting wink.

Relaxing for a few minutes back in the room, Nick thought over the evening's plan before he called Porter in Washington. He had to admit he was looking forward to confronting Alethea. Wouldn't *she* be surprised! Of course, she knew nothing about being followed, either by him or the Arabs, that much was pitifully obvious. She might have been pretty clever the way she had eluded him on the drive to Washington, but she wasn't all that smart. And, somehow, he'd like her to know it.

He could hardly wait to see her hazel eyes widen in . . . in what? Maybe fear, or maybe she would be glad to see him. But why she would, Nick couldn't quite fathom. Especially after the other night, the evening she had spent with Suliman Akmet at Le Relais de la Butte. She certainly had looked relaxed then, almost intimate with him over the candlelit table. Of course, Nick had only caught a quick glance at them through the restaurant window, but they seemed to be thoroughly enjoying themselves while he waited outside in his car, alternately switching the motor on and off for warmth, bored to distraction. And then afterward, at her apartment, Akmet had taken her in and had not come out for some time. Nick had surmised there wasn't enough time for Suliman to seduce her, or the other way around, he had thought grimly. Yet Nick was sure there had been plenty of time for a long embrace.

Suddenly, Nick knew he wouldn't miss being at the chalet tonight for anything.

He reached for the phone. He waited impatiently while it took forty-five minutes for the overseas connection.

Finally, it rang. He snatched it up.

"Nick?"

"Yeah. Listen, I'm in Switzerland, little ski resort called Leysin."

"Girl's there now?"

"Right. And so are the Arabs."

"She must be setting up a deal with them. Damn the bitch!" Unconsciously, Nick flinched at Porter's choice of words. "I'm not so sure she is," he said pensively. "It seems more like she's trying to get away from them. Point is, if I don't bring her in soon, they may make a move. That could be dangerous."

"So what do you plan? You know the situation better than I do."

Quickly, Nick related the amusing story of his invitation to the chalet.

Porter laughed. "May as well go."

"I will. Should be back in Washington tomorrow—late."

"Make damn good and sure you've got the papers."

Nick hesitated. What if she didn't have them on her? What if she had hidden them, already made contact with Suliman Akmet in Paris and sold them? He hadn't been able to watch her every move, after all. Still the Arabs were here, making asses out of themselves. Surely if Akmet had what he wanted, he'd have called his dogs off . . .

"I'll do my best."

"What does *that* mean?" Porter's tone became clearly annoyed.

"Simply that she may not have the papers on her right now." Nick paused. "And listen, Skip, I'll be damned if I'm going to force her to talk. Understand?"

Porter was silent for a long moment.

"I think you're getting a little soft. You'd have gotten the information out of her a year ago . . . any way it took."

"Not this time, Skip. I mean it," Nick said firmly. "She's not like that."

"Want me to send someone else?" Porter said crisply.

"No."

There was another pause. "All right. You handle it. But get the job done!"

"I'll be seeing you." Nick hung up slowly, pensively. Was Porter right? Was he getting soft? Well, if he was, one thing was for sure, he couldn't let Alethea know that . . . or Suliman Akmet.

Nick rose from the bed and began stripping. He'd have just enough time for a shower, then on over to the chalet. If she had the papers here, it would make things a whole lot simpler. He had been on the same train with her to Switzerland but hadn't been able to watch her too closely or she might easily have seen him. She could have made contact with someone during the trip.

Nick stepped into the white-tiled stall and began soaping himself down. What would he do if she refused to give him the papers? Sure, he could take her back to Washington, let Porter's crew drug her, get the information. But it would make him seem like an ass in front of his colleagues. Suddenly, Nick knew he would have to bring her, *and* the papers, back. If he let himself get too soft now, he would be useless to the NSC. Once you let your guard down . . . Maybe he *should* have let Porter send someone else.

Nick dressed in a pair of faded jeans, boots and a black turtleneck sweater. Over it he wore a navy-blue parka, nothing fancy. Besides, it was all he had with him; the rest of his things were back in Paris, locked in the Saab near the railway station.

He stepped out into the brisk mountain night. A light snow was falling, dampening his thick hair. The chalet was only a couple of blocks up the steep hill. The tiny shops of the town were still open; tourists jammed the narrow, winding streets; bells jingled over doors. It was a lovely spot for a vacation.

The snow crunched under his boots as he made his way toward the chalet. How different this pristine Swiss setting was from other streets he had walked. Even the air smelled pure here, scented with burning wood. It was a far, far cry from the rancid back streets of Saigon.

Ignoring the quaint brass knocker, Nick used his fist to rap on the chalet's door.

He could hear faint laughter through the heavy wood. Vaguely, he wondered if it were Alethea's.

Finally, the door swung open and Lisa stood on the threshold with the crowded, firelit room behind her.

"Oh! You made it! Wonderful!" She reached out a hand and took his warmly, standing on tiptoe and giving him a noisy, inviting kiss full on the lips.

Nick stepped up into the room. "Yes," he said, "I begged off with my friends." He smiled then, but it did not reach his eyes, which were trained over Lisa's head, intently scanning the large room.

Chapter 15

Sunday, December 11

Alethea's heart gave a great sickening lurch that seemed to burst her chest, and her knees went all watery. Her mind could not at first adjust to the reality.

Nick. Here.

His blue eyes looked soberly over Lisa's shoulder, those eyes that had looked into hers with such feeling, his strong hand was on Lisa's arm, gently turning her from her passionate greeting.

So *this* was the man that Lisa had pursued, hooked, dragged in, the one she'd raved about all afternoon!

Nick!

The joke was on Lisa this time.

And then Alethea realized, with a humbling wave of clarity, that she hadn't lost him at all, that it was no coincidence that he was here. He'd followed her every step of the way, second-guessing her at every turn. How stupid she'd been!

"Come on, Nick," she heard Lisa say, "meet everybody!" Lisa linked her arm through Nick's, walking him to the group of people around the fire.

"Hey, everybody! This is Nick . . ." Lisa looked at him questioningly.

"DeWolff," he filled in.

"Nick DeWolff. What'll you have to drink?" Lisa turned toward her sister. "Clair, meet Nick. Isn't he gorgeous?" And then, not waiting for anyone's answer, she steered him to where Alethea was standing, frozen, trying desperately to decide how to face him. Brazen it out? Lie, say she'd never met him?

The warm, firelit room seemed to become fuzzy, like the unfocused background in a professional photograph, and there, centered in the middle of the hazy picture, was Nick, standing out in stark clarity, the focal point of the scene. Nothing else existed. She could hear no distinct sounds, only a blur of voices. She could hear her blood pounding in her ears like a tide.

Suddenly, she felt like running but she couldn't. She remained mesmerized, frozen like a statue in the strange void of her perception.

Then he was in front of her and she forced herself to think, to smile, faintly, falsely. Lisa's image sharpened and the room became distinct again, words reached her ears.

Lisa rubbed her cheek sensuously against Nick's shoulder, purring like a cat in front of a fire. "Thea, this is Nick. Wasn't it nice of him to come?"

Alethea dared herself to meet his eyes. What struck her at first was that Nick looked so familiar, as if she'd seen him just yesterday: his slightly mocking, boyish grin, his rumpled dark hair, the purely male, unselfconscious beauty of him. How could she have forgotten it for an instant?

Alethea sensed instinctively he wouldn't give away the fact that they knew each other.

Unexpectedly, a wave of anger filled her—that he would let Lisa, of all people, drape herself all over him. She'd thought his taste was better than that!

Alethea mumbled a few noncommittal words to which Lisa didn't listen anyway, and excused herself. She could not help but notice Nick's penetrating blue-eyed gaze on her the whole time. What did he want?

"Not bad at all," Clair was whispering in her ear. "I think Lisa has done it this time." Then she looked closer at Alethea. "Are you sick or something? The altitude get you?"

"No, I'm just a little tired. I think I'll go up to my room."

"Sure. Take it easy," Clair said, concerned.

Alethea waited until Nick and Lisa seemed to be involved in a conversation, then she slipped quietly up the stairs, along the balcony, to her room, closing the door softly behind her with immense relief. At least she wouldn't have to watch him with Lisa anymore. She had to admit it hurt.

But most of all it made her furious. How dare he? she fumed. After he'd pretended, even said, he really liked her, that he wasn't playing games. Alethea remembered his words vividly from that night in Athens. She could almost feel his hands on her arms again, the feel of his lips on hers . . .

Damn him! How could he throw that all in her face, ignore her, allow Lisa to ooze all over him in front of her? She found herself stalking furiously back and forth, clenching her fists whitely. She threw herself onto the bed, near tears with frustration, and pounded one fist into the down comforter.

In her wrath, she failed to hear the door open quietly, then close with a smooth click. How long did she lie there, seething, before she sensed the unaccountable presence filling her room?

Her head snapped up sharply.

"I'm sorry about the scene downstairs," Nick said as if nothing of consequence had happened. "I realize it must have surprised you." His voice was low, intimate.

Alethea sat up quickly on the edge of the bed, feeling flushed and uncomfortable.

"What exactly are you doing here?" she asked tightly, trying to make her voice sound hard. "Besides using my friend to get in here?"

"Let's just say I've been keeping an eye on you," he replied coolly, walking over to the tall windows that looked out over the Rhône Valley and opening them to check their distance from the ground. He seemed satisfied that they were high enough to keep her from getting out that way.

Alethea sat in frozen silence, unable to marshal her thoughts enough to give him the scathing reply he deserved. She concentrated on keeping her dignity intact, at least those few tattered rags of it that were left to her.

Casually, dispassionately, Nick walked over to her suitcase, felt carefully through her clothes, opened the closet door, all the drawers in the dresser, oblivious to her anger that he would dare to rifle her belongings.

She knew exactly what he was after, but she wouldn't give him the satisfaction of admitting she knew.

"Okay, Alethea, where are they?"

"Where are what?"

"Your father's papers. Don't play games with me."

"They were nothing important, after all. I threw them out," she lied smoothly.

The amused expression on his face told her he didn't believe it.

"Tomorrow morning we're going to Geneva and we're flying to Washington. We're a little late . . ." he said to her, a slight smile curving the corner of his lip. It infuriated her.

"Who in hell are you to tell me where I go and what I do?" she hissed.

"I'm a representative of your government, Alethea," he stated calmly.

"I don't care! I have nothing the government wants. I'm not going anywhere with you!"

"Yes, you are, even if I have to tie and gag you and carry you over my shoulder." He laughed, evidently quite untouched by her anger. It made her even more furious.

"You can't do that, you son-of-a-bitch!"

"Watch me." His eyes suddenly turned hard.

She'd never seen him this way. It scared her, it sobered her quickly. "Why don't you go back downstairs to Lisa? Why don't you leave me alone? You bastard!"

His blue eyes narrowed. "We'll leave tomorning morning. Please be ready. My superiors have been patient so far . . ."

She couldn't miss the veiled threat in Nick's words. He didn't *want* her to miss it.

Then his expression changed. He looked like the man she had known in Athens again. "Look, Alethea, you've had your fun. It'll be better for everybody if you cooperate, especially for you. I hate to see you caught up in this mess, but you are. There's no out. All you have to do is go back to Washington with me, answer some questions. Then it's all out of your hands." He almost sounded as if he were begging her now, but she knew better.

"I don't have any answers," she replied stubbornly. "At least not the kind your boss wants."

"Okay," Nick sighed in exasperation. "We'll do it the hard way. Be ready to leave with me in the morning." And he turned his back on her, walked to the door, opened it without a backward glance.

Then he was gone.

Alethea slumped on her bed with a muffled groan. All her plans, her good intentions, all her hopes for her father's discovery! She couldn't let Nick take her back. She couldn't lose, not this easily. She had to put up a better fight, even if she was an amateur up against professionals. It wasn't in her to give up without trying, and trying again, until there was no hope at all. She knew Nick wouldn't let her out of his sight tonight, but there was always tomorrow . . . and it was a long way to Washington. A very long way.

Suddenly, it came to Alethea—crystal-clear and practically foolproof. But she'd have to ask Clair to help her, which meant she'd have to tell her friend the whole story, or at least enough of it to convince Clair to help.

It was a good plan. It would work.

Alethea crossed the room to the mirror and began to brush her honey-brown, wavy hair almost viciously. She'd show Nick DeWolff! And she'd go back to the party, prove to him that he hadn't gotten to her, that she wasn't a scared little mouse who had to hide away in her room. She might even enjoy watching Lisa suck him dry.

She slashed a line of bright red lipstick on her mouth, brushed some rouge on her pale cheeks. It would do.

Alethea left the room, stood on the balcony and took a deep breath, readying herself to face everyone at the party . . . especially Nick. When she looked down at the firelit room, her eyes fell instantly on Lisa's purple silk blouse and wild black curls. One sleek purple arm was flung around Nick's shoulder, one long white hand played with the dark curly hair at the nape of his neck.

Alethea's stomach clenched with sudden hate as she threw her head up and began to descend the stairs.

Chapter 16

Sunday, December 11

It was painfully obvious to Nick that he had not been tough enough on Alethea. And he had only himself to blame for that.

As he stood, a mug of hot wine in hand, talking with Lisa, he found his glance continuously fixing on the door of Alethea's room. Surely she wasn't going to cloister herself up there all night!

"Daddy was in shipping," Lisa was telling him gaily. "He made an absolute fortune and Clair and I have had the most wonderful time spending it!" she finished unabashedly.

Nick smiled, nodding, while Lisa toyed with the neck of his sweater with warm fingers. At least she had been too wrapped up in her hostess role to notice that he hadn't used the bathroom upstairs but had instead gone into Alethea's room. It would have been damn hard to explain.

Lisa introduced him to several more people at the party—most of them Europeans—but Nick found it difficult to concentrate on a conversation. It would be a long night and he knew he would have to spend all of it at the chalet. Of course, Lisa wouldn't be hard to convince of that!

"This is Ricardo," she was saying. The men shook hands politely. "He's from Rome—a doctor. Aren't you, *amore?*" The man smiled fondly at Lisa, who seemed to know him awfully well. "Ricardo's my 'Italian Stallion.'" She laughed huskily, then led Nick aside to a quieter corner of·the large room. "You're not jealous, are you, Nick, darling?"

"No, Lisa, I'm not," he replied, wondering when Alethea had rejoined the party. She was standing near the fireplace, her back turned away from him, talking to Clair and two rather German-looking types who seemed quite interested in the very pretty woman. Alethea wore a pair of snug-fitting jeans and a pale yellow silk blouse that molded to her trim figure. She wasn't very tall, Nick registered, but had shapely, long legs which rounded nicely, firmly, at the thighs. Her hips were semi-full, also firm-looking, and her fanny tended to stick out just enough to be extremely enticing.

He felt Lisa tracing a finger along his jawline, then lightly touch the spot near the bridge of his nose where it had been busted. "Who are you staring at, Nick? Is it Clair?"

He looked down to meet her glare. "I'm not staring at anyone, Lisa. I was thinking."

"Maybe it's her friend, Alethea?"

"Lisa . . ."

"I'm not blind, love. But it's okay." She laughed curtly. "Look all you like, as long as you remember *who* invited you."

He smiled tightly at her. Lisa was spoiled rotten and could use a good setting down. Too bad he didn't have the time or the inclination, but someday, some man would burst this female's bubble.

"Lisa," Clair interrupted, "I'm sorry to break in this way, but would you mind helping Thea and me in the kitchen for a few minutes? We really ought to feed this horde something. It's getting late."

"Well," Lisa pouted, annoyed, "I guess you're right. I told you to hire someone, though." And then she looked up into Nick's eyes. "Maybe you could help, too. I'm a horror in the kitchen and all you men seem to cook so well these days."

"Sure," Nick said, following the two women across the room.

They threw together a quick assortment of cheeses and crackers, popped some into the tiny oven, cut up vegetables to go along with dip and placed sliced *jambon de Grison*, darkly cured ham, on a platter with Dijon mustard and wonderful, freshly baked bread.

Alethea had clammed up the instant Nick had walked into the kitchen. Even now, she kept her back to him while chopping celery near the sink. All the while, Lisa chattered away and Nick ascertained from Clair's expression that the half-sisters probably fought often. Evidently, they were like day and night.

He finished piling the last scraps of ham onto a silver platter and Lisa and Clair began carrying the food out to the guests. He walked over to the sink to wash his hands.

Suddenly, Alethea gasped. "Ouch!" Quickly, she drew her hand back from the cutting board. The knife clattered to the floor at her feet.

Nick was at her side in an instant. "Here," he said, taking her hand, "let me see that."

She tried to pull away. "Let go of me!"

"You've cut yourself pretty deeply," he said, ignoring what she said.

"I can see that!" she spat.

Nick flashed her an irritated look. "Hold this towel on it," he said roughly, "and I'll go get a Band-Aid from Clair."

He began walking to the door when Alethea rudely shouldered past him, blocking the exit. "I can take care of myself," she said heatedly. "I wish you'd go away; or why not let Lisa take you upstairs!"

"Alethea . . ." He could see her eyes fill with moisture.

"Just leave me alone!" With that she was gone, heading, stiff-backed, over to Clair, oblivious of Nick's eyes following her pensively.

And then Lisa was there, nuzzling up to him again, telling him how nice it was to find a man who was handy in the kitchen. They left the room and rejoined the party. Lisa led him to the deep, overstuffed couch near the hearth and they settled into its soft comfort. After the food was served, most of the people left. Alethea had disappeared upstairs and Nick surmised it was to get a Band-Aid, then maybe she had turned in for the night.

As Lisa purred softly against him, sipping on the spiced wine, Nick couldn't stop thinking about Alethea—the girl who seemed to despise him now—and the other Alethea, the one who had warmed so easily to him in Athens and who had accepted his offer of help when she had been terrified in New York. Where was that soft, innocent woman now? Was it possible for him to have read her so wrongly? Was she really playing one side off against the other—a mercenary?

Lisa reached a hand up to the back of his neck. He turned his head, looking down into her pale, glossy eyes. Her lips parted, waiting. She placed her other hand on his thigh. It was a very open invitation and Nick wasn't certain how, under these circumstances, to resist.

One thing he knew for sure, she was going to rape him on the spot if he didn't do something, and do it quickly. "Want some more wine?" he said lamely, rising.

Lisa shook her head and seemed content to wait for him while he refilled his mug. When he returned, however, the situation hadn't changed. She snuggled even closer to him than before. The game could be funny, he thought, if it weren't so deadly serious. The hunter had become the hunted. And Nick was not at all sure he liked it, although—her marvelously supple leg inserted itself between his knees—it had its advantages for a man.

"Nick, love, let's go take a sauna and sweat some of this wine out of us. It's cozy in there, private-like." Now she was breathing into his ear with her husky voice. She knew the tricks, all right.

"Sure, Lisa, in a minute. Just want to finish this wine—great stuff." How long could he go on, letting her wrap him around her finger? And how in hell could he spend the whole night here and still avoid her?

Lisa rubbed her face against his, murmuring something about how good he felt, her wine-sweet breath tickling his neck. Everyone had left now, even Clair was nowhere in sight.

"Where's your sister and her friend? Aren't we snubbing them a little?" Nick hoped this wasn't too obvious a change of subject, but he had to find out, make sure Alethea was still here. He hadn't seen her in hours now.

"Oh, Clair's in bed, and Thea? . . . Thea's funny. She's not into men. And her father just died. They were very close. She only came to ski, she says, but to tell the truth, I tried to convince her earlier to get herself a man. Even offered Ricardo . . . But I wouldn't let her have you, love. *You're* special." She buried her face in his neck, her hand sliding up his thigh to brush him boldly.

Nick responded, needing to keep her occupied, hating to lead her on in a way, but what the hell, she was an adult. His mind, however, was still working quickly and efficiently, like the well-honed tool it was. Alethea had been dodging around Europe, seemingly innocent, amateurish, but apparently it was only to throw everyone off-guard, to confuse them. It would be difficult getting the papers from her, that is, without hurting her.

In a moment of stark honesty, he admitted to himself, Nicholas James DeWolff, you're confused by her. No rhyme or reason to her actions. Strange girl in so many ways.

And yet her face had already become so familiar to him, her graceful figure and mannerisms a well-known habit. She seemed to have a great deal of poise, an unending well of almost courtly manners and well-bred behavior from which to draw. But, he had discovered, she had a temper, too.

"Nick, you turn me on," Lisa was whispering, her hands going up under his turtleneck to stroke his back. "What's this, love?" Her finger traced a raised ridge along his ribs, reminding him of the white-hot slash of the shrapnel . . .

"Nothing," he said harshly; then, trying to cover his reaction, "Vietnam, like a lot of others."

"Oh, I bet you looked fantastic in a uniform! I *love* a man in a uniform. Oh, Nick!"

From their place on the fat, overstuffed couch, Nick could see the balcony with the bedroom doors leading off it. The bathroom door opened and Alethea's familiar figure came out, in a terry-cloth robe, a towel wrapped around her freshly washed hair. Her delicate white face glanced down at him for a second, then snatched away. She walked to her room, firmly shutting the door behind her.

Well, she's still here, he thought. She hadn't climbed out a window, down those treacherous cliffs or anything. Nick felt oddly embarrassed, with Lisa fondling him, caught with his hand in the cookie jar, so to speak. But it was a way to spend the night here, what the hell. Besides, he didn't owe Alethea any sort of faithfulness.

Finally, he let Lisa convince him to take a sauna. She gave him no opportunity to get a suit, so obviously this was to be an exercise in the buff.

Lisa undressed in the shower room, taking off her clothes like a burlesque queen, slowly, sensuously, her long, angular form gradually emerging as the pile of clothes at her feet grew. She wrapped a towel around her waist, watching Nick undress, unashamedly devouring him with her big, pale eyes until he, too, draped a towel around his middle. They let themselves into the tight little cedar-smelling cubicle and the hot, dry air singed his lungs.

"Oh, Nick, this is wonderful," sighed Lisa, taking in his lean body hungrily.

Sweat began to pop out on his skin as Lisa rose, standing above him, panting in the close, hot, burning air. He reached up and caressed a pert nipple. There would be no stopping it now . . .

In a moment, she was next to him, her sweat-slicked body pressed urgently to his, her lips moving against his almost desperately. It was funny, he noticed, but her skin was cool to the touch, even her belly, which slid up against his wetly.

Her tongue darted into his mouth with quick, demanding thrusts. Then her hand came in between his legs and began stroking him slowly at first and then feverishly.

Suddenly, he pulled his head away. He was suffocating. "Lisa," he said, half-panting, "I don't know if I'm up to this."

She drew away abruptly, her brow arched. "You don't want me?"

"It's not that, Lisa. You can certainly tell I want you." He smiled weakly. "I guess I'm just used to taking the initiative. Saunas aren't my style . . . I'm dying in here."

A smile split her mouth. "Oh! You should have said something. We'll go to my room."

But Nick knew that wouldn't help. Sure, he was plenty turned on, what man wouldn't be? But somehow he didn't want to have sex with Lisa. He told himself he was exhausted, too much wine and far too little sleep lately. Strange, he thought, this had never happened to him before—*never*—especially in this condition! He glanced at Lisa and saw her staring at the obvious bulge beneath his towel.

They stayed in the sauna a while longer—Nick's idea. He needed time to think. Sweat poured out of him profusely, but Lisa seemed unaffected, tossing more and more water onto the hot stones until he thought he would surely die. Then, when he guessed he knew why people occasionally had heart attacks in saunas, Lisa began to kiss him again. He had never had claustrophobia, but this must be it!

For the second time, he eased her away. She didn't pout or even frown. She must be anticipating a romp in her room. How would he get out of this one?

When the sauna was over, he felt more drained than ever before in his life, and he hadn't even slept with her yet. His heart beat madly; his head spun; he gasped like a fish stranded on a hot beach. The ultimate weapon, he thought fleetingly—Lisa in a sauna.

Later, after he'd sat weakly on the smooth tiles of the shower, the cold water drizzling onto his head and back, and had a long, cool drink, he persuaded Lisa to sit on the couch for a few minutes before turning in. He had to admire her staying power. She looked quite refreshed, glowing, in fact, for this very late hour. What a woman! *Formidable*, as the French would say. Now how could he keep from going to her room?

Lisa was telling him more about herself, how her shrink had turned her on to sex as therapy, what he had taught her. Nick watched the leaping flames, amused, a bit bored by her, thoroughly exhausted. He closed his eyes, only vaguely listening to Lisa's words, knowing she was trying to prep him for the inevitable and knowing, also, that she was in for a big disappointment. No way did he have the energy or will to sleep with her. It was plain and simple, he told himself. Lisa wasn't his type.

While Nick half-dozed, he slowly became aware of another presence in the room. Suddenly, he sat up, spun around quickly—a well-established habit he couldn't break. Alethea stood near the kitchen door, a book in one hand, the other holding a steaming cup of hot chocolate. She looked horribly embarrassed, rattled and maybe a touch angry still. He could feel her discomfort as if it were his own.

"I . . . I'm sorry . . . I couldn't sleep. Thought I'd fix myself something warm to drink. You were in the sauna . . ." Her soft voice trailed off.

"Hey, Thea, no harm done. See, we're dressed—all proper. You want to come talk before we turn in?" Lisa was not the least bit disconcerted and plainly did not see Alethea's mortification.

"No . . . no. I'm going up to my room now. To read." She held up her book, smiling nervously, falsely, then fled up the stairs.

"Poor kid. We embarrassed her," Nick heard himself say, wondering briefly why he had said it.

"Poor kid, my ass," snapped Lisa. "She's no kid. She's twenty-five, and if she doesn't want to take advantage of the pleasures of life, that's her problem. Embarrassed, hell! I refuse to ruin my fun for a weeping willow. I tried to cheer her up. Well, she's not staying long anyway. Guess she's hot to get back to work. She hasn't the slightest idea of how to have fun."

Little did Lisa know, thought Nick, that Alethea was hardly on her way back to work.

"Want to go upstairs now?" Lisa asked.

Nick sat up, looked at the balcony, then to Alethea's door. "Listen, Lisa," he began, "would you be terribly upset if we stayed here? I'm really beat . . . honestly."

"It's me, isn't it?" She frowned and looked down at her hands.

"No. It's not you, Lisa."

And then her eyes flew open and her head snapped around to face him. "You're not a . . . a fag, are you?"

Nick threw back his head and laughed deeply. Now why hadn't he told her that in the first place! "No, Lisa. I'm not. I'm just here on vacation, a badly needed one. I'm tired. Let's just stay right here on the couch and enjoy the fire. I'll feel better if I get some rest."

She gazed at him pensively. "Then you'll go upstairs later?"

He smiled noncommittally, drawing her up against his chest. They stayed that way for what must have been hours; Nick didn't know, he was dozing on and off. When he finally awoke fully, it was four in the morning. He vaguely remembered Lisa getting up and leaving. Most likely she went to bed, no doubt waiting for him to come to her in the early morning. She'd have a long wait.

He wondered then if it were possible that Alethea might have slipped past him while he had slept? Probably not. No matter how tired he was, he had never slept through even the slightest movement around him.

But just to be sure, he rose and quietly mounted the stairs. He found himself standing at her door, his hand resting on the knob gently. It turned smoothly, silently, in his hand.

The soft glow from the living room below fell in a stripe across the floor. He could make out a figure on the bed, but to assure himself that it wasn't merely blankets, he walked carefully over to the bedside. It was Alethea, all right. Her face was a pale oval against the sheets, and she looked so young, so childlike. But didn't people always think that about others? Still, she looked very different from the angry woman in the kitchen last night. When he had offered to help with her cut, she had instantly lost that well-bred, ladylike, slightly old-fashioned aspect of hers. He had to admit, there were many sides to this woman. But he knew from experience, it took all types. The freckle-faced boy-next-door could spatter an innocent village with deadly machine-gun fire, massacring women and children, then laugh as he cut the breasts off the dead bodies. You could never tell . . .

Nick turned slowly away from the bed, retracing his quiet steps.

It could be that she cultivated that innocent look. Don't be taken in by it, he told himself. That might be fatal.

He closed the door gently, then stood on the balcony. Lisa's room was only a few feet away. He had gotten some sleep, not much, but he did feel better. Maybe he should try her door . . . He didn't have to worry about Alethea for a few minutes, she appeared to have been soundly asleep.

Nick almost took that step toward Lisa's room, but suddenly he knew he couldn't. He saw himself, with stark clarity, holding Lisa's body in his arms but envisioning Alethea's face.

"Hell," he whispered, then turned, walking back down to the lonely couch.

Chapter 17

Alethea plopped herself down on the kitchen chair across from Clair and yawned. It had been a late night and she'd been too preoccupied to sleep very well.

"I know, I'm tired, too," Clair said. "I might bag the skiing today."

"Clair, I have to tell you the most amazing story," Alethea began. She'd better dive in. At least there was no one around right now. She'd just passed Nick, asleep on the couch. Since Lisa wasn't with him, she might possibly have finally gotten her fill. Alethea pushed the disturbing image of the two together from her thoughts.

"It's about that guy. Nick, isn't it?" Clair said.

"How in hell did you know?" Alethea asked, shocked.

"No one could miss the way you kept looking at him last night. You know him, don't you?" Clair's face took on an almost comically knowing expression. "You can't fool me, Alethea Holmes."

"Was it that noticeable?"

"Definitely."

"Well, that doesn't matter now. I do know him. As a matter of fact, he's been following me and I have to get away from him. It all has to do with a discovery my father made—"

"Your father?"

"Oh, it's all so complicated. Anyway, he wants some papers of my father's and I don't want him to have them. Believe me, it's very important, Clair, or I wouldn't even tell you anything."

"Are the papers here?"

"No, of course not."

"Well, don't tell me where they are. I don't want to know."

Alethea sighed. "And I wish I didn't know either. It's a mess. And now Nick has found me again."

"Uh-oh. Poor Lisa. She thought she had it made this time."

"That's her own fault. She chased him and he used her to get in here," Alethea said coldly.

"Who is this guy, anyway?"

"He works for the government. An agent or something."

"A spy?" gasped Clair, wide-eyed.

"Shhh!" Alethea put a finger to her lips, afraid he might hear Clair. "Yes, I guess so."

"So how are you going to get rid of him?" Clair screwed up her face into a *femme fatale* grimace. "That is, if you really want to. He's quite a catch, it seems to me."

"He's not exactly out for my body, Clair. And I do have to get rid of him, and quick."

"Okay, what's the plan?"

"I'll convince him to go skiing this morning because the next train to Geneva doesn't leave until this afternoon anyway, right?"

"Right."

"I lure him onto the Black Trail and get a little ahead of him, then take that shortcut back here. Remember, the one we used to use when we were in school?"

"Sure, the narrow one that goes off by the old barn."

"He'll never find it until it's too late, and by then he'll be so lost it'll take him all day to get back to the chalet."

"It might work," mused Clair.

"It has to!" Alethea said fervently. "When he gets back, I have another idea, and this is where you come in."

"I know! You want me to seduce him until you're safely away."

Alethea managed a smile. "No, even better. You tell the police that this stranger who came to your party stole some jewelry. You know these Swiss police. They'll jump on him as fast as a shot! After a day or so, you can conveniently find it."

"Very clever. Diabolical, in fact. Does the poor bastard deserve all that?"

"You're damn right he does!"

"Okay, okay. You know I'll do it. And you also know I'm the most accomplished liar around if I need to be."

"Thanks, Clair. I'll tell you the whole story someday. Right now you're better off not knowing anything."

"Are you really in any danger? What are they going to do to you?" Clair asked anxiously.

"Throw some questions at me that I don't want to answer."

"You sure? I mean, they aren't going to put on the ol' thumb screws and stuff?"

"Don't be silly. One more thing. Can you pack my stuff after I leave with him? I don't want to give him any hints."

"Sure. Where you going?"

"Back to Paris. I have to see somebody there."

"Okay, but I'll tell you something, if you don't call me in a week to tell me you're safe, I'll raise such a stink trying to find you that the whole world will hear about it."

"Sure, I'll do that."

"A week from today," Clair repeated sternly. "I mean it."

Alethea found it hard to talk. There was a lump in her throat. "Clair, you're really a good friend, you know that?"

"Sure, Thea. Just don't try any crazy heroics or anything."

"I won't. Now, you know what to do?" Alethea asked.

"Yes, keep the poor sod here at all costs."

"Right."

"But I still don't know why in hell you're running *away* from him!" said Clair, grinning mischievously at her.

Now came the hard part. Somehow she had to get Nick away from Lisa and convince him to go skiing with her this morning. She hoped he wouldn't refuse, or she'd have to rethink her plan. Maybe it wouldn't be so hard, though. Lisa was a late sleeper.

Alethea walked over to the couch and looked down at Nick. He lay with his forearm across his eyes, one knee flexed. He needed a shave and his hair was mussed. She sensed he wasn't really asleep. "Nick?"

His arm came down, he sat up—alert, ready, like a cat.

"Look, I thought all night." She hoped she sounded sufficiently contrite. "I'll go with you. No struggle, no trying to escape. I know it won't do any good."

He cocked his head, looked at her warily. "You don't say."

"Yes, really. I'll go to Washington. But they may be disappointed. I don't have any information . . . or any papers. But I'll go with you, so they know that, and then maybe you'll all leave me alone."

His blue eyes were still boring into hers suspiciously. "Okay, it's a deal."

"There's one thing." Mentally, she crossed her fingers and prayed.

"Ah."

"Can we go skiing this morning?"

"No." A flat, irrevocable statement.

"Please, Nick. It's my last chance. I happen to know that the train to Geneva leaves from Aigle in half an hour and we can't make it. The next one is at two. We have plenty of time to get to the airport." She tried to sound trustworthy, reasonable, female. "I'd like one more day of skiing so much. You're cutting my vacation short, you know." She pouted a little, held his eyes with hers, put a touch of honey into her voice.

Nick remained on the couch. He was silent for a long time, watching her carefully, assessingly. She hoped she passed the test.

"Come on, Nick. I've been through a lot lately." Demurely, she cast her eyes down, working on the pity end of the spectrum. Could she force a few tears? "It would do me good. Please." There, she could even feel a film of moisture in her eyes. He couldn't miss it.

"All right. But we have to be back here at noon. I won't let you out of my sight for a second."

She'd won! She wanted to whoop, to jump for joy, but instead she said, "Thanks, Nick. You won't regret it. I'll be putty in your hands."

Alethea thought she saw a slight twinkle in his tired-looking blue eyes. "I'm sure you will be. After all, you're an intelligent girl, aren't you?" he said mildly.

He made her come with him while he returned to his hotel room to change into his ski gear, even locked the door from the inside while she waited for him to change. She sat fuming in a chair while he shaved and showered, but she was all sweetness and light to his face.

And really, she had to admit, being locked in a room with Nick wasn't all *that* bad. Especially while he dressed. After he had emerged from the bathroom with only a damp white towel wrapped around his middle, and before she had cast her eyes away, Alethea had all but gasped aloud at the pure virile beauty of his body: the long, well-shaped legs covered with brown curling hairs, the broad back he showed her with its corded muscles beckoning to be stroked, savored, and his strong arms still glistening wet from the shower, strong and firm, looking as if he could crush her without batting an eye. Beneath the limp towel, she could see the slender shape of his hips and the flat, sinewy stomach above—even the bulge of his maleness was visible, and she guessed, blushing, that he was fairly well endowed.

She tried not to look, to stare so openly. It was extremely hard. But as he bent to collect his ski clothes from his suitcase, she was afforded an even better view of his powerfully built legs. Oh, he was beautiful . . . And by the time he disappeared back into the bathroom to dress, she was thoroughly relieved to see him go. In another second, he might have turned and caught the blatant wonder written on her face.

As they walked to the *téléférique*, a haze began to cover the sky, making the weak sunlight gray and flat. Not the greatest conditions for skiing, but maybe that was even better. She'd had lots of experience with weather like this. Maybe he hadn't. The skiing would be harder, the visibility tricky. Some people even got vertigo from the flat light—good.

Alethea made small talk as they rode up the gondola, trying to avoid any serious, touchy subject. No point in setting him off.

But that part of her plan fell through the floor.

"I didn't have a chance last night to compliment you on your cleverness." His tone was amused, but underneath it she could sense barely suppressed anger. "Did you enjoy making a fool of me that night on the Interstate, Alethea?"

Oh, no, she'd been trying so hard to be pleasant. "Please, Nick, believe me, it wasn't anything personal."

"What did you do, use a window?" His sapphire-blue eyes imprisoned her gaze, challenging her.

"Yes."

"Go on."

She cast her eyes down. "It wasn't so hard, really. The worst part was the ride I got."

"Oh?"

"Yes, with a truck driver. He was awful at first."

Nick narrowed his eyes. "What do you mean, awful? Why, you little fool, did he do anything to you?"

What a strange attitude for Nick to take. Why should he care? "No, of course not. I'm not that dumb." She saw his raised brow. "I told him how I'd just found out I was pregnant and had a terrible fight with my boyfriend because he wouldn't marry me, and the guy suddenly turned all protective. It actually turned out to be quite a pleasant trip."

"I'm glad you enjoyed it," Nick said sarcastically, but she didn't miss the faint tug of a smile at the corner of his mouth.

They continued the ride in silence for a while, and she sensed that he was watching her very closely, ready for any move she might make.

Alethea tried to empty her mind, pretend that she was a tourist on a holiday with her boyfriend. And sometimes it almost worked. Nick was so handsome in his bright blue turtleneck and navy parka, his tight ski pants outlining the long, lean muscles in his legs and the hard roundness of his butt. He looked totally refreshed after his shower, as if the night before had never happened.

The night before. Then it came back to her. Lisa and Nick. Their absolutely disgusting behavior together. Of course, Nick would say he'd had to use Lisa as his excuse to get into the chalet, but he didn't have to carry it that far! He'd probably use anybody to get his job done . . . and enjoy every minute of it—all in the name of duty! Alethea felt herself grow cold and bitchy.

But he couldn't know how she felt, not for a second. If her resentment showed, he'd be even more suspicious. That might ruin everything. Forget it, she told herself. He must use the same line on everybody. It sure worked on her in Athens!

They skied at the top of the Berneuse for a while, warming up. Nick was a competent skier but not great. Alethea knew she was better, but then she'd been skiing ever since she was a child in New England and all through finishing school in Switzerland. She had an unfair advantage.

Good.

The wind began to pick up, blowing in sharp gusts. A storm was advancing across the valley. The light was so flat it made the snow appear to dance in even, tiny spots of light all over. It was almost impossible to tell which way was up or down, whether you were moving or stopped.

"Hey, this is getting nasty," Nick said as they got off the top of the lift. "Think we should go down now?"

"One more, please. I love it. Don't you? It's such a challenge!"

"All right," he agreed grimly. "Just take it easy. I'm not as young as I used to be."

"Okay. Let's do the Black Trail. That will get us down to the village, but it's a good long way down." She hoped she hadn't relented too easily. The last thing she wanted to do was to arouse his suspicions at this point. So far, everything was fine. She was keeping herself under impeccable control.

They cut down behind the mountaintop restaurant to where the sign said Piste Noire, then they began turning on a steep, tree-dotted slope. The mountains fell away beneath them, the bumps hidden by the dancing, glaring flat light and blowing snow.

Alethea led, knowing the way unerringly under any condition. She waited politely for Nick a few times as he negotiated the trail a little slower than she did. Still, she tried not to underestimate him. She'd done *that* before . . .

They were totally alone on the back side of the mountain, away from the other skiers, of whom only the locals knew about this trail or dared to take it.

They traversed a steep gully, then began following a narrow trail until it finally opened up to what were, in the summer, cow pastures.

Soon the old, weathered, wooden barn was in sight, just as she remembered, across the expanse of snow. Alethea pushed on, getting farther ahead of Nick until he was still behind the trees while she quickly crossed the field in a tuck position.

There it was. The narrow path at the corner of the barn that no one would notice unless they knew precisely what to look for. The main trail continued on down past the barn in a meandering path to the bottom of the village. Nick would have a long walk back from there to the chalet, *if* he found the way at all! He could easily follow the wrong path up here, especially with the weather worsening. Meanwhile, she'd be long gone before he got there.

Filled with an anxious thrill that gave her strength, Alethea pushed her poles against the snow as hard as she could, propelling herself around the barn. Then she skied recklessly along the trail, knocking the snow off overhanging branches, falling once, going on and on as fast as she could until, finally, she came out on the road just above Clair's chalet.

Quickly, she kicked out of her skis, slung them on her shoulder, her breath sobbing in her chest as she trotted down to the chalet. She burst in, dropping the skis with a clatter. Clair appeared, white-faced.

"It worked!" Clair realized. "I've been so worried."

"It worked fine," panted Alethea. "I've got to get the cable car down to Aigle now. God, I hope I don't have to wait long."

"Here's your stuff, all packed. Get going. And trust me. I'll keep him here, don't worry."

"Thanks, Clair. I mean it."

"What're friends for?"

Alethea hugged her. "I'll never forget this."

"Remember, you call in a week! No more, understand?"

"Yes, I promise. 'Bye."

But before she could dash out of the door, Lisa's familiar, brassy voice brought her to a halt.

"Where's Nick?" She was descending the steps, pulling her robe together, searching the room.

"Go on," Clair whispered, "get the hell out of here, I'll take care of Lisa."

Alethea turned to leave again but Lisa walked up and placed a restraining hand on her arm.

"Where are you going in such a rush?" Lisa arched her brow questioningly.

"Ah . . . I'm leaving . . . I've got to get back."

"Certainly in a hurry, aren't you?" She turned to Clair. "Where's Nick?"

"He's skiing, I guess," replied Clair, avoiding her sister's intense gaze.

"Oh?" Lisa said, taking in Alethea's ski suit. "Were you skiing with him?"

Alethea answered her with stony silence.

"Well! Were you?"

Alethea turned to walk down the stairs but was shocked to feel Lisa's hand on her arm again. She whirled around. "Get your hand off me! How should I know where he is?"

"Oh, don't play Little Miss Innocent with me, kid. I saw the way you two looked at each other last night!"

Alethea pulled her arm away. "Well, you must have mistaken it. It was only your filthy mind at work!"

And then she was gone, racing down the path, but not before she heard Lisa yell after her, "Go to hell!"

She ignored Lisa, actually smiling to herself. She'd finally gotten to Lisa after all these years.

It took a few minutes to get to the Leysin-Feydey cog railway station. Luckily, it was downhill from Clair's chalet. Alethea raced on, lugging her bag, breathless, her blood pounding sickeningly in her ears. The miniature train that would take her down to Aigle was waiting. There she'd catch the train to Paris in two hours.

Alethea sat facing backward in the cog train, her hands clenched in her lap no matter how many times she tried to relax them, expecting to see a raging Nick appear at any moment. She had a couple of bad moments when the train stopped at lower pick-up points in the village. What if he'd made it down, was waiting for her at one of the two stops?

But he wasn't there, not at either one. So far, so good.

She stepped off the cog railway at the Aigle station into a different world: no storm brewing, only an overcast sky. The temperature was warmer, the people were not dressed for skiing and there was no snow. It was a solid, tidy Swiss town like a hundred others.

She bought her ticket, changed her ski boots for leather boots in the ladies' room and then sat down in the station café to have a cup of coffee and a croissant. She faced the door, watching nervously to see if he appeared. Yet if he did appear, she hadn't the faintest notion of what she'd do. Still, she watched, sweating in her black, one-piece ski suit. She kept glancing at the big wall clock—an hour to go, then half an hour, then twenty minutes. No Nick.

The last ten minutes until the train pulled in seemed like a whole day. She left the café, walked to the correct platform, paced along the bricks, watching for him, always watching.

The Orient Express pulled in exactly on time and the silver-sided cars flashed by her, each labeled as to its final destination:

Dijon, Paris, London. Quickly, Alethea climbed onto one marked Paris and pulled her bag up after her. She edged along the narrow corridor, picking an empty compartment, slinging her bag up onto the overhead rack.

Thank God, she thought, slumping into the hard leather seat. I've done it . . . I've really done it!

But then Alethea had to wait endless moments until the train pulled out. He could still find her, sitting there on the train with nowhere to go. It was possible.

It was only when the train had pulled out of the station and picked up speed along the valley floor that she breathed more freely. Now it depended on Clair to keep him from following her, because he could very easily guess that she'd gone back to Paris. Yet she had to face Suliman, to make sure of him. Only a couple of days. Afterward, she could retrieve the papers.

The train rattled through the damp, gray, wintery landscape of the Rhône Valley on its way west to the French border. Gray-green fields, lovely Swiss towns, colorful Swiss houses, even a crumbling castle or two slid by the window as she leaned her hot cheek against the cool, vibrating glass. The rhythm of the train wheels could put her to sleep if she would let it, but her mind was too busy to allow her to rest.

Alethea had many hours to sit on the train before it reached Paris, many long hours in which to remember every expression, every nuance of Nick's face, of his voice. She had misjudged him terribly, had thought he was at least a well-meaning, fair-minded person, who genuinely cared about her.

Well, he wasn't. Nick was a hard man with a job to do and he'd do it any way he could, even if he had to harm people along the way—like Lisa, like herself. It hurt Alethea that her judgment had been so very wrong.

She couldn't rid herself of the picture of Nick and Lisa on the couch the night before. Lisa had looked so sure of herself, so smug, so satisfied. It had oozed from her every pore hatefully. And how had Nick looked? Alethea tried hard to recall, to picture his exact expression. Then she thought she had it.

Hadn't he looked quite sated?

Chapter 18

Tuesday, December 13

Nick was still seething as he left the small *gendarmerie*. It was very early in the morning, the picture-perfect streets of Leysin gleaming insolently back at him under a bright winter sun. He felt grimy, he needed a shave and about twelve hours of uninterrupted sleep . . . which he wasn't going to get.

It had taken nearly the whole night to convince the local magistrate and *gendarmes* that he had not really stolen Clair's diamond bracelet, that he was in Switzerland on official business for the United States government. Even his NSC identification and his official passport hadn't convinced the heavyset, tight-lipped magistrate. It had finally taken an early morning phone call to Skip Porter in Washington to clear things up.

As he walked swiftly up the steep, winding, snow-covered street to Clair's chalet, his breath making white puffs in the clear, cold air, he couldn't help but feel a certain amount of grudging admiration for Alethea and her friend and accomplice. He knew they'd cooked the whole scheme up together. He felt a rush of outrage again at the way he'd been duped. By the time he'd found his way back to the village in the storm, she'd been gone, of course.

The little bitch! That saccharine-sweet act had been all for his benefit . . . and, unfortunately for him, it had worked.

The girl was an amateur, pure and simple, but a very smart, resourceful amateur. He'd been underestimating her all along. He'd have to stop doing that right now. Maybe Porter had been right, maybe he was getting soft . . .

Nick remembered how the *gendarme* had been waiting at his hotel room when he'd raced back there to grab his bag and get down to Aigle to see if he could catch her. Her timing had been perfect. Unbidden, a mild smile tugged at the corner of his grim mouth. He had to hand it to Alethea. She'd won round one and round two. She'd delayed him quite handily. However, round three was coming up.

Now he had to confront Clair and find out where Alethea had gone. Then there was Lisa. He hoped she wasn't there to complicate matters . . .

He rubbed a hand over his bristly face. God, he was tired. But he'd been tired before and he'd lived through it. He had to find Alethea soon. The Arabs might be on her trail. Suliman, he was sure, had been keeping very close tabs on her all the time. Maybe he should have told her that, scared her. But she didn't seem the type to scare too easily. He had to respect that in her, however reluctantly. She was gutsy. Misguided, but gutsy.

Of course, Alethea could be telling the truth about her father's research, but she sure appeared to be guilty as hell. It was academic in any case. He'd been ordered to bring her in, period.

Nick strode up to the door of Clair's chalet and pushed it open without bothering to knock. The hell with good manners. He was irritated and frustrated. And, Nick admitted to himself, worried to death about Alethea.

"Anybody home?" he yelled.

Clair appeared on the balcony above him in a bathrobe, her long blonde hair loose, her eyes wide with feigned surprise. "Nick DeWolff, isn't it?" she asked innocently. "Lisa's friend?"

"Yeah," he drawled, "Lisa's friend."

Clair descended the stairs, looking young and clean and fresh, exactly the opposite of the way he felt. "Did the *gendarmes* let you go? Did they find my bracelet? I'm awfully sorry if it wasn't you." Her blue eyes shone with guilelessness. A real good act.

"Where's Alethea?" he asked, trying to keep the anger from his voice. No sense upsetting Clair on the off-chance that she wasn't involved.

"Alethea? But I thought—" She looked genuinely puzzled.

"I need to know where Alethea's gone."

"I haven't the faintest idea," she said loftily. "She just left. I'm not her mother, for goodness sakes."

"Look, Clair, it's important. I'll forgive you the fake setup if you'll tell me."

"Fake setup? What on earth . . . ?"

"Cut the act. Just tell me where she's gone."

Clair set her chin with determination. "I said I don't know. Now, if you don't leave, I'll have to call the police again."

"Just try it." The stupid twits. They had no idea what they were up against. They were like little kids playing with matches. It chilled him to think of Alethea alone out there, in a jungle just as dangerous as any in Vietnam. He tried to swallow his wrath—it would get him nowhere—and sound reasonable.

"She could be in serious trouble, Clair. I'm only trying to help her."

"Oh, I think she knows what she's doing. I wouldn't worry if I were you. Besides, it's really none of your business, is it?" Clair's determination infuriated him. Well, he thought in growing exasperation, there were two ways to go: He could twist her arm until she squealed, or he could try to trap her with her own words. "Okay. Let's try it this way. She went home to New York."

"No," said Clair, almost giggling, "I love guessing games. Go on."

"She's still in Leysin, hiding out somewhere."

"No." Clair's bright eyes danced.

"London."

"No."

"Abjala."

"No." Clair laughed. There was no hint of recognition in her voice.

"Geneva."

"No."

"Paris."

"No."

Ah. That was it. The tiny, unconscious flick of knowledge, the infinitesimal signs of a lie. Nick knew them all, was as sensitive to them as a master safecracker was to the silent click of the tumblers. She'd gone to Paris.

"Thank you, Clair," he said quietly. "You've told me all I want to know."

"I didn't tell you anything," she replied stubbornly.

Nick's lip curled faintly, the smile not reaching his eyes. "Sorry, but I'm afraid you did." Then he softened his tone, seeing her obvious consternation. "Believe me, it's better this way." He had no time to waste. Every second counted now. He turned to leave.

"Nick!" The brassy voice fell on his ears like a death knell.

Lisa was coming out of her room in a scanty nightgown, running down the stairs toward him, her big mouth in a wide smile, her black curls bobbing. "Lover! I missed you. Where have you been?"

"Oh, I was detained," he said sarcastically, glancing at Clair. Her eyes were on the floor, but he could see that her wide mouth was trembling.

Lisa stroked his cheek, rubbed up against his shoulder. "You look tired, love. Want to take a little nap in my room?"

That was all he needed! "Actually, Lisa, I was on my way out. I have some business in Paris. Important business." He sensed Clair's head lift quickly.

"Oh, come on, just a few minutes. How about breakfast?"

"Sorry, I don't have time, Lisa."

She pouted. "What a friend you are! A regular Houdini, with the disappearing act and all." Then her expression hardened. "And how come you were skiing with that prissy Alethea yesterday? You could have waited for me."

"I didn't want to disturb your beauty sleep, hon."

"Nick!"

"Sorry, I've got to get going."

But Lisa wasn't so easy to put off. She turned her long, thin arms around his neck, put one slender leg between his and pulled his face down to hers, kissing him thoroughly.

Finally, he managed to disengage himself from her surprisingly strong embrace. "'Bye, Lisa."

"'Bye, Nick. Love ya. Come on back," she said sweetly as he turned to leave.

Then he heard Clair's shrill, anxious voice following him as he strode down the path. "If you touch one single hair on her head . . ."

Nick smiled grimly to himself. *He* wouldn't be the one to harm Alethea.

Chapter 19

Alethea's feet and calves were beginning to ache from touring the museum. But if her body was physically tired, her mind was not, and she was positive now that she had shaken off anyone who might be following her. That coup in Leysin had done it.

Wandering without direction through the Louvre was one of her favorite pastimes. It was always a refreshing luxury to take time away from the everyday hustle and bustle of modern living and roam backward through pictorial history as far as she cared to go. It was like living a marvelous, romantic fairy tale.

But today she'd had another, quite different reason for visiting the Louvre. On the train from Leysin, Alethea had decided to put her safety to one more test. She had to be certain none of Suliman's men were dogging her. But just in case, she had racked her brain for the perfect spot in Paris where she could be out in the open, on the alert for a tail. Nick could not possibly be in Paris yet if her plan in Leysin had gone smoothly. Clair would not fail her. There was one snag, however. Alethea remembered telling Clair

147

she was heading to Paris. That was stupid, she had realized on the train, for Nick might be able to get that information out of Clair. But if no one followed her here, if there were no suspicious-looking, gray-suited men, no one taking special notice of her, then she was safe. She would think quite seriously about collecting her father's papers from their safe hiding place.

The huge, sprawling palace—the Louvre—was ideal for the final test. She could stand still, ostensibly admiring a work of art, and watch the faces around her. She'd be sure to notice if anyone seemed peculiar, because the place was so huge and empty on Wednesday afternoons that she'd be unlikely to see the same person more than once.

As Alethea strolled through the basement section housing the Egyptian and Babylonian exhibits, her eyes traveling over the fine collection of stone and terra cotta statues, mummies and stylized bas reliefs, she realized that calling Suliman Akmet this morning had been the right thing to do. He must be completely convinced by now that she was ready to drop the whole thing and go back to her job. There was no reason for Suliman to think otherwise. He didn't know that she had her father's papers, he couldn't.

He had sounded so glib on the phone, so concerned with her welfare. "I'm truly glad you feel better, Alethea. The short visit to Switzerland was beneficial then?"

"Oh, yes," she had replied. "I would have loved to stay on and done some more skiing with my friend, but it seemed like getting back to work would be the best cure."

"It is an old saying, that work is often a cure. You're leaving Paris, I assume?"

"Yes. I'm booked on an evening flight. Tonight, in fact," she lied easily. "I just wanted to thank you for being so kind, Suliman."

"My pleasure, Alethea. I'm very pleased you called. I should not have wanted to return to Abjala this afternoon thinking of you alone and unhappy. And please, Alethea, try to understand why I had my men following you in New York. It was for your protection, or so I thought at the time."

"Well, it did scare the hell out of me, I've got to admit. But I can see why you did it."

"I'm terribly sorry if you were frightened but I assure you that I sent them back to Abjala days ago."

"That's good."

"Now, are you certain you'll be all right? If there's anything you need . . ."

"Oh, I'm fine," Alethea assured him, and ended the conversation soon after.

Now her eyes rested appreciatively on a five-thousand-year-old figure of a seated scribe while she tried to imagine a different sort of visit to Abjala, one in which the oil minister would escort her around his country. It might be fun once the mystery of her father's death was cleared up. Suliman wasn't the pompous Arab she had first thought him. No, in fact, he was quite handsome, in a dark way, and worldly, too. It might be an interesting visit, if she ever decided to go.

Alethea walked back up the stairs into the Grande Galerie, in awe as always of the sweeping, open beauty of the giant white hall. From there, she strolled down through one of the many wings, pausing a moment by a window to rest her feet.

She was gazing out over the busy street below when her vision suddenly focused on the reflection in the window pane. The glass mirrored several paintings on the wall behind her, but it was not the oils that drew her attention—not at all. Instead, she fixed her stare on a swarthy-complected man who stood perhaps thirty paces away, his eyes glancing from Raphael's *Madonna* to Alethea's back and then to the oil again. She was instantly alert. Hadn't she seen him somewhere before? She was dying to turn around and face him so that she could better view his features, but she remained motionless, presumably looking out onto the street. Again his eyes bore into her back and returned to the painting.

For several more minutes, Alethea stood frozen to the spot, waiting, hoping she was wrong. And then he moved forward to another painting, nearing her by perhaps ten feet as he did so. He glanced again at her back, and when he did, she got a clear picture of his face.

"Oh, no," she whispered. "Oh, God . . ."

He was an Arab—that much was plain. And she *had* seen him before. He was the same man who had stood below her window in New York. Akmet's man! He was watching her, following her! And, oh, God, Suliman had lied!

Forcing her feet to move, she turned away from the window and headed down the long hall away from him, faster and faster, while her breath snatched in her throat.

Alethea braved a quick look over her shoulder. He was following. Her heart throbbed in fear. Before she even realized it, she was half-running, passing through the long galleries of priceless paintings, not seeing the kaleidoscope of flashing colors and forms that flew by her, sensing the eerie tap-tap of footsteps on the polished marble floor behind her. And then she was racing down the massive marble steps. That heads turned and watched her fleeing the museum escaped her completely. All she sensed now was an animal instinct that told her to run. And run fast.

Rounding the corner on the north side of the Louvre, she fled down the rue de Rivoli, frantically searching the heavily trafficked street for a taxi, a bus, a Métro entrance.

Breathless, she spotted a free cab waiting at the light. She ran toward the vehicle feeling that her heart was going to burst in her chest, praying that the light wouldn't change before she caught the car.

"Attendez! Attendez!" she sobbed.

As the light turned green, the taxi remained motionless, its tail pipe spewing out great puffs of gray into the chill air. Finally, mercifully, she threw herself into the backseat.

"Hurry . . . please," she gasped. *"Vite! Rue Monsieur-le-Prince, numéro vingt!"*

As the taxi bolted forward, darting like a rabbit in and out of the traffic, she kept her gaze fixed out of the rear window looking desperately for any sign of someone following.

It was impossible to tell. There were dozens of small black sedans on the street. And the drivers' faces were invisible, hunched over the steering wheels in an all-out effort to get somewhere first.

It struck Alethea then, as she drew precious air into her lungs, that she was an idiot to return to her apartment. But what else could she do? Her purse, her passport, her credit cards were there. All she'd taken to the Louvre was cash, stuffing it along with her keys into her jeans pockets so she wouldn't have to carry a handbag. Dammitall to hell! Everyone had always told her not to leave her purse. But she'd always hated to tote around the extra weight and she never, never left money in it. Oh, why in God's name did she have to leave it behind today? She had been right in the first place . . . back in New York, when she had been in shock. Suliman Akmet was a lying, filthy murderer!

And now he was stalking her!

All the horror, all the miserable, sick fear that she had worked so hard to rid herself of, washed instantly back as the taxi sped across the bridge to the Left Bank, then down the Boulevard Saint-Germain.

Alethea felt nauseous. The predicament she found herself in left her so stunned that she couldn't think straight, much less make a decision. Once she collected her belongings, she'd take off. Anywhere, except where the papers were!

The taxi turned onto rue Monsieur-le-Prince. She felt panic rising in her throat, choking her. The cab stopped in front of her building. She had to move now, and quickly. No time to wallow in self-pity or fear. She pulled several bills out of her pocket and shoved them at the driver. Alethea did not see the black Mercedes pull up two cars behind the taxi. Nor did she see the man who slid quickly out of the car and walked toward her.

She opened the taxi door and stepped out hurriedly onto the pavement. She began to half-run toward the apartment entrance when she felt a hard, demanding grip on her arm. She was spun around rapidly and Alethea thought her heart would burst as she came face to face with *him*—with that heinous Arab.

At the precise instant her mouth was opening to scream, a hard object was jammed into her ribs.

"*If* you resist," the Arab said slowly, "this gun will go off."

The scream froze on her lips as the gun was shoved deeper into her side while he started to half-drag her down the street.

Alethea saw the Mercedes then. There was another Arab at the wheel and, as they neared the auto, she saw a familiar face in the backseat. *Suliman*. The back door swung open. Suliman was leaning over, holding it so that her captor could force her in.

Oh, God! She couldn't get in there with him! She just couldn't! Alethea tried to twist away, mindless of the gun stuck in her ribs.

"Please get in, Alethea," Suliman said mildly.

"No!" she hissed, "you dirty *bastard!*"

"I said . . . get in!"

She struggled again, frantically, but to no avail. The Arab was easily pushing her onto the seat while Suliman grabbed her free arm and started pulling.

Alethea half-moaned, half-cried, "No! Never!"

Suddenly, everything went crazy.

Chapter 20

Wednesday, December 14

The Saab tore across the bridge leading over the Seine onto the Left Bank, an accelerating blur of gray. Nick changed gears swiftly, smoothly, darting easily in and out of traffic, braking, speeding, leaving a throng of slower-moving vehicles behind as he sped down the avenue.

He had not known for a certainty that Alethea's taxi was headed for her apartment until it had taken a left onto Saint-Germain, but now he was positive, and the cab, along with the trailing Mercedes, was still a good two blocks ahead. He would have to pass both vehicles and, within a very short distance, be on rue Monsieur-le-Prince before them.

Damn the stupid girl anyway! Didn't she know that the Arabs were going to snatch her? It was the most obvious thing in the world to Nick as he shoved the clutch in, down-shifted to second, and bolted around three more cars.

The Saab responded to his expert handling like a roaring beast and, within half a minute, he was passing the Mercedes looking like any other Parisian driver in a hurry to get nowhere.

Nick allowed himself a quick glance at the black sedan in his rearview mirror. He could see the driver hovering like an animal over the steering wheel, oblivious to all else but the taxi, now one car ahead of Nick's. God help her if that snarling-faced maniac got a hold of her first!

Rue Monsieur-le-Prince was coming up fast. Nick pulled out around the Renault that stood between him and the taxi, and fell in behind for a moment. Now he could clearly see Alethea's face, white and strained, staring out the back window. Did she see him? Recognize him? No, her gaze was fixed further behind the gray Saab, probably trying to spot the Arabs. Why didn't she tell the driver to take her to a police station? He answered his own question; she was too terrified to think straight.

Her street was only a block away. Short of cutting the taxi off completely, he'd have to take the right turn behind it and pray for a spot to park the Saab before the Mercedes reached her.

There it was, an opening on the corner next to the stop sign— illegal, but what the hell—Nick pulled directly in and was out of the car before the taxi had fully stopped in front of number 20. He was already walking casually toward the cab when the Mercedes turned the corner with a squeal and braked between him and Alethea.

What a stinking mess! The Arab who had been driving was out of the sedan in a flash and a good ten yards closer to the girl than Nick was. Hell. Now things would really get sticky. There was no smooth way to handle this. Nothing in the manual . . .

Nick slowed his pace. Think, weigh, gauge the situation. He couldn't possibly reach her before the Arab—not a chance. And then the Arab was next to her as the taxi pulled away. Nick watched while the man took hold of her arm and pressed the bulge in his pocket into the girl's side. She sure as hell looked like she would faint, and Nick felt his body ready itself for action, every muscle tuned, every sense sharpened.

Forget about her terror, he told himself, clear your mind and make your move and make it good.

Nick leaned over as if to tie a shoe when the Arab led Alethea back toward the Mercedes, actually passing Nick as he did so. Quickly, Nick reached under his jacket and casually slipped the Beretta from the shoulder holster into the jacket's right hand pocket.

He straightened back up and walked single-mindedly toward

the Mercedes that now sat waiting with its back door open. If the Arab could kidnap the girl on a busy street, in broad daylight, then Nick sure as hell could retrieve her. It was absolutely amazing that people could walk straight past this whole mess and not even notice! But they did nevertheless. And the ones that might notice, Nick realized, didn't give a damn what went on around them so long as they weren't involved.

He was directly behind the Arab when he heard Alethea cry, "No! Never!"

In a split-second decision, Nick decided that the man wouldn't shoot her. Nick shoved the small, rock-hard barrel of his gun into the Arab's back and took firm hold of Alethea's coat in a literal tug-of-war for possession of the girl until the man realized what was happening.

In a second, Nick was pushing her behind him forcefully, saying, "Go into the building, quickly. Don't look back, Alethea. Hurry!"

"Mustafa!" Nick heard Akmet's panicked voice from the rear seat and automatically pressed the gun even harder into Mustafa's back.

Keeping the man between him and the car and directing his voice at Akmet, Nick said in a deadly cold tone, "I'll put a hole in Mustafa's back if he even moves, Akmet. And then I'll put one between your eyes."

Akmet was silent. Nick could feel the man's hatred emanating from the car but knew that there was no way either the minister or driver could get a shot off without Nick seeing a movement first.

Instructing Mustafa not to move a muscle, Nick took several backward steps and then turned slightly and made his way steadily toward the apartment entrance, his hand on the pistol, his eyes never leaving the Mercedes.

There was no doubt in Nick's mind that the three men would love to put a hole in him if given half the chance. However, Nick had the advantage, and within a minute he had his hand on the doorknob and had slipped quickly inside, away from their threat, his heart still beating furiously.

For several minutes, he stood quietly at the door, breathing deeply, waiting to see if they would dare to follow. He thought not. They would wait out on the street, knowing Nick would have to come out sometime, yet it didn't hurt to be careful. It didn't hurt at all.

Nick's eyes were adjusting to the dimly lit hallway when he heard a muffled sob behind him. He'd almost forgotten about Alethea.

Automatically, he turned away from the entrance and looked at the narrow stairwell. He heard the sob again and went toward the steps. There she was, sitting like a curled-up ball on the top step, her face buried in her hands.

From the bottom step, he could see her tremble and then shudder in great, quavering sobs. His heart contracted strangely at the sight.

"Lord," he murmured under his breath, taking the steps two at a time until he stood above her. He reached a hand down to touch her shoulder.

"No!" she wailed, recoiling tightly against the wall.

"It's all right, Alethea," he reassured her. "I'm not going to hurt you." He knelt down alongside her and placed a gentle hand on her chin. Again she edged closer to the wall.

"Come on. Crying won't help . . ." Tenderly, he brought her face out of her hands. "Come on . . . Let's find your keys and get inside."

Still, she did not move, but faced the wall. Nick was at a loss for what to do. He didn't want to drag her up, but they couldn't sit on the steps all day.

"Come on," he urged again, this time putting his hands on her shoulders and half-dragging her up into a standing position. Alethea kept her eyes averted from his face, continuing to sob piteously. She was acting as if he, too, were the enemy.

Then he led her toward what he guessed to be her apartment door. "I'll need your key, Alethea." He rested her shaking body against the wall and this time forced her face up to meet his with his hands. "Your key." His tone turned slightly demanding.

At last she seemed to acknowledge him, her eyes widening suddenly through the tears. He heard her sharp intake of breath.

"Nick?" she whispered.

As if she'd seen a ghost, Alethea threw her hand over her mouth and stumbled backward. Nick had to force himself to imagine this whole scene from her point of view. She had every right to be looking at him as if he'd been resurrected from the dead.

So what was he supposed to do now? Slap her in the face, like they did in the movies, until she regained control?

"We have to talk," he found himself saying, "but don't you think we should go in?"

With eyes the size of saucers, Alethea mumbled, "Yes . . . Inside."

"The key," Nick reminded her again.

"Yes . . . the key."

He watched in silence as her hand went shakily to her jeans pocket.

Finally, she pulled out her key and turned to put it in the lock. Abruptly, she laughed. "I don't think I can do it." She giggled oddly.

He took it from her hand, thinking that she must be in a state of shock or very near to it. He wondered, as he opened her door, if she had any tranquilizers.

Nick led her inside, locked the door carefully behind them and went directly to the window to check on the Arabs. They were still there all right. So much for that. They could rot there for all he cared. Not only could Nick hole up in the apartment for days, but if worst came to worst, he could always telephone Porter and have some reliable help stationed in Paris come over and take care of the Arabs. Yet, at this point, he preferred to go it alone. He'd look pretty ridiculous if he had to call for help and still didn't have the papers . . . There was also something else, a reluctance to call in other men to deal with Alethea's case. This was *his* job, and the girl was *his* responsibility. An odd feeling, but he was unable to erase it from his mind.

He turned back to the girl. "Have you got something to calm your nerves—pills or anything?"

"I've never needed them." She laughed again. "Isn't that funny?"

"A riot," he commented dryly. "Look kid, I think you better lie down."

She emitted a small sound somewhere between a sob and a chuckle. She was hysterical, he thought suddenly. Boy, was she a mess. "Look, Alethea, hadn't you better rest for a while?"

As she made no move toward the sofa, he decided to steer her there as gingerly as possible. But when he approached, she backed away, her head tilted to one side, confusion playing in her hazel eyes. "How did you get here so fast?"

He didn't bother to answer; she wouldn't understand right now anyway.

Alethea moaned and, thankfully, finally sat down on the edge of the couch, putting her face in her hands and beginning to cry again, but this time he sensed it was more from frustration than fear.

Watching her, the way the fragile shoulders heaved and shook, Nick felt lost. What the hell could he do to comfort her? Let's see—page 73 of the survival handbook: "How to Render a Subject Unconscious Without Leaving a Mark." No, that sure wouldn't do. What about: "How to Stop Arterial Bleeding from a Deep Wound?" No.

He took a couple of slow, uncertain steps toward her and tried to place his hand on her shoulder.

Suddenly, her head snapped up. "Get away from me! Get away!" she shrieked. "Don't come near me!"

"I'm not leaving here, Alethea, that's for sure. Now cry it out, do whatever you have to," he said helplessly, "and as soon as you're ready to listen, we can talk this over."

In answer, she eyed him icily, but at least she wasn't shrieking anymore. God, he wished she'd calm down, go to sleep, anything but this infernal weeping.

Nick went over to the stove, exasperated, and lit the burner under the leftover coffee. While he waited for it to heat, he again checked out the street below. The Arabs were still there and he could almost imagine how furious Akmet must be. A tight smile gathered at the corners of Nick's mouth. What a bungling idiot Akmet's man was. A true-blue dolt. Briefly, Nick wondered for the hundredth time if the hysterical girl had tried to make a deal with Akmet, and then, perhaps, changed her mind and tried to back out of the deal. Yeah, Nick would answer her questions, and she'd have plenty, as soon as she quit crying . . . but he had a few for her, too. The big question, however, was if he could believe her answers. Precisely how good a liar Alethea Holmes was remained to be seen.

Sitting down at the small kitchen table, his legs stretched out comfortably in front of him, Nick rested his eyes on the softly weeping form while he waited patiently for her to come around. He couldn't help comparing her present state of misery and fear with the woman he remembered from Athens, the one who had loosened her hair, kicked off her shoes and done the *hazapiko* with him in Philo's place. Or the woman whose lips had parted so willingly beneath his in Athens and again in New York. Where was *that* Alethea now? How many different sides to her remained hidden, closely guarded from the world?

Nick let his gaze travel over her, the bent head with the soft curtain of honey-brown hair falling over her crossed arms, the long, shapely legs curled beneath her. Things between them should have been different, he mused pensively. He should be holding her, comforting her . . . proving to her that she was far from the cold woman she had described in her diary. *Very* far indeed.

If only she'd gone along with him in the first place, none of this would have happened; she'd be perfectly safe. He'd have to tell her about Suliman and the tails in Leysin, although by now she must have figured that out for herself.

Poor kid. And why did he keep thinking of her as a poor kid?

He looked at Alethea again, huddled protectively on the old couch. Just how long could a woman cry, anyway?

Chapter 21

Wednesday, December 14

Nick remained in the kitchen, sipping a cup of coffee, waiting with seemingly inexhaustible patience, as if he had nothing better to do than to sit there—forever, if necessary.

Alethea could not help the small, hiccuping sobs of frustration that kept tearing at her chest. Her mind was filled with a vast, unending turmoil. The questions piled themselves one upon the other, opening new vistas of confusion, new questions, like the box within the box within the box.

He rose, walking—no, padding, as if he were stalking something—to the window, pulled back the lace curtain with a steady hand and glanced down at the street. There was no outward reaction from him, but she knew, as if he had told her, that the black Mercedes was still there, watching, waiting.

What kind of man was Nick?

Aside from the obvious fact that he had been the perfect gentleman in Athens and the bastard whom Lisa had enjoyed so thoroughly at her party . . . But that was no answer. Alethea's brain whirled with bewilderment over his many facets. Was there a real Nick DeWolff behind that cryptic, unreadable façade?

As the minutes passed, she felt her anger lessening. The apartment was gray-shadowed, dusky with the fall of the raw winter's night over the city. At least the familiar walls seemed to give her a kind of security, and Nick didn't seem to be dangerous to her; at least he didn't present the same threat as the horrible men below.

Unbidden, the feel of his hand on her arm returned to Alethea. She had been in a state of shock, her senses frozen, her mind numb with terror. Then his hand had come out of nowhere, his familiar voice urged her to get into the building. Somehow he had freed her from the Arab's grasp, pushed her behind him to safety. Unconsciously, her hand went to the place on her arm where he had grasped her, as if she would still feel the imprints of his fingers there.

How had he found her so quickly?

And a thousand more questions filled her head, too, overshadowing even the terror she had felt. Suliman—everything he had told her was a lie. She was surrounded, smothered by layers of lies that choked her, and no matter how many layers she pulled away, there were more sticky strata, lies parading as truth, and more again under those. The instincts she had always depended on no longer worked. They were fouled by a suffocating miasma of falsehood.

There was, at least, one thing she did know—that this man who called himself Nick had saved her from Suliman's clutches. A tremor shook Alethea again, the goose bumps rising on her back and arms. And then the futile anger returned, too.

She watched as Nick switched on the light, chasing the encroaching shadows back into the corners of the room. It registered in her mind that Nick always moved with a lithe grace, that his eyelashes were much too long for a man, that his wide mouth could be grim-looking and his face was not exactly handsome, but strongly defined, a mask of pure, unselfconscious masculinity.

Alethea wanted to ask him so many things and tried to choose the most important. Instead, she heard herself saying something entirely inane: "What would *Lisa* say if she knew you were here?"

He seemed startled by her voice, but coolly ignored her question, turning to face her as she sat up on the couch, making a vague, unconscious effort to straighten her hair.

"Are you feeling better now?" he asked.

"A little," she said, half-sullenly, grudgingly. She stood, feeling drained and giddy, and walked unsteadily to the kitchen sink, where she splashed some cold water on her hot, swollen eyes. She could sense his gaze on her, watching every move she made, causing her to feel clumsy, awkward.

Finally, Alethea turned, leaning back against the sink, trying desperately to appear calm. "I think you have some explaining to do."

He indicated the other chair at the table. "Sit down."

Instantly, Alethea felt the urge to do anything but sit down, to childishly rebel against his authority, but she forced herself to do as he said.

She found herself meeting his cool, detached gaze, remembering so well those blue eyes that seemed to hold secrets, dangerous knowledge.

"To begin with, Alethea, you were nuts to run away from me in Switzerland."

She folded her hands in her lap, twisting her fingers nervously, refusing to speak to him. If only there were some way she could get rid of him! But no. He stuck with her like glue. Obviously, he had been dogging her ever since New York. So he must know about her meetings with Suliman. What a fool Nick must think her! Her eyes flicked up to his, wide now. She had to know. "Were you in Paris before I went to Leysin?"

"Yes."

So he did know about her and Suliman . . . She digested the knowledge, then an overwhelming rage filled her, blotting out all else. "You bastard," she said, quietly, coldly. "You followed me everywhere. In Paris, in Leysin. Oh, that must have been a choice assignment!" She could hear the sarcasm fill her voice. "You dirty . . . You used me. You made love to my friend! How dare you—"

Nick came smoothly, fluidly, to his feet, hovering over the table, his blue eyes flinty now as he spoke. "Made *love* to your friend? Don't be so naive! Hell. Think what you like . . . Sure, I made love to her, why not?" He seemed to catch himself, perhaps regretting his sudden loss of control, and ran a hand through his dark hair as he eased back into the chair. "Look, Alethea, call it whatever you want. It's all in a day's work for me." His words fell like ice chips on her.

"Yes, and lying comes so naturally to you," she spat.

"I haven't lied to you."

"Oh, no? How about in Athens? You lied about your job and, I'm sure, about what you were doing there in the first place. Vacationing, I believe you said," Alethea finished smugly, her eyes holding his in challenge.

Silently, he studied her for a long moment. He sat forward in the chair, his hands clasped tightly between his knees. "Look, there was a reason I lied about my work."

"Oh? I suppose it's so top secret you can't tell anyone."

"No, not necessarily. That's my choice, depending on the situation. You see," Nick tried to explain, "I've had nothing but bad luck when I've come right out and told someone," he paused, "someone I wanted to see again, about my job."

"That makes no sense whatsoever." Again she defied him to explain away his lies.

"All right," Nick said in a firm tone, "suppose I had told you? You know what your first question would have been?" He gave her no opportunity to reply. "You would have asked me if I had ever killed anyone." He waited for her to digest this new information. "And then I could have said no, or I could have told you yes, and if I had admitted it, you would have begun to be afraid of me. It would have been the beginning of the end."

"You're so sure."

"Yes. It's happened. All you females love the idea of a James Bond, but when it comes down to reality, the idea of my job scares women, yes, even repulses them sometimes."

"Well, I may not be a feminist, but I'm also not your average giddy female, Nick. You don't know what goes on inside my mind. To me, there is no such thing as justifiable lying. I won't accept it."

His eyes held hers. "Then I made a mistake lying to you, didn't I?"

"Yes. And I won't forgive or trust you, ever."

"Alethea . . ."

"No, don't. And the fact remains you followed me around as if I were guilty of something. You cheated me out of my rights as a citizen, as a human being."

"Oh? And I suppose tricking me in New York and then that little stunt you and Clair pulled was aboveboard?"

Alethea ignored his bitter sarcasm. "How did you get Clair to tell you about Paris? You better not have hurt her!"

Nick flew to his feet, took a threatening step toward her. He seemed to change his mind, however, and spun away abruptly, going to the window with his back to her. He laughed bitterly. "I put your friend on the rack. Tortured her." And then, after a strained silence, "She's all right, Alethea. She didn't betray you on purpose. You're just both children playing adult games. You're rank amateurs."

"So, I'm learning," she said belligerently.

He turned around then, slowly, calculatingly. "The fact remains, Alethea, in case you've forgotten, that it's a good thing I did follow you back to Paris, in spite of your efforts to the contrary. Your friend Mr. Akmet had some lovely plans for you, I'm sure."

She was stubbornly silent, refusing to give ground.

"What do you think they planned for you? A picnic under the Eiffel Tower?"

"Are you trying to tell me Suliman was going to harm me?" Alethea asked tightly.

"Maybe not right away . . ."

"You're wrong. Suliman has been very kind to me. There must be a misunderstanding." She knew that was a lie . . . but was it for her benefit or Nick's?

"Then why were you running like a scared rabbit?"

She compressed her lips and said nothing.

His voice continued; his blue eyes softened a little. "I'm going to ask you something, Alethea. And I want a straight answer. It'll make it easier for everyone concerned."

She watched him intently, warily.

"Were you dealing with Akmet?"

"What?"

"Selling him your father's papers?" Nick was watching her closely, obviously trying to gauge her reaction.

"Good Lord, no! Are you joking? That filthy bastard *killed* my father!" Her true feelings were out; she could no longer hide them from Nick. Hot tears of grief and rage filled Alethea's eyes, and she rose to her feet, pacing the floor. "I can't . . . can't believe you'd even think that! That I would *sell* Akmet—anyone—my father's most significant achievement."

"You've got to admit that your meetings with him looked pretty fishy."

"Oh, go to hell," she hissed furiously, putting her face in her hands, frustrated and confused, embarrassed that Nick knew how Suliman had used her.

"All right. Maybe I believe you."

"I don't care *what* you—"

"Okay, okay, I believe you."

Was he only trying to pacify her?

"Let me put it this way. Do you have your father's papers with you now? I'd like a straight answer for a change."

Alethea whirled around to face him. They stood so close, she could smell the faint odor of his maleness. She glared at him, feeling flushed, suddenly filled with raw fury.

"No! I have nothing, *nothing!* I told you that already! You're no better than Akmet! You and your boss and Akmet, and anyone else who's nosing around, can just go fly a kite! Do you hear me, Mr. DeWolff? Get out of my life, all of you!" She spun away from him and threw herself onto the couch, beating her fist into the overstuffed pillow. "I don't have anything! Leave me alone!"

"Look, Alethea . . ." She glared at him, her eyes hot and swollen-feeling with anger. He seemed to take a step toward her and changed his mind. "You might try to see it from our point of view. You ran in New York. You looked guilty as hell."

"I was scared. And then I realized you weren't the same man I thought you were—you were some kind of a spy. I was so confused. I had to get away, to think. I needed some time . . ."

"But you had your father's papers in New York."

She thought quickly, desperately, then gave a little laugh that sounded false even to her. "Oh, those. I told you in Leysin. Well, I was so upset . . . I thought they were important but then I read them again on the plane. And—oh, I'm so embarrassed—you'll think I'm silly. They were only some old papers, nothing at all. I already told you that."

"Where are they then?" His voice was mild, slightly patronizing, as if he were talking to a child.

"I threw them out, days and days ago. I told you—"

"Before Leysin?"

"Why . . . why, yes." He was trying to trap her! What had she told him before?

"So why," Nick approached her slowly, his hands on his hips, "might I ask, did you run away again, if, as you say, the papers were nothing?"

"I . . . I was scared. How did I know you wouldn't hurt me or, well, drag my friends into this whole crazy thing!" There, she thought, that sounded reasonable.

"I see. And you're sure they were unimportant?"

"Oh, yes," Alethea said eagerly, looking at him in what she hoped was an innocent manner.

He bent his head to one side; the slight smile on his wide mouth did not quite touch his eyes. "Did you know the men in New York searched your apartment after you left? And that they've been hot on your heels ever since?"

She felt a burst of anger, threw her head up to face him. "So what? I've told you a dozen times—the papers meant nothing. I threw them out."

He shrugged his broad shoulders. "The Arabs don't seem to think so. They thought you had them before and must still think so."

"Well, they won't find anything, will they?" She could hear her voice, sullen and defiant again.

"Nope, I guess not." There was the tiniest hint of humor in his voice this time.

"I suppose you went back to my apartment looking for me, too." Alethea felt bitter at the sudden realization; then, just as quickly, mortified that Nick might have gone through her personal things. And, oh, Lord! Her diary! She always left it lying around—out in the open!

"Yes, I had to. Remember, *you* asked for help, then disappeared. Going back to New York to find you was part of the job."

"Yes," she spat, "your *job!*"

"Well, a man has to earn a living."

"All of you make me sick!"

"I can understand that. But think, there are things at stake here, possibly big things."

"The only big thing at stake for me is the fact that my father is dead—most likely murdered by that filthy, stinking—Oh, God! What am I going to do?" Alethea's control began to slip, the terror, the frustration swamping her again, pulling her under.

She put her face in her hands, her fingers trembling, hating for him to see her this way. Suddenly, she felt his hand on her shoulder, firm and warm. All of her instincts told her to grasp it, to hold onto it as if it were a life preserver. Instead, Alethea recoiled from his touch, pressing herself into the cushions, hugging her arms around her body as if to protect herself. She didn't need Nick's false pity or his comfort!

His voice was very low and gentle. "I'm sorry about your father. If he was murdered, we'll find out, It's out of your hands for the present. Let me handle things from here on. It's my job."

Oh, to let someone else take over, take the burden of responsibility from her. But she couldn't. He represented the government. He'd hand the papers over to his boss, the man he called Porter. And her father had written, expressly, that no one country should have his discovery. She would have to make sure he hadn't died in vain . . .

For the time being, she needed Nick. There was Akmet outside, waiting. She couldn't get away, she knew that now. She'd tried, twice, and it was laughable. They'd all followed her as if she'd laid a trail in fluorescent paint.

She slumped on the couch, surrendering for the moment. She was too tired, too upset even to think. Alethea rested her head on the back of the couch and closed her eyes. Nick was opening cupboards, getting out pots and pans as if he owned the place, owned her.

"You haven't got much to eat, do you?" he asked.

"I didn't have a chance to go shopping today," she replied caustically.

His movements stopped, and her breath caught in her throat as she heard him come toward her. She refused to turn her head. The beating of her heart was so loud in her ears that surely he must hear it. How far could she push this man and get away with it?

Nick sat down next to her on the couch, causing the old springs to sag under him. Finally, she braved a glance at him. He was looking at her, steadily and with quizzical interest. "Look, Alethea, let's try to get along. We're stuck with each other for a while—until we're back home. It's my job to protect you and get you back to the States alive and well. Don't make it any harder for me than it is. I'm only trying to help." He sounded sincere.

Abruptly, she felt ashamed of her childish reactions. I'm sorry," she muttered under her breath. "This isn't easy for me."

"Okay. I understand. Now, I'm going to get us something to eat. Afraid I'm not much of a cook. Hey, don't review me in your magazine!" He gave a short laugh.

Was he trying to make her feel better so he could spring another question at her? She'd have to watch him. He was better at this than she.

Nick was the perfect gentleman while he puttered around the tiny kitchen, asking her nothing more, making casual conversation, forcing her to eat something of the light, canned supper. He even made her drink a glass of wine from a half-empty bottle he found in a closet. And it did help, relaxing her instantly when it reached her head. She saw him briefly again as the man in Athens, charming, witty, warm company. It was so hard to keep her eyes open, to concentrate on what he was saying as he washed the few dishes.

It suddenly struck Alethea, clearing her brain as if a cold bucket of water had been thrown on her, that she would have to spend the night here. Unconsciously, she looked at Nick from under the veil of her lashes. It was all in a day's work, he had said. Vivid images of him and Lisa flashed into her mind: naked bodies, squirming limbs. But Alethea blanked it out deliberately. Did he expect her to . . . ?

She watched closely while he dried his hands and then walked toward the bedroom, as if he were deciding where to sleep. Some of her alarm must have communicated itself to him.

"Don't worry, Alethea. I'm not the mad rapist. I'll sleep on the couch. Just tell me where there's a spare blanket." A lopsided grin tugged at the corner of Nick's wide, sensual mouth. "I'd love to get the bag out of my car, but our friends out there," he gestured with his head, "wouldn't like it at all. Well, it's warmer in here at least." There was real humor in his expression, lighting up his deep-set eyes, relaxing the grim lines of his face. He didn't *look* like the type that would molest a girl, but she didn't know anymore—nothing was what it seemed to be.

And then she felt embarrassed that he had read her thoughts so easily, yet strangely a bit put out that he would dismiss her so lightly. He had certainly not dismissed Lisa like that! Alethea remembered them together on the couch in the chalet, his calm air of masculine fulfillment, Lisa's glowing face . . . Oh, God, what a miserable situation. She hated him for that.

Alethea went into the bedroom and changed into her nightgown, noticing how he carefully kept his back turned toward the half-open door until she was done.

"Are you decent?"

"Yes."

And then he stood in the bedroom doorway, filling it with his casual presence. She was instantly aware of his eyes traveling nonchalantly over her attire, and wasn't at all sure if he approved or disapproved. Her gown was a genuine antique, which she had purchased for a small fortune in a quaint shop on rue de Vaugirard. It was a sheer white muslin, perhaps too transparent due to its age, and trimmed at the neck and cuffs with fine Belgian lace. The gown clung to her breasts, leaving little to the imagination. The sheerness of the material displayed far too much of her body; even the triangle between her legs was partly visible through the clinging white fabric.

Alethea blushed and thought to herself that she might as well be wearing a number from Fredericks of Hollywood; the way Nick was eyeing her.

For endless moments, the room seemed filled with a pregnant silence. Finally, he cleared his throat, his eyes shifted away from her. "About Leysin," he began quietly, "Lisa and I—"

"I don't want to hear about you and Lisa. That's your affair!" Alethea interrupted harshly, feeling that she ought to cover herself somehow under his close regard.

As Nick drew his stare away, she could see a tiny muscle working in his jaw. He looked very angry.

"All right," he said sharply. "I won't mention it again." He turned, leaving the bedroom, and pulled the door partially closed.

She let her breath out and curled up on the familiar old bed, hearing, as if for the first time, the cranky squeak of the springs. She'd never be able to sleep. Not with Nick in the next room, moving around with his damnable sure-footed grace in the tiny apartment. She'd never be able to sleep, Alethea thought again as she closed her eyes, wishing for welcome oblivion.

Long after Nick had turned out the light and settled himself on the couch, Alethea tossed and turned, her mind racing, her heart pounding, much too aware of him lying so close to her in the next room, much too aware, also, of Suliman's black car waiting patiently outside in the dark jungle of the Parisian night.

Chapter 22

Thursday, December 15

For half the night, Nick had lain awake weighing Alethea's statement that she had reread the papers, found them to be unimportant and then destroyed them. No way! It had been fast thinking on her part, but a lousy story. He wasn't buying, not today.

Through the thin wall, he had listened to the soft rustle of her stirring, then the quietness of sleep. How in the hell could she sleep? Didn't she know what was in store for her—what Porter would do to get his hands on the discovery?

The light in the room turned a shade brighter, battleship-gray. It was six-thirty. Nick swung his legs over the side of the couch and stretched. He then went to peek in on her. Fast asleep . . . like a child with the blanket tucked up under her chin and her hair spread in soft tangles around her peaceful face. Well, he would soon wipe that serene look off her lips. He had decided to tell her, in black and white, exactly, down to the last gruesome detail, what was going to be done to her in Washington. Yes—he'd see how well she could take a few unpleasant facts thrown in her face.

He pulled her door closed and went to make coffee, only checking on the Mercedes afterward, knowing instinctively it was still there. Then he sat down and waited for her to wake up.

Around eight, he finally heard the squeaky springs of her bed come to life.

Peeking around the corner of the door, still in her nightgown, she saw him. "Oh . . . you're up already." Ridiculously self-conscious, Alethea hid behind the door. "I'll get dressed."

"Fine," Nick commented. What did she think he was going to do, tear her nightgown off? For Pete's sake . . .

A few minutes later, she appeared clad in jeans and a dusty-rose silk blouse, but definitely no bra, he found himself observing. The sheer silk clung to her nipples and outlined the soft curve of her breasts as she moved across the room. Her jeans were skintight in all the right places: narrow waist, firm, shapely thighs and that tight, well-rounded rear.

Damn! He was wasting time ogling her feminine charms when there were decisions to be made, actions to be taken. If only she weren't quite so appealing. It made things far more difficult, made it hard for him to concentrate at times. Well, he would simply have to forget she was female—all female. Somehow he felt Alethea was using her wiles against him unfairly, even though she hadn't really done anything to credit the thought. Still, being locked up in the apartment with this woman, and the fact that she stubbornly refused to give in, angered him. Whether he was angry at her or at himself, Nick didn't choose to examine.

"Mind if I use the bathroom? It's down the hall," she said half-sarcastically.

"Sure." Nick rose and walked down the hall, where he waited for her by the door. He'd make damn good and sure she didn't try running away.

Fifteen minutes went by before the bathroom door opened and she appeared with a towel wrapped around her head.

Walking casually past him back into the apartment, Alethea said flippantly, "Sorry, but I wash it every morning."

The faint odor of her shampoo hung in the air as she went to pour herself a cup of coffee. Wash her hair, indeed, Nick thought angrily.

While Alethea seated herself at the table, rubbing her head with the white towel, Nick rested a shoulder against the locked door, his arms folded, watching her.

It was time. "We've gotta have a little talk, Alethea. You feel up to it?" He forced himself to sound dispassionate. Might as well act as cold as possible—that way she might get the message.

"I guess so," she replied, eying him carefully.

He unfolded his arms and walked purposefully to the table. "Yesterday I tried to explain some simple facts of life to you. I can only assume you were too upset to listen. You realize we've got to get a plane soon for the States . . ."

"Why?" The towel dropped out of her hands onto the table. "I already told you—"

"Dammit, woman!" Nick pounded a strong fist on the smooth wood. The coffee in her cup sloshed onto the saucer. "You didn't really think I believed that cock-and-bull story about the papers, did you?"

"You don't have to holler at me. And . . . and it's not a cock-and—"

"Quit lying. You're wasting your breath while I'm trying to be honest with you. We can't hole up here forever. I'll have to call for help soon."

Alethea rose, turning her back to him. She went to the couch and pulled her hairbrush out of her purse and, deliberately averting her eyes from his, returned to the kitchen and began to brush out the wet tangles.

"We're far from done with our little discussion," he said slowly.

Her eyes flashed defiantly. All right, thought Nick coldly, let her have both barrels, but take it slowly.

He sat opposite her, clasping his hands in front of him, gaining her full attention. "You're going to listen now . . . and don't interrupt. Think about it." He ignored the small smirk that crossed her lips. "Somewhere down the line, you've decided you're smarter than the rest of us. No matter how obvious your dangerous position becomes, you insist on turning your back on any help. Help, I should add, from a friend."

"Friend?" Alethea quirked a thin brow at him and compressed her lips.

"Quiet," Nick reminded her. "I'm doing my damnedest to be nice to you and it's getting pretty hard. Fact is, I don't like being lied to. I'm trying to help you before my boss, Porter, gets his hands on you. Are you following me?"

"Sure." She shifted her weight and looked off-handedly down at her nails.

"Okay. Now Porter isn't quite the good guy I am. He'll go to great lengths to get what he wants—I'm talking about the papers, kid. He'll force you to talk. Those notes would be a nice feather for his cap. I'm trying to put this as gently as I can, but you're just plain stupid if you don't think you're in for a rough ride. Wise up, kid."

"That's enough!" Alethea jumped to her feet, grabbed her coffee cup and smashed it in the sink.

Nick ignored the temper tantrum, the flying chips of porcelain, and went to stand behind her. "Oh, my little innocent, we're not done yet," he said, almost in a whisper, placing his hands on her shoulders and forcing her around to face him.

"I don't want to hear!" she yelled. "I won't listen!"

"You *will* listen." He held her more firmly, knowing he was hurting her. "I'm going to be forced to call for help soon and take you back. Porter will use any method he can on you, believe me . . . and it won't be very pleasant. Ever been shot up with truth drugs? They've got all kinds now, and when you finally come to—".

"Stop it!" Alethea cried, obviously on the verge of tears.

Her face was as pallid as a daytime moon; it seemed all eyes. But he couldn't stop now, when she was so close to breaking. Nick purposely made his voice turn soft, reassuring, and loosened his grip on her arm. "Come on, Alethea. Tell me where the papers are. Save yourself that trip to Washington."

"No! I destroyed them!"

Hell. Why couldn't she get it through her thick head? "Tell me where they are. Please, no games."

"You hurt me," she cried. "Why didn't you just break my arms, you . . . you bastard!"

"I'm tempted," he lied. And then, "Stop crying, for chrissakes!"

"Let me go!"

"Not until you level with me."

"Not a chance," she spat.

"Oh, hell," Nick cursed softly, strangely finding himself wanting to pull her against his chest, to stroke the back of her damp hair, but he couldn't let himself, not now.

"Alethea," he slowly brought her face up to his, "for your own sake . . ."

"I can't, I just can't . . . Do what you have to."

Short of really hurting her, Nick knew he was getting nowhere, and beating up women wasn't exactly his style.

He searched her face thoughtfully. A muscle ticked in his jaw. "I'm not going to harm you. Take it easy."

He gave Alethea an uncertain pat on her back and led her over to the couch where she sank down onto the cushions, apparently quelled. But Nick knew this one was far from broken. For that, he had to give her credit.

Suddenly, he said, "Hey, I'm starved. How 'bout you?"

Her head snapped up. "How could you think about food at a time like this?"

"Easy," replied Nick with a warm, flashing smile. "One's got to keep up strength for the next round."

"Oh . . ."

"Do you suppose the *concièrge* would move my car before it gets towed and then fetch us something to eat?"

"I suppose so," she said sullenly, "but you'll have to give her a tip."

"Well, then, I'll be right back." He went to the door. "And please, don't try leaving . . . Your Arab pals are still outside."

"I won't," she mumbled.

The *concièrge* was quite helpful—for money, of course—and efficiently moved the Saab several spots down rue Monsieur-le-Prince, then went to the *charcuterie* to buy food. All the while, Nick ignored Alethea and watched from the window. Perhaps it was just as well they didn't talk, as it seemed as if one or the other's temper flared far too often in the close confines of the tiny apartment.

Silently, they ate the delicious pâté and camembert spread thickly on fresh bread while Nick studied her pensively. Quite a girl, he decided, finding himself unable to tear his eyes from her subdued face, from her small, thin hands that were playing with the food.

"You should eat, you know."

For a long moment, Alethea said nothing. When she finally spoke, the words fell out bitterly, cutting Nick in the face like chips of ice. "Why eat? From what you tell me, I don't have much of a future."

"Hey," he retorted, feeling her blow deeply. "Don't try to put it on me. I'm just being level with you."

"Oh, yes. How could I forget so soon? You're doing your job. I guess I can't expect any help or sympathy from you."

"Do you really think I want it this way? To see you drugged, interrogated . . . Lord knows what else?" His appetite gone abruptly, Nick pushed the meal away. "Listen, if you'd just hand over the information, tell me where it is, we could go our separate ways. No harm done."

Alethea leaned across the table. She looked desperate, frightened. "Help me, Nick. Help me get away . . . please."

He couldn't have felt worse at the moment. Dammitall, anyway. He said nothing.

"Please, Nick. I'm begging . . ."

"Stop it. I *can't* help you, that's what I'm trying to tell you."

"If you wanted to, you could. You know it."

He saw her eyes fill with unshed tears.

"Don't start crying again. I already—" He shut his mouth quickly, unable to admit his sympathy for her.

"Help me."

"No!" Nick jumped to his feet in a sudden, fluid motion. He shoved the chair back so violently that it toppled over. "Don't bother begging, Alethea. I can't help you."

"Not can't, Nick . . . You *won't!*"

For hours, neither spoke a word, nor looked the other in the eye.

It was late afternoon. Nick sat by the window staring mutely out over the Paris street, not really seeing the slanted silver winter light hitting the brick buildings. He had opened the window; the cold, damp breeze ruffled his dark hair slightly.

"Would you like some coffee?"

Nick turned around and saw Alethea standing in the middle of the dimly lit room. "What?"

"Coffee. Would you like me to make a pot?"

"Yes. That'd be fine."

So she had broken the strained silence at last. He sure hoped she wasn't planning on starting up the argument again. Still, he was depressed by her begging earlier. He wasn't used to that sort of behavior. Before this girl, he'd dealt only with men, and never had one asked a thing of him. Oh, maybe they'd asked for a cigarette, a drink, things like that. But never to let them go—they had known he wouldn't anyway. Earlier it had flown through Nick's mind that she was absolutely right—he could, if he wanted to, help her. But he had quickly pushed the thought out of his consciousness. It wouldn't do to weaken over a pretty female simply because this was a difficult situation.

Alethea poured two cups of coffee. She smiled shyly at Nick. "Look, I'm really sorry about earlier." Momentarily, the smile left her lips, then returned as if she were gathering her courage. "It was wrong of me to beg you."

"Don't . . ." Nick could hardly believe the effect her apology was having on him. He felt like a complete ass, a cheap bully picking on a defenseless girl. Steel yourself, man, he thought quickly. Don't let her get too close, so damn near . . .

"You're still mad at me, aren't you?" With trembling hands, she passed him the coffee cup.

"No, I'm not. Let's drop it. Okay?"

"All right."

Why was she so poignant to him? Her words, her manner struck a chord . . . Maybe he was a little too partial to Alethea. Yet he'd still take her back to Porter. He couldn't drag his feet much longer, a day, two maybe. That was all.

Then an idea struck Nick. He'd considered it before, most definitely, but not exactly with this purpose. It might just have the proper effect. He should seduce her—not only would it be pleasant, but women often opened up their hearts after a bedroom encounter. Would Alethea? Could he get her to trust him, to talk to him?

He glanced over at her. Damn desirable woman. Nick smiled at her then, hoping that his intentions did not play in his eyes. If Athens was any example, it wouldn't take long to get close to her.

But there was something nagging at him, in the back of his mind, something he felt he should bring to the surface. Oh, yes, recalled Nick in a moment of clarity, it was something she'd written about in her diary—what had she said? It was about her sex life, about not being able to find fulfillment. So, he thought, Alethea has not yet reached that point of womanhood where she could let go of herself fully, dig her nails in.

He should, Nick thought briefly, feel guilt for knowing such a private thing about her. But he didn't. Instead, Nick told himself it gave him an edge. He would play it that way in bed, restrain himself so that she could have every chance of enjoyment.

Cool, calculating. He really was quite a bastard, Nick admitted. Yet somehow the self-knowledge didn't bother him. Not at all.

On the contrary, he rather looked forward to the moment, to feeling that soft, translucent skin touching his, to hear her cry aloud perhaps . . .

How would he begin? With the silk-covered buttons on her blouse, of course. One by one, he'd undo them until her firm white breasts were bared to his eyes. He would take it slowly, naturally, until she was ready to accept his caresses. Alethea was like an untamed filly—wild but needing a tender hand, a gentle word, a calculated coaxing until she was ready to be mounted. He would first kiss a rosy nipple until it stood erect and waiting, and then the other, and all the while his hands would stroke her satin-smooth flesh. And then, when she was breathing shallowly and unafraid, he'd unfasten those snug jeans and ease them off. Would she be as soft down there as the fine brown hair on her head? Would she cry out his name as he hovered above her ready to possess her, ready to show her that she wasn't the least bit frigid?

Sipping on the steaming cup of coffee, forming his plan of seduction, Nick nearly laughed out loud. His new approach to covert activities was not in the manual, either—not even under Section 12, "Improvisation." They hadn't written the book yet.

"What's so funny?" asked Alethea.

"Nothing, really. I was just thinking."

"Tell me," she pried, obviously dying of curiosity.

"Not on your life." Thankfully, she couldn't read his mind, or surely the girl would haul off and slug him. And he wasn't really laughing at her, or at himself, only at the whole crazy idea that would bring them together. Still, Nick thought, funny or not, he was very much looking forward to it. He met her large, questioning hazel eyes with his—yes, very, very much.

Chapter 23

Friday, December 16

Alethea paced nervously back and forth in front of the tall window. She stopped once to pull the lace curtain back and look out. Yes, there it was, slightly farther down the block but black and stolid and silent like a horrible shiny toad. How she hated that car! It had been there for two days now, confining them in the small apartment.

What was Nick waiting for? Why didn't he just take her back and get it over with?

He was such a strange man; totally cold and professional on the one hand, but sometimes he broke into that boyish grin that sent a tingle right down to her toes. Enigmatic. That was the word to describe him.

After their initial argument, they had begun to talk again. But Nick avoided certain subjects like the plague. He refused to talk about his past much, only mentioning briefly that he'd been in Vietnam. And when he did, she'd seen a dark, hooded look come over his face. He'd changed the subject quickly.

What a bizarre situation. She'd been cooped up with this man for two days. But now she couldn't think of Nick as a stranger anymore. Alethea knew he kept a lot of secrets from her, and his past seemed a closed book, but after being forced to live with him as closely as they had in the tiny apartment, she felt, well, as though she knew him, a little at least.

Alethea understood instinctively that she could trust her life to Nick, but the papers—that was another matter. He sure hadn't bought her story about throwing them away. A man in his line of work wouldn't be worth two cents if he had, she supposed.

And now more than ever she had to get away from him, *and* from Suliman, and lose herself somewhere, someplace they couldn't follow this time. Change her name, wear a wig, whatever it took. Nick would take her back soon now. Suddenly, Alethea wondered why they hadn't left already. Nick must have a reason for waiting. He didn't seem the type to do anything without a very good reason. And he had a gun. No doubt they could walk straight to his car without trouble. Or he could call for help as he had mentioned. She felt he was getting edgy, impatient. And Alethea knew that the NSC would get the information out of her. She sure wasn't any Joan of Arc, and the Maid of Orleans had never had to contend with mind-altering drugs. The thought sent a dismal shiver down Alethea's spine. She had to get away!

Yet Nick was with her every second. He was uncanny. She couldn't even go to the bathroom down the hall without finding him casually leaning against the doorframe of the apartment, that lopsided grin on his face, waiting for her to return.

If she woke at night, his shadowed form was padding around the apartment, checking the door and windows. It seemed as though he never slept.

But he always looked fresh in the morning, clean-shaven, neatly dressed. Like a machine. She'd found no Achilles' heel, no trace of weakness.

Suddenly, Alethea couldn't bear the tension anymore. She stalked into the kitchen where he was reading the *Paris Soir* that the *concièrge* had given them.

"Nick."

He looked up at her quizzically, obviously catching the barely controlled hysteria in her voice. His blue eyes crinkled at the corners.

"Nick." She could think of nothing sensible to say.

"You already said that."

"Oh, damn you! How come you're always so cool . . . so damn controlled?"

He pushed the chair back from the table, searching her face carefully. "You got cabin fever?"

"Yes," she replied tightly. "If I don't get out of here, I'm going to go crazy. I'm not used to it. I can't stand it!" Alethea could hear her voice begin to grow louder, shriller. She caught herself, clamping her mouth shut, willing the hysteria down.

Nick put a hand on her arm. It felt strong, reassuring, warming her, sending small tingles of sensation along her skin. "Hey, take it easy. It won't be long now. I'm working on it."

"How long, Nick? I feel like I'm about to burst. I can't take much more of this. Can't we get out of here, just for a little while?" She was begging now. "Isn't there some way?"

"Let me think about it." He narrowed his eyes. "Now, I'm not promising anything."

"Please, Nick."

Alethea tried to keep herself busy then, tidying up the apartment, washing a few dishes that were left in the sink from breakfast, anything at all to forget that she was virtually a prisoner. She even dusted the few bookshelves and washed some underwear in the sink. If Nick didn't like female undergarments hanging around, too bad. He was the one keeping her here; he'd have to put up with it.

Finally, she went into her bedroom and propped herself up with pillows. When she decided to bury herself in *Les Misérables* as a last resort, she heard Nick push his chair back and stand up.

"Alethea."

"Well?" she called. "Do you have some brilliant plan to get us out of here?"

"As a matter of fact, yes." He was leaning against the door-frame, his arms folded.

"Well?"

"Now don't laugh."

"I'm not exactly in the mood to laugh, Nick."

"You might be when I explain what I have in mind."

She felt her heart begin to beat a little faster with near-excitement. "Explain away."

"Okay. We dress up like an old married couple, with the help of your *concièrge*, and walk out in the middle of the day."

"Come on, Nick." She was skeptical.

"It'll work." His blue eyes filled with boyish mischief. "Look, you can borrow a coat and put a pillow over your stomach."

"What?"

"Sure, they're not looking for a pregnant lady. And I'll rub some burned cork on so I'll have a mustache." He grinned at her. "The only hitch is if your *concièrge* and her husband will agree to help us out."

"Oh, they'll help," replied Alethea dryly, "if they're paid."

"Money is no object."

Alethea giggled suddenly. "How about a baby carriage? No self-respecting French couple goes out without a baby carriage. I noticed one on the ground floor."

"A baby carriage *and* a pregnant wife? I'm not sure I can handle it . . ."

"Sure you can, Nick. It's all in the line of duty," Alethea said sarcastically, noticing with satisfaction his sharp look at her words.

"Okay. Call the *concièrge* . . . *and* the lady with the carriage."

She did, settling on three hundred francs for two old coats and the *concièrge*'s cooperation. The carriage was thrown in free.

Laughing like carefree souls, they got ready: Nick rubbed on his mustache, donned a beret and the moth-eaten coat while Alethea belted a pillow around her stomach, pulling her sweater over the whole thing, tied a drab scarf on her head and put on the other black wool coat.

"God," she said, surprised, seeing herself in the mirror, "we really look like one of the couples I've seen on the street and made fun of since I was a kid. The French bourgeoisie." Then it occurred to her in a vivid flash of insight. She eyed Nick for a second. "Hey, if we can get out of here so easily, why can't we just hop in your car and drive away? Or get a cab to the airport?"

"Very simple." Nick imprisoned her suspicious glance with his own suddenly hard one. "I'm not taking you back to Porter without the papers."

"I told you—"

"Sorry, Alethea, guess we'll simply have to wait till they turn up then."

"But I don't—"

"Do you have any idea what some people will go through to get your father's research?" he interrupted harshly.

The happy smile was gone from her face; a stubborn expression narrowed her big golden-brown eyes and hardened her sensitive mouth. "There are no papers, Nick," she said softly, but with steel underlying the velvet, as if she could will him to believe her.

"Okay, sure. Forget it. Right now we're going out, that's all. That's what you wanted, right?"

"Yes."

He walked over to his tweed sport coat and pulled something out of the pocket, checked it, stuck it inside his ratty disguise. "All set."

Alethea didn't even need to ask what it was; she'd seen the dull gleam of metal.

"Now, remember, we're not the people they're watching for. Don't even breathe nervousness. And don't skulk. We belong here," he instructed.

They walked out of the building without a hitch. It felt dangerous—childish and excitingly dangerous with Nick at her side—strolling along the narrow street pushing the wickerwork carriage with the rolled-up towel in it that should have been a baby. Sedately carrying an empty string bag, she walked behind Nick on the narrow *trottoir* as he pushed the carriage. Alethea held her breath for so long she was beginning to see spots in front of her eyes. Is this what it was like being an undercover agent?

"*Ça va bien,*" Nick was saying quietly into her ear. "They're still watching the building."

She breathed an immense sigh of relief.

"You okay?" came his quiet voice again.

"Fine, lovely."

"Where to?"

"Let's just walk down to the Seine for now."

Alethea couldn't help smiling as she gave Nick a sidelong glance. His fake mustache gave him a silly, rakish look and the beret accentuated the image. He looked like a kid dressed up for Halloween. Then she remembered how she must look herself. She giggled.

"I could laugh, too, you know," he said out of the corner of his mouth, "but I'm afraid the mustache will smear."

"Oh, Nick, you look so funny!"

"Hey, this was all your idea, now act like a French housewife—a pregnant one."

But Alethea couldn't stop smiling as they crossed the Boulevard Saint-Germain and continued on down the old streets to the Seine. Maybe everyone would forgive a pregnant lady her ridiculous grin, she hoped.

When they reached the embankment above the river, the pavement widened and Nick told her to link her arm through his. It felt kind of nice, pretending to be a married lady with her husband—warm and comfortable. It was a foolish fantasy, but Alethea enjoyed it anyway.

It was a chilly day, damp and weakly lit, but she enjoyed the caressingly cool, fresh air after the stuffy apartment.

"Thanks, Nick," she finally acknowledged, "this is wonderful. No one following us? I'm terrified to turn around."

Nick stopped the carriage, bent over to tuck in the nonexistent baby in such a way as to look behind them. Alethea almost laughed out loud.

"Nope," he said, giving her a rakish wink.

They walked on and she drank in the sights and sounds of the Left Bank as if she'd never seen them before: the booksellers that lined the embankment with their tattered old volumes among which it might be possible to find a first edition of Zola or Dumas; the wonderful antique shops filled with dark oil paintings and gilded furniture; the tiny black doorways squeezed in between high walls housing, perhaps, a whole clan of Moroccan immigrants; the scruffy students on their way to classes at the Sorbonne or one of the art schools in the area; the delectable *patisseries* that had windows filled with beautifully arranged pastries; the *charcuteries* whose window displays were stuffed with cheeses, sausages, ducks, *pâtés*, salads and dusty bottles of wine. And the aromas: French cigarettes, damp cobblestones, strong coffee, freshly baked bread—that certain indefinable odor that was Paris.

Today Alethea loved it all with a passion.

They passed a café, a small one, with a few workingmen standing at the bar, several other customers at the few round-topped tables.

"Oh, could we stop and get some coffee and a sandwich? I'd give anything . . ." she asked wistfully as they walked past the entrance.

"Why not?" Nick responded lightly. "Let's find one where it's not so obvious leaving this silly thing." He meant the baby carriage.

So they continued along the river, then up a narrow, crooked ancient street to the Boulevard Saint-Michel. They left the carriage parked in the doorway of a building and walked into a bright café that was large enough to hide them in the crowd.

They sat inside and ordered *café au lait* and sandwiches: camembert and *pâté* on long, golden-crusted *baguettes*.

"I must have died and gone to heaven," Alethea remarked, sighing as she licked the last crumb off her plate with her finger.

"It sure doesn't take much to keep you happy, does it?" Nick observed lazily.

She shot him a quick glance from under her lashes, not sure if he was being facetious or sarcastic. Was there a double meaning to his comment? But no, he was only looking at her, smiling a little under the fake mustache. Nick seemed quite content, like a husband out with his wife—fond, relaxed. His acting was quite good. And really, why was he bothering with all this? He could have easily taken her back to the States.

Alethea studied him intently. Was he embarrassed to face his boss, Porter, without the papers? Or did Nick think he was going to get them out of her still? He certainly didn't seem to be in a hurry right now.

"Tell me something about yourself," she found herself saying. "I hardly know you. I'm curious."

"There's nothing much to tell. You've heard it all already." He gazed at her steadily with his deep blue eyes. She tried to ignore the mustache.

"Come on. Tell me about your mother and father. Any sisters or brothers?"

"Yeah, one sister—older, married, two kids, rich husband."

"Is it that boring?" she asked lightly.

"Can't say, as I haven't tried it, but she seems satisfied."

"Hmmm. She must be terribly well dressed and Establishment. Am I right?"

"Sure." He grinned at Alethea in amusement.

"And your mother is gracious and ladylike and belongs to the D.A.R."

"Almost right, except for the D.A.R. part. Pretty clever, aren't you?"

"Yes." She smirked coyly at him. "And your father." She concentrated hard. "He's tall and distinguished and totally forbidding."

"How did you know?" Nick was looking at her more sharply now.

"Easy."

"I bet you don't know his nickname."

"You're right. I don't. But tell me."

"Among the lower echelons of the legal profession in Philadelphia, he's known as 'old iron pants.'"

"I love it! He must be an absolute ogre. Now I know where you get that tough-guy façade from."

"Façade?" he asked, arching a dark brow.

"Well, I don't know how deep it goes yet. That'll take more time. So far, it seems to go pretty deep."

"Maybe," he said, musing. "I never thought about it. I guess you get a hard shell in my line of work."

"Do you like your work?"

Nick thought for a minute. "Sure. It's better than a lot of things I could think of. I guess it satisfies some of my needs."

"Such as?"

"Hey, what is this? A cross-examination?" he asked jokingly, but Alethea could tell he was uncomfortable.

"No, it's only that I've never met anyone like you before."

He leaned his chin on his hand, a faraway expression in his eyes. "I've never discussed this with anyone. It's kind of hard coming up with an answer, at least one that you'd understand."

"Try me," Alethea said flatly, feeling for the first time she'd really hear the truth from him, enabling her to put together some pieces of the puzzle that was Nick DeWolff. It made her heart beat faster. She leaned over the table to be closer to him, as if that would help her understand.

"Well, when I got back from Nam, I couldn't settle down. After all the violence, you can't settle into a humdrum job very well. You crave action, you're obsessed with it. Some of the guys went in for illegal action, some for just plain kinky stuff, I guess. I went in for legal violence, talked myself into believing it was a necessary job, one that someone had to do."

"Do you feel that way now? That it's a necessary job?" Her voice was taut with feeling.

Nick turned his gaze on her. She saw something deep in his

eyes, in the grim lines that ran from his nose to the corners of his wide mouth, a kind of implacable regret. "Yes," he said softly. "It's another way I can use my skills to help my country."

"I see," said Alethea, feeling somehow disappointed, yet respecting him, however reluctantly.

"Come on, we better be getting back," he said, breaking the spell that had bound them together so closely for a few short minutes.

Alethea felt empty, a little sad, but not quite as confused about Nick as she had been. She could see a faint glimmer of logic in what he said and what he did . . . even if she didn't want to.

It began to rain, a cold, fine mist, as they walked back to rue Monsieur-le-Prince. They were both quiet, pensive. Alethea felt curiously purged of her previous anger and frustration.

It had been a pleasant interlude, a fleeting truce in their battle.

Chapter 24

Friday, December 16

Nick leaned a casual shoulder against the doorframe while he pensively watched Alethea as she paced in front of the darkening window. He seemed to have an inexhaustible wellspring of patience.

"Ready for another game?" he asked, grinning.

"Oh, no, not again. You know I'll whip your pants off. Are you a masochist or something?"

"It's good for my French."

"Okay, then, sure. Why not?"

They sat down at the kitchen table in their accustomed places—they'd already fallen into a comfortable routine—and Alethea pulled out the old box of Scrabble, dumping the pieces face-down in front of them. She'd told Nick time and time again that her mother had raised her to speak French, that he didn't have a chance, but he insisted on playing in the foreign language. She always won.

They moved pieces in silence for a while. Well into the game, he crossed her *étranger* with the not-so-bad *mystère*. He was getting better.

Nick sat back from the table, scraping the chair legs across the floor, and looked at her, a slightly triumphant smile on his face. Calmly, she spelled out *effroi* on the "e." He cocked his head questioningly. "Fright, horror," she said, staring straight into his eyes, feeling bold.

He nodded, frowned, then arranged his pieces: *vérité*.

"Truth," Alethea said thoughtfully. "That's funny."

"What's funny?"

"My name means 'truth' in Greek."

"Ah, I see. And who was so learned as to choose that name?"

"My mother. She was a great fan of the classics."

"A lovely name. Different."

"Thank you but I wasn't fishing for compliments," Alethea said, vaguely embarrassed, irritated that he was so damn condescending.

"I know," Nick stated evenly.

She met his eyes, slightly surprised at the assurance of his words. He was measuring her, almost insolent in his unequivocal gaze.

"*What* do you know?" she asked archly, feeling like pushing Nick a little, like wiping that infernal knowing look off his face. What in hell did he know about her, after all?

"I know you don't fish for compliments," he said flatly.

"And how do you know that?" she snapped.

"I'm a mind-reader," he replied, straight-faced.

"Oh, hell!" Alethea rose, exasperated, and stalked around the kitchen. Suddenly, everything grated on her nerves again. "I'm sick of sitting here, waiting. I can't stand being cooped up . . . with you! Why don't you let me go? I don't have anything you want!"

"We've been over all that."

"Well, call the police to escort me somewhere. Or pull your little dressing-up routine again. I'm sure you have ways. It's your *job*, isn't it?" she demanded, sneering.

"Simmer down."

"Dammit, why should I?" Her temper flared, ignited by the worry of the past few days. She swept her hand through the pile of wooden Scrabble pieces on the table, scattering them everywhere. "I just want to be left alone!"

She felt tears near the surface again and her cheeks flushed with anger and shame. Alethea ran from the kitchen and flung herself on the bed, mortified to have had such a childish tantrum. She lay there for a long time, her face buried in the pillow.

She heard his chair scrape, then the sound of the little square pieces being picked up and dropped into the box. Then there was silence.

Why doesn't he ever get angry? Alethea wondered. If anyone did that to her, she'd want to spank him. She realized, though, it was all in the line of his work. Like with Lisa. Alethea squeezed her eyes shut even tighter, somehow still hating the thought of him and Lisa.

It was then that the notion came to her. Instantly, Alethea was aware that it had always been there, lurking under the rippled surface of her thoughts.

She would seduce him.

He was extremely attractive. It wasn't so much his actual features, but more his manner, his way of moving, his calm self-assurance. He had, as Lisa had so aptly mentioned, sex appeal. Alethea felt it. She had felt it all along. But she had fought the attraction because he was the enemy. Now she analyzed it from another angle. What better way to put him off-guard, confuse him, lay his suspicions to rest? And when she had him where she wanted him, she'd escape, and he'd never find her.

Fleetingly, Alethea wondered if she weren't rationalizing, structuring this whole thing to gratify her own desires. No, of course not. She was the frigid one, the one who never responded properly, never got any pleasure out of it. Why should she suddenly desire a man?

She made up her mind. There was no choice, anyway.

Her only weapon was her body. How sick, how trite, an old, old joke. But it just might work . . .

Alethea sat up and glanced through the doorway. He was sitting on the sofa, reading a newspaper. He looked unruffled, uncaring.

Well, she'd make him care. She'd play Judith to his Holofernes. And she'd have his head—in this case, her own freedom.

But would she have the guts to go through with it? She wasn't Lisa. She'd had a little experience, mostly unsatisfactory, and she wasn't sure of herself in this respect at all.

Would he compare her, unfavorably, to Lisa? What a terrible thought. Alethea put it from her. There was more at stake here than her ego, much more. And what if Nick weren't receptive? Maybe she wasn't his type. Maybe she absolutely repulsed him. You couldn't tell from his smooth, professional demeanor. But she didn't think so. There had been flashes of pure kindness on his part. She didn't *think* she repulsed him. He certainly hadn't seemed put off in Athens.

Alethea rose, smoothing her hair back, straightening her black sweater as she walked into the other room. She hoped her eyes weren't red and swollen. But he'd seen her in worse condition.

"I'm sorry," she said, trying to sound contrite, standing before him.

Nick looked up from the newspaper and her heart began to thud with the enormity of her plan. He said nothing but continued to watch her, expressionless.

"I'm sorry," Alethea said again. "That was ridiculous." She found herself unable to meet his level-eyed gaze.

"The penitent doesn't suit you," he noted dryly, then waited deliberately.

Why was he making it so hard for her? It wasn't fair. Her heart was fluttering in her chest.

"You must think I'm awful."

"No."

Alethea fell silent, then tried again. "I know it's your job. It's just that I'm not used to this sort of thing. I'll try to be more . . . pleasant." Her voice trailed off. This was too difficult. She couldn't go on.

"All right, what exactly do you want?" Nick asked, his face blank, his voice tightly controlled, cold, too cold. "Don't play games with me."

Alethea heard herself gasp. She felt as if he'd struck her in the face. The hot flush of shame rose to her cheeks, and she whirled around, ready to run, to get away from his cruel words, his hard, ice-blue gaze that saw right through her.

A hand seized her arm, hard and unrelenting as a vise; then, slowly, Nick pulled her around to face him as he stood over her.

"Is this what you wanted?" he asked softly, pulling her to him and bending so that his lips met hers. His mouth moved on her own and her heart stopped. "Is this what you were after . . . Alethea?"

And then his lips closed on hers, warm and hard and soft all at the same time. She felt as if she were submerged in sensation, melting. The anger in her turned into passion, the shame into desire. Surprised at the strength of her own feelings, she tried to fight them, but they were too strong. She felt herself relax in his arms. He felt so strong, so warm, so good.

"Yes," she whispered when he drew back a little. Their eyes locked. "This is what I wanted." His lips closed on hers again, blotting out all thought.

Nick simply stood there kissing her and doing no more until she was weak with longing to feel his hands on her. Finally, when Alethea thought she would have to tear her own clothes off, he led her into the bedroom where, with that boyish grin on his lips and the late sun lighting his eyes to an azure shade, he eased her onto the bed and lay down next to her.

"Are you sure?" he whispered, tracing a finger along the line of her chin and neck.

She nodded, closing her eyes. Yes . . . she was very sure.

Slowly, he pushed the tight black sweater up over her breasts and lowered his head until his lips brushed the sensitive peaks.

Alethea gasped at the instant warmth which spread from her stomach downward. For the first time in her life, she was experiencing a pleasurable reaction to a man's touch—before she had felt nothing more than a curious desire to be fulfilled. Timidly, she brought her hands up and ran her fingers through his thick, curling hair until she found herself pressing his head to her breasts, wanting to feel him, his mouth, against her impatient flesh.

Nick responded equally, tasting her nipples, pushing her breasts up to meet his tongue with growing urgency, and then his head came up, their eyes met briefly, and his mouth closed over hers in a hard, demanding kiss.

Endless moments later, he raised his head. "Let's get out of these things." He stood, undid his belt, all the while watching her, smiling at her in the afternoon light.

For a fleeting second, Alethea wanted to run. What if she couldn't respond? What if she could react merely to the preliminaries at which he was so obviously expert, only to be left cold and empty in the end?

Oh, God, she prayed, please let me know what it can be like . . . please!

Nick was undressed and standing over her before she had even gotten off her sweater. "I'll help you," he said, reaching down and easing it over her head. She helped him with the jeans and her tan lace underwear, feeling terribly naked and unsure of herself. Despite her self-consciousness, Nick drank in the beauty of her translucent white flesh against the pale blue spread.

She was afraid to look at him fully but he coaxed her with gentle words until she gazed at the pure, raw virility of his body.

The breath caught in her throat. He was so perfect, so utterly beautiful that Alethea could barely believe she would soon lie beneath that magnificent body. It would be like sleeping with Apollo—a Greek god—she thought fleetingly while the blood pounded in her head and her breathing grew ragged.

And then he was next to her on the bed, his warm, strong hands stroking her flesh, searching the curves and hollows of her body. His mouth followed the path of his hands and she grew excited beyond imagination at his touch. He kissed the sensitive pulse on her neck, drew his mouth across her taut nipples, flicked his tongue across her belly and hips, sending waves of pleasure throughout her body until she thought she would cry aloud with longing.

Yet still, as he poised above her and she yearned to feel him plunge into her body, a small doubt nagged at Alethea's mind. Could she reach a climax or would he enter and cause her to recoil?

Slowly, patiently, Nick teased her body at its entrance until Alethea raised her hips to meet his thrust. And suddenly, she was filled with him and then emptied and filled again in the age-old rhythm of love. Each time she raised and arched her back to meet his thrust, her passion grew. She lost all thought of her actions, all reservations, all care for the words which came involuntarily from her throat. She sought only that secret, unknown peak which loomed before her, beckoning with rapturous torment.

Nick was whispering in her ear, taking her mouth with his until she moaned. At moments, he almost hurt her, and then he would tenderly brush her lips until the pain subsided. Alethea became oblivious to time and space. Nick began to take liberties with her body that before would have repelled and horrified her, but now, mindless of all else save the desperate urge to be fulfilled, she cried with pleasure as his hands molded her flesh and he twisted her into positions she never dreamed possible.

Her passion and search for release grew until she felt as if she were spinning uncontrolled within a dark cloud. At any moment, she would break out into the sunshine. With each passing second, she realized that she was about to emerge into this glorious, unknown world. And when she finally dug her nails into Nick's back and cried out unashamedly, Alethea knew the miracle of a woman and a man together—the joy, the thrill, the bliss were hers now to cherish forever.

Finally, she closed her eyes in weakness, holding him close to her.

Later, the winter sun spread its rays weakly across the quilt, touching his naked torso with pallid light. Alethea rested her head on one arm and watched him sleep. He was beautiful. That was the only way she could think of him now. His face was relaxed in sleep, and surprisingly it made him look older, a little worried. She loved the vulnerability it lent him.

Alethea smiled, feeling foolish, for there was no one around to see her. This man, this Nick DeWolff, this enigmatic human being that she sought to escape . . . What a joke! She had seduced him all right, or was it the other way around? And to her endless wonder, he had made glorious, slow, awesome love to her. Yes, she thought, still smiling, he had made *love* to her. It couldn't be called anything else.

And this was what she should abandon when she'd just found it. She could go right now, while he was still asleep . . .

Instead, Alethea snuggled closer to him, nuzzling his face with her mouth, nibbling at him until he stirred. Nick opened his eyes and looked at her unblinking for a long moment, then rolled over to face her, reaching out a hand to push her hair back from her face. He grinned lazily at her, the laugh lines showing around his eyes, as if they shared a secret, charming her anew. She caught her breath at the look of him, the feel of him. This was all so fresh to her. She reveled in it.

Nick caressed her, tenderly at first, then hungrily, and she returned his kisses fervently. Then she felt his hands on her, seeking, burning, awakening her to sensations she never knew existed. And her hands, unbidden, searched his hard, lean body, felt the scarred ridges that seemed right on him. She gasped for breath as if she had been racing, and the pulsing ache began in her loins, a welcome pain, for she knew that soon it would be relieved gloriously.

When he entered her, she gave a glad cry of joy and pulled him ravenously toward her. As he moved with her, she moaned in pleasure and arched higher to meet him.

And then she could feel it coming, building to a crescendo, until her body took over, fulfilling itself, knowing precisely how to respond.

And then they just held each other; she could sense the sweat on his body where it pressed close to hers, the rise and fall of his ribs, the man smell of him.

Now! Now was the time to run, the moment when he was at his lowest ebb, his least suspicious, now, when he trusted her. But it was too hard to tear herself from him. Alethea felt as if she would be ripping away a part of herself, leaving an open, bloody wound. She lay quietly in the timorous winter dawn, waiting for the strength to make her move.

He dozed. Quietly, reluctantly, she rose from the rumpled bed, snatched her clothes from the pile on the floor and walked out. Even if Nick heard her, he'd only think she was going to the bathroom. She felt chilled and sad as she dressed, jamming her money, credit cards and passport viciously into her pockets. As the walls were paper-thin and the bathroom was next to her apartment, she turned the water on full blast in the sink to make it sound as if she were still in the bathroom, detachedly admiring her cleverness, then slid on the black coat, certain it would fool them again.

The cool musty air of the hall hit her face as she ran to the rear of the building, down the rarely used back stairs and out into the littered alleyway that surely Suliman didn't know about. She ran as if the devil pursued her, more afraid of facing Nick than of anything else. The terror of a confrontation with him overwhelmed her. He would hate her now. Oh, how bitterly he would hate her!

A sudden, sobering thought struck her. Maybe he had only been doing his job. She vividly remembered his remark about Lisa—"all in a day's work." Could it have all been a well-rehearsed plan? Was she just another body, a sort of coffee break?

She wouldn't think of it. It didn't matter. She'd never see him again, anyway. But she'd never forget the feeling as long as she lived.

Alethea reached the street and paused, looking around for a chance taxi.

There weren't any.

Instantly, Alethea knew that she couldn't go through with it. Thank goodness there hadn't been a cab. Now she could go back to Nick's warm, wonderful body, his strong, reassuring arms. She wouldn't have to go on alone. She turned, began to walk purposefully, quickly, back into the building.

Chapter 25

Saturday, December 17

The sun was burning pleasurably hot on Nick's back. The sky was a cloudless, pellucid blue where it met the sparkling Caribbean water. He could hear the waves gently licking the pink sand at his feet . . .

No. It wasn't waves, thought Nick hazily, it was the water running in the bathroom pipes next to the apartment. It was Alethea washing her hair.

A smile gathered at the corners of his mouth. He willed himself to doze on, trying to ease back into his dream. Maybe one day he would take Alethea to the Caribbean, far away from the cold of Paris . . .

Alethea. Unconsciously, Nick gathered his pillow into a ball under his head. He added the pretty, delicately featured girl to the delightful scenario. He mentally undressed her on the baking sand, his hands caressing her soft flesh, the water barely touching her white skin, then receding again . . .

Suddenly, Nick jolted into a sitting position.

The room was brighter, less dull and gray than when she had slipped out of bed. But, straining his ears, he could still hear the water running.

At first he refused to acknowledge the possibility. She wouldn't have—not after a night like that! But an instant later, a gnawing apprehension began to crawl up his backbone. Hell!

He leaped out of bed, racing to the front room window while dragging on his pants.

Tearing aside the curtain, he was just in time to see the smaller Arab shoving the figure of a woman into the backseat of the Mercedes.

The stupid little bitch!

Nick dashed back into the bedroom, grabbed his shirt and coat, slipped into his shoes, sockless still, and was down the apartment stairs in less than fifteen seconds.

He tore the front door nearly off its hinges in time to see the Mercedes roll by down the street, sputtering out great black puffs of smoke. So they hadn't warmed it up; no wonder they hadn't gotten away yet. Thank God!

On the slim chance that he might succeed, Nick pulled his gun out of the jacket pocket, dropped to one knee in the middle of the street and fired twice at the right rear tire as the car turned the corner.

He missed both shots.

Quickly exchanging the gun for the keys in his pocket, Nick ran breathlessly to the Saab, now parked near the corner where the *concièrge* had moved it last night.

The car was pointed in the right direction. It came roaring to life immediately. He could have kissed the purring engine.

As he sped around the corner in the same direction as the Mercedes, Nick could see heads hanging out of windows on the rue Monsieur-le-Prince. The two shots had drawn a lot of attention but he'd be long gone if anyone summoned the police.

The Mercedes was a black blur some four blocks ahead. There was no early morning weekend traffic. Nick blew two red lights in a row and saw the Mercedes continue straight south. Several seconds later, he down-shifted into second and squealed around a wide traffic circle.

He was gaining on them fast, and was certain they could see him. The only question was if Akmet would instruct his driver to lose Nick or continue on and wait for a shoot-out further on.

Probably the latter, Nick surmised. They outnumbered him three to one, after all.

Down the wide boulevard they raced, and Nick suspected that Akmet would continue onto N20 south, a main highway, out into the country, probably to a safe house. If Nick were Suliman, that's what he would have done days ago—rented a quiet, out-of-the-way place, just in case.

The poor girl. But as quickly as the thought touched his mind, Nick swore under his breath. It would serve her right if Suliman hurt her. Alethea thought she was so clever—and maybe she was, Nick admitted grimly. But this time her scheming had backfired and he doubted she knew the price she might have to pay. It was, of course, as much his fault as hers. She had managed to find a weak spot in him and was using it to her best advantage. Porter had been right—Nick was getting soft. The simple fact that Alethea had managed to pull the wool over his eyes three times now was damning proof.

The Mercedes swerved left, rocking on two wheels, heading toward the autoroute that led southeast toward Orleans. If it were him, he would have rented a spot within thirty or forty miles. An isolated location within easy reach of the city.

Nick slowed the steel-gray Saab. Yes. They made the turn up the ramp, southeast. He down-shifted again. Maybe he could hang back, let Akmet think he'd been lost. The Mercedes would be easy to spot for a long distance ahead now on the empty autoroute.

Nick guessed the car ahead to be doing well over a hundred kilometers, or seventy miles per hour. He'd go along at this lower speed for a while, then pick up his pace.

He reached over and flipped on the heater—without socks, his feet were freezing. Damn that girl!

He could barely see the Mercedes now. It looked like a tiny black speck on the horizon before rounding a wide curve and disappearing. The next side road wasn't for several kilometers, he would still hang way back.

Nick's eyes took in the overcast day. The sky was gun-metal gray—the same color as the Saab. No way could they see him this far back, not with the small size of the Saab Turbo and its indifferent color. Good choice, thought Nick. He relaxed a little back into the comfortable bucket seat and listened to the steady drone of the engine.

Taking a few moments to think, he was actually amazed that

he'd let his guard down so low. No, he'd let it totally collapse, he admitted in self-disgust. My God, he'd had women before, plenty of them, but he'd never become so relaxed and engaged in his lovemaking that he'd forgotten all else. Even with Mei Ling, he'd always had other things on his mind. In fact, hadn't she complained of that very thing?

"Nick . . . when you are with me, still I think you are somewhere else. No?" she had said many years ago.

And it was true. Now he had to wonder what in hell had gone so wrong back in that Paris apartment that he'd come apart. How could he have let himself be so completely duped again? Alethea probably planned that very thing all along. Nick's face clouded with anger. Of course she had. Just like him, she had manipulated the whole seduction to gain her own ends. And her with those damn big, scared hazel eyes—

"Hell," he muttered.

Unexpectedly, it occurred to him that maybe she had faked her response, too. Thinking hard on the possibility, Nick swore under his breath and felt like an ass.

Finally, trying to regain his concentration on the task at hand, he managed to put the thoughts of their lovemaking aside and gradually picked up his speed. The Mercedes was nearing the Arpajon turnoff and he wanted to be certain it didn't make the exit without him seeing it.

Nick closed the gap some when the countryside became less flat and open with more soft, rolling brown hills. The turnoff was probably five kilometers ahead of Nick, maybe two kilometers in front of the black car.

Glancing down at his speedometer—ninety kilometers per hour—Nick saw something on the dashboard that made his heart lurch to a stop.

Empty.

The damn gauge was reading empty!

How in hell?

And then he realized . . . of course it was. The Arabs had seen the *concièrge* move the car twice and had all but drained the tank. Probably last night, Nick speculated furiously. And here he had thought they were so utterly unprofessional! It had occurred to him that they might let the air out of his tires but he had dismissed the idea, thinking they wouldn't plan for a car chase. Now, because *he* was unprepared, it might cost Alethea her life. Quickly, Nick shut the notion out of his mind.

So how much gas was left? That was what he had to think about now.

Before the exit, Nick got his answer—sput, sput, sputter.

The car slowed rapidly. The Saab coasted for a short distance before it choked to a complete stop. He jumped out and raced up the slight incline until he could just make out the intersection in the middle of a long stretch of highway.

No Mercedes.

Nick gulped in the cold, wet air and strained his eyes, searching the gray road ahead, squinting madly at the horizon where the autoroute met the sky maybe a mile or so in front of the intersection. There was no sign of a car. It couldn't have gotten over that rise so quickly, could it?

Had the sleek black Mercedes taken that turnoff, or was he grossly mistaken about the distances ahead of him? Was his eyesight that good anymore? A million questions tortured his mind. Nick felt like a bloody fool standing in the middle of the pavement, his chest heaving madly, nervous sweat pouring off his brow, and no goddam socks!

"Okay . . ." he gasped. "Okay. You took the turnoff. I'll find you bastards! You're not *that* smart."

He retraced his steps back down the incline, suddenly feeling the sweat on his body turn cold. And now he couldn't even turn on the motor and warm up.

Once back in the car, only slightly protected from the chill morning air, Nick watched the rearview mirror intently, ignoring the cold, ignoring his growing worry about the girl's future. He would do everything humanly possible to save her—not because he felt something for her, but because it was his stinking job.

Five minutes passed. Still no sign of another car, or bus or even a truck. Should he get out and walk to a farmhouse? Maybe there were services at the intersection? Would they be open this early on a Saturday morning? Wasn't anyone at all alive in France on a Saturday morning?

Seven minutes had passed. Nick stayed in his car. He needed it and would simply have to wait until someone came along and either carried spare gas or could give him a lift to the nearest station.

Eight minutes. Not a soul on either side of the road. Hell. Everyone in France must be dead. Once he got gas, if he ever did, how hard would it be to find the Mercedes? How many farmhouses lay nestled in the valleys around the exit? And was he correct to assume Akmet would use a farmhouse? Was anything being overlooked, forgotten? Too damn many "ifs, ands and buts."

Nine minutes. In the rearview mirror, Nick saw a large blur. It grew by the second. It was a truck; another one raced behind it.

He sighed deeply and opened the car door, stepping back out into the bone-chilling air. His breath came out in rapid white plumes. He was breathing far too hard. He was tense with repressed fear for the girl.

Nick put his hand up and waved it slowly back and forth. God, please, make one of them stop. I know we don't talk often, but please, God . . . for her sake.

Chapter 26

Saturday, December 17

Surprisingly, Alethea appeared at peace, tranquil as she lay asleep on a narrow cot. Occasionally, however, she would whimper and a frown line would crease her brow, but she couldn't quite grasp reality and would slip again into a foggy unconsciousness.

At moments, she would swim up out of the murk, her eyelids fluttering, and find Suliman Akmet sitting beside her, his weight tipping the small cot toward him.

It was so cold in the room.

She groaned and tried to roll over.

Suddenly, she felt a hand on her arm. "Alethea? Wake up!"

She squeezed her eyes tightly shut, trying to push his hand away with her weak arms. Why did her muscles feel so limp, so ineffectual?

"Mustafa!"

Who was Mustafa? she wondered in confusion. And then she sensed another presence in the small room and heard a door closing.

"Yes, *effendi?*"

"I think you have overdosed her. She is too drowsy. I cannot wake her."

"She will awaken soon, *effendi*. I beg your forgiveness. I have no experience with this drug."

Drugged! Of course . . . And then small snatches of reality touched her. She had been running from Nick, yes, and she had worn that coat to be certain the Arabs wouldn't recognize her. But then she had changed her mind and they had grabbed her and she could remember the rough hand on her mouth and her arms and legs flailing uselessly.

Then Suliman. Not the man who had treated her so carefully, but a different man: frightening, cruel, desperate.

"How long do you think it will be before I can question her, Mustafa?" She heard Suliman's voice sift through the fog.

"I cannot say."

Suliman's tone changed, angry now, Arabic words rushing out at the other man.

Where was Nick? He had crouched on the street and had shot at the car.

Suliman had laughed then. "As you Americans say, a clean snatch!"

On that terrifying ride out of Paris, his whole personality had changed. No longer was he the urbane oil minister with his almost poetic speech. He had been furious with her, his dark eyes shadowed, frenzied.

"The game has ended, Alethea," he had said bluntly. "You will now tell me where the papers are or I shall be forced to harm you." He had searched her white face. "No? Then so much the worse for you. Do you think I relish having to hurt you, my dear? I do not. But my country shall have the discovery. Your life means nothing in the course of events. Your father's life meant nothing."

"Murderer!" The word had exploded from her lips.

"Your father was a stubborn man. He did his work in secret. He was also stupid. He should have known that his lab assistant was loyal only to me."

"I don't understand."

"It is very simple. His assistant informed me of his secret work. I then gave your father every opportunity to share his research with me. But Dr. Holmes lied to me." Suliman had paused then. "You see, Alethea, when my man questioned him, the doctor, although brave, admitted that he had already sent the papers out of Abjala. It was not difficult to guess where."

"You're wrong! You have no proof!"

"Please, my dear, give me a little credit. Of course you have them."

"I don't. I swear it! Please . . . let me go."

"No. Not until I have the papers."

"And then?" The words had been torn from her throat. "What will become of me, Suliman . . . the same thing that happened to my father? An accident?"

"That, my dear, was unfortunate. Your father could not withstand the . . . questioning."

"You tortured him!"

Suliman had met her accusation with icy silence.

"And then you set a fire to cover it up! You filthy murderer!"

Suliman had laughed abruptly. "*I* . . . dirty my own hands? Don't be ridiculous, Alethea. It was not me. After all, an oil minister must remain above any suspicion . . ."

But he wasn't laughing now. He was angry, hurting her arm, shaking her. She didn't want to wake up!

There was a sharp, stinging sensation on her cheek then, and another. He was slapping her!

"Alethea! I know you can hear me."

She felt a harsh grip on her chin turning her face. Her eyes fluttered open. Suddenly, there was an impression of a heinous face suspended over her—dark threatening features, black forked beard, wild black eyes—the devil. She closed her eyes in horror, willing the vision to disappear.

"You'll pay for this, Mustafa! By Allah, I swear you'll pay. Now wake her up!"

And then there were hands under her arms, and she was being lifted, her feet barely touching the floor. Someone was trying to make her walk, but she couldn't. She drifted into unconsciousness, only to feel a slap on her cheek again, but oddly it didn't hurt. She felt numb.

She tried to open her eyes.

"*Effendi!* She awakes!" Those hands were gone and she was lying down again. Suddenly, her head was pulled back by the hair, shaking her slightly.

"Alethea, I am your friend, Suliman Akmet. You can trust

me," came his voice through the miasma that clouded her brain. "Alethea, I know you have your father's notes. I want to know where they are."

This time her eyes opened fully and she tried to focus on his face. It was still demonic but she recognized him.

"Alethea?"

"Mmm."

"Where are your father's papers?"

". . . don't have them," she mumbled.

"But where are they?" he asked, his voice growing excited.

"Not supposed to tell anyone . . ." She felt like laughing suddenly.

"Alethea. You may tell me. I am your friend. You will tell no one else, but you *will* tell me."

She was fighting the heavy effects of the drug. It would be wrong to lie to Suliman. He was such a kind man. "I mailed them—safe place."

"Yes, you mailed them, but where?" His voice emerged slowly, controlled.

"Safe place . . ." She heard his long, quavering breath. It was wrong of her not to tell him, but wasn't there a reason? Yes, she wasn't supposed to. That was it.

"Where, Alethea? Where are the papers?"

"Mailed them . . . to . . ." Her voice trailed off, the muscles of her face relaxed again, her breathing became deep and even. It was too hard to stay awake, too hard . . .

"Alethea?"

"Sleep. I'm so tired," she mumbled incoherently. It was so hard to talk.

"You bitch!" Suliman shook her, hard.

"No, please . . ." Why was he hurting her?

"Look at you!" his harsh voice cut into her. "Whore! Do you think I am blind? Your lips are still swollen. From that agent's kisses, no doubt. Tramp. I treated you so carefully, yet you turned to him!"

"No . . ."

"Do you think I am going to let you get away with this?" He pulled her up to a sitting position; her head rolled from side to side. "Where are the papers!"

"Mailed them . . ."

"Filthy whore!" He shoved her fiercely back onto the cot and she sensed that she had bitten her tongue. If only she could sleep awhile . . .

And then she was slipping, being dragged under by the overdose of the drug. There was a vague, strange sensation of her turtleneck being pulled over her head. Then there were cool hands on her, touching, kneading her breasts. She would have cried out, but no sound emerged through her lips now, and instead she went under, deeper and deeper.

Alethea swam up through thick layers of fog, knowing somehow that she had to fight desperately to get somewhere but not knowing where, or why. It was like a nightmare. She tried to run, but her legs wouldn't work and something was chasing her.

Gaps showed through the fog occasionally: a small, bare, whitewashed room with a shuttered window, a small table with an opened pack of Gauloises on it, a dim electric bulb suspended from a wire, a wooden chair.

As the images floated in and out of her mind—Alethea was aware that she dozed on and off—she felt extremely weak and relaxed. It was hard to concentrate.

Slowly, the fog began to recede, allowing her to wonder vaguely where she was. Then, suddenly, it all flooded back. Her skin rose in goose bumps and her heart raced in a hot burst of fear.

Suliman! The ride in the car out of Paris! The farmhouse! The needle slipping so easily in, burning for a second; then, shortly, oblivion.

Had they given her one of those horrible truth drugs Nick had told her about? She searched her mind and found there only a great lassitude, endless apathy.

Alethea wondered how long she'd been here. It seemed to be night—the same night, the next night?—she didn't know, had no way of telling.

She felt she ought to be terrified, more frightened than she was, but it was too hard to summon up the energy. Her head ached and her mouth tasted terrible. She raised a hand to rub her eyes, then abruptly realized her arm was bare.

Quickly, she felt for her clothes. Gone. She was stark naked, lying under some sort of a rough sheet. A sick fear began to gnaw at the edges of her mind. Had they taken her clothes to keep her from escaping? Or was there a different reason? She shuddered, picturing the hulking Mustafa, and the smaller, rat-faced man who had caught her. Would they have . . . ? Or was it Suliman himself who had undressed her?

Then, vaguely, the way a forgotten dream sifts slowly back in bright, disjointed images, she recalled something: Suliman, sitting close by her head, his mouth moving too slowly, the sounds emerging from his dark beard like a record played on the wrong speed, asking her questions, trying to drag something from her. The papers, he kept saying. Where were the papers? She could hear his voice in her mind, even its undertone of desperation, but her own answers did not come to her.

She couldn't remember what she'd told him, and it didn't seem worth the effort to try anymore.

She felt so tired and drained. It must be the drug, Alethea realized. She fought it, searching her mind for memories, but they receded before her every time, just as she thought she'd caught up to them. Then, abruptly, a clear image exploded in her brain— Suliman slapping her face, but not hard, and then he was touching her body, but she was paralyzed, and his hands were on her, all over her flesh and she couldn't do anything about it. Oh, God, what had he done to her? She shuddered, feeling sick. She couldn't remember anything but the hands. Tears squeezed out of her eyes and rolled down her temples. With trembling fingers, Alethea explored herself. A great wavering sigh of relief escaped her lips; there was no evidence of a rape. If he had touched her there, wouldn't the proof be left behind?

If you don't remember it, did it really happen?

Lethargy overwhelmed her. Let it go, she thought, it's too hard. Later, later, when she felt better, she'd think about it.

Alethea dozed, only to wake with a start at the sound of a man's laugh in the next room, then a rapid stream of Arabic.

She heard the deeper, fluid tones of Suliman. They were out there, waiting for her to wake up so they could question her some more or—the thought chilled her—maybe she'd already told them all they wanted to know and they were going to get rid of her, kill her. She tried to fight the rising panic.

She had to escape. It would have to be the window.

Alethea wrapped the sheet around her and sat up. For a moment, dizziness overwhelmed her and nausea rose in her stomach. It passed. She forced herself to walk to the window, carefully, slowly, feeling as feeble as an invalid. The shutters unlatched easily, revealing a small, double-paned window. that swung inward. It was fastened with a bolt, which looked as though it probably hadn't been opened in years. After repeated yanking, the bolt finally released, but the windows were stuck firmly, as if they had been painted shut.

Alethea pulled at them frantically, afraid to make any noise.

At last one pane began to swing in, squealing in protest as it did so. She froze, her heart drumming in her ears.

Slowly, ever so slowly, Alethea pulled on it until the cold night air hit her face. The window would be open in a second, just enough for her to crawl out into the safety of darkness. Surely there would be someone who would help her, even if she had to walk some distance.

It was open! She gathered the sheet around her and rose on her toes to climb out.

Suliman's voice, soft and low and deadly, cut her in the back like a knife blade. "Alethea, my dear, where on earth are you going on such a cold night?"

Chapter 27

Sunday, December 18

Nick had been absolutely right, the Mercedes had exited at Arpajon, but it took him practically a full day of dead ends and frustrated searching to locate the half-concealed car. There had been times that day, lots of them, when he nearly gave up the hunt, positive he'd been wrong about the turnoff. He'd been ready to go to the nearest police station and have them put out an APB on the Mercedes. Nick had given himself a limit of one more hour before bringing in help when suddenly his headlights reflected off a half-hidden car bumper. Instead of backing up and checking, he had driven ahead a hundred yards, turned off his lights and killed the engine.

Now he waited, crouched on the far side of the Mercedes from the farmhouse, to make his move. He had already disabled the Arabs' car. There was nothing left to do but crawl across the open meadow in front of the old stone house and pray to God that Akmet hadn't killed Alethea.

Nick removed his jacket—to give himself more flexibility—

and laid it carefully under a tree, tucking his gun securely under his belt. It was essential to get across the open field undetected by the Arab standing on the front porch. There was no other way to go in. The farmhouse stood completely alone in the middle of a field. A well-chosen spot, thought Nick.

There would be no problem until he was within earshot of the Arab, and then Nick hoped the man would follow his previous pattern of circling the house so that Nick could be waiting on that same porch by the time the Arab returned.

Nick's elbows ground painfully into the frozen earth. Pushing with his knees, he inched forward, silently, deliberately. For a moment, he stopped and dug his nails into the hard earth, collected what dirt he could and rubbed it into his skin.

There were several frozen haystacks in the unkempt field that Nick used to partially conceal his advance, but more often than not he was out in the open, praying his quiet movements would mix with the night shadows and some good old-fashioned luck.

He was approximately forty yards from the northeast corner of the house when the Arab moved to the front rail and seemed to stare in his direction. Nick could almost feel the man's eyes resting on his shirt, which was many shades lighter than the grayish earth.

Nick's heart skipped a few beats. Imperceptibly, he reached a hand toward his belt and got a good grip on the gun's butt. May as well go down fighting, die with his boots on and all that, he thought with dark humor.

Finally, the man moved . . . away from Nick, toward the steps.

Nick let out his breath in a low, muted hiss while he watched as the guard disappeared behind the house. If the man kept to the same pattern as before, he would take about a minute to make the round.

Nick tensed his muscles for the forty-yard dash.

He was breathless but well hidden on the creaky boards when the guard turned the opposite corner of the house.

The Arab guard walked slowly back up the three steps and reached both hands up to pull his coat collar more snugly around his neck.

He never saw what hit him.

Nick had come silently up behind the Arab. He merely gave him a quick, calculated blow on the back of the head with his gun and then eased the inert body onto the boards. The Arab would have a nasty headache but he'd live.

Now for the two inside, Nick thought. That was a different story.

He readied himself. He felt every nerve, every capillary in his body; the pounded-in months of training came back in a flood.

With his gun in his right hand, Nick turned the loosened door handle with the left. He planned to enter quickly and with as little fuss as possible. He was banking on the fact that Mustafa and Akmet would not be armed, that they would naturally think it was the other guard reentering the house. Nick would have the advantage. And if both weren't to be found together, then the odds would be even better . . . He'd take on one at a time.

The door opened with a loud, drawn-out creak. Nick was inside in an instant, the heat from an old stove slamming into his body, his eyes quickly adjusting to the light.

Immediately, he took in the whole scene. Mustafa was alone in the main room. He was sitting in a broken-down, overstuffed chair; he might have been dozing. At first his expression was blank, and then surprise spread up from his mouth until it reached his eyes.

Nick had the gun pointed directly at the Arab's face. Still, Mustafa reached, almost as if in unconscious reaction, to a pistol lying next to him on the table.

Damn. Nick fired a single shot. He had no choice whatsoever. He barely watched as Mustafa's body slumped down into the cushions. The man was dead.

It could only have been a second after Mustafa's head sagged onto his chest that Nick heard a shrill scream.

Alethea!

He raced, crouched, toward the room where the sound had originated.

Nick had no idea what to expect when he burst into the tiny bedroom. Akmet might be holding the girl in front of him for protection. He might be ready, pointing a weapon straight at Nick's face. It didn't matter . . .

The scene, however, that met his eyes was welcome but surprising nonetheless. Alethea stood in the middle of the room, clad only in a sheet, swaying as if drunk, a hand pressed to her forehead, her eyes wide in horror, but quite alone. Not a soul was in the room with her.

From his bent position, with the gun still pointed forward, Nick's eyes swept the room swiftly and came to rest on the open window.

He rushed to it. A man was moving across the field, stumbling, regaining his balance and moving away again in and out of the secret night shadows.

Nick rested his gun arm on the paint-chipped windowsill and aimed carefully at the figure's legs. Then his mind flashed on the girl behind him, terrified, hardly dressed. Coldly, calculatingly, he raised his aim higher, squeezed off a shot and then another.

Akmet was quite far away. Nick guessed he had probably missed even though the man seemed to falter momentarily, then disappeared into the heavily shadowed woods. He knew he should pursue Akmet but the soft sound of weeping reached his ears and somehow he couldn't bring himself to leave her alone in the house with a dead body in the next room.

Nick came slowly to his feet and turned around to face her. His clear blue eyes were dark now in both anger and a sudden flash of helplessness. She looked so damned scared, so alone standing there, clutching that sheet.

For a long moment, he stayed frozen to the spot, his eyes traveling over her carefully, like a mother counting a newborn's fingers.

She looked okay—pretty drugged judging by the unfocused gaze, but okay. It didn't seem like she recognized him. She looked terrified . . .

He took a hesitant step forward. Alethea backed away.

"It's me, Nick," he whispered gently.

Her mouth opened to form a word, but in her retreat she stumbled over the dragging sheet and gasped aloud instead.

Taking a long stride, he caught her before she fell. The sheet sagged down over her breast. Deliberately, he pulled it back up and stretched her out on the crude cot. He ached to hold her to him, to comfort her, but she was twisting away.

"It's Nick, Alethea . . . You're all right now."

Her eyes half-rolled up into her head. What in hell had that bastard given her, anyway? Briefly, Nick wished he hadn't missed his shot at Akmet and was glad now that he had raised his aim to kill. But there was no time to dwell on that. He had to get them both out of there.

"Alethea." He shook her gently. "Can you hear me?"

Her mouth opened. "Please . . ."

Dammit! It was no use. Even if he could get her to come around, she'd still be pretty helpless. Maybe it was better this way. Dress her quickly, without a fuss. Get her out to his car.

Glancing around the room, he found her clothes sticking out from under the bed. He got the sweater half over her head, trying to keep his eyes averted from her defenseless body, trying even harder to keep from wondering how she had gotten undressed in the first place. Did he really want to know? Oh, hell . . . Nick tried to stick her limp arms into the sleeves, then pulled on her hands until the sweater was on. Now for the pants. Exasperated, embarrassed, he wondered how to dress a female. He'd undressed a few in his time, but this was absurd. Everything about this case was ridiculous from the beginning. Another one for the manual— "Dressing a Drugged Female."

Chapter 28

Sunday, December 18

It felt as though someone was bumping the cot beneath Alethea. A low drone filled her ears. She tried to place the sound but she couldn't pin it down.

Then she had it. A car. She was in a car! Oh, God, where were they taking her now? She refused to open her eyes, afraid to accept the awful reality.

But the sun pressed on her eyelids and Alethea knew she'd have to open them soon. The light made her eyes water and her head ache. How long could she feign sleep? She tried licking her dry lips and swallowing; her tongue felt thick and dry and fuzzy.

"Alethea?"

She gasped with shock and her muscles flinched instinctively in a protective reflex action. Warily, she turned her head toward the voice.

She saw his profile at first. His dark curling hair was mussed, as if he hadn't combed it, his blue eyes under the too-long lashes were focused straight ahead, intent on the road. His nose with its slight marred line looked so familiar, so welcome, that she wanted to cry in relief.

Then he took his gaze off the road for a second, and when he saw that her eyes were open he gave her that wide, boyish grin.

"How you feeling?" he asked.

"I . . . I don't know. What happened? How did you get me?"

"Whoa. One at a time. First, are you all right? Feel sick or anything?"

She was sore and tired and her head hurt. "No, I'm okay . . . I think I'm okay."

"Good." He smiled at her again.

"How did you . . . .? They had guns . . ."

"It's my job, remember?"

"Oh."

He was silent for a moment, as if weighing his next question carefully. "Did they . . . hurt you?"

"No," Alethea said too quickly, and then the horror and fear and nightmarish feel of those hands, the questions . . . It all came back, overwhelming her as the images piled one on top of the other and she couldn't stop them from coming at her like the horrible flying demons of a childhood fantasy.

She buried her face in her hands and began to sob, unable to stop, ashamed of losing control, but far beyond the ability or desire to command it.

He pulled smoothly off onto the wide shoulder and stopped. Then he turned to her and drew her into the comfort of his arms. She let herself go, crying against his chest, feeling safe, secure. She felt his hand smooth her tangled hair back from her face, and somehow a handkerchief was in her hand and she sniffled and wiped her eyes.

After a while, Alethea was quiet, staring unseeingly out of the car window, lying against Nick's broad, hard chest, not having the energy or will to move.

His breath whispered warmly on her hair and then his lips pressed lightly on the same spot. She shivered a little in reaction.

"Feel better?" His voice was low, soothing.

"Yes . . . I'm sorry. I just—"

"Hey, don't be. I've seen strong men cry after a dose of that stuff."

"How did you know where to find me?"

"I followed their car."

"But how could you?" A flush of hot shame blossomed under her skin and Alethea suddenly remembered how she'd left him and then changed her mind.

"Yes, you did leave me in rather a . . . compromised position." Nick laughed ruefully. "Luckily, my innocent little temptress, I woke up in time. But I never did have a chance to put on my socks."

He thrust out his foot and she saw his bare ankle above the shoe. It suddenly seemed comical. His socks! How could he think about his *socks* at a time like this! She found herself giggling, uncontrollably, almost hysterically.

"It's not *that* funny," he said dryly. "My feet have been freezing."

"I know . . . I'm sorry," she gasped out, half-crying, half-laughing.

"I wish you'd quit apologizing. You get me into trouble every time you start that stuff." He smiled at her again and Alethea was surprised at the simple caring evident in his face. How could he like her after what she'd done, so deliberately, to him?

Her mood sobered instantly. Abruptly, she felt shy and uncomfortable. The memories came crowding back: the feel of his body on hers, the strength and tenderness of him, the glorious, new, bursting love they'd made. She felt horribly embarrassed and slid away from his embrace, not able to meet his eyes.

"Alethea," he said quietly, "I don't hold anything against you . . . for trying. I don't blame you a bit. I would've done the same thing. But you should have taken Akmet more seriously. You have a lot to learn about this cloak-and-dagger routine."

She looked up at his face. He was serious, dead serious. Then he didn't hate her? She studied his face solemnly. Did he mean it, could she trust him, or was his speech merely another untruth, another way to deceive her?

"Will you leave it to me now?" he asked lightly, but his expression was quite grave. "You have no choice, you know. It's either me . . . or them. He's still out there somewhere. I doubt if Akmet will give up so easily."

"I don't know . . ."

"You'll have to tell me now, anyway," Nick said softly, "because you probably told him."

"No! I couldn't have," she cried, confused, scared again.

"Yes, you could have. I warned you about the drugs. We don't have a monopoly on them. I hate to push at a time like this but it may be very important. See what you can remember," he said quietly, off-handedly.

Nick turned the key and the engine roared to life. He gave her hand a quick pat, then concentrated on his driving as he pulled back into the light traffic of the autoroute.

Alethea tried desperately to remember what had happened in the dimly lighted little room. She did recall Akmet asking where the papers were, but any answers she might have given were completely elusive. Maybe she'd said she mailed them, but she wasn't sure. The images faded in and out, so fuzzy black around the edges, confusing her. It was possible she'd told him, but she had a faint, inexplicable notion that she hadn't.

She went over it again, trying hard to recap the events, but all that came to her in stark, line-bright, distinct, surrealistic detail was Suliman's hands on her, violating, prying.

And then it dawned on her. She had been naked. It didn't seem likely she could have dressed herself and not remember it now. It must have been Nick who had gotten her clothes back on her, Alethea concluded.

She braved a timid glance over at him. He was concentrating on the autoroute. She felt the blood flow into her cheeks as her train of thought continued against her will. And what had he thought about her nakedness? Did he suspect that Suliman might have . . . She couldn't stand to continue. Suddenly, Alethea felt so mortified that she almost wished Nick hadn't rescued her. What would he think of her now? Even if she dared to bring up the subject, how could she make him believe that she honestly didn't remember a thing? Maybe nothing at all had happened. Better to say nothing. If he thought Suliman had touched her, so be it. Tough. It didn't matter to her, she told herself. Let Nick think what he must and to hell with it.

He treated her like a porcelain doll that would break with rough usage all the way back to Paris, through the rest of the strangely sunny afternoon, until she almost grew impatient with his deliberate avoidance of any sensitive subject.

Alethea still felt knocked out, weepy, vaguely drugged, and she dozed most of the way back in the car. He woke her gently when they pulled to a stop in front of 20 rue Monsieur-le-Prince. Walking up the familiar stairs, she could hardly believe the last day had happened. The bed was rumpled, the covers trailing on the floor, the way he must have left it when he'd realized she was gone . . .

They ate, and Alethea was surprised that she was ravenous, until Nick pointed out that she hadn't eaten in over twenty-four hours.

She found herself dozing off again after the meal, and then she felt his arms around her, lifting, carrying her to the bed. There he helped her undress, like a small child, and kissed her chastely on the forehead while he lay down beside her, held her gently in his arms. It was so good to be taken care of, so easy to let go.

She woke with a start at six in the morning. She felt much better—brisk, clear-headed. Where was Nick? She was alone in the bed. Tiptoeing into the living room, Alethea found him asleep on the couch, one bare arm flung wide, trailing on the floor, his dark hair tousled with sleep. So climbing into bed with her last night had only been to comfort her. He must have been exhausted, up that whole dreadful night, all on her account.

Quietly, Alethea made coffee and buttered an end of a stale *baguette,* sat down to eat and watch him sleep as if it would somehow give her an answer. There would be a showdown with him today; there was no avoiding it. He'd ask where the papers were, and if she refused to tell him, he'd take her back to Porter— no fooling around this time. Alethea was quite aware that he had already jeopardized his mission by almost losing her once. On the other hand, if she told him, he'd probably go there and get the envelope . . . but she'd have more time, more time to think of a way out, a solution. Amazingly, she felt she wasn't ready to give up yet. But she needed Nick; she knew that now. He'd saved her twice. Of course, it was his *job,* but still, he'd been there and a damn good thing, too. Yes, she needed his strength, his know-how, his calm acceptance of the risks, his gun.

And he needed her, too. She knew where the papers were, *exactly* where they were. She still didn't think Suliman knew the whole story, but if he did, she would have to get to them first. It was that simple. And, Alethea suddenly thought, they'd lost a whole day!

She grew impatient for Nick to wake up and rattled her plate unnecessarily in the sink.

He sat up with a jerk, looking around quickly.

"Don't worry. I'm still here," she said, feeling guilty now for her childish trick.

He didn't answer but put his face in his hands and rubbed his eyes with his fingertips, then scrubbed them through his hair.

When Nick looked at her again, he was grinning sheepishly. "I overslept. Bad habit." He paused, looking keenly at her. "You're feeling better." It wasn't a question.

"Yes."

"Good." He stood, stretched like a jungle cat, and she saw the lean muscles pull tight across his ribs. He wore only a pair of jockey shorts. She felt vaguely embarrassed.

"I need a shower." He looked questioningly at her and she blushed.

"I'm not going anywhere," she said, feeling like a fool.

She was standing at the window, dressed, looking down into the street, when he returned. He fixed himself a cup of coffee.

"Our friends down there?" he asked casually, too casually, as if he already knew the answer.

"No, I don't think so."

Unexpectedly, the phone rang. They both tensed as if they'd heard a gunshot and looked questioningly at each other.

"I'll get it," Nick said coolly.

Alethea could only hear his side of the conversation.

"She's fine," he was saying. A pause. "No, we weren't home yesterday. Took a little drive." He winked at Alethea over the receiver. "Sure, you can talk to her." He held the receiver out. "It's Clair."

"Clair, hello. Why are you calling? I thought I had till—let's see—tomorrow."

"I couldn't wait anymore," came Clair's familiar voice over the line. "I tried all day yesterday and there was no answer. I didn't know if you were still in Paris or what. I got so worried . . ."

"I'm fine, honest. And no one's twisting my arm, either."

"I see he found you."

"Yes."

"I'm sorry, but he got back here the next morning and somehow he knew. I tried my best, really I did." Clair sounded sorry, upset, relieved, all at once.

"Hey, it's okay. It's just as well he got here. Now don't blame yourself."

"You sure? I was afraid you'd be furious."

"Well, I'm not."

"Look, are you managing with the papers and all?"

Alethea hesitated. "Oh, sure, don't worry!" she said gaily.

"I see. You can't talk. Okay. Hey, is that guy shacking up with you? What's the story?"

"I'll tell you some day, Clair. It's awfully complicated."

Then Alethea could hear another voice in the background, talking to Clair. "Hey, what's going on?"

Clair's voice came on again, muffled, as if she were trying to keep from being overheard. "Oh, damn, Lisa's heard. She wants to talk to Nick. She knows he's there. What do I do?"

A surprising chill settled on Alethea; she could feel her face go all cold and stiff. "Let her talk to him. I don't care. Here, I'll put him on. No doubt he'll be delighted."

She held the phone out to him. "It's Lisa." Alethea's voice was as cool as smooth metal, and just as hard. She deliberately turned her back on him, refusing to look at his face. She couldn't help hearing the conversation, though.

"Yes, I'm in Paris," he was saying.

Did he sound a little exasperated? Impatient?

"She needed some help with a problem she had. Naturally, being the gentleman I am, I couldn't say no."

Alethea turned toward him angrily. He shot her an amused glance.

"I'm sorry I had to leave in such a hurry, but actually, I'm doing a little work here. It's not really a vacation."

He was silent for a long time. Obviously, Lisa had something to say.

"Following her? No, of course not. We just ran into each other."

Lisa was talking again.

Then: "Lisa, I don't think I'll be making it back to Switzerland, not this trip. And really, I've got to go now."

Lisa was talking again.

"Sure, I'm in the phone book. Washington, D.C. Any time. 'Bye, Lisa."

He hung up. "She sure is persistent, isn't she?"

Alethea didn't answer. She stood with her back to him, facing the window, pretending that she hadn't heard a word of the conversation, pretending that she wasn't even in the same room with him. Then she felt his hand on her shoulder. Unbidden, her body tensed, as if for flight.

"Hey, what's the matter?" Nick asked softly.

"Nothing." She whirled to face him, finding, to her consternation, that he was even closer than she'd realized. She couldn't back up; the window was right behind her. She looked down, unable to think. He was too near, his warm breath on her hair, his broad shoulders blocking her view of the room, his blue eyes smiling at her, slightly mocking but warm, full of intimate knowledge. Damn him!

Alethea moved sideways, out of his reach. She felt his eyes on her back, questioning, burning.

She turned, then, too quickly she knew, but she didn't care, and began the speech she'd prepared, bursting right into the middle of it. "My father didn't want the United States to get the papers, Nick. What I mean is, he didn't want any one country to have them. He said his discovery was for everybody, the whole world. It was important to him. It was so important he died for it." She looked imploringly at Nick. "Don't you understand? I have to try to do what he wanted . . . It's all I can do for him now. I have to try." She looked down at her hands. "I know I've caused you a lot of trouble already, and I can't get them alone."

He sat very quietly, so still she almost wondered if he'd heard her. His expression was unreadable. She wondered if he was whooping in triumph inside. She forced herself to go on. "I need your help. I admit it. And I'll tell you where they are. But I want to ask you one thing. Don't think I'm a dumb kid, or naive, or . . ." She couldn't think of anything else, and gave up. "Just consider. Please, Nick," she locked her gaze to his, "just consider that when we get them, you won't turn them over to Porter. We'll give them to someone else—for the world. Just think about it, please."

Nick was waiting. The tension in the air was like electricity, and Alethea almost lost her nerve. Her carefully cherished secret— it was painful to be forced to tell him; it was a kind of defeat. He was the enemy, she was fighting a war and felt like a traitor.

"I mailed them to Ravello," she blurted out, glad in a way to get it over with, but sad, too, at her need to do it.

"Ravello."

"Ravello, Italy. It's a little place near Amalfi—"

"Yes, I know where it is." He looked slightly puzzled. "Far be it from me to question your motives, but why Ravello? I was always under the impression that the Italian mail was none too swift. Why not someplace dependable, like England or Germany?"

"It was the only place I could think of. I spent a week there once with my parents—oh, ten or so years ago—a vacation. We had such a wonderful time, I never forgot. It stuck in my mind."

"Ravello, sure, why not," Nick said, as if to himself. Then he became totally professional, efficient. "Tell me exactly where and I'll call and get an agent on it right away." He smiled, a cool, thin smile. "Then I'll take you home."

"No." She could hear the stubborn sound of the word.

"What do you mean 'no'? You said you'd tell me—" He was trying to remain detached but she felt a slight prick of pleasure at her ability to get to him.

"I won't tell you exactly where, not until we get there."

"*We?*"

"Yes, we're going to get them. No agents, nobody. Me and you." Alethea leaned back against the wall, folded her arms and waited. "Or I won't tell you and you'll have to send me to Porter, and you've told me you'd hate to do that, right?"

Nick watched her unwaveringly.

"Don't try the old evil eye on me," she said flippantly. "You'll never get them without me. It'd take weeks, and by then everybody would know something was going on. There'd be questions, lots of questions." She paused and looked straight into his now opaque, dark blue eyes. "It's the only way, face it. Think of it as a business proposition. I need protection and you need information."

"You stubborn little—"

"Flattery will get you nowhere," she said, smiling archly at him.

"How do I know you'll tell me when we get there?"

"You don't. And how do *I* know you won't ship me off to Porter?"

"Okay, okay. It's a deal." Nick looked at her admiringly. "Truth, hell. I'd say 'trouble' would be the name for you." He hesitated, then began to plan out loud. "We'll take the Saab. It should only be . . . what, a couple, three days? I'll phone Porter, tell him I'm onto something, put him off for a few more days." He turned his gaze onto her, the lopsided grin coming to rest on his lips. "Just tell me one thing, Alethea."

She quirked an eyebrow at him questioningly.

"Do I ask for one room or two when we stop for the night?"

Chapter 29

Tuesday, December 20

The soft purr of the Saab's engine lulled Alethea as they drove south out of Paris. It was a bleak winter's day, gray, misty, but she felt lighthearted. They were on their way to Ravello and shortly the whole nightmare would end.

"How soon will we be there?" She glanced across at Nick, whose eyes were fixed on the road ahead.

"It'll take a while."

"I thought you said a couple . . . maybe three days was all."

"You want me to drive a hundred miles an hour?" he snapped.

"No."

Nick reached over and flipped the heater on high. "Then it'll take a few more days. Relax."

Alethea thought he sounded needlessly curt. If he was mad at her, that was just tough. She wouldn't talk to him and that way he couldn't spoil her good mood.

"I still can't get over your choice of countries to mail the papers to." His tone was sharp, irritable. "Any fool knows the mail service in Italy stinks."

"We've been over this ground before, Nick. I just did it. I didn't think. I'm *so* sorry," she ended sarcastically, her good mood evaporating abruptly.

"Well, you better hope the papers are there. That's all."

"They will be."

Nick shot her a piercing, sidelong glance. "Very confident, aren't you?"

"Yes. There's been plenty of time for them to arrive there. They're not lost. I can feel it in my bones."

In reply, he snorted with disbelief.

"Oh, go to hell," she muttered under her breath, truly angry now.

"What?"

"Nothing. Let's not talk. You know the old saying. If you don't have anything nice to say, then don't—"

"Say anything at all," Nick finished, then surprisingly forced a smile. "I believe Thumper said that. Look, let's stop and get something to eat. I don't mean to be short with you. Maybe I'm hungry."

"We've just started." At this rate, she thought, they'd never get there!

"We'll get some bread, cheese, maybe a half-bottle of wine. We can eat while I drive. Okay?"

"Fine."

Nick pulled off at a small village, typically French, with an antiquated gas station, a post office, a bakery and the omnipresent gray stone-façaded houses lining the narrow street. It had begun to rain lightly, almost a thick mist, really. Alethea waited impatiently in the Saab while Nick entered the warm *patisserie*, the *charcuterie* next door, and returned with a bag of groceries.

He handed her the food, then turned the motor back on. "You fix lunch while I drive."

Alethea peered into the bag and was suddenly starved, too. There was nothing better than freshly baked French bread with thick, hard yellow cheese. He'd even purchased a jar of tangy brown mustard. Her mouth watered as the doughy aroma assailed her.

"Got a knife?" she asked as he pulled back onto the main road south.

Nick shifted his weight toward the door and reached into his pants to search for his pocketknife, and as he did, Alethea couldn't help but notice the round, muscled shape of his thigh and buttocks. He was really built beautifully, she couldn't stop from noticing— lean and well muscled, no extras. And then a thought struck her, making her smile broadly. She was become a leg and butt woman, fascinated by his maleness.

"What are you grinning at?" Nick handed her the Swiss Army knife.

"Oh . . . nothing." She laughed, busying herself slicing the bread and cheese.

The lunch was wonderful, perfect, but as they shared the small bottle of strong red wine, passing it between them, Alethea began to wonder if it was a good idea for Nick to mix driving and drinking, even if he'd only had a very few sips.

"Want me to drive for a while?" she asked.

He turned his head and glowered at her. "Think I can't handle it?"

"I didn't say that."

They fell silent again. What was wrong with him today? Had he tired of her company so quickly? Maybe she didn't satisfy him, maybe he preferred the aggressive type. A Lisa. The thought made Alethea cringe inwardly. She could never, never behave like Lisa, fawning all over him, pawing him constantly like some kind of monkey. But maybe a man liked that. How was she supposed to know, with her limited experience?

The bleak landscape rolled by, monotonously the same: hilly, the road banked by bare trees, the tiny villages alike. The drizzle continued lightly; Nick switched on the wipers. They squeaked. Occasionally, they drove through a thick bank of fog lying heavily, like a gray mire, in the ravines. Oh, what she wouldn't give to be on a sunny, tropical beach right now, with the perfect man lying next to her—a man who could make her body respond like Nick had—perhaps rubbing suntan lotion onto her sun-warmed flesh. And then he would smile, his parted lips would brush hers softly . . .

Alethea turned her trancelike stare from the window and looked at Nick. It was a pity he could never be that man, but still she guessed she should thank him for being the first to awaken her body to pleasure. At least now she knew what to look for.

But she had to admit, it would be damn hard to find a man as attractive as Nick. It galled her that he was so handsome, and that he seemed not to know it. Was it possible that he failed to see the female heads turn in his direction admiringly? How many women had seduced him? Did he have a girlfriend or two? Maybe there was one waiting right now. He wouldn't be the first man to fool around . . . and lie about it.

While these thoughts drifted through her mind, Alethea studied him closely: the strong line of his jaw, the generous nose with that wonderful bump, those blue, blue eyes . . .

His eyes! "Watch it!" she cried suddenly, realizing in shock that his eyes were closed, and she simultaneously grabbed at the wheel. "Oh, my God!"

She held firmly onto the wheel with her left hand while Nick snapped his eyes open and began to pull the wheel away from her. In a split second, she saw in horror that their tugging motions had caused the car to swerve onto the soft shoulder.

Nick slammed on the brakes. "Let go of the goddam wheel!" he shouted.

She did, finally, gasping for breath as the car mercifully came to a stop.

"You nearly killed us!" she cried. "I asked you to let me drive. Dammit, you're drunk!"

Nick released his breath in a low whistle. "Calm down. That's stupid. I only had a couple of sips—"

"The hell you're not!" she interrupted in fury. "I'm not going another foot in this car unless I drive!" She folded her arms tightly across her chest defiantly.

"Look, Alethea." He turned toward her. "I swear I'm sober. I'm just tired as hell."

"Ha!"

"Give me a break, will you? I've been practically doing without any sleep at all since I met you!"

"Oh?" She raised a curved brow. "Are you trying to tell me *Mr. Macho* is exhausted? Why, I thought you super-types were invincible."

"Well, we're not. Now get off my back."

"Not unless I drive," she said firmly, ignoring his snarl.

"I'm fine now. I'll drive." He began to shove the gear shift into first.

"Oh, no." And Alethea had the door open before he could stop her and was standing beside the car, shivering in the light drizzle.

"Get back in here."

"Not unless I drive."

He studied her for a long minute. Finally, he said, half under his breath, "Okay, drive then!" He was out, rounding the back of the Saab before she even realized that he had given in.

Smugly, Alethea walked past him and sat in the driver's seat. "I *do* have a license, you know," she muttered, still angry as she pulled the car smoothly back onto the pavement.

He growled something unintelligible, which she chose to ignore, then turned his back toward her and rested his head against the glass.

Let him sleep, Alethea thought. He must need it badly. But she refused to feel guilt for his admitted exhaustion. It was, after all, his damn job!

She glanced over at Nick. She could faintly hear his soft breathing; he was out cold already. An involuntary flash of pity for him seized her, and then she forced it aside. Going without sleep was his fault, not hers. She thought back on the morning, before they had left Paris. He had looked awfully tired. Even when he had phoned his boss in Washington, his voice had been uncharacteristically weary.

Nick had been very evasive with Porter on the phone. At the time, she had thought to question Nick's side of the short conversation, wondering why he had purposefully misled his boss.

She furrowed her brow in concentration, trying to recall his exact words.

"It's Nick . . . Yes, I'm still in Paris." A long pause. "No, I don't actually have them yet," he had said, obviously referring to the papers. "I'm not sure exactly where," he had replied, "but we're going to fetch them today. It may take a week, I'm not sure." There had been a long hesitation on Nick's part after that, and he had turned his back on her. His next words had been muffled but she had caught the word, "Switzerland," and wondered if Nick had lied to Porter, telling him the papers were there. Next, he had quickly given Porter the location of the farmhouse and asked him to take care of the body that might still be there. "You know how touchy the French are about things like that," he had said.

One thing was for sure, he hadn't ever mentioned their intended destination. Had he lied deliberately to Porter to put him off the trail? And if so, why? She didn't, couldn't, dare to hope Nick would help her find an agency or someone without prejudice to whom she could give the papers. That was hoping for too much.

Alethea drove for a couple of hours longer while Nick slept and the rain grew steadier. It was only midafternoon when she passed a road sign: *Varennes, 13 kilomètres*.

She cast Nick a sidelong glance. He really ought to have a good night's rest. Not in a car, but on a bed, in a hotel. Maybe if he were rested, they'd make better time in the long run.

Alethea turned off the main route and drove into the center of Varennes, pulling up in front of a gray stone hotel which looked warm and comfortable.

The car jerked to a stop. Abruptly, Nick sat up, alert. "What . . . ?"

"We're stopping. No arguments, please."

He took in the hotel, then checked his watch. "It's only two o'clock."

"I know." She opened her door, then turned around to face him. "You're going to sleep for as long as you need to. We can go on later," she said firmly, leaving him little room for argument.

"Yes, Mother," he said half-mockingly, tilting his head in obedience.

Once they were warmly ensconced in a small but clean room, Alethea relaxed, sitting in the single, straight-backed chair while Nick stretched out on the bed.

"You're starting to lead me around by the nose," he observed, folding his arms behind his head. "Gonna join me?"

"Not yet." Alethea ignored his thoughtful gaze while she looked casually around the room.

"All right." He laughed, closing his eyes.

Alethea sighed to herself. He was like a cat. He could lie down and go to sleep anywhere, any time. She could use a nap, too, but she decided to wait until he was asleep. What had happened between them in Paris was in the past. She wasn't sure it was at all wise to let it happen again.

Nick dozed finally; she could see the peaceful rise and fall of his chest and found herself staring at him unabashedly, from the top of his dark head to his socks. He had the most wonderfully tight body. Her eyes touched, then rested on his lean muscles: his calves beneath the corduroys, his long thighs, his firm flanks and the flat, hard stomach. She even allowed her gaze to rest on the masculine bulge of his crotch. She knew, suddenly, shockingly, that she wanted to walk over to the bed and touch him there.

A warmth spread through her stomach and her breathing grew heavier. My God, she wondered, what have I become? Still, the self-knowledge, although bringing rare color to her cheeks, no longer surprised her. She wanted him, wanted that thrill he had brought to her.

Several minutes passed. Did she dare? Calculatingly, she stood up and pulled her turtleneck over her head, mussing her hair. The jeans were next, falling to the floor, then her underwear. Naked, forcing all thought from her mind, Alethea walked carefully to the bedside and looked down at his face.

She could put her clothes back on but that was the last thing that she wanted to do. It crossed her mind fleetingly that Nick might reject her, be too tired, but she shoved the ghastly thought aside.

She sat gently on the edge of the bed. The springs squeaked. He didn't awaken. With an unsteady hand, she touched the top button of his flannel shirt. Her cheeks flaming, she hesitated. Did she dare?

"Don't stop."

Alethea's heart leaped in her breast. He had been awake all along!

"It's all right," Nick whispered. "Go on. I'm all yours, lover."

"I . . . I've never . . ." she began.

"I know you haven't."

Was he serious, was he laughing at her, or did he really want her to?

Slowly, her hazel eyes averted from his face, she began to unbutton his shirt. She was acutely aware of his gaze on her nakedness, her breasts, her stomach and lower yet. No man had ever seen her this way—sitting nude in broad daylight. It was strangely exciting, and suddenly she felt no shame . . . only a hot, tingling sensation where his eyes rested on the half-hidden triangle between her legs.

Alethea finished with his shirt and slowly laid it open, exposing his tan chest, the dark curling hairs that extended in a line down to his flat stomach above the belt.

"Go on," Nick urged, and she knew he meant his pants.

"Maybe you should—"

"No," he said quietly, "you do it."

And she did, unable to help staring openly at the growing bulge between his legs. Was this really her, shy, self-conscious Alethea, undressing a man and causing him to rise so magnificently? The knowledge fortified her, making her grow bolder.

When she had finished loosening his pants, she freed him, trying not to actually touch his flesh.

Nick chuckled softly. "It won't hurt you. Touch me. I want you to."

She carefully touched his hard shaft, then she began to stroke him, tentatively.

Suddenly, Nick moaned and she withdrew her hand, unsure.

"God, don't stop now."

She helped him off with his clothes, almost laughing out loud at the role reversal. This was certainly the first time she had ever stripped a man, and she had to say it was fun, a very powerful sensation to suddenly know what she could do to a man with a simple touch here and a light stroke of her fingers there.

When Nick was as naked as she, Alethea wasn't quite certain what would come next. Wasn't he supposed to draw her into his arms, kiss her, press her body down into the mattress?

She paused, sitting next to his outstretched body, waiting.

Nick laughed, placing his arms behind his head again. "You started this, lover," he teased, "now what are you going to do with me?"

"What should I do?" she asked in a whisper. "Tell me."

"Oh, no." His eyes crinkled at the corners. "I'll give you a hint, though. Be bold, do whatever comes to mind. I'm sure I'll just love it."

But would he? Or would he think her unfeminine if she took the initiative?

She sighed, realizing how ragged her breathing was now. How transparent she had become.

Alethea laughed lightly at herself, then leaned over and began kissing him, gently at first, and then, as her sensitive nipples brushed his chest, with a passion she couldn't deny. But Nick wasn't about to make it easy for her. He kept his hands under his head and still refused to help.

Abruptly, she took her mouth away. "You asked for it, Nick," she murmured, kissing him on the neck, on the strong cord that ran up the side, on his ear, and then lower to his chest, where her hand lingered in his curling hairs, teasing, touching, exciting. With her other hand, she stroked his stomach until the lean muscles tensed. And she knew then that she was driving him wild.

Her mouth followed her hand down along the thin line of dark hair which spread and thickened at his groin. She wanted desperately to kiss him there, too, but paused, her head suspended above him.

"Lord, Alethea, don't stop now!"

But she couldn't . . . not yet . . . it was too new.

She raised up and searched his eyes. He understood. Oh, he didn't look like he appreciated it, but he wouldn't press her.

"Oh, Nick," she said, wanting suddenly to say a whole lot more. She kissed him again with a desire that shook her whole body. "I want you."

He moved his hands and crushed her to his chest while their mouths moved against each other, their tongues touching, tasting, exploring in a growing hunger.

His hands came down and encircled her waist as she felt him lifting her on top of him. For a moment, she was confused, until she realized that he wanted her to sit astride him.

He must have sensed her bewilderment. "There's more than one way to skin a cat. Let me help . . ." He guided her body down to meet his hardness and she eased her weight onto him, feeling him touch her, enter her waiting flesh and then fill her.

She gasped. "Oh, Nick!" It seemed so natural to move against him as he rose, thrusting, to meet her hips. Her movements were excruciating, a wonderful pain that alternately filled and emptied her. Her desire for release grew to meet his own, and mindlessly she sat up and arched her head back while Nick's hands took her breasts, crushing them almost painfully.

Low, soft moans escaped her lips as their rhythm increased, their bodies pressing together urgently, parting only to seek the hot warmth of each other once again. Alethea felt a frantic urge to be released from the exquisite agony she suffered, but her passion only seemed to grow stronger until animal sounds emerged from her lips and sweat trickled between her breasts.

It had been great between them in Paris: warm, caring, tender. This time was different. It was primitive, savage lust. Alethea thought she would go crazy if it didn't end soon—but contrarily, she'd scream if it stopped.

Nick helped her with his own driving desire. His movements

became quicker beneath her thrusting hips until she cried, "Yes . . . oh, yes!" and fell onto his chest almost sobbing with the blessed release of her body. She felt the tiny tremors of relief while her body throbbed, refusing to let him go.

"Alethea," he whispered into her hair, "I think I'm going to die."

Finally, she relaxed on top of him, her breathing returned to near-normal but her heart continued to pound. "If this is death, then I'm all for it."

Nick laughed tenderly and helped her to roll over and lie next to him, holding her warm body against his.

Alethea sensed he was near sleep again. She turned her head upward and looked into his smiling eyes. "Did I do all right?"

"Are you kidding? Now can I get some sleep?" He laughed gently.

"For a few minutes . . ."

They both dozed. It was dark by the time Alethea opened her eyes again. Nick had an arm flung casually over her breasts and her leg was lying on top of his. Amazingly, where his forearm touched her breasts she began to feel warm again and knew what that could lead to if she let it. For an instant, she thought to move a little, to try and awaken him, but then she told herself firmly that it wasn't fair—at least, not to him. And so she lay quietly next to Nick, knowing that if he so much as sighed right now, she could cup his hand to her breast and press her body hungrily to his.

And then a thought seized her: Once they got to Ravello and their relationship ended, how would she bear to live without him?

Suddenly, Alethea knew that she had just fallen prey to her own trap.

Chapter 30

Wednesday, December 21

"This seems like a cozy little place," said Nick as he swung the Saab toward the curb in front of the hotel. "Looks real clean, too." He didn't have to see Alethea's face to know that she was surprised at the fact that they were stopping so soon.

"But, Nick, we could get to the next town—"

"I like the atmosphere here," he said, hoping that she didn't push it. At least yesterday there had been a good excuse.

"Okay," she sighed. "I'll wash my hair, I guess. But can we leave early tomorrow?"

"Sure," he lied. Then he turned to her and smiled, shaking his head. "You and your hair."

She pouted a little. It made him want to grab her right then and there and kiss the tantalizing swell of her lip. How could a girl look so chaste, so modest, and yet be so passionate in bed? The combination increasingly fascinated him. She was like no one he had ever known: a blend of cleverness and naiveté, old fashioned propriety mixed with wantonness, strength and insecurity. She was like a drug to which he was growing addicted, needing more and more of it each day. And, Nick thought ruefully, she was just as lethal as a drug, too.

The room was cute—high up under the roof with dormer windows that looked out over the chimney pots of Avignon to the hills and wintry gray-green of Provence. The walls were covered with flowered wallpaper and cheap reproductions of famous French Impressionists. Still, it had atmosphere.

Alethea sat on the edge of the bed, looking at Nick pensively. He hoped to hell she wasn't going to start in again about their being in a hurry. He could tell her that Suliman was following them, and he might need to eventually, but he hated to terrify her if it wasn't really necessary. He was enjoying her more relaxed mood too much. He suddenly remembered yesterday and his knees went rubbery on him. The memory of it was enough to enervate him! Cool it, Nick told himself, there's time for that later . . .

"Hey, I just remembered something," Alethea was saying. "There's a restaurant here that was reviewed by our rival magazine. I'm not mentioning any names, you understand, but it was supposed to be so fantastic. I'd love to try it myself—on an unofficial basis, of course. Let's see, it was called . . . I've got it—La Maison du Paysan, the peasant's house." She looked at him. "Do you think we could try it tonight? It might be awfully expensive but we'll go Dutch treat. What do you say?"

He couldn't have said no even if he'd had a reason to—not with those big, black-lashed, ale-colored eyes looking up at him like that, the long white neck that curved up so enticingly, the pink mouth that was half-open, expectant.

"Sure," Nick said, trying to sound off-hand about it, hoping she didn't notice that he was melting inside.

"Oh, good," she cocked her head, looked at him worriedly, "but you'll have to wear a tie. Do you mind?"

"I'll survive," he said dryly. "I think I can dig one up."

"Great. Let's go early as long as we're here and order all sorts of different things. I'd love to compare it to that article."

"Should I tell them who you are?" Nick teased.

"Good Lord, no! That'd ruin everything." She laughed. "Now, what should I wear? All my clothes are in New York and everything I have here is all wrinkled. Damn. It'll just have to be my skirt and same old pink blouse."

Nick went to her as she bent over her suitcase, searching

through her clothes, and placed a single gentle kiss on the back of her neck. "You'd look fine in anything," he said, his voice husky, "even in nothing, if it comes to that."

"Nick!" Her voice was barely a whisper and her body seemed to melt where he touched her. She kept her head down, bent over the open suitcase. "Nick."

Slowly, he turned her in his arms to face him. Her eyes were almost unfocused, her cheeks pink, her mouth open slightly. "Yes?" he asked, nuzzling her neck. It smelled sweet; her hair tickled his cheek.

"Oh, Nick," she breathed.

"You already said that," he noted before kissing her thoroughly, unhurriedly, feeling her begin to breathe faster, to gasp.

He'd better stop or else things would go too far. They couldn't spend all day in the sack.

Gently, he held her at arm's length. Her eyes were glazed, her chest rose and fell quickly. He knew his voice was shaky as he gave a short laugh and said, "Enough of that stuff . . . for now. We'd both starve to death in here and not give a damn."

Alethea laughed weakly, glancing up at him through a veil of dark lashes. "I'm sorry if I'm too . . . forward. It's just that I've never felt this before. It seems to take over . . . everything."

"I know," he said soberly, "and you're not too forward, not a bit." He put a finger under her chin, lifted her face up to meet his. "You're just right. Perfect, in fact." Then, briskly, "Now let's get dressed and go to this Maison place and see if the opposition's opinion is worth anything."

They asked the woman at the desk how to get to La Maison du Paysan. It was a few kilometers out of town, she explained, then kissed her fingers in a typical Gallic gesture.

It was indeed a *maison,* an old fieldstone country house that had been made over into a restaurant: dark beams festooned with braids of garlic and bunches of herbs, checked tablecloths. All very rustic, full of charm. Nick held Alethea's hand as they were led to their table. The place was nearly empty at this early hour and they were seated in a discreet corner. Had they been put there because they looked like newlyweds? he wondered. Amazing.

The menu was formidable but Alethea knew her way through it like the pro she was. She ended up ordering *gigot d'agneau en croûte,* leg of lamb in a pastry crust stuffed with kidneys, mushrooms, *foie gras*, truffles and armagnac, and *gratin dauphinois à la crème*, potatoes in cream and parmesan cheese. Nick decided on *langouste*, crayfish, in a cheese sauce, and *petits pois provençales*, a vegetable dish, and chantilly cream cake topped with grilled hazelnuts for dessert. It all sounded delicious.

Perhaps they didn't notice the length of time it took for their food to come because they were talking or gazing out the window at the misty, darkening hills, quite lacking in the scorching, hellish sun of summer in Provence.

Suddenly, Alethea frowned. "What time is it?"

"Seven."

"And we've been sitting here for forty-five minutes, haven't we? That's lousy. I'll remember that."

"Compulsive workaholism," he said, mock-seriously. "A debilitating disease, gets progressively worse. The only cure is getting pregnant, retirement or a vacation."

"Sorry," she said sheepishly. "I can't help it. Ignore me."

"That isn't easy," Nick said to her, raising one dark brow.

"Oh, Nick." He loved the way she flushed, lowered her thick fringe of lashes, smiled shyly.

The food arrived on gleaming silver trays, served with an artistic flourish. The wine steward was correctly pompous. He suggested a local rosé, a Lirac, which he said was bottled in the hills a few miles west of Avignon. Nick noticed Alethea begin to make a face.

"Come on," he said, "let's try it for a change. It might be interesting. Remember, you're not on the job this time."

They dove into the fare. The crayfish was rich, the sauce terrific. Nick was enjoying himself thoroughly. Alethea's expression became vaguely distracted, he noticed. "Anything wrong?" he asked, sucking on a tiny claw.

"The lamb's overcooked and the kidneys are too strong. They weren't soaked in brine long enough." Her brows drew together. "And I could swear the potatoes are old."

"Unforgivable!" He smiled.

"Nick. This place costs an arm and a leg! Old potatoes, for goodness sakes!"

"Okay. Here, try mine. It's great." He piled a whole crayfish on her plate.

She tasted it, chewed carefully, considered a moment. "Frozen."

"Shocking!"

Alethea threw him an impatient frown. "How could they have said all those great things about this place? It's mediocre, that's all. I'll have to tell Alan—"

"Who?"

"Alan Dunbar, my editor. He'll love it. Maybe I can write a little paragraph or so in my column, sort of an aside. You know, 'by the way, I just happened to be passing by.'"

"I think it's great food."

"It is *not* great. It *is* all right. I've had better in a lot of places."

"Athens, for instance?"

She shot him a quick, laughter-filled glance. "Yes, definitely in Athens."

"The wine is good," Nick offered.

"Yes, it is."

"Ah, we agree on something."

"Oh, I'm spoiling your dinner," Alethea said suddenly. "I'm sorry."

"Not a bit. I'll eat your lamb if you don't like it. It smells divine."

They drove back to the hotel slowly, as mist filled the valleys and dips in the road. Everything had a ghostly, silent look until they drove onto the city streets. Even there, the lights had halos of tiny water droplets around them that hung in the air. The cobblestone streets were empty even though it was still early, although the cafés were well lit and full of people, their glowing windows steamy and opaque.

Nick felt restless when they got back to their room. Alethea had borrowed an iron from the lady at the desk and proceeded to press her clothes and wash some things out in the sink. Nick felt definitely superfluous and a little uncomfortable in the face of such intrepid female behavior.

"Mind if I take a walk?" he asked.

"Why?" Her head shot up, her face was scared and white again. Damn! He hadn't wanted to do that.

"Just routine. Keep the room locked. I hate open doors," he said, trying to sound reassuring. "It's a thing with me."

"Where are you going?" Alethea asked, and he knew she was worried but trying to hide it.

"Just for a walk. Maybe I'll stop in a café for a little while."

"How long?"

"Look, I'll only be gone an hour at the most. I promise. And I always keep my promises, don't I?"

"Yes." She sounded subdued. "Well, at least you trust me not to run away." She tried to smile.

"Implicitly. I'll even leave the car keys." Negligently, Nick flung them onto the dresser, walked over to her, gave her a chaste kiss on the forehead. "I'll be back before you know it."

The street was misty and cool, caressing his face with damp fingers. It was nice to get away from the girl for a while, to get his thoughts in order, see where he was going clearly without the smokescreen of her attraction to confuse him. She muddled his brain. Women! Now he knew why Porter wasn't in the field anymore. You couldn't do it and worry about a wife and kid at the same time. He'd always been able to separate work and play before. Now he was not so sure.

He should, by all rights, have been racing down to Ravello to get the papers back to Porter as soon as possible. But he wasn't. Nick wasn't certain why he had lied to Porter on the phone about their destination. He was clear about his priorities. The United States needed the papers and would use them more fairly than anyone else. Right? He was only doing his job. But the thought didn't convince him this time; the words were stale by now. What about Alethea's father and what *he'd* wanted? Dr. Holmes had been willing to die for *his* beliefs. What about Alethea herself?

Well, he still had time. That's what all this procrastinating was about—to put off the inevitable, to buy time before making the final decision. He wouldn't think about that now though. He still had a few days left to enjoy her trust, to enjoy *her*.

Automatically, he checked the street for Akmet's car, the black Citroën that Nick had seen in Paris the morning they left. He'd waited until Suliman's partner got out of the car that morning, looking sick as hell, probably from that blow on the head, and then he'd left with Alethea quickly, before the man could return. Akmet either had to follow them alone or lose them.

He'd followed.

Somehow Nick had known he would, had even wanted him to.

Yes, there it was—the Citroën, parked around the corner from the hotel. He couldn't tell if it was occupied or not. It was dark and the only streetlight glared off the wet windshield.

Nick strolled down the street, looking for that café on the next block that he'd noticed earlier. It had looked warm and inviting—full of men—a relaxing change from the unaccustomed strain of dealing with the feminine mind. He walked in. The place exuded comfort—the curved wooden bar where men stood to drink their quick coffees or anisettes, the round tables, the smoke, heavy and stronger than American cigarette smoke, the middle-class Frenchmen in their bulky sweaters, vests, wool jackets that never looked like American permanent-press clothes, even when new.

Then his trained eye noticed the man sitting at the corner table by the window. There was something about him . . . Casually, Nick walked to the end of the bar, leaned against the smooth wood, turned slowly.

Yes. It was Akmet. He was sitting with a brandy snifter in front of him, hunched over, his attention focused in the middle distance between the back wall and his table. He looked tired, even ill, his goatee unkempt, his once-impeccable clothes wrinkled as if he'd slept in them, which he probably had, thought Nick. How long could the wounded man keep this up?

A glow of power, of danger, and the need for a thrill shot through Nick. He'd never actually seen Akmet face to face, never spoken to him. Nick suddenly very much wanted to *know* the man. He was sick of watching him from a distance, through windows, in rearview mirrors. He craved confrontation. And he wanted to know what it was that Alethea had found attractive enough about this man to spend time with him.

Slowly, deliberately, savoring the anticipation, Nick walked over to Suliman's table, stood for a second as the man looked up, startled, then slid easily into the chair opposite his.

Akmet straightened up, seemingly with a struggle. He was a handsome man—typical Arab type. But now his eyes were bloodshot, his normally olive complexion flushed as if from a fever.

"Ah, the American agent," he said finally, smiling, showing even white teeth, flicking the ash from his Gauloise carelessly.

"Nick DeWolff, at your service." He held out a hand.

Akmet took his hand, moving his arm stiffly, as if it hurt. Nick noticed how warm it felt. "A worthy opponent." The thin lip curled a little. "Is this the honor of the battlefield being enacted here?"

"Sure, why not?" Nick leaned back in the chair, stretched his legs out in front of him negligently. In reality, every muscle and nerve in his body was revved up, waiting in neutral for the touch of the gas pedal.

"And where is the girl? I will try to resist the urge to call her our . . . common property." Akmet shook another Gauloise out of a gold case, lit it with an awkward movement of his right arm, drew in the smoke through flared nostrils.

Nick saw the man's face through a red haze of fury. "It's none of your business where she is. She's safe under my protection, and she's taking me to her father's papers." His voice was low, as hard and dangerous as the blade of a knife.

"And I don't suppose you'd care to tell me exactly where they are and end this farce?" asked Akmet, deliberately blowing a stream of smoke from his nostrils.

"No," Nick said tightly, angry at himself for rising to the bait so obviously thrown at him. He couldn't let Akmet rattle him. Control was the thing. "Keep following if you choose but I want to let you know one thing. When I get the papers—and I will get them—no one, I repeat *no one* will get them away from me. Anyone who stands in my way will be eliminated. I've done it before and I'm very good at it."

Suliman sipped at his brandy, his large dark eyes never leaving Nick's, then he put the glass down. "And the girl, too, will be eliminated if she, as you say, stands in your way?"

Nick shot him a wary glance, not answering the question. How much did the man know? Just what had Alethea told him in Paris, or under the drug? "Look, Akmet, I know you're hurt. You're alone. Why not give up, back off. You've given it the old college-try. I've won. You may as well admit it now. Get yourself to a hospital."

Suliman shrugged. "The wound is a mere nuisance. I, also, do not give up, Mr. DeWolff. So let us continue our little game. Your move next."

"All right. Have it your way. And now, if you'll excuse me, I'll return to my hotel and get a good night's sleep," he said pointedly, realizing how childish he was being, filling his words with double meanings as if it were a personal battle between Akmet and himself. A battle not so much over the papers but over a woman—an age-old rivalry, and to the victor belonged the spoils.

He stood, nodded to Suliman and left the bar. When the cool air outside touched his face, Nick realized that he was as tense as a coiled cobra. He forced himself to calm down, to relax. Then Suliman's words returned to him: "common property" he had called her. Of course, he had just been trying to get Nick mad, at which he'd succeeded admirably. Nick admitted to himself that he would have done the same thing. But was there any truth to it? There could be. He thought he knew Alethea, but maybe he didn't, really. She'd had plenty of opportunites in Abjala, even in Paris. And there was the way he'd found her in that farmhouse—nude. She'd never explained that at all, had avoided the subject like the plague. He'd just have to put that all out of his mind entirely. It had no bearing on this case. It only confused matters.

The shower was going when Nick let himself into the room. Suddenly, he had an overwhelming urge to touch Alethea, to try to feel the truth by holding her close to him. He needed to possess her body in a way that Akmet could not. Silently, he moved toward the half-open bathroom door, shedding his clothes as he went. He felt as if he would burst if he didn't hold her body in his arms in a second. He pushed aside the shower curtain.

"Nick!" Alethea cried. "You scared me!" Her eyes were wide.

The water streamed off her hair, her breasts, her round hips, down to the softly furred triangle between her legs. She looked at him, only surprised now; then, gradually, her eyes took on that glazed look as she saw his naked body. She reached out a hand, drew him into the shower.

He kissed her wet face, her mouth, then her neck and breasts. The water hissed and streamed off his back. She was slippery and warm and glistening. Slowly, he moved his mouth over her, sinking to his knees as his lips reached lower, moving down across her stomach, then lower still.

"Nick," he heard her say, as if from a great distance. "I'm not sure . . ."

"I am," he said, and found the place that made her moan and writhe. He felt good then, as if he had some kind of power over her. Her whole body shuddered and he rose to his feet, took her in his arms and leaned her up against the wall of the shower.

Now she was his, all his, and he took her ruthlessly, almost savagely, with the hot water of the shower cascading down their steaming bodies.

Chapter 31

Thursday, December 22

Alethea rubbed the steam away from the bathroom mirror with a hand towel, revealing her red-splotched cheeks, and her lips, swollen and bruised from Nick's demanding kisses. In the adjoining bedroom, he was sitting in a chair, a towel wrapped around his waist, staring out the window into the inky-black, wet night.

What had come over him just minutes ago in the shower? His almost brutal lovemaking had left her satisfied but somehow afraid of him. This was a side of Nick she had never witnessed and she sensed that his apparent anger had something to do with the walk he had taken earlier.

She slipped into a sheer, shell-pink, sleeveless nightgown which accentuated her high, rounded breasts. As she drew the gown down over her waist, she could see red marks on her hips from Nick's fingers. A tremor of fear shot through her—why had he treated her so cruelly?

Alethea slipped into bed silently. Nick seemed not to notice; or if he did, he certainly didn't care.

She was still awake an hour later when she felt his side of the bed sag, and then his naked body was next to her but not touching.

Alethea turned her head and saw his profile outlined in the darkness. "Is something wrong?" she managed to ask.

"No."

"Nick . . ." she began again, "I know something's bothering you. You've never treated me . . . well, the way you did in the shower. Have I done something . . . ?"

He turned to look at her then, propping himself up on an elbow. "I'm sorry about that, Alethea. Did I hurt you?" A gentle finger traced the ridge of her nose, but she could still feel his tenseness in spite of the tender touch.

"I'm all right, Nick . . . really."

Slowly, Nick kissed her in apology but she held back, wary of his mood. Eventually, and with infinite care, he took her again, and Alethea finally responded to his tenderness, reaching a height of passion which left her weak and breathless. And again, sometime just after dawn, when the small room was bathed in a pearly pink, Nick kissed her awake and entered her quickly, holding her body to his with urgency, driving himself into her flesh until she gasped and cried for release.

There was a power he held over her when they were making love, yet Alethea sensed Nick was still troubled. There was a new facet to the way he reacted toward her that she couldn't quite put her finger on. As she lay on her back waiting for the sun to rise, she knew, however, that their relationship really didn't matter in the long run. What *did* matter were the papers. And for the present, she would have to play along with him at any cost.

Nick took his eyes off of the road ahead for a moment and caught the embarrassed look on her face.

"Is there, well . . . I don't mean to pry," Alethea hesitated, "but is there someone back home you'll miss on Christmas?" she finished quickly.

He laughed. "Sure. Everyone I know will miss me."

"Oh! You're infuriating, Nick. Don't play games with me!" She flipped down the visor and began to check her hair in the mirror.

"Who's playing games?" he retorted. "Why don't you just come right out and ask me."

"What?"

"Ask me if I have a girlfriend." His eyes crinkled along familiar laugh lines.

"Well . . . do you?"

For a long, maddening moment he didn't answer. It was kind of fun to have the upper hand on Alethea for once. Let her stew.

"Nick. Don't tease me."

"I've got six steady women and twenty-seven illegitimate children."

Alethea shoved the visor back up and folded her arms tightly in irritation. "You just can't be serious, can you? Well, I don't really give a damn if you have a girlfriend or not," she spat. "And if you do . . . I pity the poor woman! And another thing," she went on quickly. "why are you driving so damn slow? We haven't got forever to get to Ravello. Maybe *I* might want to be back in New York by Christmas. I happen to have someone waiting there for me."

Casting her a sidelong glance of amusement, Nick let his laughter tumble out. Sure she had someone waiting. Like hell. He'd read the diary . . . Now he couldn't resist turning her words back on her. "Too bad there's someone waiting. I'm pretty much alone—not seeing anyone special—and I was going to ask you to spend Christmas with me. But if you've got other plans . . ."

"You bastard!"

"You love it, Alethea. Admit it. A day without a challenge for you isn't worth living."

"That's not true," she defended herself. "I don't want any more challenges for the rest of my life! I'd like to just sit back on a front porch in a rocker right now."

He quirked a dark brow. "Really?"

"Yes. I mean it. I'd give anything to have this burden taken off my shoulders—anything. Oh, what I wouldn't do for a day's rest!"

Nick concentrated on his driving. They weren't even in Cannes yet. She had been right. He was taking his time. And for all the reasons he'd gone over in his head so many times in the last few days that they swirled around his brain incessantly like so many ugly, black, croaking ravens. But he couldn't tell her all that. It was his problem.

Then, too, there was still Suliman Akmet.

At first, after leaving Paris, he had made it easy for Akmet to follow. Nick had planned to drive far out into the French countryside and rid himself of the Arab once and for all. But then that had seemed almost too easy—unsatisfying—and Nick had kept driving slowly down toward the French coast, letting Akmet follow them closely. And what was unbelievable was that Alethea didn't even know he was behind them. For all she knew, Suliman Akmet was still back at the farmhouse.

Nick had admitted to himself yesterday, finally, why he didn't simply do away with Akmet. It was really uncomplicated. It was because he wanted to savor the moment . . . to draw out the pleasurable anticipation as long as possible. Plainly and simply, Nick was jealous as hell—bent on killing Akmet for what he suspected the Arab had done to Alethea in that dim little room. It was not hard to admit. Nick was falling more and more in love with the girl. It was impossible not to. And he wasn't exactly pleased with himself for letting it happen. After all, it had been a deceitful affair on both parts from that first time in Paris when they had slept together, each to gain their own selfish end. But then again, did it really matter? When they got to Ravello, he knew it would be over between them. It had to be. She could never accept his job, the fact that he would turn the papers over to Porter. That alone would destroy any feelings she had for him. And he couldn't blame her.

"Nick."

"Yeah?"

"Are you angry at me? I mean, well, you know, about asking you personal questions?"

"Nope."

"Then why so quiet?"

"No reason. Just enjoying the drive. It's been years since I was last here. I like this part of France. Remember how dreary it was in Paris?"

She sighed. "I sure do. I hate winters there. In New York, too, though."

"You know, that's funny . . . I just remembered something. Back in New York, before I got to your apartment, I was wondering why you didn't live somewhere sunny."

"That's really weird. I ask myself that all the time, too. I've often thought of moving to a warmer climate. I'd love to live in the Bahamas or the Caribbean. Did I say something funny?"

Nick was smiling, remembering the dream he was having the morning in Paris she'd run away. "Funnier than you know."

"Tell me."

"You'll smack me."

"No, I won't." She giggled. "Oh, come on, tell me . . ."

"I had a dream about us." He glanced at her face and couldn't resist revealing the rest. "It was the morning Akmet nabbed you. You'd left the water running . . . We were on a Caribbean beach. I was undressing you."

"Oh," she commented pensively, a bit embarrassed. "And I liked it?"

Nick grinned wolfishly. "You adored it."

On an impulse, thinking what a laugh it would be to see Akmet's face when he did it, Nick stopped the Saab on the far side of a bridge over a deep gully. It was a beautiful spot, ideal for what he had in mind.

"What are you doing?" Alethea asked.

"I'm stopping the car. We're going to get out, walk back to the edge of the ravine, take a quick look at the splashing river below, the blue perfect sky, the tiny, chirping birds."

"I don't see why—"

"And then I'm going to take you in my arms and kiss you. Don't ask why. I just feel like it. Okay?" He pulled on the parking brake.

"Well . . . okay."

He took her hand and led her back, across a stony path, to the bridge. The sun felt fantastic on his shoulders. It highlighted Alethea's hair to a wonderful golden color, reminding him of Kansas wheat in August. While they stood, breathing in the fresh country air, he couldn't help reaching out and touching the windswept curls, crushing them under his fingers.

Alethea turned her face up to his. Her lips parted irresistibly. The sun lit her skin a glowing pearl color. He brought his mouth tenderly down onto hers, covering her lips lightly at first and then more urgently, demandingly, while his arms came around her waist and carried her up to meet him.

Her response was instant. She locked her arms around his neck and met violent kiss with violent kiss until he felt her lean weakly against him, ready to fall on the sun-warmed earth beneath him.

Suddenly, Nick tore his mouth away. Her eyes flew open questioningly. "Nick . . ."

His breathing was ragged. "Tell me, I know the last couple of times we slept together things were good, but . . . honestly, no lying, did you fake it back in Paris?"

"What?" The word exploded from her lips. She tried to pull away.

Nick grabbed her arm roughly, spinning her back to face him. "Answer me, goddammit! I want to know."

Defiantly, hurt and ashamed, she finally whispered, "No. I didn't. For me . . . it was the first time I'd ever felt anything. You can think I'm lying. I don't care. Leaving you that morning was . . . was . . ."

Before she could finish the sentence, Nick kissed her again, feeling foolish, knowing now how much more difficult it would be to deceive her.

He ended the long kiss gently this time and held her at arm's length. "We'd better go."

If his behavior confused her, she wasn't saying so. Alethea followed him back to the car with a blank look on her face.

Once back on the highway, Nick finally spoke. "I was an idiot to ask you that. You shouldn't have answered."

"Oh, Nick," she cried, "stop it! Stop being so damned unreachable! So cold! I'm glad you asked. I wanted you to know and I didn't think, until back at that bridge, that you even cared!"

The whole damn thing between them was getting too far out of hand. But could he, did he want to, stop it? Under any other circumstances, another time, another place, she would be the one. He knew that now. It hurt . . . hurt all the way down in the pit of his stomach to know what he had to do, to know that he'd probably lie to her, tell her he'd help her make the discovery available to the whole damned world if necessary, anything to get those papers in his hot little hand.

He should stop torturing himself, Nick thought silently—steel himself. It wasn't all that bad. There were other women, other fish in the sea. It was purely physical with Alethea, just electricity. That's all it was. Love was for decent people, the ones that could allow happiness to come into their drab lives. For now, if he was strong, he could simply stretch out the days and let a little happiness touch him for a moment—forget all else, forget what a lying bastard he would have to be to finish this rotten job.

Nick drove on into Cannes in silence. Alethea, obviously trying to cheer him out of this dark mood, made light conversation about the scenery, the milky-blue Mediterranean, the pastel houses dotting the hillsides, the quaint outdoor cafés and intimate, cozy restaurants she'd written about. Nick barely heard her. He didn't want to.

When he took a sharp left onto a side street off the waterfront, next to a hotel with wrought-iron balconies, she asked, "What are we doing now? I'd say, in this mood of yours, we may as well keep driving and—"

"Look, Alethea," he barked harshly, "let me do the thinking, okay?"

"Whatever you say," she replied, mock-sweetly.

But the undisturbed front she was trying to display fell apart once they were inside the hotel lobby when Nick hired two rooms for the night instead of one.

Immediately, when they were away from the desk, she snapped, "Why? Why two rooms?"

Nick felt her confused pain as if it were his own. Dammitall, he didn't really know why himself! Maybe it was because he liked her too much to deceive her so miserably. Maybe she wasn't the kind to be used. Maybe he was just a heel. How the hell did he know? Nothing seemed the same since meeting her. All his values were topsy-turvy now, thrown out into the harsh light, needing badly to be examined.

They reached the top of the narrow steps. He felt Alethea's hand on his arm. "Nick, please . . . let me help you . . . open up to me! Don't close me out this way."

He turned around to face her. The hall was close, dark. He could almost feel her breath on him, smell the light fragrance of her hair. He could let himself get close to her if he wanted to, but the distance loomed between them—vast, limitless.

He put her key in the lock and swung her door open while he remained in the hall.

"Nick?" she whispered.

"Look. I don't feel like talking right now. Drop it, will you? I'll knock on your door in an hour. We'll have dinner. And don't answer a knock unless it's me. I'll be right next door if you need anything."

Alethea went into the room, tossing her bag roughly onto the single bed, her eyes flashing anger. She spun on him. "I *won't* be needing anything. And I'll take my dinner alone, if you don't mind!"

Nick didn't know what to say or do. She walked purposefully to her door and slammed it in his face. The wind that was pushed in front of the door struck him hotly, the sound reverberating in his ears. An ugly sound.

He went to his own room and lay down on the old creaking bed. The room smelled humid, musty, and the yellow-flowered wallpaper was faded and peeling. It suited his mood just fine. It made him feel sick and disgusted and alone.

Chapter 32

Friday, December 23

They'd driven all day through the fairyland scenery of the French Riviera, then into the subtle distinctness of the Italian coast, coming back to reality only when they hit the smoggy industry and dock area of Genoa.

Nick had been strangely quiet all day, making Alethea uncomfortable, causing her to withdraw into herself after a few unsuccessful attempts at casual conversation. If she cared to glance over at him, all she could see was his now-familiar profile: the forehead covered with a wave of dark hair, the slightly crooked nose, the strong, clean line of his jaw, the shadow of his eyelashes on his cheek.

She knew he was thinking a lot, thought it very well might be about what he'd do when they reached Ravello. Or maybe she was assuming too much. Maybe he wasn't the least bit worried about what he'd do. Maybe she was flattering herself, thinking she'd got to him.

How could Nick be so hard, so withdrawn now? It was difficult to picture the flashing boyish smile on those grim features, or imagine his tenderness toward her.

And why in hell was he dawdling, dragging his feet—a late start, a long lunch stop. Why, they could have been there already!

Could it be, she asked herself tentatively, that he didn't want to get there, *dreaded* facing the decision that he must make? Was he feeling guilty, knowing he'd betray her? Or could it be that he was dragging it out so that their relationship didn't come to a quick, dismal end? She was only kidding herself, Alethea laughed silently. He was a man with a job to do, trained, professional, and he'd do it.

And that will be the end of us, she thought. A quick, deadly blow. Maybe it was better that way, cleaner. Alethea knew she could never accept his betrayal of her . . . and her father. It was so important, so vital . . . to her, to the world, to the future. Couldn't he see that?

Maybe she should try to get away from him somehow, get to Ravello first—her original plan. But the chill hand of fear closed on her heart when she thought of running again, alone, unprotected. No, she couldn't do it. Anyone could be out there, waiting for her, like last time. She gave a little involuntary shudder.

"Cold?" Nick asked.

"No," she said quickly. "No, it's beautiful here."

"Well, I'm glad you like it, because we're stopping in a little while. Portofino's coming up. Cute place."

"So soon? It's still light. We could go another hundred miles."

"We're stopping," he said harshly, then fell silent, his face set in grim lines again.

She sighed. He was probably still angry after she'd slammed the door in his face last night. Well, he'd deserved worse, but it hadn't really been worth it. She'd lain in bed, burning with fury, then with a yearning for a hard, male body next to her. Nick's body. She'd been so restless she couldn't sleep. Finally, she had risen to stand at the window, watching the long, gracefully curved line of the shore, spangled with a necklace of lights as it swept to the horizon. This was not a place to be alone. Even in December, it was a place you'd take a holiday . . . with someone you loved.

They were pulling up at a conveniently located *pensione*. She noticed that Nick preferred a certain kind of hotel: not too large, so he could keep an eye on the guests, a clear, open square in front, a back entrance. He was just being professional, she guessed. It was routine.

The white stucco buildings stepped up the hills behind the town in gentle, Mediterranean order. A promenade followed the shore, spiky palm trees lining it. There was a little shop across the street advertising *gelati*, ice cream. It looked so peaceful.

Wordlessly, she followed Nick into the hotel, arriving at the desk in time to hear him requesting two rooms. Was he too proud to back down until she begged him? Or had he just plain lost interest in her? Alethea did not know what had happened between them. She was totally confused as to whether she'd done something wrong or if it was completely his doing.

This time she refused to eat alone. When he hesitatingly started to ask her to meet him downstairs in the dining room, she quickly agreed, trying to ignore his apparent coldness.

The dinner was extremely mediocre. Nick pushed his half-eaten, leathery *biftec* away finally and ordered a brandy. Funny, he hadn't had anything but a glass of wine up to now. Alethea couldn't bear the way he avoided her eyes, sipping glumly on the sweet-smelling drink.

"Nick."

"Yeah?"

"What's the matter?" She tried to keep her voice level, reasonable.

His deep blue eyes met hers, and she saw what they held—pain, questions, anger—all mixed up, each vying for ascendancy, each losing.

"You," he said roughly, softly, almost a growl. "You're the matter. You damn stupid kid, you shouldn't have come along. They could have sent someone else to pick the stuff up. Haven't you caused enough trouble?"

Alethea refused to back down, stung that he'd called her a kid. "If you ask me, I've been a lot more mature than you were today. You've been sulking like a baby. Listen, you creep, I've got more at stake in this wild goose chase than you have. Who in hell do you think you are? I'm a free citizen of the United States and you have some nerve to push me around, insult me. I don't care whom you work for!" She felt her cheeks grow hot, her voice rising. God! He made her so mad.

"You look beautiful when you're angry," Nick said incongruously, suddenly smiling at her, teasingly.

"Oh, shut up!"

"It's true."

"Nick!"

251

"I guess I need to be yelled at to put me in a better mood, mellow me out a little." He was still smiling. "There aren't too many women who've dared to. Could be what I've been lacking all these years."

Alethea rose, exasperated, and turned to leave the table. She wasn't about to stay there if he couldn't be honest with her, not for a second! She walked quickly up the stairs toward her room, her back stiff, her heart pounding, wondering whether he was following, wondering whether she even wanted him to follow, knowing deep inside that she did.

And then she felt his hand on her arm, his brandy-sweet breath tickling her ear.

"I'm sorry," he said. "See, now it's my turn to apologize. Shall we see if it gets us into as much trouble as when you apologize?"

Nick took both her hands and held them, looking at her for a long moment in the hallway until she felt like squirming under his scrutiny.

"What are you staring at?" she asked finally, her voice much softer than she'd meant it to be.

"You."

"Oh, Nick . . ." She couldn't help herself; all he had to do was say the word, and she knew she'd be in his arms. It didn't matter that he'd been deliberately distant for a whole day. All he had to do was smile once, relent a tiny bit, and she melted, like there were no bones in her body, like there was nothing but molten desire filling her skin.

He kissed her long and thoroughly, then stopped and gazed at her again. "I can't get enough of looking at you," he said, as if in wonder. Then, in a brisker tone, "Will you be insulted if we use my room instead of yours?"

Alethea couldn't pretend. She wanted him as much as he wanted her. And she felt no prudishness, no shame with him. Oh, how she loved the feel of him, the long, lean muscles, the jutting hip bones, the strong tendons of his neck, his lovely flanks and his thighs thickly covered with hairs. And the center of his glory— the wonderful, pulsating proof of his desire that brought her aching, exquisite relief. Oh, how trite, she thought fleetingly. She hadn't known it could be like this! She hadn't known!

Afterward, Alethea had to touch him with the entire length of her body, hold him, run a finger over the place where his nose had been broken.

"How did you get that?" she asked.

He kissed the hollow of her neck, tickling her. "If you must know, I got it in a brawl in La Grenouille Bar in Saigon. There was this big marine, and he was madder'n hell—"

"Why was he so mad?"

"I don't know. Big marines are always mad, aren't they?"

"Nick, really, tell me."

"Sorry, that's all there is to the story. It's true." He rose on an elbow and looked down at her, his eyes shadowed.

"Tell me all about it," she pleaded. "I want to know you. I can't believe you have a past. It seems you should only have started existing when I met you. How could you have lived all those years before . . . when I didn't know you?"

"It wasn't easy." He laughed, then she could see the lines in his face turn hard. "Oh, I have a past, all right," he said with sudden bitterness.

"Tell me, please. *Tell me,*" she urged. "Everything you did made you what you are now, don't you see? I want to know, Nick."

He watched Alethea in silence for a time, then sagged back onto the bed and put an arm over his eyes. "Oh, yes, it made me what I am now, all right. The betrayals, the killing, the burning. Did you ever see what napalm does to the skin? Like a chicken on a grill too close to the charcoal. The jungle is full of bugs, disease. Nice a place as any to fight a war, I guess. Men's bodies blown apart—friends." He paused.

"Nick, I'm sorry . . ."

"And the funny thing is, the whole thing was a waste of time. There was no reason. It was all a big waste." He turned on her, almost brutally. "You wanted to know, didn't you? Do you like it? It isn't pretty, is it?"

"No," she whispered, "but maybe it'll help if you talk about it."

"Help! That's a laugh. It didn't help the ones who died—shot to pieces, mangled, roasted, poisoned. It didn't help Mei Ling—" Nick stopped abruptly, filling the room with the sound of his ragged breathing.

"Who was Mei Ling?" She was almost afraid to ask, he sounded so tortured.

"A girl," he said finally. "A beautiful Vietnamese girl, gently bred, educated, went to a convent school run by French nuns."

He stopped for so long that Alethea thought he was done. She held her breath. But he began again, slowly. "She loved me, I thought I loved her. I was young in those days, thought it could work, that we'd marry, go back to Philly, have kids, live happily ever after. What a joke!" He gave a short, bitter laugh.

"The Viet Cong got her, said she was a traitor, hanging around so much with an American soldier. Her lousy *uncle* turned her in! They tortured her. She died. An old story. It happened to a lot of them, the innocent ones. I was away, some useless mission. When I got back, her mother came and told me. It was too late . . ."

He was silent for so long then, Alethea thought he'd fallen asleep, but he hadn't. She turned, finally, to watch his face, wishing she could say something, anything, to help him, and she saw that his eyes were open, staring at the ceiling, reliving it all.

"Nick?"

He turned his head toward her; his eyes were desolate.

"Thank you for telling me. I'm glad you did."

"Thea," he said, inadvertently using her father's pet name, "Thea." He pulled her to him, holding her tightly, and she tried to will some of her happiness into him.

He seemed calmer after that, and even told her a little more about his family, his father—"old iron pants"—his sweet, ineffectual mother.

"My job is getting a bit old," he said later. "This cloak-and-dagger routine is wearing on the nerves. I think I'm outgrowing it." He looked down at her in the darkness and smiled. "I'm only a kid, after all. I still have to mature a little, don't I? Maybe I'll turn to law eventually, who knows? It's not a bad profession."

Then, finally, she watched him sleep. He *was* beautiful. Wounded inside, perhaps, but he could be made whole again, with understanding, with love.

Love? Did she *love* him—this stranger, this agent, sent by an impersonal government agency to "bring her in"? Did she actually *love* him?

Would she love him when they got to Ravello, when he took the papers from her to send to the United States government, where bureaucrats would use her father's secrets for their own greedy ends? How could her love exist after that?

Did she love him? she asked herself again.

Oh, God, I hope not, Alethea thought. I hope not.

Chapter 33

Saturday, December 24

Once they were through the Amalfi traffic, the road narrowed perceptibly as it followed the contours of the ravine that led to Ravello. Nick steered the Saab expertly around the dangerously curved mountain road. It was only a mile or so up from the sea, up a lush green valley, before they would reach the small village. Alethea clearly remembered the quaint Italian resort town as if it were only yesterday that she'd holidayed there with her parents. Even before the car rolled into the cobblestoned square, she could picture the bright white stucco buildings and shops with their red-tiled roofs and vine-covered walls. Even the blue-tiled fountain in the center of Ravello's square was pleasantly implanted in her memory.

And then they were there, at last, in Ravello, parking the car in a narrow, dirt alleyway next to the Hotel di Salerno, which sat facing the town square. There weren't very many people around. It was midday. Perhaps they were a mile below the hillside town, sunning themselves on the pebbly Mediterranean beach. Alethea couldn't help but be glad to be away from the dismal cold of northern Europe. This was the place to spend winter—in an out-of-the-way town that painted its buildings and flower boxes yearly and smelled of pristine, salty air.

Climbing out of the car and stretching her legs, she commented to Nick, "Don't you just love it here? I wish we never had to leave . . ." But then she turned and saw a dark look cover his features. She wished she hadn't brought up the subject of leaving. It wasn't over yet . . .

"It is wonderful," Nick said, relenting. "Come on, let's see if we can get a room."

She smiled faintly as he came around the front of the car and placed a reassuring hand on her back, leading her into the hotel lobby.

Before approaching the desk, Alethea drew him aside, a bit embarrassed. "Let's get one room. To be honest, I don't want to be alone." She paused, then blurted it out. "It's Christmas Eve, you know."

He grinned broadly. "I almost forgot. In that case, only because you insist, one room it is!"

While Nick turned over their passports to the clerk and signed the register, Alethea walked back to the door and stared out over the sun-drenched square, remembering the small clothing shop across the way where her mother had purchased a ridiculous straw hat covered with plastic flowers. How they'd all laughed over the hat. It seemed just yesterday . . .

A Citroën pulled up in front of the shop, blocking her view, and parked. Alethea was about to turn away when something familiar about the driver struck her. As the figure stepped out of the vehicle, her brows knitted together.

"Suliman . . ." she whispered, her skin rising in bumps from the cold breath of fear.

Unconsciously, she backed away from the door, her feet dragging, her hand pressed to her mouth.

"Alethea?"

She jumped.

Nick touched her arm lightly. "What's wrong? You look as if you'd seen a ghost!"

"I have," she gasped, pointing a shaky finger out the window. "Look!"

He took a few steps toward the door, then returned to Alethea. "Let's get upstairs. Come on."

Once they were behind the door of their hotel room on the second floor, Nick surprisingly tossed the keys casually on the dresser and plunked himself into the single chair as if nothing had happened.

"How can you be so . . . so relaxed about this!" Alethea cried, pacing the room like a caged cat.

"Calm down. Akmet's been right behind us since Paris. No point getting hysterical."

"What? And you knew . . . You never let on!" She went to the window overlooking the square and drew the drapes together cautiously. The room was semidark now. She felt silly, foolish, acting like a cheap spy.

Nick laughed. "Hey, come on now, I'm not going to let him near you."

She tried smiling, too. It didn't work. "Oh, Nick," she sat nervously on the edge of the bed, "how can I get my father's notes with him here? What are we going to do?"

"We're not going to worry about Akmet until we've got the papers, and then, if he tries anything—"

"Of course he will! That's why he followed us all the way here!"

"I said, don't worry. I'll handle him." Nick leaned forward and clasped his hands in front of him, nonchalantly, between his legs. "Now. Let's get down to business. The papers, where are they, Alethea?"

She felt the blood rush to her head, pound in her ears. She looked down at her lap mutely. Nothing was turning out right. She hadn't expected to need Nick once he got her here but now, with Akmet outside, waiting, watching . . .

Then it struck her, like a bucket of cold water thrown in her face, that was precisely why Nick had let Akmet follow them— to make damn good and sure she still needed him for protection when she got the papers. Oh! Nick had it all planned, even down to the last detail—making love to keep her docile and unsuspecting. He was using her! God, why hadn't she seen it?

Without thinking, Alethea turned on him. "You bastard," she hissed. "You let me believe you actually cared! I thought . . . I thought by now maybe you'd have seen things my way, my father's way."

"I never said any such thing," Nick snapped quickly. "I have a job to do. You knew that all along. What the hell did you expect?"

"A little honesty." She flew to her feet, placing her hands on her hips in anger.

"Honesty? Were you honest when you used *me* to get you here, to keep Akmet off your back?" He rushed on, his face lined in rage now. "And don't tell me it was anything more. You used me as much as I did you."

"Like hell I did! Back in Paris, I told you exactly why I needed you to get to Ravello. I never lied! Never!"

Nick rose slowly to his feet. "Look. Maybe you're right. Maybe I haven't been as honest as you, *Saint* Alethea. Well, I'm no goddam saint, kid! And I'm not exactly enjoying this, either. I knew this was going to happen. Damn! You're just too vulnerable." He strode stiffly to the window and drew open the curtains. "Women don't belong in this sort of life. They can't handle it."

Tears were burning her eyes. It was so bitterly plain now. It was always his job; even the romance, the sexual attraction, that was part of it, too. And all along, she had known it deep down inside. She should not have let him affect her, get near her. Even his expert lovemaking was so well played out. They were on a stage—the play was over—it had all been a game, and now they would smile, take their bows for a great performance and go their separate ways. End of show. Closed for the season. *La Commedia è finita.* Alethea sat on the bed, frozen, her cheeks flushed, her eyes hot and swollen with unshed tears.

Suddenly, she felt his hands on her shoulders, his face low over hers.

"Alethea. Listen to me. Please."

"No! I hate you! I hate your guts!"

"Hate me then. I can't stop you. But you *will* listen."

She glared her loathing up at him and fought back the tears. She wasn't going to cry over him anymore. It was bad enough falling apart in front of him like this. She had to stop right now. To hell with him!

"Ready to listen?"

"Yes," she said slowly, evenly now, coldly. "But get your hands off of me. I mean it, Nick, I don't want you to touch me again."

For the first time since they'd met, Alethea had the satisfaction of seeing *him* hurt—seeing him look as if a knife had been stuck in and twisted. Good.

He eased off the bed, rose and turned his back on her. "I don't blame you for feeling that way. Okay, I won't touch you again. We'll leave it like that. I just think you should know that it started out all wrong between us. We both used sex as a means to an end . . ."

He was right. It was such an ugly, ugly truth, but he was absolutely right.

"I'm really sorry it's come to this. I'm sorry about my job . . . I'm sorry about a thousand things lately, it seems."

"Oh, Nick . . ." She wanted so badly to reach out to him, to draw him tightly up against her. But she'd just told him not to touch her. Oh! Why did it have to be this way? Why was everything falling apart? Alethea took a deep breath. Everything depended on his reaction now. She had to make him understand. "Please. I'll tell you where the papers are. We could even go get them now, right now, if you won't give them to Porter. You don't have to! Surely you can see that. I just know I'm right. You know it, too, don't you? The whole world should have this knowledge. Oh, please, Nick?" She didn't let her eyes waver for a second, but held his gaze prisoner with hers.

He fell silent. What was he thinking, standing there with his profile so strong, so deep in concentration? And now, thought Alethea, he must make a decision. They'd come to the bitter impasse. She prayed he would do it her way.

The moments ticked by, endlessly long, pregnant, as he stared straight ahead like a statue. She couldn't bear another second.

"Nick."

He said nothing but his head turned toward her.

"If you'll read the papers and my father's letter, you'll see what I mean. You'll understand then. Promise me that you'll do that before you decide anything."

"Okay," he said slowly, his voice strangely distant. "I'll think about it seriously. I'll sleep on it."

"You'll see," Alethea said passionately, tears brimming in her eyes. "You'll believe me then."

Chapter 34

Sunday, December 25

Nick awakened to the sound of church bells tolling serenely over the square. It was Christmas. The chiming and clanging bells were marvelous, like something out of a medieval pageant. He felt sure that if he peered outside, he'd see ladies dressed in rich red silk gowns, their heads covered with wimples. The men would wear colorful velvet surcoats and long hose, and best of all would be the soldiers in their coats of chainmail. It would be wonderful! He stayed in bed. It would be no fun to look out on the square now.

Alethea rolled over, nestling snugly up against his naked body. Back to reality, he thought grimly. Back to the cold, painful decision he'd finally come to late last night. If he were strong enough to carry the lie through, she'd detest him forever. But, of course, none of that mattered now. His path was laid out clearly before him, had been since Porter first sent him to get the papers. Nothing had changed.

Nothing much, Nick thought miserably, just the simple fact that he'd fallen in love with the girl he was about to betray. He was about to kill their chance for happiness as surely as she lay there breathing softly against his chest.

Well, no point in putting it off. Might as well wake her up and get it done with. Now, how was he going to put it? Dearest Alethea, I've decided not to give the papers to Porter, I'll help you do whatever you want with them, trust me, I want you. That much at least was true, he thought.

"Hell," he whispered aloud.

She stirred then, murmuring in her sleep. "Nick?"

"I'm here," he replied quietly, wishing he faced a horde of screaming Zulu warriors, anything but this. Anything!

Slowly, he rolled over toward her; he brushed her hair gently out of her face. Oh, Alethea, he thought, don't hate me too much. It's my duty. I can't betray my government, even if your way is better. Don't you see that?

"Feels good," she whispered.

He bent his head and kissed her chastely on the cheek. And then, amazingly, he felt choked up inside, as if he were about to break down. Nick had broken before as a man; he saw no shame in it. There were times when he'd lost a friend, and then Mei Ling, when it had been the only outlet—cry or go crazy. Lots of them had wept back then. But not now. Self-pity was a poor reason. He breathed deeply for a few seconds, then rolled out of bed.

All at once, he remembered the present, the small Christmas gift he'd bought for Alethea back in Cannes. Would she think of him in the months to come when she dabbed the perfume on her wrists, behind her ears, in the cleavage of her breasts? Or would she hate him still?

Nick fetched the present out of his leather bag and went back over to the bed, placing it next to her on the lamp table.

Alethea must have heard him stirring, for she opened her eyes. When she saw the package, she moaned, threw a hand over her eyes and exclaimed, "It's Christmas! I forgot . . . Oh, Nick, I'm so sorry . . . I didn't think to get—"

"Hey, it's okay. Really. And it's nothing."

"Nick, you're so sweet . . . But I shouldn't. I'd feel guilty. I just can't accept it."

"Well, if you're sure." He reached for the gift teasingly, delighted when her eyes widened in surprise.

"Don't you dare, Nicholas DeWolff!" She snatched up the

package before he could playfully take it back. And then she ripped it open like a child. "Shalimar!" Her eyes flew up to meet his. "How did you know? I haven't worn any in weeks!"

"Easy. Stop looking at me as if I were a mind-reader. Back in New York, there was a broken bottle of it in your bathroom. That's all. The Arabs busted it in their search. The place smelled like hell, but I figured you liked the stuff."

"Well, I'll be," she said, smiling. "And you remembered."

Nick glanced over at her, but the amusement was gone from his face now, replaced by a new look, one of desire, longing. The bedsheet had fallen half off her body and he couldn't wrench his eyes away.

He knew she recognized the look on his features. He asked, "Want to?"

When he slipped back into bed next to her, a thought flashed across his mind: This was completely unfair to her—dead wrong—when afterward he would have to spring the lie on her. And even if he didn't, she would ask and he couldn't postpone it any longer.

Still, as he drew her yielding body under his own, he managed to put all thoughts away, all thoughts save one, that he wanted her. That they were entitled to have this much before he . . . Nick closed his eyes and began a rhythmic motion in her body, savoring each movement, each response of hers, as if it were the last. And, he knew, it *was* the last.

When they were done, exhausted and covered with a sweet sheen of perspiration, Nick propped his arms behind his head. He couldn't put off their talk any longer. It was a crime, a filthy, low-down crime to catch her at her weakest, after love, but what better time?

"I've been thinking about your father's wishes. Maybe he was right." He felt Alethea's body grow taut with suspense. He did not look her in the eye. He couldn't. "I've been wrong about the importance of the discovery. It does belong to the world, to mankind."

"Nick," she began hesitantly, "are you sure? I mean . . . what about Porter, your job?"

"My job's important, Alethea. But it hardly compares to something like your father's discovery, something that would benefit all humanity. Now does it?" God! He almost believed the lie himself! It did sound right . . . Forget it, man! Don't give in now! Stand up for your principles.

"Oh, Nick! Nick! Are you certain?" She pressed her body against him, wrapping her arms around him and covering him with kisses that seared his skin.

"I'm sure," he managed to mumble, feeling like he was going to have to throw her off him and run to the bathroom and vomit out his sickness.

Nick controlled his self-loathing and returned her embraces. This must be what hell is like, he thought, when you hate yourself so damn bad nothing else matters.

The church bells tolled again outside in the square and he squeezed his eyes shut and breathed deeply.

Finally, Alethea propped herself up over him, studying his face, her finger tracing a line over his whiskers.

"Guess I need a shave." He forced a laugh. Don't let her suspect now. "Then we'll go get the papers. By the way," he felt his heart pounding, "where are they?" It was said. Somehow he'd managed to get the words out.

For a long moment, she was silent. "You're sure? You won't . . . I hate to ask . . . I've got to know, Nick . . . You won't betray me?"

Her face seemed all eyes—large, trusting, imploring, gorgeous hazel eyes. They pinned him under their regard, and he felt sick and weak with disgust for what he was doing.

How could he keep up this lie? But he had to. There was no turning back. He steeled himself. "I told you I was sure. Don't you believe me?" Still, he couldn't meet her eyes; his stomach rolled over.

"Yes. I do believe you, Nick." There was assurance in her tone. "I mailed them to the Pensione Stella. It's not far from here, overlooks the sea. I spent a vacation there with Mom and Dad years ago. The people were so friendly. I even got a card last year from the woman who owns it. I knew she'd keep the papers safe and ask no questions."

"I see." He forced the words out calmly. "Well, let's get dressed and fetch them. That is, if they got there. Okay?" Sound casual.

"Yes." She rolled out of bed. "Nick?"

"Yeah?"

"What about Suliman? I mean, did you really let him follow so I'd need your protection?"

"Partly, I guess," he answered honestly. "But maybe I was a little jealous, too, wanted to string him along for a while."

His eyes met hers for a moment, then she looked down quickly at her hands. Alethea frowned. "So what about him now?"

"Don't worry. I have a feeling he might just hang himself."

"Well, I don't really understand, but I'll leave it to you."

Before they left the room, she said, "Wait a minute." She walked toward him, her heels clicking on the wooden floor.

"What?"

She came up to face him. "This." She kissed Nick then, a thorough, warm caress of her lips. Finally, she said, "I can't tell you how nice it feels to have you on my side—not to think of you as the enemy and all. It's so good to trust you, Nick."

That was the clincher—her statement of trust that he sure didn't need to hear. His guts felt like she had put a barbed knife in and wouldn't stop turning it. He couldn't talk.

And then Nick knew something. It came to him suddenly. As soon as he got back to Washington with those damned papers, he was going to hand in his resignation. He would never be a part of something like this again. He was through, finished. And all his years in the service of the United States had left him nothing, nothing but a permanent, bitter self-hatred that no time or distance could wash away.

He followed Alethea down the steps in silence, a grim, unreadable mask cloaking his features. If he could have looked in a mirror, he would have thought he'd ~d ten years in the space of an hour.

Chapter 35

Sunday, December 25

They were well out of Ravello, twisting along the tortuous, serpentine curves of the Amalfi Drive above the sparkling Mediterranean, when Alethea spotted Suliman's car.

"He's there . . . behind us," she gasped, unable to tear her eyes from the rear window.

Nick made no comment. Suddenly, she realized he hadn't spoken a single word since entering the Pensione Stella. How odd. Maybe he felt bad about his job, about Porter. That must be it.

Another question occurred to her then. "Where are we headed?"

Finally, he broke the strained silence. "Naples."

"Naples?" She thought a moment. "Why there?"

"There's an airport."

Why was he being so mysterious, so cool? "Are we flying somewhere?" she asked hesitantly. Maybe he knew, had decided, which world organization should receive the papers.

"Sure, we're flying somewhere," he answered dryly.

"Well, where? And what about Suliman?"

"Just sit back and relax, Alethea. Quit questioning me, for godsake. You're giving me the third degree," he snapped.

"Sorry." It was so unlike him to bark at her like this. What was wrong with him, anyway? It was as if he couldn't stand her presence, couldn't even look her directly in the eye. It was as if he were acting . . . guilty. But guilty about what? His job, the papers, shooting Suliman, or—the thought pounded in her brain— had he lied to her?

She shot him a quizzical sidelong glance. His face was twisted, as if in pain. Alethea glanced down at the manila envelope lying between their seats. She knew then, intuitively, it was too obvious to miss.

He *had* lied to her!

There could be no other explanation for Nick's behavior. She should have put two and two together back in the hotel room. First, he had not touched her or looked her in the eye; then, later, when they'd made love, it had been different somehow. He was harsh with her, almost fierce, desperate, as if it were the last time, Alethea realized abruptly.

Her heart pounded savagely while her fists opened and closed nervously in her lap. What a fool she had been! What a blind, lovesick fool!

Unexpectedly, the Saab picked up speed. Nick had his foot pressed to the floorboard. Alethea turned quickly and saw Suliman's car gaining on them. The breath caught in her throat. What would Nick do if Suliman caught up?

Nick answered her thoughts. "I'm going to put distance between us on the next straightaway. When I reach the next rise, just out of his sight, we're coming to a quick stop, so hold on tight."

She looked back. Nick was pulling way out in front of the Citroën now. Alethea turned around and put her hands on the dashboard for security. She felt her face grow slowly white with dread.

"When I stop, Alethea, get out as quick as you can. Take the envelope . . . Find cover behind a boulder, anything, and stay flat on your stomach. Don't worry, you hear?"

"But . . . but what if he . . . what if Suliman . . ."

"He won't."

Oh, how confident you are! she wanted to scream.

But what if Suliman got Nick, killed him? she thought in terror. What would Suliman do to her once he had the papers?

She watched the next steep incline coming up. The Saab was hurtling along. They'd be there in a minute, less.

Suddenly, Alethea had to ask, had to know before it was too late. "Nick," she cried. "Did you lie to me? Were you going to take me back to Washington? Tell me! Tell me, dammit!"

They were speeding over the rise. She saw his hands whiten on the steering wheel.

"Hold on tight!"

And then her body was thrown against the door, brutally, and the sky seemed to spin against the rocks, and then the sea, and she heard the horrible squealing of tires on asphalt, and smelled the burning, pungent odor of rubber.

Abruptly, everything was deathly still.

"Get out! Hurry!" he commanded.

She forced her hand to open the door. She seemed to be moving in slow motion, like when she had been drugged.

"Hurry the hell up!" She barely heard him shout.

Then her feet moved, carrying her across the hot pavement, to a pile of boulders shoved against the cliffside. And she was behind them, crouched, clutching the envelope to her breast, trembling violently.

A shot rang out clearly, crashing in her ears. She jumped involuntarily. And then it sounded as if a car were skidding— more squealing, more burning rubber, more sweet-sick odor.

Had Nick shot at Suliman's tires?

She was supposed to be on her belly, she remembered. Nick wasn't hurt . . . It was all right, wasn't it?

She barely breathed now and her body was shaking uncontrollably, but she had to look. In spite of her terror, she had to see . . .

Peering around the rock, it was as if she were looking through a stop-motion camera lens. Nick was crouched on one knee in the middle of the road, his gun trained in front of him with both hands pointing at the Citröen, which was just rocking to a stop.

Had it really only been a split second ago that Nick had fired that shot? Wasn't it hours?

In mute horror, she watched as the scene began to come slowly alive before her eyes. Nick moved slightly. He was perhaps only thirty yards from the Citröen. He fired a shot. Then she heard another shot, a slightly different sound. Her eyes moved to Suliman, still in his car. He must have fired at Nick.

The picture sped up quickly now. Nick seemed to roll onto his side. Was he hurt? Her heart lurched. But no, he was up onto a knee again. Another shot.

She hadn't realized it, but sometime, probably when Nick had rolled once, she had come to her feet and was standing, holding the envelope tightly, in full view of the men.

And then she saw Nick roll again. A moving target—that's what he was doing.

Why didn't he just take cover!

Suliman opened his door, crouched behind it and fired again. It was all happening so fast she couldn't see clearly.

Nick was darting sideways.

Suliman stood upright. He was taking careful aim! Surely he wouldn't miss this time! Oh, God! Fire, Nick! Fire!

Without her knowing it, Alethea screamed, her eyes wide with horror, fixed on the gun in Suliman's hand. The gun moved then, quickly. And dear God! It was suddenly trained directly at her!

She heard a shot. It mingled with another scream—her own, Alethea realized. Was she hit? But no, she wasn't. Suliman was. Yes . . . Nick had shot Suliman! The man's body was slumping now, the revolver dangling from his hand, dropping to the pavement. She heard the metal clang to the hard asphalt and watched in agonized fascination as his body followed the path of the gun, making a terrible thud as it, too, fell onto the road and was still.

"Are you all right?" She heard Nick's voice as if from a great distance.

For a long moment, she couldn't speak, her eyes wouldn't even move; they were fixed on the body.

Then the voice seemed nearer. "Alethea . . . you damned crazy kid. What were you trying to do?"

"I . . ." She tried to move her mouth. It was so hard. "I . . . thought you were shot. Oh, God." She wept.

She looked toward Nick. He was standing near Suliman's inert body. He motioned for her to come. She forced her feet to move. It was all right now, Alethea realized slowly, the enemy was felled. Gone. The danger, the horror, were over.

Halfway between the rocks and Nick, she stopped. Her feet froze. Was the enemy *really* dead? Of course Suliman posed no threat to Nick now, but what about her? Slowly, painfully, she wondered, was she, too, the enemy?

She squeezed the envelope. It was wet with perspiration where she clutched it. Fear crawled up her spine.

"Come here," she heard Nick say. "It's all right now."

Alethea moved again, forcing her feet to step one in front of the other. It was Nick calling her. He would never hurt her, would he? He might betray her, but hurt her? They loved each other, after all, she thought suddenly.

And then Alethea was beside him. She could smell the animal scent of him, the scent of sweat and danger and maleness, the lingering acrid odor of gunpowder. She looked hesitantly up into Nick's eyes, clear, crystal-blue now, unreadable as they met and locked with her own.

Chapter 36

Sunday, December 25

Her hazel eyes were wide and terrified, as if she had seen something that was too awful to contemplate. It wasn't Suliman's death—no—the expression had occurred as their eyes met over his body. Nick could see her fingers clutching at the envelope as if it were a life preserver in a high sea and she were drowning.

He reached out a hand to reassure her, to calm her. It was over now. But she gave a strangled cry, whirled and began to run toward the narrow, twisting road as if the devil pursued her. He stood there, stupefied. His mind raced in the anticlimax of violence, of flirting with death once more. His body was still high on adrenaline, but her action defeated his logic.

Wasn't she supposed to throw her arms around him, welcome the conquering hero home?

Abruptly, it struck him: She knew. She knew he had lied about the papers, about agreeing with her, and she figured she was next on his hit list. She was running for her life. It made sense if you cared to look at it from her point of view. He didn't blame her.

It hadn't occurred to him because he was trained in a perverse sort of logic and never really trusted anyone, ever.

He could let Alethea go. He could let her hitch a ride and run to safety with the papers, tell Porter he lost her. Or he could catch her, take the papers and still let her go. Or . . . He stood over the body still. The sun touched Nick with warmth, the Tyrrhenian Sea washed on the rocks below the road, a fly buzzed angrily somewhere nearby.

He knew then that he couldn't let her go, not like this. There had to be a confrontation. Alethea had, at the very least, to know that he would never harm her. She'd been chased, hounded, lied to enough. It had to end. He had to see her, if only once more, finish it off in a civilized manner, not let her run scared, forever looking over her shoulder. And he had to touch her just once more, look at her face and memorize the quiet beauty he'd grown to know so well.

He began to move, walking after her faster and faster, then finally breaking into a sprint. He could see her when he rounded the curve in the road. She was still running, but slowly, as if she were exhausted, tripping over a rock, almost falling.

It was very easy to catch up with her, grab her arm, spin her around to face him. She was still terrified but she didn't struggle. Her chest heaved with effort. She'd been crying, her cheeks were streaked with dirt and tears, like a child.

"Alethea," he said softly, at a loss.

Her shoulders sagged, she looked down. Her voice came in a sobbing whisper. "Do whatever you have to, just do it quick. I tried. I did my best. I can't do any more."

"Thea. I wouldn't hurt you, ever. I just killed a man to protect you. My God! Don't you know that?"

She looked up at him. Her eyes were angry now, shooting golden sparks. "You lied! You got me all softened up and I believed every word you said and then you lied to me! How can I believe you now?"

Nick's only answer was to pull her unresisting body close to him, put his arms around her, hold her, stroke her soft brown hair. "You have to believe me now. I lied. It's true . . . I thought it would be better that way. I was wrong. But . . . the other things. I never lied about them . . ." He tipped her head up to meet her eyes with their tear-soaked lashes. "Look at me, Alethea."

She looked scared—hoping, yet despairing, too. Doubt and

love combined forces in her eyes. It stabbed him with a poignancy he'd never felt before.

He groaned in his turmoil, buried his head in her fragrant hair. "Thea, I love you." The words, even as he said them, gave him an immense sense of relief, but they frightened him, too. They meant commitment, emotional responsibility.

"Nick?" Her voice cut across his fears, quavering, uncertain. Her eyes, huge and golden, questioned him endlessly.

"Do you believe me?" he asked, watching her carefully.

"Yes," Alethea breathed, "But what good will it do? How can I love a man who betrayed me and my father? Betrayed everything I've tried to do? It won't work. You're my enemy."

"All I know is that I love you and I won't let you go. There's got to be a way out of this mess."

"Oh, Nick, I hurt inside, like I'm going to break apart. I hurt so bad . . ." She buried her head in his chest, held onto him.

"I know, Thea."

"What are we going to do?" she cried, turning her face up to his. Agonized tears welled in her eyes.

"I don't know, Thea," he said bitterly, feeling the weight of his betrayal sit heavily on his shoulders, weighing him down with its onerous burden. "I just don't know."

Chapter 37

Saturday, December 31

Alethea wondered if she'd been this nervous when she'd first seen that dark Arab face looking up at her from the street below. It seemed like centuries, eons ago. Actually, it had been less than a month. Incredible. How could a person change so much in a month?

But that had been before Nick. She had been a different person then, in so many ways. She had succeeded in her goal—to give her father's discovery to the world. And she had revenged his death, although she would have wished for a less violent way.

The government of Abjala had even sent her an official apology for the death of her father, regretting actions by their now-deceased oil minister that were "deplorable and mistaken in intent."

Yes, she had succeeded, but Nick—What about him? From the National Security Council's point of view, he had failed miserably. He'd let the papers get away, let a girl outsmart him. Not only that, but he had actually aided and abetted her. They'd be after his neck!

God, when would he return? He'd left for Washington yesterday, promising to be back in New York by tonight, promising her that they'd celebrate the New Year together. It was nearly eight o'clock and she hadn't heard from him! Had they arrested him? Or, God forbid, had they killed him and tucked his body away in one of the top-secret, off-limits basement rooms in the maze of the Pentagon? They could also be torturing him in one of their fiendish ways.

He'd told her he'd be all right, hand in his resignation, explain to Porter what had happened, that's all. But Alethea was afraid. Now that she'd found Nick, she couldn't bear the thought of losing him.

A knock on the door startled her. Instantly, she became alert to danger . . . She'd given Nick the spare key. Alethea feared it might be one of Porter's men, coming to bring her in.

She opened the door a crack, keeping the chain on, but all she could see was a pair of arms around some packages, a bunch of green, tissue-wrapped flowers, a garish pink satin box of candy, a black and silver gift-wrapped liquor bottle.

"For godsakes, Alethea, let me in! My arms are ready to break! Those damn stairs of yours!"

"Nick!" Her voice cracked with relief. She felt like a fool.

"Who in hell did you think it was? Peter Rabbit?"

She laughed then, adoring the sound of his voice, so familiar now, so beloved, and unhooked the chain.

He lurched into the room and dropped the presents onto the couch, but he saved the flowers, holding them out to her.

"Happy New Year, Alethea," he said, smiling, his cheeks slightly flushed from the cold, glistening snowflakes melting on his dark hair.

She took the blossoms, burying her head in them to smell the hothouse aroma for a second, then she threw herself on him, nestling her face against his cold, wet-wool-smelling coat.

"Oh, Nick, I love you!"

"Me, too, Thea."

"But . . . Porter . . . what did he say? I was so worried!" She pushed Nick away and held him at arms' length, the frown line back on her brow.

"They're coming for me in a minute!" he stage-whispered conspiratorially, bending close to her ear. "They just gave me time to say my last goodbye."

"Oh, Nick! Don't tease! Tell me!"

"Hell, Thea. I told you. He's dropping the whole thing. It never got beyond him and if he lets the story out, *he'll* be the fool. The U.S. government will now celebrate the discovery as the best thing that ever happened to the world. They're preparing a press release already stating how *happy* they are that it will be shared by all."

"He wouldn't try to follow you, get them after all?"

"I'd like to see him try!" said Nick, his face falling into the grim lines she knew so well. "Don't worry, they're safe. I have a friend very highly placed in the UN. He's completely trustworthy. He's having hundreds of copies made. Everyone in the General Assembly will get them simultaneously. And last week, I took the precaution of getting some copies made myself and putting them in a safety deposit box. I also sent some to my father's law office, under seal, with a letter to be opened in case anything happens to me or to you."

"Oh, Nick, have we really done it at last?"

"Yep, I think so." He flashed his bright grin at her. "And now, let's get down to really important matters—things that eclipse the mere discovery of an oil substitute . . ."

"Like what?" Alethea asked, grinning back at him.

"Like this." He drew her into his arms and kissed her deeply, unhurriedly.

She pushed him away then and studied him for a long moment before asking, "In Leysin—tell me the truth, Nick—did you like Lisa? Did you think she was attractive?"

He looked down at her in amazement. "Are you still hashing that over? That's history! That was—"

"I know, part of the job. But tell me, really . . ."

"I thought she was stunning, gorgeous, sexy," he said mock-seriously.

"Oh." Alethea's voice was very small and quiet. She began to turn away but his voice stopped her.

"But I love you, Alethea. That's different."

"So, what about that night in Leysin? You and Lisa . . ." She couldn't go on.

He threw back his head and laughed. "I guess I better 'fess up. I didn't sleep with her. I couldn't." Then the laughter fled from his eyes. "Since we're laying all our cards on the table . . . what really happened between you and Suliman in the farmhouse?"

Her eyes slid away from his intense gaze, then returned to meet his squarely. "Nothing. Maybe he wanted to, maybe he even took my clothes off for that reason, but . . . a woman knows these things."

"I'm glad to know for your sake, Thea. I must admit, it half-killed me to think of him harming you." His blue eyes met hers with love.

"Oh, Nick!" The happiness returned to her voice. "I'm so glad nothing happened between you and Lisa."

"And I never asked Lisa to marry me, either, did I?" he said, still staring down into her eyes seriously.

"Nick?"

"Are you in the market for an old, beat-up spy-turned-lawyer for a husband?" Gently, he pulled Alethea into the warmth of his embrace.

"Oh, yes, Nick, yes! You bet I am!" she cried, hugging him tightly, then raising her lips to meet the passion of his kiss.

Epilogue

Tuesday, January 3

OIL OUT—WATER IN?

Incredible Discovery Presented to United Nations

At 10:15 A.M. yesterday, under mysterious circumstances, members of the United Nations General Assembly each received a photocopy of handwritten papers outlining a method for using the hydrogen in water as an inexhaustible source of fuel, replacing oil as the major source of energy. The papers are purported to be the lifelong work of recently deceased Dr. Craig Holmes, the renowned rocket engineer, who had been working in Abjala on the project.

Says the foremost expert in the energy field, Dr. Jonathan Burgmeister, of Columbia University, "The papers appear genuine, and in my opinion the method is quite probably workable. Dr. Holmes has made the

277

great breakthrough. I think he deserves the Nobel Prize if the tests prove his theory. It is amazing. Totally amazing."

Officers of the Security Council are still checking on the source of the papers, but so far there are no leads.

About the Author

Lynn Erickson is the pseudonym for the writing team of Carla Peltonen and Molly Swanton, who live in Aspen, Colorado. Each has always been an avid reader, and when they got hooked on romances, they decided to try creating their own stories. *This Raging Flower*, *Sweet Nemesis*, *The Silver Kiss* and *Gentle Betrayer* have been the result.

Carla is responsible for the research, Molly for the plot development. They write alternating chapters, which are then revised for uniformity of style.

The friends make an interesting picture of contrasts. Carla has dark hair; Molly's is blond. One is a gourmet cook; the other is all for TV dinners. One is totally committed to physical fitness; the other laughingly says she must have weighed sixty pounds at birth. They also share similarities. Carla freely admits to a fear of flying, while Molly is scared of heights; yet neither will permit her phobia to dominate her. Early American furniture is adored by both, and they enjoy restoring antiques together.

Their love of skiing and taste for worldwide travel form strong bonds between them as well. Molly was en route to California when she decided to spend a weekend in Aspen. The first night she was there, she met her husband. And Carla met her husband while skiing in Leysin, Switzerland.

You Have a Rendezvous with Richard Gallen Books...

EVERY MONTH!

Visit worlds of romance and passion in the distant past and the exciting present, words of danger and desire, intrigue and ecstasy—in breathtaking novels from romantic fiction's finest writers.

Now you can order the Richard Gallen books you might have missed!

These great contemporary romances...

Continued next page